"NOT HERE," SHE PLEADED.

"Come to me, Eleanor," he said softly. "It is time."

"Nay," she repeated, her voice trembling.

He drew her deeper into the shadows of the grove and spread his heavy cloak on the forest floor. She tried to still the pounding of her heart. It was her duty, she mentally repeated, her duty. She choked back a sob as his mouth took hers. His hands released the clasps of her gown, pulling the garment down to her waist. Slowly, as his kiss deepened, he began to stroke the full softness of her breast. Then he lowered her to the ground. He lifted her skirts and his fingers slipped to the softness between her thighs.

It flashed across her mind where they were, that he was taking her like an animal. But she was lost to caring. She groaned, arching her back to his caresses, wanting him to touch her, wanting what he was giving her. Distantly she heard the sound of her own voice, pleading, still pleading . . .

*   *   *

"Five stars. A must for your summer reading pleasure."

—Affaire de Coeur

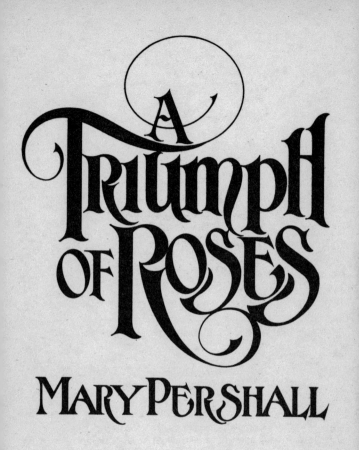

A Triumph of Roses

MARY PERSHALL

BERKLEY BOOKS, NEW YORK

Mail to the author
may be addressed to:
Mary Pershall
P.O. Box 1453
Soledad, CA 94960

A TRIUMPH OF ROSES

A Berkley Book / published by arrangement with
the author

PRINTING HISTORY
Berkley edition / July 1986

ISBN: 0-425-09079-5

A BERKLEY BOOK ® TM 757,375
Berkley Books are published by The Berkley Publishing Group,
200 Madison Avenue, New York, New York 10016.
The name "BERKLEY" and the stylized "B" with design
are trademarks belonging to Berkley Publishing Corporation.

PRINTED IN THE UNITED STATES OF AMERICA

For
Theodora Ellen Carson Nelson,
a grand lady of vision, great faith, and pluck

MARSHALS

Earl of Pembroke
WILLIAM MARSHAL ⟨M.⟩ **ISABEL deCLARE**

- Will
  Earl of Pembroke
  Marshal of England
  ⟨M.⟩
  Eleanor
  Plantagenet

- Richard

- Gilbert

- Walter

- Anselem

- Matilda
  ⟨M.⟩
  Hugh Bigod,
  Earl of Norfolk

- Isabella
  ⟨M.⟩
  Gilbert deClare
  Earl of Hertford

- Sybile
  ⟨M.⟩
  William deFerrars,
  Earl of Derby

- Eve
  ⟨M.⟩
  William
  deBraose

- Joanne

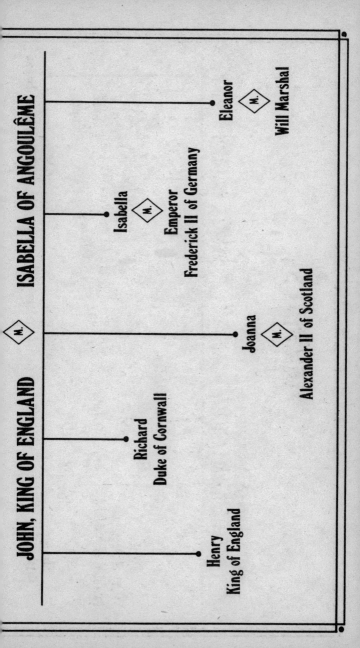

JOHN, KING OF ENGLAND ◇ M. ◇ ISABELLA OF ANGOULÊME

Henry
King of England

Richard
Duke of Cornwall

Joanna
◇ M. ◇
Alexander II of Scotland

Isabella
◇ M. ◇
Emperor
Frederick II of Germany

Eleanor
◇ M. ◇
Will Marshal

PROLOGUE

October 28, 1216
Gloucester Castle, England

A small child with raven hair and large blue eyes watched with fascination as her older brother slowly walked the long hall between the tall knights to ascend the throne of England. She knew that he was nervous by the way he pulled at his ear and the tight set to his mouth; the signs were comfortingly familiar to her. Her gaze shifted to the tallest of the barons, who had stepped forward wearing the golden spurs of England, and her eyes widened as they fixed on the fierce red lion rampant on his coat of arms. For a frightening moment she envisioned that the knight, surely as fierce as his device, would devour her beloved brother. After all, Henry was hardly older than her own five years. Stifling a whimper, she stepped back behind the fullness of her nurse's skirts and grasped their folds. Then, unable to contain her curiosity, she peeked out behind the voluminous skirt of her broad-hipped guardian. She looked away suddenly as she found herself staring into eyes as blue as her own.

Dancing eyes, crinkling with amusement, were watching her. He wore the same coat of arms as the knight who had terrified her so, but somehow she was not afraid. He was as tall, but younger. Everyone else was watching her brother, or

1

listening intently to those who were speaking. She felt lost; she didn't understand what was happening—not really. She only knew she was supposed to stand still and act quite grown-up—as her older sisters, Joanna and Isabella, were doing, but she knew they were as uncomfortable as she was.

She tried not to look again, for she knew she should be watching her brother, but she couldn't help herself. She looked, and as she did, he winked. Before she could stop herself she giggled, to the horror of her nurse, who grasped her hand—and to the horror of her mother, who threw her an angry, disapproving stare. But for once she did not care that her mother was angry with her. Warmth entered her heart and she felt suddenly happy. She had a friend, a wonderful friend, a tall, handsome knight with warm, laughing eyes.

PART ONE

Kings, Bishops, And Pawns

1

1225
In the Ninth Year of Our Reign
Henry III, Plantagenet

ELEANOR squinted into the sun, shading her eyes with her hand as she scanned the far side of the wide meadow and the fringe of elder and ash beyond. She scrambled over a low stone wall, ignoring the scraping of the rough stone against the knees of her britches. As she ran through the meadow, with the small bow and quiver bouncing against her back, she was thankful for the thick leather boots she wore, for the dense dry grasses were full of cockleburs and foxtail. She felt a surge of excitement as she ran, momentarily forgetting her purpose in the freedom she felt from those who watched her, as well as from the restraints of skirts. The late summer sun was warm against her face, and the air smelled heavily of honeysuckle and sage. As she filled her senses with the heavy fragrance, she felt wonderfully unfettered and euphoric.

Finally reaching the cover of trees, she stopped, darting into a shadow of a large spreading oak to catch her breath. Her face was flushed with exertion and excitement, but her eyes darted about as she plotted her next move. The clearing just beyond, she reasoned, that was where they would come. She had to reach it before they did, or all of her plans would be undone.

She found the clearing and smiled to find it empty; moreover, there were no signs that anyone had been there before her. The hard-packed floor of the clearing, framed by a large copse of thickly set trees, carried only the signs of past activities. Even the evidence of previous campfires had long since been obliterated. She glanced about, and her freckled face broke into a grin as she found what she needed. A low-slung branch of an ancient oak reached out over one edge of the clearing, and she made for it, swinging herself up. Settling herself in the crook of a sturdy branch, she leaned against the trunk to wait.

Leave me behind, would they, she thought. She reached into the pocket of her short leather tunic, extracting a piece of dry jerky, which she began to chew on thoughtfully. Not this time, she reasoned, savoring the taste of the heavy spices as they tripped over her tongue, giving emphasis to her thoughts.

Shifting on her perch, she adjusted the bow slung over her shoulder and the quiver of arrows at her back to make herself more comfortable. Familiar visions began to float through her mind, stories told to her of women. Wives of great earls who had led armies in the absence of their husbands who had gone to the Crusades. Women who had defended their battlements in the absence of their men. Stories of her own grandmother, her namesake, who had gone on a crusade with her first husband, Louis of France. Eleanor of Aquitaine had gone not as a follower but as a participant, leading her own small army of women who sought to join in the battle against the Saracen. Yet she, Eleanor Plantagenet, was not even allowed to join the men on a hunt! She, who could use the bow as well as any of them! She flushed angrily as she recalled her brother's parting volley. "This time you must stay, little one," he had said with a laugh. " 'Tis time you put aside this nonsense and began to develop arts which will better suit you." Little one, he had called her! How she had come to detest that nickname! King of England or not, he was only four years older than she, barely eighteen, yet he treated her as such a child! Pah, she thought. She knew all too well to what arts he referred. The art of idleness and gossip!

She had dutifully attended mass that morning, her mind already in rebellion. She had given the proper responses, her eyes downcast in supplication, but her thoughts had been with the small party that had left Windsor before dawn. Now, thinking on it, she felt thrilled by her daring, amazed by how easy it had been to escape the long morning hours she faced listening to the stern admonitions of the priest. She shifted uncomfortably on her perch as she remembered the previous day's lessons with the good father. She did not know why it had disturbed her so; she only knew that she could not abide another like it. Each day of her life, as far back as she could recall, had been spent so, the morning hours after mass listening to the teachings of the priests. The switch had been used to enforce lessons when she was caught daydreaming, the stern voice shifting quickly from Latin to angry French with the burning sting against her hands or shoulders.

But yesterday had been different, stirring her with an anger she did not understand. She reached into her pocket and withdrew a small scrap of needlework, holding it thoughtfully to her lips as her eyes darkened with doubt. Opening it gently, she held it to the light of late afternoon which filtered through the branches above her, and she felt an inner softness ease over her as she studied the scene depicted. Why had Father Latius been so angry? she wondered. The tapestry had been beautiful, how could he destroy it? She spread the material on her knee and touched it reverently with her small hands, her fingers outlining what remained of the head and shoulders of a beautiful white unicorn.

Eleanor had entered the morning chamber to find her ladies gathered about Lady Elizabeth, widow of a northern earl who had recently come to court. As the small group had drawn apart to admit her, Eleanor had been struck still by what she saw. A breathtakingly beautiful tapestry lay on a frame before her, finished but for a few remaining bordering stitches. A lovely young woman, draped in white, sat in a shaded copse of trees. A sleeping unicorn lay in repose, its magnificent head in her lap. Behind them, in the shadows, stood a knight, a drawn sword in his hand.

Admiring the work of art with her companions, she had been unaware of another presence in the room until a shadow fell across the tapestry and a large hand suddenly reached forward to rip the material from its frame. What happened next was a blur, and even now Eleanor could only recall flashing words, anger, cries of outrage from Lady Elizabeth, and the rage of Father Latius as he tore the tapestry into shreds.

Lady Elizabeth had fled from the room in tears, and Father Latius had ordered the girls to their places. Flinging the torn fabric into a corner, he had launched into a tirade on the baseness of women, reminding his charges that they were born from sin, into sin, their essence to lead man from the purity of his soul, finally repeating the words of Saint Jerome, that "woman is the gate of the devil, the path of wickedness, the sting of the serpent, a perilous object."

Eleanor tried to listen, though she could have repeated the admonishments by heart, but her attention was drawn to the discarded tapestry. Upon the end of the lessons, Father Latius recovered the object with a great show of distaste, taking it from the room with a promise that it would be reduced to the ashes it deserved. Heartbroken, though she could not have said why, Eleanor remained behind when the others left. No sooner had the door closed, than she rushed to the needlework frame, dropping to her knees as she began to search about frantically, hopefully. Then her heart filled with joy as she found the treasured remnant overlooked by the priest in his fury.

Her finger lightly traced the unicorn's head. How could such a beautiful creature be sinful? she wondered. And what had it to do with the sinfulness of women? But none of that mattered. The tapestry had touched something deep within her, and she was mad at Father Latius for destroying it. She had known upon arising that morning that she could not abide the thought of spending the coming hours listening to more of his endless lectures. It was then that she had heard the commotion beneath her window as the hunting party prepared to depart for a day's hunt, and her mind had turned boldly to the adventure. Rushing from her room, she had encountered Henry coming from his chambers. She had pleaded with him to allow her to come, but he had only laughed, touching her face affectionately even as he had refused her request. As he strode off toward the courtyard, dismissing her in his lively amusement, her plans had been laid.

She shivered suddenly and realized that while she was lost in her thoughts, the evening fog had begun to settle about the copse. Rubbing her arms against the sudden chill, she regretted that she had not thought to bring a mantle with her. The afternoon had been so warm that it had not occurred to her how cold the night might be. Lud, she thought, what if they did not come? She leaned back against the trunk of the tree and hiccuped against a sob that threatened to escape, frighteningly aware suddenly of how alone she was.

She bit her lower lip, sniffling as she tucked the precious piece of tapestry into the pocket of her tunic. She would not cry! Those early years spent at Corfe Castle where her parents had left her those nights with no one—she had cried then, wishing, believing that someone would hear her tears and come. But no one came. She promised herself never to cry again. Ever.

Then *he* had come. The Marshal of England. It was he who brought her away from that lonely, windswept castle. He brought her into light, into warmth. She sniffed again, her despair turning into a small smile as she remembered how silly she had been then, how terrified when she had first seen him—tall, fierce-looking, overbearing—at Henry's coronation. She had been struck dumb with terror when her mother had told her that *he* would be her guardian. She had tried to understand all that her mother was telling her: that her father had died, that her sister Joanna would be going to Scotland and Isabella to Germany, to marry the king there, that her brother was now king of England, that her mother would be leaving for the Continent, that the Marshal was now Regent for her brother until he reached his majority—but all that she could focus on was that he would be her guardian also.

But there had been another, one so like him, yet a younger version. Warm blue eyes filled with lively amusement, a wink offered to a terrified child, filling her with laughter—and her life had changed. A handsome young knight, named William like his father the Marshal, soon coaxed her from her fears. Gently persuading, he showed her that his father's fierce facade covered a tender concern for the little maid. And she found herself among the first family she had ever known. The younger Marshal brothers, Richard, Gilbert, Walter, and Anselem, were brought to court as companions to the nine-

year-old king. Under Will's watchful eye she found herself immersed in the all-male court, finally coming to know her own
brothers, Henry and Richard, and the joy of the love of a
family.

The sound of barking dogs brought her from her reverie,
and then she heard the sound of men and horses approaching
through the trees. She sat up, scratching her leg abstractedly
against the harsh wool of the men's chausses she wore, and she
peered through the growing dusk in the direction of the approaching party. As the dogs ran into the clearing beneath her,
the sound of men's laughter carried to her and she smiled,
easily recognizing their voices.

Eleanor's smile widened as they began to emerge into the
clearing. Her eyes moved eagerly over the group, noting
those who had accompanied her brother on the hunt. As the
squires moved apart to tend to the comforts of their knights,
she felt increasingly comforted by each recognition. She spied
Henry's blond head among the group, but her eyes moved on,
searching for another. His voice brought her to him, and she
felt a small thrill of excitement tremble in her. She pulled
herself instinctively back into the shadows of the branches as
she watched and listened, even as her eyes never left him.
Would she ever tire of looking at him? He was tall and broad-
shouldered, and she could imagine the muscles of his back
beneath the leather of his surcoat as he pulled the saddle from
his mount. Rich chestnut hair feathered about his forehead
and curled about his ears. They still spoke of the handsome
countenance of his father, but Will fully matched his father in
looks, she thought proudly. And his eyes. They were the first
thing she had noticed about him those many years before.
Vibrant blue, warm, laughing, containing a depth of wisdom
that drew her into them in an undefined longing for security
and protection.

As she watched, doubt overtook her. Henry would be
angry when he found her here, she was certain of it. But her
brother's anger did not concern her, he was never angry with
her for long. But Will would be angry too, and he would not
be so forgiving. Oh lud, she thought, perhaps she should not
have come. The men's voices suddenly blended into a blur as
she pressed against the trunk of the tree. It was far too late to

worry about such things now, she reasoned. Besides, she had every right to be here! After all, Will Marshal was her husband. In name, if not in fact.

"O sweet lord, my bones do protest!" one of the younger knights groaned as he slipped from the saddle. He leaned heavily against the side of his palfrey for a moment before he reached for the reins and handed them to his squire.

"Perhaps you would prefer the comfort of a warming hearth, Gilbert Marshal." Henry Plantagenet chortled as he gave the reins of his mount to another. "Have I been guilty of leading you on a merry chase? We were not totally unsuccessful," he added, glancing at the sumpter horse bearing a six-pointed hart across his back. "But 'tis a pity we did not discover the source of those last tracks we discovered. 'Twas a mighty pig; I warrant its tusks would have made a handsome trophy."

"Leave off, Henry," Will tossed. "Some of us have better sense than to track a boar of that size when we are tired."

Henry spun about and eyed the Earl of Pembroke through narrowed eyes. "Do you admit that you are beaten?" The tall knight paused as he pulled the saddle from his mount, and he turned to his king as he fought a smile, knowing that Henry was baiting him on an earlier bet of who would be first to call it a day. "I admit that it is the worst folly to pursue such an animal with tired men and horses, Henry. You were most correct in giving the order to cease in the hunt," he added, quietly pressing the last point.

Henry paused for an instant, then laughed. "Point taken, Will. But, oh, how I would have loved to have taken the beast."

"In the morning," the other agreed. "I will see you to the task at first light. For now, all I wish for is the warmth of that fire and some sleep." He glanced at the efforts of his squire, who was striking a flint to a gathered pile of leaves and kindling.

The hunting party stretched out before the tender blaze on their blankets and soon succumbed to the aroma of roasting hare. Stories came with the supper, lies of their hunting expertise growing with the comfort gained from the fire and full bellies. Chortles of laughter denied outrageous claims, and the men relaxed with the stories. Soon the events of hunting were dismissed and other claims came forth, those of a more personal nature involving exploits with the more gentle sex. Will stretched out, giving way to his fatigue, as Henry launched into a factually detailed accounting of a previous conquest. Will's lips moved silently with the often-told recounting even as he shifted his body and sought comfort, wanting only sleep. He folded his arms across his chest and closed his eyes. Then, suddenly, his eyes flew open and he moved in one fluid motion. Instantly he was on his feet, sword in hand. He stood blocking Henry as his eyes turned upward, searching the depths of the darkened branches above them. The clearing quickly became mass confusion; a mayhem of startled voices and a scurry of activity filled the camp as men struggled to their feet, swearing profusely as they stumbled over one another and sought their weapons.

"Come down and perhaps, if your hands are empty, we will spare your miserable life!" he barked.

Deathly silence followed as the men braced themselves for attack. It never occurred to them to doubt him. They had moved quickly about Henry, protecting him with their bodies, swords in hand, as they faced the dark void which surrounded them.

"Now!" Will roared, facing the blackness, "Or your life is forfeit!"

A rustle of leaves and a mutter of profanity emanated from above them. Skinny legs clad in form-fitting wool chausses suddenly appeared. Feet swung at the air, and then there was a sharp woosh as the form dropped to the ground. Without hesitation, Will stepped forward, bringing his sword about to pin the figure where it landed.

"Dammit, Marshal, get that thing off of me!"

Will's mouth dropped open and he blinked. As the other men began to identify the visitor, eyes widened and two voices began to bellow simultaneously.

"By the breath of God, Eleanor!" Henry Plantagenet roared.

"Sweet Mother! Eleanor, how in God's name . . ." Will raged, his face flushing with fury. "I could have killed you!"

"Well, for heaven's sake," Eleanor tossed off the words as

she struggled to her feet and brushed herself off. "Calm down. I'm hardly a threat to you big, strong men."

Henry began stomping about the grove, visibly trying to control his rage as Will froze, afraid that if he moved he would strike her. The thought flashed through his mind that he had the right. Even Henry could not protest. He had never wanted to beat a female before, but at the moment the thought was strangely appealing. "Eleanor." He ground out her name. "What—were you doing in that tree?"

"Waiting for you, of course." she answered, rubbing her backside.

"Waiting for us," he parroted lamely. "In a tree?" He swallowed, forcing himself to be calm. "How did you come to be here? We left you at Windsor."

"Not for long," she answered cheerily. "And that is all that you will learn from me." She tossed her head and turned toward the warmth of the fire. She knew that Henry and Will were likely to forgive her—well, at least Henry would—but it would not go as well for the luckless young knight she had coerced into bringing her from Windsor. If there was one thing Eleanor felt strongly, it was loyalty to those she counted as friends.

Will turned toward her, but before he could open his mouth to speak, Henry appeared on the other side of her and jerked her about to face him. "What in the devil were you thinking of to come out unescorted? Anything could have happened and no one would even have known where you were! By the Blood, Eleanor, I swear I'll lock you in the tower, swallow the key, and leave it to Will to decide whether to ever let you out! If he has any sense he'll forget that you're there!"

Eleanor had dropped her gaze as he raged, and she placed her small hands on his broad chest. She looked up at him through tear-filled eyes. "Henry, I am truly sorry. I did not think clearly—I—I did not mean to worry you."

Henry's face softened at the sound of his sister's tender plea, and he drew her into his arms and hugged her to him, missing the rolling of Will's eyes as he listened with disbelief. He looked past Henry's shoulders to the others, who were watching with interest, and he met their looks of amusement with a wince, knowing the certain ribbing that would come from his brothers and Hugh Bigod, his brother by marriage.

"We cannot return you to Windsor tonight," Henry was saying quietly as he held Eleanor from him and gazed down at her tenderly. "There is no moon, so we will not be able to travel until daybreak."

At the note of apology in Henry's voice, Will's temper snapped. He reached out and pulled Eleanor sharply from her brother. "Do not concern yourself further, Your Grace," he said smoothly as he glared down at her. "She is my responsibility and I shall see to it that she is returned at first light."

"Aye, Will!" Henry said brightly, obviously pleased to be relieved of the problem. "I would like to go after that pig in the morning. As you say, she is your responsibility," he added with a grin.

"Aye, Your Grace," Will muttered as he pulled Eleanor about and led her to his blanket near the fire.

"Will, you're hurting my arm!" she gasped as she tried to pull away from his grip.

"I'd like to do more than that, you little fool," he growled as he pushed her down onto his blanket. Stepping around her, he grabbed his cloak and wrapped it about himself, then lay down beside her. Reaching over, he pulled the blanket about her shoulders. "Now go to sleep and try not to cause any more trouble tonight."

The camp gradually grew quiet as the others again sought their bedrolls. Soon the only sound heard in the grove was the crackling of the fire behind her and the even breathing of the sleeping men. But sleep eluded Eleanor. She lay on her side, an arm tucked beneath her head, and she watched Will's profile in the dim flickering light of the fire. She had been right to come, she thought with sleepy contentment. She was here, in this wonderful forest, with those she loved best—except for Richard, but he rarely left his lands in Cornwall anymore —and she was lying next to Will. Watching him, she felt her chest contract, and for a moment it was hard to breathe for the bittersweet pain she was feeling.

She had loved him since the first moment she had seen him, and she knew with every part of her that she would never love another. It had taken little urging on her part to persuade Henry to betroth her to Will. He had proven all too willing to give her to his best friend, but then Henry never could say no to her when it was something she really wanted. Dear, sweet Henry. Then, suddenly, another thought entered her mind and her brow knit into a frown. "Will?" she said softly.

"What is it?"

"If—if I were locked away, would you forget about me?"

"No, Eleanor. I would not forget about you. Now go to sleep."

Satisfied, she snuggled up against him and sighed contentedly at the familiar scent of musk he wore. How good life can be, she mused, closing her eyes. And then she remembered a moment not so pleasant. "Will? Why would Father Latius become enraged over a unicorn?"

There was a long moment of silence. "Eleanor, what are you talking about?"

"This." She fought the tangles of the blanket to reach her pocket, pulling the tapestry from her tunic.

He took it from her and opened it, leaning it to the dimming light of the fire. He turned back to look at her and his brow creased into a frown. "Where did you get this?"

Whispering, she told him what had happened in the morning chamber. "He was furious, Will. He started lecturing us on the evils of being female."

Will's eyes sparked with anger. "Did he strike you again?"

"Nay, but what does being a woman have to do with this?"

"O Lord, Eleanor." He yawned. "Look, suffice it to say that there are those who do not view the role of women as they have been. The tapestry, as you described it, depicts a woman as the Virgin Mary, one of purity and innocence. Not the role of Eve, steeped in evil."

"No wonder Father Latius was so angry," she mused. "I do not think he would like it very well if women were not as he had always thought them to be."

Will grinned at her quickness, and he chuckled softly. "Aye, I am certain that you are right. If women begin to be thought of as models of the Virgin, our esteemed priest would find himself in a rather awkward position as the redeemer of their tortured souls. But enough. It is late and we both need our sleep."

Moments later Will glanced down to find Eleanor already

asleep. Shaking his head with bemusement, he tucked an arm behind his head and stared into the blackness above him. Lifting the piece of tapestry to the light of the fire, he rubbed his thumb over it thoughtfully. So it had come to England. Such thoughts had been developing on the Continent since the First Crusade, stirring a great deal of controversy among the clergy. Actually, he was indifferent to the matter. In his mind women were not objects of purity any more than they were steeped in evil. But he could smell trouble, rising like the stink of rotting carrion. Heresy was the stuff the Poitevin priests thrived upon, and such were now in power within the Church in England.

Eleanor moaned softly in her sleep, drawing his attention. He reached over and drew the blanket up about her shoulders. His gaze passed over her tender features, the light sprinkling of freckles across her cheeks and nose, the dark lashes, and the small mouth now softened into a childish pout in her sleep. Sighing, Will lay back, knowing it would be some time before he found the peace of sleep.

His thoughts drifted back to the day, five years before, when Henry had announced that he was giving Eleanor to him as wife. He had been appalled, but each argument he had offered, Henry had countered. The fact of being betrothed to a child of nine, and thirteen years his junior, was not uncommon. Henry had commiserated with his friend that there would be many years before Eleanor reached her maturity and the marriage could be consummated. Will had finally allowed Henry to believe that to be the basis for his reluctance to the betrothal. He would not discuss his true reasons for his objections to the marriage, not with anyone. His memories of another belonged only to him. His ghosts were his alone.

There had followed an expected outcry by many closest to the throne when the betrothal had been rumored. Protest had been led with vehemence by the Bishop of Winchester, Peter desRoches, and it was this that had convinced Will to accept the marriage. Will confirmed his decision yet again as he glanced down at the sleeping girl at his side. His father, Marshal of England and Regent upon the death of John Plantagenet, had mistrusted the wily bishop, with good cause.

Upon the Marshal's deathbed, desRoches, who had served as assistant to the Regent, had stepped forward to claim guardianship of Henry, and thus the power of the throne. One of the Regent's last acts was to turn to Pandulfo, the papal legate who stood nearby, and commend young Henry into his hands, thus placing the young king under the protection of the Holy Father and out of the grasp of the power-seeking bishop. But it had not ended there, and gradually desRoches had gained more and more control over the impressionable Henry. Thus, when desRoches began to eye young Eleanor, protesting loudly against Will as a choice for her husband, Will knew he was plotting to betroth her to his own son, Peter desRevaux. As Will also knew, the only thing that stood between desRoches and control of the throne was the power of the Marshal family.

Will had consented to the betrothal then and thrown the forces of his power into the removal of desRoches from influence over the young king. Eventually, desRoches became convinced that a pilgrimage to Compostela was advisable. It proved all too easy to encourage Henry to support desRoches's leavetaking for the Continent, as the young king had become increasingly stifled under the strict tutelage of the bishop.

Henry. Will took a deep breath which turned to a sigh as he stared sleeplessly into the intertwining branches above his head. Will recalled his first meeting with the frightened nine-year-old who had suddenly become king of England. His father had ridden out to meet the young prince in the meadows of Milford Haven, where he had been brought from Devizes upon the death of his father, King John. The Marshal had brought the boy to Gloucester Castle, where the barons had gathered to give their oaths of fealty to their new king. Within hours after the simple coronation, the barons had pressed William to become Regent for the child, and in the hours William Marshal had struggled with his decision, Will had kept the young, terrified boy company. Their friendship had been struck in those hours, through games of backgammon and plantains, and an unshakable loyalty had developed between them. But Will's own remnants of innocence had been lost during those hours, as he began to sense that whatever freedom he had enjoyed in his life had become a thing of the past.

Eleanor mumbled in her sleep, bringing Will's attention back to the present. He reached down and again pulled the blanket back around her shoulders as she tossed restlessly in her sleep, causing him to wonder momentarily about the manner of her dreams. Were they the dreams of a child, or the dreams of the young woman she promised to be? Will stirred uncomfortably, feeling trapped by the responsibilities he felt for the girl who lay at his side. A sadness enveloped him as he thought of the years ahead and the grief they were almost certain to cause one another. He knew that she was confident and firm in her love, as only a child could be. What would happen to it, to her, when she looked at him through a woman's eyes; when she discovered that he could never love her in the manner she wanted, needed, had a right to expect?

He slipped his arm about her and gathered her to him protectively. I never want to hurt you, little one, he thought. But God help us, it is almost certain to be.

2

AT the first light of dawn the camp began to stir. As the grove lightened to a soft grey, the squires rekindled the fire to a warming blaze and prepared a breakfast of cold meat and wheaten bread for the knights. The hunting party's clothes were dampened by the ground-drenching fog that had settled in during the night, and movements were stiff even beneath the fur-lined cloaks that they wore.

Will watched Anselem with approval as the youth tended to Hugh Bigod's needs. Though it had been less than a year since the youngster had been elevated from the position of page to squire in the Earl of Norfolk's household, Will was proud to note that his little brother had taken to his new responsibilities readily. The fourteen-year-old's body had begun to fill out, showing promise of the man he would become. Will's brow knit at the thought, and his gaze shifted to Eleanor. She was huddled by the fire as she chewed on a crust of bread and a generous chunk of the meat left from the previous night. She was the same age as his youngest brother, and the realization caused Will to frown deeply. It struck him that it would not be long before she would reach her maturity and he could no longer continue to treat her as the little sister he felt her to be.

"Shall I ready our mounts, Lord William?"

Drawn from his thoughts, Will nodded absently. "Aye, Landon. As soon as Princess Eleanor has finished breaking her fast we will be leaving for London."

"I think not, Will." This came from Henry, who strolled over to them, his mouth full of roast hare and his eyes bright with a mischief Will recognized all too easily. "I have been giving it some thought and have decided that the hunt can wait until another time. Indeed, as I have the Marshal clan all together, what better time than to see us to Oxford to look into that little matter with the good friars there?"

Henry ignored the groans that came from Richard and Gilbert and the rolling of Walter's eyes, but his own eyes continued to dance as he saw Will wince. Henry had committed himself to build a new chapel at the university and, ever pressed for funds, he had been steadily urging the Marshals to contribute a more than equal share to that of his own purse.

"I must of need see Eleanor to London, Your Grace," Will protested.

"Nonsense!" Henry chortled, so well pleased with himself that Will began to wonder if the hunt had been a ruse all along. "Eleanor can accompany us. She will not cause any trouble!"

"Nay, I promise that I will not!" Eleanor exclaimed. She jumped up and ran to Will, tugging his sleeve. "Oh, Will, say aye, please! I have never been to Oxford!"

"And you will not do so now." Will frowned as his eyes swept over her. "Your attire would cause a scandal among the good brothers."

"Only if they were to know who she is." Henry chuckled. "Since she is dressed as a page, she can certainly be one. Landon, 'twould seem that you have assistance in serving your lord!"

Will groaned inwardly. "Henry, the trip to Oxford and the return will take many days," he tried, even while knowing the matter to be settled. "There are matters of importance awaiting you in London. . . ."

"Pah!" Henry waved off the protest. "DeBurgh is justiciar; he can see to whatever is needed. Surely a new chapel for the spiritual comfort of the good friars is of equal importance to whatever awaits me in London!"

As camp was broken Will observed the barely concealed amusement on his brother-in-law's face, and he made the point to pass by him before mounting his palfrey. "I hope that you continue to find the matter to your liking, Hugh, for I fear that your own purse will be lighter before this journey ends."

He fought a smile at the look of dismay that crossed the Earl of Norfolk's face, and he took the reins from his squire and swung into the saddle. Turning, he held out his hand to Eleanor. "Take my hand, Eleanor," he ordered.

"But—there is no pillion."

"You expect to ride on a soft cushion behind me, as a lady would?" he offered in mock dismay.

"But—I cannot ride behind you—astride!"

"What would you suggest?" he asked, leaning down to her as he arched a brow to her shock. "Should I let you ride in my lap? That would be a fine sight. Eleanor, a page does not ride in his master's lap—it just is not done. In normal circles, at least. Nay, 'tis a page you wish to be and you shall have it. Now give me your hand—boy."

Her lower lip pushed out into a pout, but she reached out so that he could pull her up behind him. As she settled uncomfortably on the wide girth of the palfrey's hindquarters she turned and looked down at her. "Hold on to me—and try not to wiggle. We have a long ride ahead of us." As he turned back he fought a grin, knowing that by the end of the day Eleanor would surely long for the comforts of Windsor, with serious second thoughts about her eager decision to accompany them to Oxford. "It is not too late, Eleanor," he said as he led the palfrey from the grove. "I must see Henry to Oxford, but I can send you back to Windsor with Landon."

"Oh no, you don't," she gritted. "I am going to Oxford with you."

"As you will. Do not say that I did not give you the opportunity to change your mind."

The day began blissfully for Eleanor. Her arms clasped tightly about Will, her cheek pressed against his broad back, she closed her eyes in happy dreaming. There was nowhere else in the world she wanted to be, and her fantasies soon took the shape of a great adventure. She imagined that she and Will were alone at last, but for the company of their faithful retainers, ever on guard against the sudden appearance of the Black Knight, who, also desiring her favors, might appear at any moment to pluck her from the arms of her lover. As they rounded a bend in the road she imagined that he was there, blocking their path, dressed in his black mail and surcoat, a fierce red dragon emblazoned on his tabard. Waving his sword above his head, he challenged the party, calling for Will to surrender Eleanor to him. Their faithful retainers rode forward one by one to meet the knight, each falling beneath the mighty sword, even to the last, a brave knight who looked somewhat like Henry. And then, in the grasp of her fantasy, Will pulled her across his lap to embrace her with a kiss, then set her upon the ground before he turned to meet the knight in battle.

"You will have privacy for your needs, just beyond in those trees." She vaguely realized that she was indeed dismounted and standing at the edge of the road. Will stood beside her, holding the reins of their mount and was looking at her strangely. "What?" she asked numbly.

He repeated himself and she flushed, painfully aware of sudden reality, his meaning, and the sharp pains that ran up the back of her legs. She turned and walked stiffly toward the trees, unaware of the concerned look that followed her. "Eleanor, are you all right?"

"I am fine," she gritted. She forced herself to move, missing the amusement that passed over his expression as she disappeared into the trees.

They stopped just long enough to rest the horses, and to Eleanor's dismay they were all too soon once again upon their journey. The following hours proved to be a sore trial to Eleanor, each mile increasing the pain in her legs and backside until she thought she could not bear it. Her thighs chafed miserably through the thin wool of the chausses, and any fanciful thoughts had long been forgotten.

They stopped late in the morning at a small inn near Wycombe. What Eleanor had felt that morning was nothing to compare to what she felt as Will lifted her from the mount before the inn. She clung to his arm as he helped her up the steps and into the warmth of the tavern room, and her mood did not improve as he leaned down to her. "For heaven's sake, keep that cap about your hair and do not speak," he muttered as he led her through the doorway.

He helped her to a table before an immense hearth which filled half the wall of the taproom. She began to lower herself to the bench, but he pulled her up. Pulling his fox-lined cloak from his shoulders, he folded it onto the seat before allowing her to sit.

The innkeeper had appeared upon the entrance of the visitors, his face beaming with the prospect of profit. Although the party was dressed simply, in leather tunics and plain woolen chausses and cross-garters, the quality of their garments and the fine weapons they wore did not miss his eyes. With a bellow and a snap of his fingers ale was already being placed on the tables even as his expression grew doubtful when he noted Eleanor's discomfort. "Is he ill?" he growled doubtfully. As much as he desired profit, the thought of sickness in his establishment drew fear into his heart. Even rumors of sickness had been the cause of many an inn's demise.

"Nay, good man," Will offered with deliberate casualness. " 'Tis the first time the lad has spent a full day behind the saddle and he is rather the worse for wear for the experience."

The innkeeper guffawed good-naturedly, in understanding and not a little relief. "A hearty meal will see him well. If, of course, you've of a mind to spend the coin," he added, glancing at William, knowing that many knights would be reluctant to do so.

"Aye, he's a good lad. See to it, though I doubt that he is worth the coin. He comes from a poor family of no particular merit. Oftentimes I wonder why I bother with him."

The innkeeper turned to issue orders to his help, and he missed the gasp from Eleanor at Will's words and the stony glare she threw at him. However, the laughter of the men brought him about, particularly to the tall blond knight who chortled the loudest at the parry. Puzzled, the innkeeper shrugged and went about his business, counting their unexplained humor to the idiocy of the nobility.

Eleanor picked at her food, too exhausted and sore to eat more than a few bites. But she was not too wayworn to notice the attention that was paid to the men, in particular to Will. The fact that the tavern maids were slovenly and ill-kempt went beyond notice. They were women, full-breasted and round of hip, and their attentions were fixed upon those Eleanor thought as belonging to her alone. When an auburn-haired wench with full red lips and interested green eyes paused as she served Will, leaning against him as she refilled his tankard, Eleanor had to clench her jaw to keep from saying what sprung to her mind. She turned her attention to her bowl and attempted to study the bits of roast fowl even as she visualized various means of torture that might be appropriate.

A peal of feminine laughter brought her eyes up and they fixed upon the doxy perched in her brother's lap. Amazingly, even though the woman proceeded to play with the laces of Henry's tunic, he seemed not to be terribly concerned.

"Is that all you are going to eat?" Will asked, staring at the nearly full bowl in front of her as his eyes sparkled with amusement. She flushed, remembering a time not long before when she had been allowed to attend a court banquet. Will, who had been at her side for the occasion, had remarked with humor that she ate "just like one of the men."

"I'm not hungry," she said sulkily.

"You had better eat something," he admonished, tearing off a hunk of bread and putting it on her bowl. "This is likely to be the last full meal until we reach Oxford."

"I'm not hungry!" She leapt up from the bench to take a place near the far wall in the shadows of the trestle bar.

"Fine." Will shrugged. "Go hungry and sulk if it suits you better." What was bothering the chit now? he wondered, turning back to his own meal.

The tavern wenches continued to bat their eyes and ply their wiles, even as they pointedly ignored the fresh-cheeked page who was throwing surly looks at his lord. Aware of similar glowers sent in their direction as they gave attention to the handsome knight, they wondered as to his tastes. Passing in the kitchen, they discussed the matter in some detail, but the auburn-haired wench insisted that the knight preferred women and she was determined to prove it.

Accepting yet another draught of ale, Will's eyes fixed on the low-cut bodice of the well-set barmaid as she leaned unnecessarily close to him to refill his tankard. The warmth of the inn, his full stomach, and the hour passed with the ale had dulled his senses pleasantly. He smiled wickedly at the redhead, and the grin deepened as her breath drew in sharply. As her tongue flicked suggestively over her lips, he reached out and pulled her toward him slowly until her body came against his side, her full breasts open to his lusty gaze above the low-cut bodice. His mind was already fixed upon a pleasurable conclusion to the encounter when he heard a soft mumbled oath from the shadows. Good God, he had forgotten Eleanor. He glanced about the room and his eyes widened. Richard and Gilbert had wenches curled up in their laps. Walter's face was buried in the bosom of his buxom companion while the girl giggled and squirmed suggestively. And Henry . . . in a few moments the wench in his lap would have his breaches undone. The redhead gasped with surprise as he pushed her away and leapt from his chair. Crossing the room in a few strides, he grabbed Eleanor's hand and pulled her from the bench, dragging her toward the door to the court-yard. "Oxford awaits!" he bellowed over his shoulder as he pushed her in front of him and into the bright afternoon sunlight toward the waiting horses.

The morning fog had lifted and the air gave heavy promise of a warm afternoon. As they rode, Eleanor kept her eyes closed and her cheek pressed against Will's back. She half listened to the banter tossed back and forth by the men, accompanied by excited barking of the long-legged raches, or running hounds, and the smaller harriers as they raced ahead and back to their party as if urging them on, occasionally departing to chase an unsuspecting bird. She felt totally miserable. The joy had been lost from the adventure, her thoughts now matching the aching muscles in her back and legs.

Eleanor was not totally ignorant of the matters between men and women. Her mother had returned to the Continent soon after her father's death and had shortly remarried, thus leaving her daughter's fate to the Good Knight and to the very male court in which she had been raised. Thus she had been continuously exposed to male ways, even if the particulars had remained somewhat mysterious. But she knew enough to recognize Will's attraction to the barmaid. Not that she was shocked by the knowledge. She was not jealous of what the woman had offered, only by what the woman *could* offer, while she could not. After all, men satisfied and found relief as a matter of normal course. But lud, as things were, where did that leave her? Never was she more aware of her slim hips and small breasts, mere buds just beginning to swell. I might just as well be the page I pretend to be, she thought miserably, for I have nothing else to offer him!

Lost as she was in the misery of her thoughts, it was a moment before she was aware that Henry had suddenly shouted in alarm. Will's arm went behind to catch at Eleanor as he pulled the palfrey's head about, and, grasping with his knees to control the horse, he reached his other hand across his body to pull his sword from its scabbard. The horse tossed its head and sidestepped, and Eleanor could hear Will swear under his breath, damning it for not being his destrier. As they came about, the others were at ready, swords drawn to confront the subject of Henry's alarm.

"Look!" the youthful king shouted again, pointing at the far edge of the meadow bordering the road, now exposed by a break in the trees. The men, who had been scanning the road, gaped doubtfully at Henry's expression of obvious glee, then followed his fixed gaze. Across the field a group of local yeoman had set up targets and were practicing with the bow. The knights exchanged puzzled glances. The sight was common enough, as each yeoman who earned less than one hundred pence a year was obliged by law to practice daily, to be ever ready to serve his lord or king.

Will caught Richard's eye and they exchanged looks of incredulity, while the others could be heard to grumble angrily as they resheathed their weapons. "Dammit, Henry!" Will snapped as he slid his sword into its scabbard. "You nearly unhorsed me, as well as Eleanor! What is so all-fired important about locals practicing with the bow?"

"Look again!" Henry enthused, ignoring his friend's anger. "They are using the longbow! By the blood, I've of a mind to try it!" Before anyone could stay him, Henry had spurred his mount forward.

"Well, I do not think I need to fear for my purse," Hugh commented. "I doubt that at this rate we shall ever make it to Oxford."

"You may be correct." Will chuckled. But his humor

turned to alarm as they sought to catch up with Henry. He saw the men across the field stop in their practice. He could only imagine what they must have been thinking to see a madman bearing down on them and an armed party following behind. "Damn," he muttered, urging his mount forward to an even faster pace.

"What is it?" Eleanor exclaimed. Alarmed by the tenseness she could feel in Will and the fury of his expletive, she leaned out away from him to see what was happening.

"Eleanor, sit back!" he shouted, thrusting an arm back to push her behind him. "You'll unseat us both!"

But it was too late. Adjusting to the shifting weight upon his back, the palfrey turned sharply to counterbalance. Will grasped wildly in an effort to catch Eleanor, but he was met with air as they were flung in unison in a wide arch from the horse's back.

The yeomen stood in dumb silence, their mouths agape. Looking up to find an armed party bearing down on them, they had swiftly drawn arrows to their bows and had stood ready to confront the threat. There was nothing to give identity to the rapidly approaching group, and they could only conclude that it was a small band of outlaws, bent on taking what they could. Even so, doubtful glances were exchanged. Why were the attackers riding toward them so haphazardly, without having drawn their swords? And then one of the riders seemed to lose control of his mount as he and a slender boy riding behind were tossed off. Their companions pulled in their mounts, their shouts drawing the tall blond youth ahead of them as he pulled about and spurred his horse back to the fallen pair. The yeomen watched with amazement as the pair struggled to their feet and the boy's cap fell to reveal a mass of long, thick black hair which tumbled to the waist. Even at the distance between them, the men could hear the bellowing rage of anger from the taller of the two.

The amazing events became apparent to the men as they watched and one of the men was heard to drawl, "A lass, is it? Methinks she's in for a right beating."

" 'Twould be unfair, Rolf," said another calmly, easing his arrow from the string of his bow as he lowered it from his shoulder. "I warrant the lass has saved at least one life today, if she is the cause for unhorsing them both."

Grunts of agreement followed as the men lowered their bows. Fascinated, they leaned against their bows as they waited to see what would happen next. A few eyebrows were raised as the lass did not receive the expected beating but was lifted onto the back of the retrieved horse, and the party continued toward them, now at a more sedate and reasonable pace. Their eyes became guarded as the party approached and their hands stood at the ready upon their weapons, but as the arrivals kept their hands well away from their swords, the yeomen waited.

Henry, unaware or ignoring the guarded look in the yeomen's eyes, pulled his mount to a halt before them and slid from the saddle, his gazed fixed eagerly on the bows. "Those are fine weapons!" he enthused. "It would please me to try one!"

Will had approached near enough to hear Henry's careless request, and he groaned. It was the ultimate of bad form to ask use of another's weapon, particularly when the request was issued as a demand, and he wondered for a moment if they were going to have to fight themselves out of the situation. His hand moved subtlely toward the hilt of his sword as he drew Eleanor half behind him while attempting to keep both of his movements natural.

Henry's natural enthusiasm and his guileless expression saved the moment. While the yeomen were shocked by the request, there was something infectious and unthreatening about the young noble's manner. Tentatively, the one called Rolf held out his bow. Henry accepted it with a reverence that did not go unnoticed by the yeomen. He stroked the hard yew of the bow, which fully met his six feet of height, and then lifted it to his shoulder and drew back the string, whistling softly in appreciation of the resistance to his pull. An expectant glance at the bow's owner brought forth an arrow. Henry placed the arrow's shaft on the belly of the bow and notched it, drawing the string back to his ear as he sighted down the shaft to the target some 150 yards in the distance. The three fingers holding the string relaxed and the arrow jettisoned forward, arching toward the target. Henry and his companions watched with held breath, even as an unmistakable chortle was heard from one of the yeomen. As the missile approached the target it began to wobble wildly and seemed to stop midair, then dropped to the ground a full fifty yards short of the straw-filled target.

Frustrated and puzzled, Henry swung on the yeomen. Their faces were placid, but a few of them were busy studying their feet. "What happened?" he exclaimed.

"Ye did not hit the target, milord," one of the men drawled. " 'Haps you'd like to step closer."

"Give him an arrow matched to the bow," Will said quietly as he studied the men.

The yeomen's gazes shifted in unison to Will. Their usual stoic faces relaxed with surprise, and there was a glimmer of guarded respect in their eyes. Nothing was said, but a new arrow was produced from Rolf's quiver and handed to Henry.

The second arrow shot through the air, landing in the ground just before the target. "Better!" Henry shouted, "Much better!" Then realization dawned on him and he spun on Will. "What was wrong with the first arrow?"

"It had too much spine." Will shrugged.

There was no pretense in the looks of respect the yeomen now gave to Will. " 'Haps you'd like to try, milord." The apparent leader of the group, a large burly man with a thick, unruly thatch of black hair peppered with grey, offered his bow to Will.

Will stepped forward and took the man's bow as an arrow was produced. He set the nocked end of the arrow in its place on the string. Locking the arm which held the bow's belly, he raised his hand slightly above his eyes, then lowered it to sight the target as he pulled the string back, all in a single, smooth motion. Hesitating for a moment against the incredible pull, he allowed the string to slip through his fingers. The arrow left the bow with a breath and arched through the air in silent flight, striking the distant target with a soft thud, only inches from the center.

"Well done, Will!" Hugh laughed, joined by the others as Will turned back to the man and handed him his weapon.

"There is a slight quartering wind," he said to the stunned yeomen as a smile touched his mouth.

Dumbfounded, the man frowned. This man they called Will was obviously noble; it told in his bearing and his attire. The

sword sheathed at his side was that of a knight, and all knew
that a bow was not a weapon favored by such. Yet perhaps
this was one of those rare men who had at some time found
favor with his lord and had been allowed to improve himself,
eventually to the rank of knighthood.

"By the blood, Will!" Henry bellowed with frustration, the
import of what had happened finally hitting him. "Explain
yourself! What do you mean by a matched arrow—and how
the devil did you learn to shoot like that?"

"Perhaps you would like to answer the first question."
Will's gaze settled on the owner of his borrowed bow.

The man glanced at Henry and had the dignity to look
sheepish. "Each arrow is different, milord. Each has its own
life and, as a living thing, acts differently. One that is perfectly
in tune with the bow will pass without touching it. If it is not,
it will touch and deflect. Your . . . first arrow thrust well to the
left as it passed the bow. We must know the traits of each that
we carry."

"Impossible!" Henry snorted. "You have too many arrows
between you to know them all!"

"Not impossible, Henry," Will said. "They would know
however many provided by their lord—hence a wise lord will
provide them with as many as would be needed for battle, in
spite of the cost."

Henry's brows gathered for a moment as he wondered if
Will could be pulling his leg, and then they lifted. "Which
reminds me! You have not answered the second question.
How did you learn to shoot like that?"

"You forget that my family was part of Wales when all of
England still regarded them as mere barbarians." He did not
miss the shadow that passed over the young king's eyes at the
mention of Wales, but he ignored it. "My grandfather, and
his father before him, did not gain the name of Strongbow for
naught."

Will saw recognition and respect dawn on some of the yeomen's faces. He knew that it made little difference if they
knew his identity, however, as long as they did not recognize
Henry. It was understood in such situations as this—and with
Henry there had been many—that he wished to be treated as
his companion's equal. If the yeomen were to know that they

were in the company of their king, the easy companionship that was beginning to develop would rapidly disappear—and Henry's pleasure would thus be lost. Will could not but reflect upon his sovereign's pleasures. As much as he enjoyed them himself, he could only wish that Henry would give the same measure of attention to the serious needs of his realm.

As the afternoon progressed each knight took his turn with the bow, and soon any thoughts of continuing their journey to Oxford was forgotten. Though speculative glances were thrown in her direction, none dared to question Eleanor's presence. Stern glances from Will and Henry kept her from interjecting herself into the day's amusement, and she spent her time sitting to one side on a grassy slope edging the meadow, sulking in boredom.

A light meal of bread, cheese, and jerky was shared from their saddlebags with the yeomen, and conversation turned to matters of interest to the freemen, with light prodding by the knights. Henry, growing bored by the turn in the conversation, brightened considerably when a hard leather ball was produced by one of their guests. Instantly the meal was forgotten as they took up a rousing game of bandyball, each rushing to find a suitable stick and sides quickly drawn by a balance of size and agility. The two teams rushed about the field in a harum-scarum pattern of the rules of the game, amid shouts of laughter and grunts of pain as bodies were ruthlessly struck in an attempt to move the ball to either side's goal at opposite ends of the wide meadow.

Eleanor watched from her place on the sidelines, her mood shifting between petulance and laughter as the men provided occasional comic amusement from the field. Reasonably, she knew that she had nothing to feel sorry for; there was no way she could participate in the brutal game, even as, had they allowed her to try, she could have pulled the longbow. But it rankled nonetheless. Lud, she thought, first the inn and now this. Left out again. But then, watching Will as he struck the ball between two of his opponents with a shout of laughter, the sound of his deep voice carrying across the field, she felt washed with a confusing feeling of warmth. The odd feeling had begun as she had watched him at the inn. The look he had given to the barmaid—the touch of his hand when he had

pulled her from the taproom. Suddenly she did not really mind
not being able to play in the game. For the first time in her life
she did not just want to be Will's best friend, at least not by
itself. For the first time in her life she felt rather feminine.
And she liked it.

The game ended soon after, the men collapsing beneath the
trees, their hair and clothes damp with their efforts, as they
gasped to catch their breaths. Good-natured banter was exchanged about the game and the expertise of each side, though
the score was deemed to be a draw. Eventually fatigue had its
way as the party stretched out, gaining what comfort they
could on their blankets and cloaks, and the soft rhythm of
their slumber soon was the only sound heard.

When Eleanor awoke, the sun had lowered to the beginnings of dusk, and for a moment she merely stared into the intertwined branches above her as she wondered why she had
awakened. And then she heard a sound and realized that she
had not awakened of her own accord. She rolled onto her side
and stroked Will's shoulder softly, not wanting to startle him
from sleep. "Will," she whispered, trying to keep her voice
calm. "Will, wake up, I think I heard something."

He opened his eyes, focusing sleepily on her as she leaned
over him, and then as her words registered he was instantly
awake. "What is it?" he asked softly even as he sat up and his
eyes were moving about him.

"There was something—someone in the trees—there . . . ,"
she whispered, pointing to a spot behind them.

His hand was on the hilt of his sword, which lay next to
him, and though she could feel the tenseness in his arm which
lay beneath her hand, his manner was calm. "Wait here. And
wake Hugh, as you did me," he said, rising silently. In a moment he was gone, disappearing into the dense foliage.

She did as he bade, and Hugh moved to the others until all
were awake, including the yeomen, who took up their bows in
readiness though they instinctively deferred to orders from the
knights.

The men were tensed as they fixed warily on the fringe of
trees, but their expressions changed to wonder as they heard
the sound of laughter. To their amazement, Will appeared
with another man, engaged in pleasant conversation. Weap-

ons were lowered as the band of men recognized the newcomer
by his garb, the short red bardy coat of the goliard, or wandering minstrel. Some of the men eyed the stranger with
displeasure, knowing the type to be frowned upon by the
Church. The priests were forever admonishing the populace
against the manner of these renegades, too often talented,
educated men of the clergy who had forsaken their vows to
spend the remainder of their lives in wastefulness and the evil
pursuit of drink and wenching. Worse, traveling from tavern
to tavern, they imparted the most inflammatory manner of
song and story of Crown and Church, using their exceptional
talents, which far surpassed those of the ordinary bard who
might maintain residence within castle or court, in giving
pointed, though treasonable and blasphemous, utterance.

"We have our evening's entertainment!" Will laughed, the
easy sound of his tone encouraging the men to put aside their
weapons. "I give you Darcy, for he will give me no other
name, but he does promise to pleasure us with his song and
wit. What say you, shall we allow him to sup with us?"

More enthusiasm met Will's question than the disgruntled
comments that were passed among a few, and the stranger was
welcomed warmly. The harriers were taken out and hares were
caught for supper, quickly gutted and skinned, and put upon
the spit.

As the supper was readied Eleanor had the opportunity to
study the goliard objectively. She had never seen his like
before and had to stifle a giggle. If her priest was to be believed, the man would bear horns and a tail. While she could
readily dispute the former, she could only speculate upon the
latter, though reason defied it. To her view he looked like any
other man: perhaps more handsome than most, but normal in
any event. He was taller than average, slim, with warm brown
eyes and dark, curling hair which clung about his ears. His
nose was chiseled over well-formed lips, and his strong, firm
jaw was much like Will's, except that it bore a fascinating cleft
which drew the eye as he spoke. 'Twas said that the devil—or
an angel—made such a mark upon birth, Eleanor could not
recall which. A sudden rush of pleasure washed over her.
Truly, life was grand. She had only sought to join them on a
day's hunt and it had turned into an adventure!

As they finished supper, Eleanor retreated to the shadows, taking Will's fox-lined cloak for warmth. In her situation she feared not that they would exclude her from their company, but that the manner of the evening would change to accommodate her presence. She was far too curious about the ways of men to call attention to herself and ruin the uniqueness of the moment—and what she might hear if they forgot about her. The events of the evening did not prove disappointing. Occasionally Eleanor had to stifle a gasp at a comment or the amorous subject of the bard's song, which was offered in a mellow, appealing voice, but she managed to maintain her silence.

As the bard finished his last song, the mood suddenly changed. Eleanor had not understood the meaning of the lyric, enjoying only the haunting melody, but as he finished she sensed the tension in the glade and she looked about to each man, wondering what had happened. The yeomen's eyes were guardedly fixed on the noblemen, apparently waiting for something. The squires' expressions were filled with horror as their eyes were on their lords, who were watching Henry. Eleanor's breath drew in as she realized her brother's face was blood-red and he was staring at the goliard with murder in his eyes.

"Is your meaning to criticize the Throne of England, bard?" Henry asked in a low, barely controlled voice.

"Nay, milord," the goliard answered offhandedly. "King Henry is not to blame for what has happened. Moreover, when he is aware of the situation, I am certain that he will take steps to rectify it."

The anger in Henry's face eased at the bard's soothing comment, even as the tension in the glade relaxed. But Henry was not completely appeased. "I think you are overstating the matter in your verse. England sends what share of funds she can to support Rome; we cannot do more. The Holy Father will not press us."

"The fact that Pope Honorius does not demand payment does not mean that the funds are not owed, milord," Darcy pressed. "The debts build, and one day they will be called due."

"Pah, Peter's Pense has been with us since my—since King John's time, and it has served but a mere annoyance."

Eleanor noticed the angry lines that formed about Will's mouth, and she wondered as to their meaning.

"King John made us vassal to Rome, hence our portion owed to the Church is greater than other countries," Will said evenly. "Darcy is correct; eventually the debt is certain to impoverish England."

"It is only a matter of time before the Holy Father will demand the funds," Hugh agreed. "He has already begun to put pressure on Philip of France for his share, and it is a far lesser amount than what England owes."

"More than that," Will pressed. "Can you be unaware of the preference that is being given to the Florentines who have come here? The cardinals of Rome give favor to their own, nepotism reigns, and England is becoming filled with new houses of banking. When nobles are unable to pay, loans are made with unreasonable interest—"

"There be nothing new," Henry protested. "The Jews—"

"The Jews be our own," Richard countered. "They—"

"You count the Jews among the English, Sir Richard?" Henry asked, turning to the knight with amazement.

"Aye, milord. They be of England, with her welfare as their own. But these Italians are for themselves."

"Enough!" Henry snapped. "This conversation is ended. I will speak of something else!"

Exasperated by Henry's blindness, Will tried again. If Henry wanted to rule, he had to realize the importance of what they were saying. "We have far more reason to fear these Italians than ever the Jews. The Florentines are under papal sanction, the protection of the Church—"

"Enough!" Henry cried. "I said well enough! You, of any in this land, are in no position to plead of injustices! Your own father sold me out, nearly gave my birthright, the very Throne of England, to France!"

Breaths drew in at the outburst, and each looked to the other in disbelief. The yeomen blinked with confusion, then, as Henry's words began to sink in and they at last realized the identity of their companion, to a man they blanched. Will ignored the others as he fought to control his outrage. "How so, milord?" he asked softly.

"He had the French invaders within his grasp, yet what did he do? Did he squash the menace? Nay, God's breath, he sued

for peace! Sending them home with little more than a warning!''

Will took a deep, even breath as he struggled to control the
rage he felt at Henry's stupidity—more than that, at his lack
of loyalty and understanding for the one who had saved his
throne for him. "He cast the French from your shores, Your
Grace. Moreover, he did so when England was bankrupt, the
Holy Father was pressing for control, and the barons were
split in their loyalty to you. England's greatest need was peace,
a time to heal her wounds.'' He cast a warning glance to his
brothers, who wore open looks of horror and outrage.
"Perhaps, Your Grace, you are referring to the fact that when
my father died, even Louis of France, England's most bitter
enemy, paid tribute to him. Upon learning of his death, he
would ask each he met, 'Did you hear that the Marshal has
died? He was the most loyal man I ever knew.' Often has that
tribute been used against the Good Knight's memory. But
anyone who knew William Marshal accepted the tribute in the
manner it was given—the respect of an opponent for a cour-
ageous foe. Only my father's most bitter enemies would seek
to use it to damn his name.''

A heavy silence hung over the small copse. None dared
speak as all awaited Henry's response. Only one among them
did not feel the fear of what might happen which passed
among the company. Eleanor could no longer control herself,
and her voice was heard in the ensuing silence. "Henry, you
are an ass.''

Faces blanked with horror. Gazes shifted to the king, who
had paled. Then Henry's mouth began to twitch. Suddenly, he
threw back his head and bellowed with laughter, and was enjoined by the others as the thicket reverberated with relief. In
the laughter, Will sighed as he glanced at Eleanor, for once
grateful for her presence.

The remainder of the evening passed more pleasantly.
Henry, his temper now cooled and his curiosity piqued, encouraged Darcy to sing of other matters of the realm and news
carried from distant parts of England.

Fighting a yawn, Eleanor struggled against sleep, not wanting to miss a moment, but her lids grew heavy and there
were moments when she realized that she had been dozing. She

pulled the cloak more tightly about her as she felt a moment of chill and fought another yawn.

"I've laid my blankets out for you," a soft voice said near her ear.

She lifted her head sleepily to find that Will had appeared at her side in the darkness. For a moment she could not fathom it; she had not seen him move from his place near the fire.

"Come, Eleanor, it is time for sleep," he said quietly.

She did not resist the gentle firmness of the order but gave in to it gratefully. She found herself tucked into the comforting weight of his blankets and snuggled into their warmth. "Darcy speaks of treason," she murmured, giving a last moment to lingering thoughts.

"Nay, little mouse, not treason," Will's soft voice said as a light hand touched her brow. "He speaks the truth, however painful it might be. Now sleep."

Will returned to his place near the fire. A soft smile lingered as he speculated on the manner of Eleanor's dreams. She had heard things tonight beyond her years and reasonings and had spoken of her confusion even as she slipped into sleep. She was bright—he often thanked God for that fact. Whatever might come to be between them, he knew he could not bear to be wed to an insipid creature who would never question or seek truths. His smile came from realizing what she had heard—indeed, he had never lost sight of the fact that she sat nearby in the shadows, even before her outrageous outburst, however much she might try to remain unobtrusive. He alone had heard her soft gasps in response to the blatant conversation exchanged among men, and he had struggled not to laugh aloud. Grow, Eleanor, he thought. And you have much growing to do.

The thought sobered him and he sighed softly. God's breath, she is such a child, and I have ever known her as such. Can I ever think of her as a woman, however much I might try?

3

"You seem restless, milord. May I join you?"

Will looked up to find the goliard standing near. He realized then that the camp had grown silent. Lost in his own thoughts, he had not been aware of when the others had taken to their bedrolls, and he was amazed to find that a fog had drifted in about them, shrouding the bodies of the sleeping men so that only dark forms could be made out in the low flames of the campfire.

He pulled himself up against his saddle, which he had been using as a back rest, and gestured for the bard to sit next to him. He was glad that the goliard had chosen to speak to him. Sleep resolutely avoided him, and the man's words—and his courage to say them—had stirred him. "Where is your home, Darcy? I would venture it to be Northumbria; your accent is of that area."

"Milord, you know that a goliard has no home. We are born of the sea and travel on mist. No mother suckled us, no father gave us succor."

"Humph," Will snorted, settling himself more comfortably. "You mean that you are a pack of renegades leaving hearth and home behind you, as you cannot return for fear of the rope. What was it, Darcy? A disgruntled husband, a sheriff, or the Church which cast you out? What are you running from?''

"I run from no man," the bard countered, enjoying the exchange. "Rather, I merely seek truth."

"Is that what you profess your night's song to be? The truth? If what I heard tonight to be of evidence, I fear you may yet find the rope."

"Ah, should I fear to sing a song, innocently given? I offered my words to a simple group of men who gathered for—what would it be—a hunt, I believe you said? Was I to know that I sang for the king?''

Will's head jerked about and he studied the man in the dim glow from the campfire. Darcy's face remained placid, but somehow Will knew that behind that look of innocence the bard had known from the start with whom he had shared his supper. "You insist that your songs were innocently given?" he pressed softly.

"My words are received differently by each man, milord. I cannot be responsible if one, due to his torment and guilt, puts his own interpretations upon them."

"Indeed." Will snorted. "I will give you the point, goliard, as I am too weary to debate the matter with you."

"I agree, milord." The bard chuckled. "We have been given too little precious time in this life, and it should not be wasted. In point, it was why I left Newcastle, having spent a fortnight there entertaining the guild members of that town, having been tossed only a meager portion of their table by reward."

"What did you expect, to sit above the salt?" Will laughed.

"Generous rewards from a merchant? Never." Darcy grinned. "However, there is nothing which causes more dismay for a bard than to have his song overlooked. When no reason is caught by his words. Alas, it was so with those good folk. My time was wasted."

"So you moved on, until the fates brought you here," Will observed, his eyes narrowing.

" 'Twould seem so, milord," Darcy offered with a shrug. "But not until I passed by Bedford Castle. And happy I was to find myself on the demesne of William deBeauchamp. By the reputation of his other holdings, he is known far about to be most generous to those of my stripe. There I sought refuge, a replenishing of my soul, as it were, from the kind citizens of Newmarket. Tired and footweary, imagine my dismay to find myself turned from its gate."

If the minstrel's intention was to gain Will's attention, he had it now. "Turned from its gate?" he repeated. "Why? What reason was given? As you say, deBeauchamp is known for his generosity to the traveler. Perhaps his bailey was filled. The pilgrimages have increased—"

"Nay, milord," Darcy interrupted with a sad note. "No one is admitted. DeBreaute's man has sealed the portcullis."

"DeBreaute!" Will sat up. The sleeping men stirred in their sleep at the sound of his uplifted voice. "What has Fawkes deBreaute to do with Bedford Castle?" he added in a hoarse whisper.

"I cannot imagine." Darcy shrugged. "I had been led to believe that upon King John's death deBreaute had fallen from favor and the demesne had been returned to William deBeauchamp, its rightful owner."

"So it had!" Will growled. "That damned mercenary lost what he had taken under John! God's blood, Darcy, what is it that you are trying to tell me?"

"Tell you? Milord, I am merely recounting my journey."

"Dammit man, enough!" Will snapped, his patience lost. "I well understand the position of your kind, but you need not fear from me! You know full well the identity of the one with whom you supped. Enough of your game, tell me what you know!"

A veil seemed to slip from the goliard's eyes and his manner became serious. "Is it not true that our good king sent a royal judge to secure the holdings for deBeauchamp at Bedford?"

"Aye, he did."

"Then it is true." Darcy sighed. "Milord, deBreaute has refused to release the holdings. Even now his man holds the king's justice a prisoner and he has sealed the gate against deBeauchamp and his claim."

"DeBreaute holds a king's man hostage?"

"It would seem so, milord."

"Darcy, you have done well," Will ground out, barely controlling his anger as he considered the outrage. "I promise that the Crown will reward you most generously for this news."

"I do not wish reward, milord, apart from justice," Darcy countered.

Will's brow gathered suspiciously. "No reward? Why?"

"Let us just say that I am content to see justice found."

Will studied the man for a long moment. "So be it." He glanced at the sleeping form of his king. "Will you be willing to repeat your story in the morning?"

"Aye, milord, gladly if you see the need."

"I do. For now let us sleep," Will added grimly. "There is nothing more to be done for the moment, but in the morning we will need clear heads about us."

Will awoke to an awareness that something warm and wet was nuzzling his ear. He opened one eye to find one of the silver-grey raches curled up next to him, stealing his warmth. He fought a yawn as a glance about confirmed that the other dogs had been released and the squires were busy breaking camp. The aroma of roasting meat assailed his senses, and he struggled to sit up as he wondered how he could have slept so long. And then he remembered the late conversation by the campfire. Tensing, he cast his gaze about the camp until he spied Darcy across the clearing talking with Richard.

His eyes narrowed as he watched the bard with his brother, and he turned again to the thoughts he had had just before sleeping. What would Henry's reaction be when he was told of Fawkes's duplicity? Their young king was hotheaded and impulsive, as his forebears had been. That in itself did not disturb Will overmuch, but it had yet to be proved *which* of his line he would most resemble. The wisdom of his grandfather, Henry II? The military prowess of his uncle, Richard Coeur de Lion? They had both been impulsive and hotheaded, the bane of their father's existence. But their Plantagenet weaknesses were compensated for by their strengths. Or . . . Will shifted uncomfortably as he considered another possibility. The rache lying by his side whimpered softly as if sensing the disturbed thoughts of its master. He scratched the dog's ear absent-mindedly as he watched Henry wolf down his breakfast. Will's real and abiding fear was that Henry would be like his father, John—greedy, ambitious without direction, cruel, and the worst of characteristics in a ruler: faithlessness to those he needed to trust the most. In youthful petulance —Will prayed that it was all it had been—Henry had been quick to forget the loyalty he owed to Will's father. The words thrown the previous night had hurt, but, more important, they had stuck a note of fear in Will. It was the kind of thing John would have said.

Will sighed heavily as he rose and stretched against the stiffness in his body. He moved toward Darcy, knowing that whatever happened, it had to be faced. He had barely taken a step when Eleanor seemed to materialize from the copse of trees beside him.

"Will! I need to talk with you!"

"Not now, Eleanor."

"But it's important!" Her mouth slipped into a pout.

He looked down at her and, noting the expression, so like her brother's when he did not want to face an issue of importance, felt something snap. "Damnation, Eleanor, I said not now!"

He ignored her gasp and the hurt expression that came over her face as he stepped around her. Somehow, at the moment, something about it gave him a perverse feeling of pleasure.

"Darcy." The man turned toward him as he approached and the conversation with Richard ceased abruptly. Richard frowned at the dire expression on his older brother's face, and he looked at the goliard curiously, wondering what the man had done to gain Will's obvious wrath. "Are you prepared to repeat what you told me last night?"

"Certainly, milord," the man answered smoothly, apparently unruffled by Will's manner.

"I warn you, Darcy, it had better be as you presented. If your tale was told only to gain reward . . ."

"Reward, milord?" Darcy smiled. "I assured you that I desired none."

"Indeed." Will smirked. "And still I wonder why." He started to turn away and paused. "I warn you to mind your words, Darcy. Simply give the facts of the matter, nothing more."

"Aye, milord." Darcy gave a small smile. "I will say nothing to infuse the situation."

Will startled slightly at the man's perceptiveness and frowned as he wondered about the manner of the man who had wandered with such apparent innocence into their camp.

"Your Grace."

Henry looked up with surprise at the tone in Will's voice and the formality of the address. His mouth was full of bread, and it was a moment before he could speak. He swallowed, wincing slightly at the lump that passed his throat. "What is it, Will?" He coughed, glancing at the others who had gathered silently to listen to the exchange. Suddenly he realized that he was sitting before a campfire, his hands filled with bread and greasy roast meat. And with it, the air had suddenly become quite formal. Damn, the thought passed him, why did things always work to make him appear the fool? "Risley!" he bellowed at last. The squire appeared instantly, his young face open with sudden fear that he had done something to displease his lord and king. "Take this!" Henry handed him the remains of his breakfast. "And give me something with which to wash my hands!" A towel was produced, and Henry wiped them absently as he looked at the men crouched about the warmth of the fire.

"Well, what is it?" he demanded in a tone he thought appropriate.

Will nodded at Darcy, and the bard launched into his story. As he had promised, it was told without embellishment, but the reaction was significant. The knights were outraged, but none more than Henry, who jumped to his feet before the final words were spoken.

"Damn that deBreaute! I will have his head!" Henry raged, his face turning blood-red. "How dare he kidnap one of my men! By the blood, how dare he defy my order!"

"My lord," Will said soothingly. Inwardly he was pleased that Henry had not merely dismissed the matter, as it was an unavoidable, treasonable offense. But it was also a time for clear heads. "DeBreaute will be punished, of that there is no doubt. And it has been a long time in coming." Will could feel pleasure at the prospect radiating from his brothers. Indeed, there was much for the mercenary deBreaute to answer for. Given enough time, justice did find its way. "DeBreaute is not without power; plans must be cautiously made."

"Aye—aye." Henry waved him off as he paced about the campfire, nearly bumping into Eleanor, who had been listening intently from the sidelines.

"Take it from him," she hissed with fury as she stared up at her brother. "But do it well. Send to London, tell deBurgh that you shall lay siege to Bedford. Order deBurgh to send men and arms. Let this be evidence that you are King of England and no one shall take what is yours!"

Henry's brow gathered as he stared down at his sister, and then his face seemed to lighten at her words. He spun back on the waiting men, his face filled with excited purpose. "Aye, and that is how it shall be! By God, all shall know that no one will commit treason against the Crown and go unpunished! See to it!"

Will nodded at Gilbert, who turned to his squire, shouting orders to ready his mount, and Will turned back to stare at Eleanor. His eyes darkened as he regarded her, but she did not notice as she beamed with satisfaction, obviously pleased by what had happened. She jumped as he took her arm roughly and spun her about. She had been so absorbed in her moment of victory that she had not noticed when he strode across the clearing toward her, and she did not catch her breath until he had led her from the grove, into the privacy of the trees beyond. She spun about, her face filled with anger and shock, but the words froze in her throat at the rage that he turned on her.

"You little fool! How dare you!" he choked as he attempted to keep his voice down.

"How dare I?" she squeaked. "I only said what I thought—"

"You have no right to express your opinions in such matters!"

"No right?" she gasped as she tried to wrench from the painful grip on her arm. "I have every right!"

He drew in his breath through clenched teeth and fought for control. How could he explain to her, how could he compete against the cloistered existence in which she had been raised where her every utterance was considered an absolute? "Nay," he gritted. "You have no rights, but as given by me! You wanted our betrothal, Eleanor, and you won it. You are my wife, not the queen you could have been. But if you had gained the reason and the maturity such a position would require, you would know that you must not meddle in something which you know nothing about!"

"I don't know what you are talking about," she cried softly as tears welled up in her eyes, as much from the fact that Will was angry with her as much as from the pain in her arm.

He hesitated for a moment, then released his grip slightly as weariness passed over him. "Nay, I know that you don't." He sighed. "But you must learn. Eleanor, it was for Henry to decide. It was imperative that he reach those same conclusions on his own."

"But—what difference does it make?" she sobbed, unable to hide her hurt. "As long as it is done—"

"It makes a great deal of difference," he interrupted. "He is the king, Eleanor. He must learn how to rule like one." Seeing her face work with what he had said, he felt a moment of compassion, again aware of her tender years, and he drew her into his arms in comfort. Perversely, the realization struck him that she, even as the child she was, had seen to the heart of the matter with a quickness he could only wish upon her brother. And then he recalled another matter. Brushing the top of her head with a light kiss, he squeezed her lightly. "Now what was it that you wanted to speak to me about? Before I put you off."

"Oh." The small voice was muffled in his tunic where her face was pressed. She leaned back, her face brightening through her tears as her thoughts swiftly turned to more pleasant matters, and noting with relief that he no longer seemed angry with her. "I lost my tapestry. Have you seen it?"

"Tapestry?" He frowned for a moment. "Oh, aye, it is in my saddlebags. Now hurry and eat, for we leave immediately for Bedford."

"Will you take me with you? Truly?" she breathed hopefully, leaning back against his arms to see his face. "Oh, Will, really?"

"I do not have much choice." He frowned, clearly displeased by the prospect. "But I plan to send you back at the first opportunity," he warned. "Some days will be taken to measure the situation, and you should be safe enough. But I warn you, Eleanor, do what I say, in all things."

"Oh, Will, I promise!" She could barely contain the impulse to jump up and down. Instead, she wrapped her arms about him and pressed her cheeks against his chest as she tried to contain her happiness. "I promise, Will, you won't even know that I am there."

4

THE bright afternoon sun rested heavily on the mounted and armored knight. The heavily padded gambeson near his skin was soaked in sweat beneath a rigid hauberk of fire- and water-hardened leather, covered by a weighted chain-mail shirt of silvered interlocking links of pressed steel covered over by a sleeveless tunic of gold samite. His long legs were similarly encased with mail, and overlapping steel plates protected his knees. Boots of chain mesh covered his feet and his heels were girded with the golden spurs of his warrior order.

The coif of his chain-mail shirt covered his neck and hair beneath a rigid steel helm, shadowing his face beneath a broad protective noseguard, which added to his ominous appearance. The helm was crested by the bright green and gold plumes of his colors. Thus protected, the identity of the knight was known by the coat of arms on his chest above the wide earl's belt from which hung the heavy two-handed sword at his side. A brilliant red lion, rampant with open feral mouth, marshaled with red chevrons of like color, and the matching coat of arms on the shield which hung from his saddle, identified him as the Marshal of England.

Will's eyes moved slowly over the growing mass of human-

ity before him. The view from the small knoll afforded him a
vantage point over the flat landscape. His gaze noted the
movement below him in the encampment which rounded the
tall circular stone keep elevated on its motte, a rise just slightly
higher than the one on which he stood.

The afternoon sun at his back lit up the ancient stone of the
keep, lending a pink aura to the battlements. A feeling of the
invincibility of the keep touched him, but he quickly dismissed
it. Few keeps were invincible, he reasoned with a grin he could
not contain, except those as his own Chepstow, which lay far
to the west on the Welsh border. I will beat you, Fawkes, he
thought grimly. Hide behind those walls, seal your portcullis,
I will beat you. Aye, even as you peer around the merlons of
your walls each morning to see if we are still here. Does your
mind burn with the truth of it as you fix upon the Marshal
coat of arms? There are four of us out here, Fawkes. Four of
us to make you pay for stealing the honor of our lands at
Huntingdon. For using that moment when my father lay dying
and we could not come to the defense of our lands. You knew
we were vulnerable then, just as you knew my father would
plead for us to keep the peace at that tenuous time. But we are
not vulnerable now, deBreaute. We are here, waiting.

His eyes narrowed beneath his helm as he studied the
machicolation of the keep, the jutting corbels of the upper
tower which reached out over the walls. He visualized the large
iron kettles which were even now being set over open fires to
heat whatever noxious liquid could be gathered to be poured
through the slatted floors onto the attacking forces—but not
oil. Nay, not oil, nor even animal fat, he thought, for surely,
Fawkes you are in dire shortage of those precious items.

A cruel, satisfied smile touched Will's mouth as he pictured
what the conditions within the keep were certain to be after the
five long weeks following the appearance of their forces
before the walls. Windows shuttered, allowing only meager
light from arrow slits, the interior was no doubt depressing to
its occupants. Endless days of darkened gloom. Smoke-filled
rooms. The overpowering stink of overburdened privies.
While water might be in plenty, as Will had been unable to
discover its source, food was certainly becoming scarce. Has
your diet been reduced to horseflesh, Fawkes?—for you al-

ways did relish your banquet. Divine Justice, it had finally
come. He closed his eyes for a brief moment, thanking God
for delivering Fawkes deBreaute into his hands.

His eyes moved to the activity outside the walls of the keep
and fixed with satisfaction on the siege machines, even knowing that they did little more than give added discomfort to
those within. The massive trebuchet and smaller mangonels
were for propelling stones over the battlements—or decaying
animal remains, to add discomfort and, it was hoped, disease.
A tortoise was set in place against the covered portcullis, the
shedlike structure protecting the activity of the battering ram
against whatever mayhem could be inflicted from those on the
ramparts above. To Will's left a belfray, or giant tower, was
being constructed with four levels and ladders leading to each.
When completed, the structure would be wheeled to the wall
of the keep, its roofs of water-soaked hides repelling an attempt to fire it—and the men-at-arms loaded within would
seek to take the walls.

Henry was having a fine time, Will mused. Knighted at his
coronation by Will's father, the youthful king had found his
first opportunity to earn his spurs, and he was relishing every
moment of it. Have your amusement, Henry, but none of this
will prove Fawkes's undoing, thought Will. He knew, as the
unseasoned king could not fully appreciate, that Fawkes could
hold out indefinitely against any such ploys. He well knew the
determination and resolve of the man within, a fact of which
he could not seem to convince Henry. Will had learned well at
his father's knee. He could hear the Marshal's voice across the
years: know your opponent. The measure of the man weighed
far heavier than whatever obstacles you might throw against
him. Nay, Will's experience reasoned that they would have to
starve deBreaute out, and that could well take months—and
Will was growing impatient. But perhaps there was another
way. . . .

"Easy, Hamal." Will said soothingly to the restless destrier
as the animal shifted beneath him, impatient against the en-
forced inactivity. The mean-blooded animal had been named
tongue-in-cheek for the Arabic word for "lamb," a left-
handed tribute to Will's father, who had been the only one of
his family to go off to the Crusades. That fact had given rise to

long hours of heated discussion before the fire at Chepstow. Will felt it to be a gross waste of English manhood, while William had defended the action in his loyalty to King and Church.

The horse sidestepped, tossing its massive head as Will's attention was momentarily taken in controlling him. Setting his rowelspurs to the animal's flank, he leapt forward, riding down into the valley toward the cluster of brightly striped tents at the center of the encampment.

Pulling the horse before the largest of the tents, he waited as an experienced farrier came forward to grab the reins before he could slip from the saddle. The trained animal's eyes rolled wildly as it was released from the weight of its master, and Will could feel the nervous ripple of the horse's skin as he dismounted. Seeing that Hamal was in good hands, Will nodded at the posted guards and slipped into the coolness of the tent.

His face slipped into an easy grin as he noted those in the king's company. Two tall, muscled knights had turned at his entrance, one bearing the coat of arms of the Earl of Gloucester and the other the device of the powerful deBraose family. "Gilbert . . . William," Will acknowledged with a grin. "I am glad that you are here."

"I am plagued by the Marshal family," Henry growled. "If not by blood, then by marriage."

Will winked at his brothers-in-law and then turned to his king, who he noticed was slumped in his chair and wore a decided pout. "I gather the news they bring has not pleased you? You come from deBurgh?" he added, turning back to the others.

"Aye, Will," Gilbert deClare confirmed. "The justiciar is in a nettle over what you do here. There are matters in London which—"

"There are matters in London which deBurgh is well capable of handling without me!" Henry shouted as he leapt from his chair and grabbed up a pitcher of ale, which he sloshed into a tankard. He took a long draught before turning back to the men as he wiped his mouth with the back of his hand. "Our esteemed justiciar would have me return to London so that he may place me under his thumb!"

Besides, Will thought, you are having a much better time

here. But for once Will agreed with the youthful king. It was time, beyond time, for Henry to learn the arts of warfare. "It matters not, milord," Will offered soothingly. "Soon we will have matters settled here."

"Humph," Henry snorted as he took another draught. "If the tower does not do the trick, we may be here unto winter."

"I think not, your grace." Will smiled. "There is more than one way into that keep. Did you bring them?" he asked deClare.

"Would I not?" The russet-haired knight grinned as his dark brown eyes lit up.

"Bring what?" Henry blurted, his eyes shifting among the other men.

"Twenty-three of the best miners in England!" Gilbert crowed. "Snatched them right out of the tin mines in Cornwall—I don't think Prince Richard has noticed their passing as yet."

"Saint George!" Henry gasped. "You took men out of my brother's mines—without consulting with him?" The question went unanswered, but by the looks on the other men's faces there was no need. Slowly a grin began on Henry's face, then widened as he gave in to a great bellow of laughter. Though a year younger than Henry, Richard of Cornwall already excelled in talents of administration and business. Everything the young man touched seemed to turn to gold, and the mines he had inherited brought forth wealth unthought of by their predecessors. While Henry's fierce feelings of loyalty and love for his family took precedence over anything else in his life, undoubtedly the result of an unloved, lonely childhood, it touched a humorous chord within him to know that Richard had been surpassed in his own game.

"See that they are well fed and comfortable," Will ordered. "Tomorrow their service to their king will begin—and everything depends upon them."

"It has already been done," William deBraose countered.

"Why, Will?" Henry asked as he wiped tears of laughter from the corners of his eyes. "We had already discussed the possibility of undermining the walls and had concluded that it would be ineffective."

"Not exactly, Your Grace. We know that deBreaute will

begin countermining the moment we hit the walls. Further, in
that we do not know the angle of the walls beneath ground
level, we are at a disadvantage. We know that the walls were
built with a considerable batter, the angle of slope resisting
undermining. Both facts give deBreaute the advantage. His
counteroffensive is certain to win out against us—unless we
can move with speed.''

A light was kindled behind Henry's eyes as he grasped
Will's meaning. "Thus—experienced miners. They will see to
the task before deBreaute's men can counter to meet the tunnel before it has done its damage."

"Exactly—or so we hope."

"When do we begin?" Henry's eyes widened with anticipation.

"In the morning, I should think." Will laughed. "Give the
men a chance to rest; they have traveled a goodly distance. For
now, milord, with your permission there are matters to which
I should attend." At Henry's absent nod, his mind filled with
the prospect of the morrow, Will turned to the others. "I
would hear of my sisters." he said, moving to the opening of
the tent. "I trust that they are well? And my nieces and
nephews?"

The three men stood before the king's tent exchanging
pleasantries. Will truly liked the men his sisters had chosen for
their husbands—indeed, for that is how it had been, even
though Will suspected that the men thought the choices had
been theirs. However, as soon as the well-being of his family
had been confirmed, Will found his mind wandering. He
realized that he had not seen Eleanor that day. Normally she
was ever underfoot. He had tried to send her back to London
since the day of their arrival, but Henry—moreover, Eleanor
—had persisted. Thus, it had become a part of his day to
check on her whereabouts. Often as not he found her mixing
in the business of men: hanging about the crews managing the
trebuchets or ballistas. She was particularly on his mind, he
realized with a growing discomfort, because of the heated row
that had occurred between them the day before.

He had moved through the lines of men, dodging the arrows
and javelins from the battlements of the keep to reach the tortoise. Reaching the elongated structure, he edged along the

battering ram until he located the sergeant who was bellowing orders to his men, his face running with rivulets of sweat in the heat of the tight enclosure. After questioning the man briefly and taking a moment to watch the progressive damage inflicted upon the thick oak door of the keep and its iron bandings, Will turned to make his way back to the entrance. Then, with a sweep of incredulity, he had become frozen to the spot. Shock was quickly replaced with raging anger as he spied Eleanor, again dressed in the attire of a lad, among the men who were checking lines holding the massive iron-tipped ram. Ignoring her squeak of surprise, followed by shrieks of protest, he grabbed her arm and pulled her toward the end of the tortoise. Reaching the bright light of the entrance, he shouted for protection for their backs, drawing a group of men-at-arms about them, as he protected her with his body and rushed for the safety of the rear guard.

He feared his mind would split with fury, and a dizzy fear for her safety, the thought of her lying wounded or worse, coupled with the realization of the danger in which she had placed the men who had protected them. And it was all so unnecessary! He couldn't speak as he glared down at her, his fingers biting into her arms. He wanted to shake her. It took all of his control not to land the blow that every fiber in his being called for to release his deep fury. She took that moment to scream at him, protesting his unasked-for and, to her mind, untimely interference. Twisting her about, he pulled his hand back and it dropped swiftly to her thinly covered posterior, where it landed with a sharp snap.

The sizable crowd which had gathered burst into laughter, shouts of encouragement from the men adding to the pain of Eleanor's rump as she spun back on him, her large blue eyes filling with tears as her mouth worked silently in an effort not to cry. She drew in her breath sharply in a loud, gasping sob and spun about, fleeing from her embarrassment and hurt.

He had not checked on her that night, realizing that his own anger was still too raw to allow him to handle the situation well. Damnation, he thought, she needed a father, not a husband!

"Will? Are we keeping you from something?"

"What?" He realized that Gilbert had been speaking to

him. "I am sorry, my friends, my mind is on other matters."

"Understandable," William deBraose offered. "Do not let us keep you. For me, I am of a good supper and some rest. By the way, I had not asked, how is Eleanor?"

Will, whose thoughts had already begun to drift again, turned back to the question and he shrugged. "Eleanor? Eleanor is—Eleanor." With that he left their company, moving to his waiting destrier. Fortunately he missed the looks of sympathy which followed him.

He rode to her tent, his thoughts filled with misgiving as he struggled with what he would say to her. She would understand her position and his once and for all! If only he could decide how to say it.

Eleanor had spent the morning in her tent. Puzzled glances had been exchanged by her women over her unusual behavior, but they had quickly become silent, even in their own chatter, in the face of her petulant mood. They knew, indeed word had spread rapidly through the camp, of the confrontation between the princess and her husband. But it was not like Eleanor to wallow in anger or unhappiness. She was quick to temper and, like her Plantagenet predecessors, her wrath could bring all about her to trembling. But normally Eleanor was as quick to forgive as she was to anger; it was totally out of character for her to remain moody for so long.

They were all too willing to make themselves unobtrusive. Their positions with the little princess suited them well. Unlike other mistresses, Eleanor was never demanding, and they enjoyed a life tending to laziness.

Eleanor had never felt so alone. Ever surrounded by people, never alone since the moment of her birth, she had no one to confide in. Will was mad at her. She had never seen him so angry. She had not meant to anger him. She hadn't even thought of what he would think when she had gone to the tortoise. She only wanted to see how the battering ram worked. Day after day, night after night, she had heard the echoing sound of it as it struck the portcullis barrier. She just wanted to see it.

Two days ago she had begun her monthly flux. She had wanted to tell Will. But how could she blurt out something like that? But he was her best friend. Who else could she tell? Besides, he was mad at her now.

Restless, she sighed raggedly and moved to the opening of the tent. Leaning against the heavy support pole, she looked out over the activity in the encampment and frowned. Everyone was busy; even the lowliest of the camp followers had a reason for being here. And then it struck her—she had never actually seen a camp follower, not up close. Her interest perked.

Sounds seemed to take on a different quality as she neared the rim of the camp. The air of urgency seemed to be gone. Tension felt released, replaced by a feeling of relaxed disorder. Tents were shabbier, what there were of them. Hasty hovels of brush and scraps of wood were the rule, shelters constructed from whatever could be gleaned from the surrounding countryside to offer protection from the elements. She picked her way among campfires set with spitted pieces of meat and iron pots bubbling with unrecognizable food; even the odors which assailed Eleanor's nose seemed strange. Shabbily dressed women stopped to watch her pass, their eyes hostile. Feeling the anger emanating from the women as they paused in their endeavors and stared, their unfriendly eyes moving blatantly over the quality of her blaiunt and cloak, she began to feel a tinge of regret that she had come.

"What is this? The need of an adventure, or just curiosity?" A sharp voice came from behind her, and Eleanor spun about. A woman sat in the shade of her tent, her lips curled in a mixture of amusement and anger as her eyes fixed upon Eleanor. It was impossible to tell her age. Her skin was coarse with heavy lines about her mouth beneath cheeks tinted with rouge, yet there remained a ghost of former beauty, dominated by hazel eyes which seemed to burn at Eleanor as she watched her. Her hair was deep auburn, touched with light streaks of grey, hanging loosely about her face and the shoulders of a grey wool kirtle.

"Pardon?"

"Pardon?" the woman parroted. "She asks my pardon!" Her eyes crinkled with amusement. Other women had gathered and now joined cruelly in the jest. "Tra-la! Maggie, quick now!" she tossed at one of the women. "Fetch us some hippocras! We shall sup on swan, methinks, the best shall be laid as we have company!''

Eleanor's face burned at the joke and she swallowed heavily, even as she felt her own ire pricked. "Enough!" she snapped, spinning to glare at the other women before her eyes settled on her tormentor. "I have done naught to warrant such! Keep a civil tongue in your head, woman, or I shall have it snatched out!"

"Indeed, I think you could. Is that why you are here?"

"Nay, I—I only wished to . . ." Eleanor stumbled on the words. She was totally at a loss of how to answer. She had not thought out her reasonings for coming to this place; as usual she had only reacted. Seeing the confusion written in the younger woman's face and sensing her discomfort, the harlot sighed with disgust and snapped at the others to be about their business. "Sit down," she ordered Eleanor. "It is cooler here in the shade." Something about the woman compelled Eleanor to comply, and she sat while glancing about nervously at the others who were watching with hostile curiosity.

"How old are you, child?"

"Fourteen," Eleanor answered.

Fourteen. Oh, Lord, what did it feel like to be fourteen? She had never been this child's age. Her eyes passed over the girl and she smirked. "Your nursemaid must be frantic."

"I have been well on my own since I was five!" Eleanor snapped, irked by the older woman's contemptuous attitude.

"On your own?" The whore chortled. "I do not think you have been alone until this moment."

Eleanor frowned. "You are talking nonsense!"

The woman studied Eleanor for a long moment. The large blue eyes of the child were innocent, and she fought off the feeling of resentment that accompanied the realization, even as another part of her reached for that innocence. Damnation, she thought, who needed it? "Go back, wherever you came from," she snapped irritably. "Now!"

"But—why?" Eleanor asked. Why did this strange woman resent her so?

"Do I need a reason? You do not belong here!"

Eleanor braced herself against the woman's sudden anger and she stiffened in sore-won pride, "I meant no harm. In honesty, I do not even know why I came—except, perhaps, curiosity. I wanted to know why the men are so drawn to you."

The woman's eyes widened at the statement. Her first response was anger, but as she looked into the young face, fresh, open, without malice, she bit it back. The child promised great beauty. Obviously noble, apparently with every advantage, she had something indelibly sad about her, a loneliness which the harlot recognized with startling clarity. "Go back to your mother," she said roughly. "This is no place for you."

"I have not seen my mother since I was five," Eleanor countered. "Why will you not answer my question?"

"Because you are a child. And I am *not* your mother."

"I am not a child!" Eleanor protested. "I have been married since I was nine!"

The woman's eyes swept with surprise over Eleanor's slender body, and she did not attempt to hide her disgust. Men, she thought to herself. She doubted if the girl had even begun her flux. She felt a surge of rage toward the man who would possess this child, even as the emotion startled her. After all, she was hardly a stranger to the fact; she had been taken by her own uncle when she was not much older than this one. But then, she had had a mother to comfort her. "There are ways, child, to make it less painful," she said more gently.

"If only there was." Eleanor sighed. "But I fear that he will never give me the chance."

"Men never will." The woman answered with spite. "You must be responsible for your own life, and your own body." At least now she knew why the child had come. "Does he beat you?"

Eleanor looked up with horror. "Nay! He would never—" And then she flushed as she remembered the whack he had applied to her posterior. "Well, almost never. But—" she flushed—"I deserved it, I—"

"Nay, no man has the right to lay a hand on you! They would like us to think that they do, as it gives them power. Listen to me, luv. Any man who needs to feel power by beating a woman is no man at all. He is worth less than nothing. Such a man does not deserve your consideration."

"Really, he does not beat me!" Eleanor protested. "He—

he hardly notices me at all. In fact that is what I—''

Her words were altered by the sounds of laughter, and their attention was drawn to the men who had suddenly appeared at the edge of the camp.

''It is late,'' the woman observed. She looked back at Eleanor with honest concern. ''You must go now.'' Seeing the look of interest in the young girl's expression as she watched the women about move toward the new arrivals, her manner became firm. ''Now. You must go now.''

But even as Eleanor rose to go, the woman laid a hand on her arm to stay her. It surprised the harlot even as she did it. It was a reaction to something—a word, perhaps, the sound of the girl's voice, a look of sorrow. ''Life is never perfect—do not look for it,'' she said quietly.

Eleanor paused and looked back at the woman, uncertain that she had heard her correctly. ''It has never been so for me.''

''You think so? Little one, you believe that you bear the worst of it, yet you have not even begun. You have only yet to discover pain. But you can survive. While only death brings total release from the pain of living, life comes with each morn and brings hope. Perhaps, you think, today it will begin. Never let go of that hope, hold to it. . . .''

Eleanor realized that the woman had ceased speaking and a strange, almost frightened look had come over her face as she stared at something over Eleanor's shoulder. Eleanor frowned at the woman's strange expression, and she twisted about to see what had distracted the harlot. She fixed on the four massive black legs of a destrier. Her gaze swept up the body of the restless horse and its rider until Will's eyes were glaring angrily into her own.

''Your husband?'' The woman whispered.

''Aye,'' Eleanor answered as she stood up slowly.

Will's furious gaze shifted from Eleanor to the harlot, and he startled at the look of hatred which was focused on him. Sloughing off the look, he glared back at Eleanor as he held out his hand to her. She stood and approached him slowly, to Hamal's blind side as Will pulled the animal's head about. She lifted her arms to him, and he reached down and his arm went about her waist, lifting her into his lap.

The woman watched as the knight bore the girl away, and she was filled with anger and despair, facing that which she had not thought about in a long, long time, all of the unfairness and cruelty she had felt in her own life. Suddenly she startled as she felt a hand on her arm. Looking up, she found warm brown eyes staring down into hers.

"What is it, Leona? I told you I would come."

"Oh, it is you, Darcy," the woman said distractedly. "When did you get back from London?"

"Only moments ago. What is wrong?"

"It is nothing. Only—that." She looked back as her large eyes glittered with anger. "Who is he?"

Darcy followed her gaze and his eyes widened in surprise. "What is he doing here with her?"

"Answer me. Who is he?"

"He is the Marshal of England, love," Darcy answered. "What was he doing here? And what was *she* doing here?"

"She came to me for help." Leona shrugged.

"She came to you for help?" Darcy blinked. "What kind of help?"

"Help from him, evidently," the woman snapped. "The bastard comforts himself with a mere child—what is more, he beats her!"

"He what?"

"You heard me."

He almost burst out laughing. Then his eyes narrowed as they shifted to the departing couple with interest. "Leona, my love, I think we need to talk. It's damnably hot out here—shall we go inside?"

5

WILL pulled back the flap of the tent and pushed
Eleanor in before him. "Out!" he roared to her women.

They looked up in shock, their startled gazes passing between the furious Marshal and the pale and trembling princess
who had spun about to face him. There was a scramble of activity as they sought to do his bidding. Will snapped the tent
flap behind them and turned back on Eleanor. "By the blood
of Saint George!" he bellowed. "How could you do such a
thing?"

"Do what?" she cried. "I only wanted to talk with other
women!"

"Other women? They are whores, Eleanor! What is more,
many are thieves, murderers! It is a miracle you were not
stripped for the clothes and jewelry you wear!"

She stiffened as her eyes grew wide, and she glanced down
at her betrothal ring, a large sapphire set in heavy gold.
"But—they did not try to harm me—they never threatened—"

"That is only because you were incredibly lucky," he told
her severely. "If Leona had not befriended you, the outcome
would have been quite different, I assure you."

"Leona?" she asked numbly.

"The harlot I found you with."

"You know her?"

"Everyone knows her."

"But you know her too?"

"The subject of this discussion is you, Eleanor!" He snapped irascibly. "Do not attempt to change it!"

"Why is she so much better than the others?" she persisted.

"She isn't. But no one crosses her—you can thank God that she took a liking to you."

"Then—I was perfectly safe," she observed haughtily.

His face took on a choleric expression. "Nay, by the blood, you were not!"

"But, you said—"

"Never mind what I said!" he bellowed. "Eleanor, this must stop! I have better things to do with my time than chase you about, extracting you from trouble! My God, I did not know where you were—no one did!"

She lowered her gaze to fix on his belt buckle, knowing better than to let him see the pleasure in her eyes. He had worried about her! "I am sorry, Will. Truly, I am. I did not mean to worry you," she answered softly.

"Oh nay, Eleanor. That trick might work with Henry but not with me. Moreover, I know that you will do it again, as soon as my back is turned."

Her eyes flew up to his and she winced at the anger she still read there. "Oh, please Will! Believe me, I won't—I'll be good! I'll stay right here. I won't leave my tent unless you give me bid—"

"Enough, Eleanor!" Without another word he turned to the entrance and lifted the flap as he shouted for her women. "You will pack your mistress's things," he snapped at the cringing maids. "Have them ready by first light." With that he ducked beneath the tent entrance, ignoring the sound of Eleanor's cry which followed him.

He strode from the tent, too angry to notice the dumbfounded expressions of the farriers who held Hamal as he passed them by. The destrier's eyes rolled as he caught Will's scent. Baring his teeth, he began to bite at the hands which were attempting to hold him, the animal's only thought to join and protect his master.

Will's long strides took him across the length of the camp
toward his own tent. Mumbling to himself, he was oblivious to
the strange looks of the men as he passed, and to the shouts
and curses behind him as the men, joined by others who were
rushing to help, struggled to calm the crazed horse. He nodded
curtly to the guard outside his tent, not noticing that the man's
gaze was fixed on the commotion across the camp, and he
ducked into the coolness of the striped canvas.

Landon and Meryle looked up upon Will's entrance, and
their faces blanched at their lord's expression. "Wine!" Will
barked. Landon pressed a goblet into Will's hand in an instant
and then went to work with Meryle on the laces on the sides of
his surcoat. Taking a long draught of the beverage, Will fixed
his gaze on an empty point before him, ignoring the sure
assistance of his squires. The eyes of the young men met over
Will's shoulders, but they astutely kept their silence as they
helped Will to disarm.

"Send Alan Wadley to me," Will growled as he settled into
a chair.

A knight with the Marshal badge on his shoulder soon
ducked into the tent and came before Will, who was moodily
staring off into space. Finally Will looked up at the beefy
knight who stood at rigid attention, his weathered face held in
a stoic expression. A slight frown deepened the line of the
grey-flecked black brows beneath a thick ruff of greying black
hair which was dampened by the helm he had removed and
now held beneath his well-muscled arm.

"Well?" Will snapped, irritated by his master-at-arms's
odd behavior.

"You sent for me, milord?" the knight asked, still staring
straight ahead.

"Dammit, Alan, what is the matter with you?" Will asked
churlishly.

"I had it to believe that you were in no right mood,
milord," the knight answered. "Don't want to push you while
your nettle's up. Nay, milord, I don't."

Will's eyes widened, then snapped to Landon and Meryle,
who had settled in the farthest corner of the tent to clean
Will's armor. His gaze shifted back to the knight and his eyes
narrowed. "Let's have it, Alan. What is on your mind?"

"My mind, milord?" The man feigned surprise. "You sent for me."

"Aye, I did," Will grumbled, holding out his goblet, which was rapidly refilled. "At dawn you will take your men to escort the Princess Eleanor to Windsor. Remain there, assuring that she does so, until I return." He saw the look of dismay that passed over the knight's face, though it was quickly concealed. "I know, Alan. I would not ask you to absent yourself from what is going to happen here unless it was important. I am entrusting you with a princess royal of England. Moreover, my lady. While I shall face a mere battle, I fear that you have the more difficult task."

The knight's face cracked on the last words, and Will noted the glimpse of a smile. "Aye, Will, I vow that she shall not leave Windsor."

"Hummm." Will grunted. "Watch her closely."

As the knight turned to go, he paused and looked back, his dark brown eyes now filled with laughter. "You might like to know that it took eight men to wrestle Hamal to his tether, but they managed it."

"What?" Will looked up, puzzled. As Alan's meaning sunk in, he blanched. "Oh, my God, Hamal—I forgot."

"Thought you might have." The knight chortled. "But you need not worry. Bruises and bites heal eventually." He was still laughing at Will's dumbfounded expression as he left. Will slumped down in his chair as depression settled firmly over him. Inexcusable! A stallion at best was volatile. A trained warhorse was more so. High-strung, the animal became a fighting machine when his master was firmly settled with his familiar weight in the saddle, his instincts and training poised to respond to command. But should a knight become unseated, the animal was trained to protect his master, lashing at anyone near. Farriers were trained to handle the high-blooded animals, removing them as rapidly as possible from the scent of their masters, the only possibility of controlling them. Realizing what he had done, Will groaned.

"It would seem to be not the best of days."

Will looked up through his fingers to encounter Darcy's off-sided grin. He merely growled in response and took another long draught of his wine.

"That's what I thought," the goliard chuckled. "May I join you?" Without waiting for an answer, he crossed to the small table near Will and helped himself to a generous measure of wine before he settled himself into a chair next to Will's.

"Where have you been?" Will queried, drawing from his goblet. "You are usually about when things are happening."

"Oh, here and there," Darcy answered.

Will snorted at the typically vague answer, but he left it alone, settling to a comfortable silence between them. In the two months since they had met in the forest near Wycombe an easy relationship had developed between the two men. Neither demanded anything from the other, a comfortable situation for both of them and one too seldom found.

"DeBreaute is not in the keep," Darcy said at last in a soft drawl.

"What?" Will's head jerked up.

"He's not there," Darcy repeated as he stretched his long legs out before him. "He's in London. And furious that you are attacking his keep. Even now he is appealing to the justiciar for succor."

"The devil you say!" Will roared, jumping up to spin back on the relaxed minstrel. "I was assured that he was there! Dammit! He must have known we were coming and slipped out, the weasel!"

"Nay. It seems that he was never there. Moreover, he insists that his castellan acted without his knowledge or approval."

"Damnation, Darcy! Are you certain?"

"Aye, Will. I saw him at Winchester. He was as close to me as you are. He has issued a complaint with the justiciar."

Will spun about, throwing a rapid stream of curses at the peaked roof of the tent before he spun back on the goliard. "What was deBurgh's response?"

"He refuses to give audience." He shrugged. " 'Twould seem that even our esteemed justiciar will not openly defy the king."

Even in his frustration and rage, Will felt a wave of pleasure rush over him and he ventured a smile. In honesty, in spite of his hatred for deBreaute, he had no desire to physically harm an old man. But the thought of deBreaute waiting endlessly in deBurgh's antechamber, pacing those halls while suspecting he would be too late, filled him with intense satisfaction. Indeed, almost as much as having the man's throat beneath his fingers years ago. Taking a deep breath, Will resettled himself into his chair and stretched out his long legs comfortably.

An easy silence settled once again between the two men. As William's squires left the tent to see to his supper, Darcy turned his head to watch Will's reaction to what he would say next. "Are you going to send her away?"

Will looked up with a glint of humor in his eyes. "What is this, Darcy? No disguise? No subtle inference? Could this be you, coming straight to the point?"

Darcy shrugged as he gave in to a smile. He took a sip from his goblet, then stared into the ruby liquid as he turned the vessel in his fingers. "Did she tell you why she went to the fringe of the camp?"

Will regarded Darcy through narrowed eyes. Was there anything the goliard didn't know? "She said that she merely wanted to talk with another woman," he gritted, remembering his fear for her safety. "But somehow I imagine that you will tell me the true reason. Out with it."

Darcy looked at Will evenly and did not flinch at the anger that was flashed at him. "She wanted to know why men were attracted to whores."

Will came near to choking on the swallow of wine he had taken. "What?" he gasped, painfully drawing in air as he turned horrified eyes to Darcy.

"You heard me well." Darcy smirked, turning to his own goblet.

"Why?" Will coughed. "Why would she want to know such a thing?"

"Why indeed?" Darcy observed quietly.

"How do you know this?"

"Leona—who else?" Darcy shrugged.

"I should have reasoned that for myself." Will growled. "She would have stricken me down with a mere look when I came to claim Eleanor. God's breath, you would think I was the devil incarnate."

Darcy's eyes crinkled and he gave a shout of laughter. "What would *you* think of a man who couples with a child and beats her for measure?"

Will stared at Darcy, bereft of speech. "Eleanor told her that?" he finally managed.

"Not in so many words, but enough that Leona could conclude nothing else." Darcy answered, wiping the tears of laughter from his eyes.

"I hope that you resolved the matter!" Will retorted indignantly.

"Why should you care what a whore thinks?" Darcy countered with a grin.

Will shifted uncomfortably, unable to answer that question. "I don't," he muttered, and then a brow arched. "Evidently you did not come directly from London."

"Wherever the breeze takes me," Darcy quipped.

"More like an ill wind."

"Well," Darcy took a deep breath to bring his humor under control. "Be as it may, 'twould seem you have a problem and I thank the gods it is not mine. There are distinct advantages in not being responsible to anyone."

Particularly to a Plantagenet, Will finished silently. "I am sending her back to London in the morning."

Darcy pursed his lips at the comment, and he drew on his wine without offering comment.

Will watched him for a long moment, knowing that disapproval lay behind that placid countenance. He should have felt anger. The man was a mere minstrel. But even as many of his kind would have rejected Darcy's kind in hand, Will recognized the man's depth. "What would you do?" he asked quietly.

"Me?" Darcy turned and regarded Will evenly with a smile even as he shrugged. "London seems far away. I heard you say that your sisters were in residence at Hertford while their husbands attended you. Perhaps it would do as well."

Will regarded Darcy for a long moment, then he shook his head with amazement at the simplicity of the solution. "And at Hertford she would be in the company of women—those who would watch her closely but with care."

"If you say so, milord," Darcy countered, drawing from his goblet.

Will laughed suddenly. "By the cross, Darcy. You plead

that you are a simple bard. I vow that someday I shall know who you really are!''

As the sun broke over the battlements the sound of heavy wooden wheels creaked painfully against the still morning air. The belfray had begun to move. At first seemingly fixed to the ground by its ponderous weight, then pushed and pulled by the masses of men and horses, the giant five-level tower jerked, protested, and suddenly began to move forward.

A line of armed and mounted knights stood at the ready, watching with anticipation. At the center of the line the King of England watched, eyes burning with tense excitement, their bright, vibrant blue moving from the belfray to the tops of the battlement. "What if we do not take the curtain wall and the outer bailey before nightfall?" he asked Will, who sat at his side.

"Then we must begin all over again tomorrow. The mining must be done under the cover of night."

A nod from Will passed along the lines to his lieutenants, and the siege machines began their work. A high-pitched whine filled the air as javelins were propelled from the ballistas, the large crossbow-type weapons. The teeth-aching sound of the trebuchets competed as the heavy ropes lashed to the frames of the machines were twisted and tightened against their counterbalances, then released with a heavy thud as the arms flung forward to release the ponderous stones set in their spoons, flinging the small boulders with the ease of pebbles beyond the castle walls. The sickening, rhythmical thud of the battering ram sequestered beneath its tortoise reverberated across the span which separated the two opposing forces. All were engaged to cover the advancement of the belfray, which had been covered with thick layers of raw, wet hides to deter the burning grease which was certain to be cast down upon it from the parapets when it finally reached the walls.

Movement was seen on the battlements, and Will smiled grimly. He realized the dismay which must be felt behind those walls as they recognized the intensity of the assault. Yet at the moment they could do nothing in defense, for the opposing army was either too well protected or out of reach. Knowing

that everything had been done, Will mumbled his excuses
to Henry and pulled Hamal's head about. Henry nodded
absently, his attention on the field before him, hardly noticing
the departure of his Marshal.

Will rode back to the lines of the encampment, passing by
the neat triangular stacks of weapons which stood at ready for
the pikemen and by the groups of men-at-arms and yeomen
who lolled about, waiting, dicing, talking, cleaning their
weapons, ignoring the building tension as they waited to be
needed. His thoughts were pulled behind him to the coming
events of the day, yet mixed with what he was riding toward,
conflicting pressures which only served to intensify his desire
to have both matters over and done with. As he approached
his destination, those thoughts were pushed from his mind,
however, as he pulled in Hamal abruptly and stared at the
scene before him.

To his left Eleanor's party had assembled, prepared for
departure amid carts and sumpter horses packed heavily for
their journey, and nervous palfreys saddled and waiting as
they pranced and shifted against the commotion of the leavetaking. Yet directly ahead a long column approached: double
rows of men-at-arms and yeomen followed by mounted
knights. Will's jaw tensed in surprise as his gaze fixed on the
banner which whipped and snapped in the light morning
breeze, recognizing it to be that of the Archbishop of Canterbury.

Will's face broke into a grin as his eyes moved beneath the
shadows of his helm, tracing the approaching party to its
center and the slight crimson-cloaked figure that rode at its
center. He pulled off his helm, setting it on the broad pommel
of his saddle, and pushed back his coif. Speaking soothing
words to Hamal, who was shifting nervously beneath him, he
found himself immersed in memories of the elderly man who
now approached: Stephen Langton, Archbishop of Canterbury, whose fine hand and mind had shaped the Magna Carta.
Will recalled the man's fire, its heat infusing the young man
Will could now only vaguely remember having been. Years
spent at Stephen Langton's side through that time of England's desperate turmoil; the outcome heading at Running-
Mead. Uncomfortable memories came as well. A time of es-

trangement from his father, moments of tension between them, pain-filled memories as he faced his father across the Thames where Will stood with the barons and William Marshal rode to the signing beside his king, John Plantagenet. Even now, all of these years past, Will felt choked by the hatred he had felt for that despotic monarch. A hard lump of distaste formed at the back of his throat as the memories returned.

As the Archbishop drew aside of Will, the column was halted. Will's eyes fixed on the crimson cloak of heavy samite embroidered with gold and silver threads of hunters and women bearing urns, and his eyes widened as he realized where he had seen the cloak before.

"You remember." The pale blue eyes of the cleric smiled in acknowledgment, holding Will's with unconscious effort. The lean face was lined with time and the heavy responsibilities of experience. The frame beneath the heavy cloak seemed to have shrunk to Will's memory, while the manner of the man bespoke strength and confidence, giving comfort to Will in his reluctance to acknowledge the passing of time and the final release of his youth.

"Aye, Your Eminence, I remember," Will offered softly.

"I have not worn it since that day," the Archbishop said as he fingered the edge of the rich, brilliant garment. "Though I cannot say why. Perhaps because there had never been another day like it. The day I returned to England to become Archbishop of Canterbury; the day of John Plantagenet's capitulation. The only moment when he bent his knee before something far greater than himself—until the signing of the Charter."

"As I recall he was still under an edict of excommunication and he could not touch your holy ring of office. You must admit that he took the moment when instead he chose to throw you a kiss."

"Aye, 'twas his moment." The Archbishop chuckled deeply, remembering. "One must give the devil his due. John always did have a flare for the dramatic, in spite of his other shortcomings."

"Why have you chosen to wear the garment now?" Will asked softly, gesturing toward the cloak.

"I cannot say. Perhaps it is only that I feel the pressure of time." Langton smiled. "But tell me, Will, how are you, my son? It has been a good while since we have had the pleasure to spend time together."

"Aye, Your Eminence, and it is I who have been the worse for the oversight. I have sorely missed our talks."

"Perhaps, when this matter is done, we shall be able to rectify the matter." The Archbishop smiled. "Are you aware that the king sent for me?"

Will's surprise was apparent. "Nay, he had not mentioned it." A feeling of hope rushed through Will at the knowledge. It was an important gesture, one that would not have occurred to Henry's sire.

"It is so. I would have been here before this, but other matters were pressing. How goes it?"

"We will have the bailey before sunset," Will answered with a grim smile.

"Then perhaps I shall be able to effect peace with those who withdrew within the keep, the Good Lord willing," Langton replied. "Let us pray that peace will be effected without further bloodshed."

"Perhaps." Will grunted without conviction. "But first, there is time for you to rest." He turned to snap orders to those who had gathered about. Ordering a tent to be set up for the Archbishop and refreshments to be brought, he turned back to Langton to find the aging cleric's attention drawn to another point. Following the Archbishop's gaze, he realized that Eleanor stood at the edge of the gathering before her tent.

"Rest?" Langton shrugged. "Rest is coming soon enough. I would rather talk with you. See to whatever matters press upon you, my son, then see to me."

With a slight nod from Langton the column moved forward, and Will's attention was again drawn to the slight figure who stood expectantly in the wake of the activity from the departing Archbishop.

Will dismounted and handed Hamal's reins to a waiting farrier as he turned to Eleanor. "Are you ready?" he asked as his gaze passed over her company, determining the matter to his own satisfaction.

"Aye, Will," she answered in an unaccustomed timid voice. The sadness he heard in her voice stirred him uncomfortably, and he reached out to touch her.

"I have decided that you shall not return to London," he said gently. "Alan shall take you to Hertford and to my sisters, who await you there. A message has been sent ahead advising them of your arrival. They will care for you, Eleanor. Do not fear them."

"Oh, Will!" she breathed as her eyes widened with pleasure. "It was my wish to come to know them! I shall not be afraid—I have heard that your lady sisters are kind and wise." She did not add that from them she hoped to learn how to please this man who was her husband.

"Kind? Aye, ever that." He laughed. "Wise? There are moments when I could differ with you on that point. But termagant, tenacious, I will give you. I fear that you may only learn ways to discomfort a husband. But, whatever else, there I know you shall be safe, and that is why I send you to them." He turned to Alan Wadley, who had approached and was waiting. "See that she is cared for." He turned back and bent to brush her cheek with a light kiss, then led her to her waiting mare and lifted her into the saddle. "I expect to find you at Hertford when I arrive there, Eleanor," he added with an admonishment.

"I shall await you there, milord," she said with forced lightness, trying to keep her voice even.

As if sensing her true feelings, he grunted as he passed the reins to her. "See that you do, Eleanor." Nodding to Alan Wadley, he returned to Hamal and mounted, not looking back, as his mind had already turned to other matters.

He rode to the area behind the camp to check on the progress of a new tortoise that was being hastily constructed, spending moments with the sergeant who was supervising the organized commotion, then rode to the area which had been set aside for the new arrivals. A soft grunt of approval came from him as he noted that the Archbishop's tent had been struck and the cleric's men had taken on the look of settling in. Dismounting before the main tent, he waited to be announced by the cleric's guards, and he ducked beneath the low entrance, his eyes sweeping about the shadows of the enclosure to assure himself that Langton had been given every comfort.

Stephen Langton turned at Will's entrance, a goblet in his hand, and he smiled with pleasure as he nodded to his attendant. The man poured a like goblet of watered wine and offered it to Will before he departed. Watching the man go, Will turned a puzzled glance on the Archbishop.

"I wished to speak to you alone," Langton explained as he lowered himself into a chair. "Sit with me. From what I have heard of your morning's plans, we have a time before either of us shall be needed."

"The king . . ."

"I have sent a message to Henry that I shall attend him presently." Langton smiled. "Be easy, Will, I have experienced a lifetime of handling Plantagenets." He waited until Will had taken the chair across from his. "Now, tell me how it goes with Henry."

"That is difficult to say," Will answered with equal bluntness. "He shows moments of being greater than his father. We can only wait."

"Well, at least desRoches's influence has been removed." Langton grimaced. "That one wanted England only for himself."

"Aye, Henry showed maturity in agreeing to his retirement."

"Aye—that or the petulance of stifled youth," Langton mumbled, less convinced. "How does he settle on deBurgh?"

"At first with eagerness," Will answered, thinking on Henry's response to the justiciar. "But lately with impatience."

"I feared so," Langton said thoughtfully. "DeBurgh is a good man, Will. He has his faults, as do we all, but he is a man for England. You must do what you can to convince Henry to work with him. Henry is young and he needs a guiding hand, even as he may dispute it. He could do far worse than Hubert deBurgh."

"And he could do better," Will countered.

"Not again in our lifetime." Langton smiled.

Both men's thoughts turned to the one they were speaking

of. It was Langton who spoke first as he reflected on the memory of a dear friend. "Will, do you recall what I said when we buried him?"

"Aye," Will answered, drawing in his breath as he remembered. "I shall never forget the words you said for my father."

"Then think upon it now. 'You see what the life of the world is worth when one is dead. One is no longer more than the slightest bit of earth. Behold all that remains of the best knight who ever lived. You will all come to this as each man dies on his day. For you and I, this is the reflection of each of us.' Will, do you understand what I meant?"

"I thank you for the tribute to him. It has stayed ever with me."

"It was that, assuredly, but it was more. He was my friend, Will. Moreover, I have never known one who was greater; each of us pales by comparison. But . . ." Langton sighed as he reached for meaning. "There is an old Italian saying that whether pawn or king, each returns to the same box. William Marshal is gone. While he leaves his inheritance and influence, our thoughts filled with his remembrance, he is no more. It is for those who survive to make their own way, to leave their mark, for good or ill."

"I miss him," Will answered, shaking his head. "But his memory does not haunt me. I accepted his death. We disagreed, we fought over principles, but I have no guilts."

"I know that, Will. You have the strengths I would wish for you."

"Then what is this about?" Will's eyes narrowed as he peered at the Archbishop. "I do not know you to mince words."

"I want you to think upon your father. Guilts? Nay, I know you, Will Marshal, you are a man unto yourself. But still, you are your father's son. If one word could sum up William Marshal's life, it would be loyalty, and for him no true justice could be found beyond that sphere. It gave him his strength and set him apart from other men. You cannot be your father's son without those principles affecting your direction and life. Yet we have reached a time when matters of men cannot be viewed with simplicity. The Great Charter, that document which your father helped me to write, effected the change along with the forces which brought it about. No man can give such total loyalty again to a king as was given before its writing. We have been granted the right to question, to ask why, to doubt. Never again can that privilege be taken from us. Your father knew it. He brought John to the table at Running-Mead in order to protect the throne and avert civil war, but his first act as regent upon John's death was to reinvoke the Charter, which had been dissolved by the Holy Father. Will, he knew what I am telling you now. He was a man of his time, but he knew times were changing. Man can no longer live under the total rule of another. It matters not whether Henry is a wise king or nay. Man must determine his own destiny, he cannot leave it to another.''

"Would you have me dispute Henry's law? Your Eminence, you are speaking treason.''

"As we often did together under John. Treason? A word too carelessly used when one disagrees. Will, do not ignore your conscience, it is all you have to live by. Your family holds incredible power; you must not misuse it. Guard the words of the Charter well, my son. Man cannot afford to lose its essence in his greed and apathy.'' He paused and smiled. "Lose it? My last prayer shall be that, in time, it shall be improved upon.''

6

SHE had been born lucky. She was a princess of England, her brothers loved her, and she was betrothed to the man she most wanted. And it was a beautiful day. The wide meadows which stretched beyond the sides of the road were sprinkled with yellow dandelions, the pink blossoms of dogrose, and white cow parsley. The heavy mauve and white heads of foxglove swayed gently in the cooling breeze, and flowering whitethorn edged the road, to lend the comfort of their shade to the traveling party. Indeed, she sighed, there was no reason to feel so unsettled.

Soon, within hours, they would arrive at Hertford. She had assured Will that she was glad to be sent to his sisters, but she was terrified. What if they did not like her? She had not seen them since the betrothal ceremony years before, and she recalled very little of that day; a sea of faces, voices, and very little else. Which one had been Matilda? She was the eldest of the Marshal sisters; could she have been that stern-looking harridan who had stood by in a group of ladies, their well-coifed heads bent together as they buzzed in apparent disapproval? Eleanor knew that many did not approve of William Marshal's being so tied to the royal family. The Marshals were powerful enough, it was said, for Will to also be the King's brother-in-law.

A pox on them, Eleanor thought spitefully. What did she care for what others thought? Including the Marshal sisters. They, too, probably disapproved of her for the criticism the betrothal brought upon their family. Or because she was so young. Grownups always seemed to be bothered when young people were about. And now she was being thrust upon them with little warning. Oh lud, how could she have been pleased, even excited, to visit them without Will? If only he were with her! He would have made them be nice to her.

She had almost put her nervous qualms aside when Hertford suddenly loomed ahead of them. She turned and glanced at her maids. No help from that quarter. Elva looked completely spent from the long ride and seemed to be using all of her effort to stay ahorse. Amala and Mave were engrossed with the attention of two young yeomen and probably would not have noticed if their young charge had been left miles behind. She turned back and fixed on Sir Wadley's broad back as she chewed at her lower lip. There was no escaping her fate. She would have to face it. She began to fantasize about the women who awaited her: their stern, pinched faces, cold and calculating eyes, and sharp, ringing voices. Repressing a shudder, she gripped the reins and sat up straighter, preparing to meet her doom with stoic determination even as she tried to suppress the butterflies which were playing havoc with her stomach.

The party clattered across Hertford's drawbridge, passing under the heavy iron portcullis, which had been raised by a call from the yeomen stationed on the towers of the gatehouse. The large outer ward was in total mayhem. Eleanor stared wide-eyed at a profusion of carts and stalls manned by hawkers shouting their wares. The din was increased by protesting sheep, cattle, and pigs and squawking fowl competing with the hundreds of people who were wandering through the stalls. The laughter and cries of children added to the voices of adults as they loudly argued for the best bargain.

"By the blood," Sir Wadley swore. "It passed me that this would be market day." His men began to clear a path for them, pushing at the crowd, which reluctantly moved from their way. As they progressed slowly across the bailey, Eleanor noted the vast array of merchandise that was being offered and wished that she could have moment to join the buyers. Among the array of stalls were those of brightly dyed cloth, artisans with handsomely worked leather, the heavy richness of the spice traders, and the succulent smells of roasting meat, reminding Eleanor that she had not eaten since early that morning.

The smaller inner bailey was only slight better. The massive, fifteen-foot-thick walls which surrounded the inner ward normally contained quarters for the household knights, the armory, laundry, and storehouses. There were chambers for guests who were not of high enough rank to be quartered within the towering keep which was centered in the furthest wall. With the exception of the household staff, those required to run the large manor, the yeomen, slaughterers, poulters, brewers, candlemakers, and carters, were quartered in the outer curtain wall of Hertford, along with the stables and those required to maintain them: the farriers, grooms, and smiths. It seemed to Eleanor that each of these who were not without must certainly be in the inner bailey, availing themselves of the additional merchandise found there.

"Does this happen often, Sir Wadley?" she shouted over the din. It reminded her of the markets in London, but she had never seen such mayhem in a castle yard before.

"Nay, milady," he roared back to her. "Only once or twice a year. The lady Isabella—"

Whatever he would have said was lost as an air-piercing shriek was heard over the commotion. Eleanor's head jerked to the sound, and she saw a slender woman of medium height railing at a cowering merchant. The man had retreated as far as he could, his back against a wagon, as the woman bent her fury upon him. Suddenly, to Eleanor's shock, the woman turned and pulled a short sword from the scabbard of a knight standing near and proceeded to flail the merchant with the flat edge. The man protected himself the best he could, ducking his head as he tripped around the end of the wagon bed, and rapidly two-stepped off in the direction of the gate. Passing by their party, Eleanor saw the terrified look on the man's face, but her attention swiftly returned to the woman. To her fur-

ther shock she saw that the knights who stood about the
woman, and had done nothing throughout the tirade, were
now laughing uproariously in the wake of the departing merchant. Eleanor turned to Sir Wadley, but her questions froze
in her throat as her guardian roared with laughter. Seeing
Eleanor's puzzled expression, Sir Wadley wiped tears from his
eyes with the back of his hand. "My Lady Isabella," he
gasped.

Eleanor's mouth dropped open as her eyes darted back
to the woman. *This* was the Countess Isabella, her sister by
marriage? From where she sat Eleanor could not see her face
clearly, but the woman's thick, chestnut hair was uncovered,
pulled back by a ribbon where it hung loose to her waist. The
Countess wore a plain, sleeveless blaiunt of rust wool over a
long, loose-sleeved chemise of light blue linen. Unadorned,
the garment had a thin gold girdle of filigree links which hung
over her hips. The woman had begun to turn away, but as a
knight bent to her ear she paused, then turned back to spot the
approaching party. Setting her hands on her hips, she waited.

Oh, Lord, Eleanor thought, Will, what have you done to
me? Her small hands trembled on the reins and she looked to
Sir Wadley for assurance, but he had already started forward,
obviously expecting her to follow. His broad back hid further
view from Eleanor as she followed reluctantly behind. When
he stopped, swinging abruptly from the saddle, she was
afforded her first clear view of the woman, and she gasped
softly in surprise. Could this be the woman who had only
moments before single-handedly attacked the merchant, a
man a good head taller than she? The Countess Isabella was
the most beautiful woman she had ever seen. The thick
chestnut hair framed a delicately boned face with a creamy
complexion, a small, well-turned nose, high cheekbones, and
soft, gracefully formed lips. Large, long-lashed eyes of startling blue-green fixed on her with interest, but there was
humor in them—and kindness.

"Eleanor, you've arrived!" The Countess gifted her with a
lovely, warm smile. She turned to her men and waved them
toward the mounted women. "Where are your manners? Help
the princess to dismount, quickly!"

Eleanor had barely touched ground when Isabella's arm was
about her shoulders and she was being ushered up the wide

stone stairs to the elevated main floor of the keep. "We are so glad that you are here, Eleanor," Isabella enthused, giving Eleanor a squeeze. "I've been telling that brother of mine that you should spend some time with us. Seaton, there you are, come here!"

A thin, rangy man with an unruly thatch of bright red hair came to a halt as he emerged onto the steps above them. His shoulders seemed to slump at the sound of Isabella's voice, and the expression he turned to her was harried. "Aye, milady," he answered with the touch of a sigh as he approached them.

"Seaton is my husband's seneschal," Isabella explained to Eleanor, apparently unaware of the man's pained expression. "Seaton, see that the Princess Eleanor's things are taken to my chamber, she shall be with me until the men return—and see that a bath is readied." With a curt nod the man was departing almost before Isabella's last words were spoken. "Now," she continued, turning to Eleanor. "I fear that with everything that is happening it will be some time before I can expect a bath to be prepared for you, but perhaps you like to rest awhile?"

It was a moment before Eleanor could find her voice. "Nay, Lady Isabella. I am not too tired—but I am rather hungry."

"Of course. Come, then, food will be brought soon." She laughed at the doubtful look Eleanor cast in the direction of the parting steward. "Do not doubt Seaton. He loves to affect the role of the overworked and put-upon. But he does the job magnificently. Now come."

Eleanor was totally unprepared for what met her when they entered the great hall. Three women sat before the hearth. As Eleanor entered on Isabella's arm, they rose from their chairs, their eyes fixed speculatively upon the new arrival, and Eleanor had never felt more like a mouse. She cringed, hesitating in her steps, as those three pair of eyes fixed on her. Shades of blue to grey, to her mind icy cold with disapproval. They were slender, graceful, decidedly poised. Their hair, free of wimple and coif, was of the same shade as Isabella's, the deep, rich chestnut of Will's. Each had her own measure of beauty. Separately they were lovely; together they were stunning.

"Ladies?" Isabella chirped. "Our sister has arrived!"

The next few moments were a blur as Eleanor found herself surrounded and hugged amid sudden chatter and happy laughter until finally the mayhem was brought to a halt by a whip-cracking voice.

"Sweet Mother, what are we doing to this poor child?" The ladies quickly deferred to that voice, and Eleanor found herself led to a chair and a goblet of warm watered wine pressed into her hands. "Now then," the one who had brought the hubbub to a halt said calmly, glaring for a moment at her sisters. "Please excuse us for such an unseemly greeting, child. The only possible excuse is that we are thrilled to have you here with us. While you catch your breath, allow me to introduce you to this unruly brood. I am Matilda, Countess Bigod, and, I fear, the eldest of the Marshal sisters. Isabella, Countess deClare, you have met, the one of us who must be continually surrounded by confusion and mayhem to feel her soul fulfilled. I fear you met the measure of that upon your arrival." Eleanor smiled at the mock horror on Isabella's face in light of the obviously true observation, and she felt herself begin to relax. At least they did not seem to dislike her. Perhaps this was not going to be so difficult.

"Now then, Sybile is the third eldest of our feminine covey. Sybile would be a knight, if her husband would overlook the fact that she is a woman. She takes to all matters of men and warfare—much to the dismay of her husband, William deFerrars, Earl of Derby." Answering her sister's mock glare with a smile, she stepped behind the next chair.

"This is Eve, the most spiritual of the lot. But do not allow her knowledge of the scriptures to fool you; she has no inclination toward a convent, nor has she ever been so. Indeed, she enjoys her husband too well for that, as William deBraose would attest." The group laughed as Eve looked for a moment to be painfully embarrassed by her sister's remark, then punctuated it with a lusty flare of her eyes.

"And then there is Joanne, whom I fear you shall not meet for some time as she is in the west, at Chepstow, with our mother. It is unfortunate as she is the one of us sweetest in disposition. I am certain that you would meet our youngest sister well."

"And you?" Eleanor ventured, forgetting the unease that

had plagued her since she left Bedford Castle.

"Me? Why, I am quite perfect," Matilda responded loftily.

"Perfectly bossy, you mean," Isabella parried as the others let out a hoot of laughter. "Matilda, as the eldest, attempts to run everyone's life—our brothers included. I reason that her husband, Hugh, is grateful for it as it draws her tongue from him."

Before she could catch her breath, midmeal was announced and she was hustled to a place at the dormant table. Bowls of warm water perfumed with marjoram and lavender were placed before them for washing their hands, and soon they were enjoying a light midmeal of venison and frumenty, a thick pudding of whole wheat grain and almond milk, blended with egg yolk and saffron. Eleanor half listened to the banter exchanged over the meal, finding that it took almost all of her energy to eat. In spite of her hunger she longed for the comfort of a soft bed. As she chewed slowly on a piece of well-flavored meat, she stopped and swallowed with surprise. A knight, whom she had not notice enter the hall, cut off a measure from the roasted haunch and, tearing off a generous piece of manchet bread, left again without saying a word. She glanced at the other women, who had not broken stride in their conversation, apparently not noticing or caring about the man's odd behavior. It was then that it struck her that they were taking midmeal alone. "Do the men not eat with us?" she blurted at a break in the conversation.

"Of course they do—normally," Isabella replied.

"Normal at Hertford is a contradiction in terms," Matilda countered. "But even for Isabella this is not a usual day. You may have noticed the market in the wards," she added with a smirk. "Twice a year she holds such a market, allowing any riffraff who will come to enter—"

"They are not riffraff!" Isabella protested. "I merely encourage a large market for the benefit of those on our demesne. Why should they not have the same advantages as those who live near cities such as London?"

"Then answer Eleanor's question, dear sister. Why do your household knights not take midmeal with us? Why have even your sisters' vassals been reduced to rushing in here to ward off starvation."

"Well . . ." Isabella's mouth twitched. "It serves well for our men to mingle with the crowd, seeing to it that all goes smoothly."

"Smoothly?" Sybile snorted. "You mean to say that they must be there to avoid a full-scale riot. Last year—" she began, turning with a smirk to Eleanor.

"Never mind about last year." Isabella interrupted. "Eleanor, would you care for some manchet?"

"My thanks, nay," Eleanor answered, her interest in food disappearing with her comforted stomach and the turn in the conversation. "May I ask—that is, I could not help but to notice your displeasure with that man as I entered the bailey. What had he done?"

"Oh, that." Isabella helped herself to the manchet and honey butter. "That rogue, Gaston, was up to his old tricks —mixing juniper berries with his peppercorns," she added in a way of explanation to her sisters. "He is quite a disreputable merchant, Eleanor. He deals in spices and often as not mixes his herbs with cuttings. I warned him never to do so again, at least not where I could catch him."

Eleanor could not understand how she could have failed to notice or remember these women, even at the tender age of nine. She felt completely out of her depths. Never, sitting among the friendly, warm, and shocking Marshal women, had she felt more like an awkward, gangly child. She became acutely aware of her straight, unmanageable hair and the contrast of its lifeless black to the rich, warm shades of the other women's. Her chest had never seemed so flat, her hips so narrow, her legs so shapeless. She had never hated herself more than she did at this moment. The ugly duckling among the swans. And she was betrothed to their brother. How could he ever come to love her when he was ever surrounded by such beauty?

Isabella's gaze, ever alert to what was going on about her, fixed on the trio of Eleanor's women who sat below the dormant table. As she watched them, her fair brow furrowed. Slovenly gluttons, the three of them. Aside from their lack of manners, they had made no attempt to see to their lady upon their arrival. Entering the hall, they had simply plopped down and helped themselves without so much as a by-your-leave to their hostess. She felt indignant anger stir within her toward the King. How could Henry be so blind to the needs of his sister? She had been shocked to learn from Will that Eleanor did not have a household of her own, a situation that should have been remedied years ago. Was it any wonder, she mused, the poor child has been surrounded by soldiers and priests, with no woman to guide her. Henry's love for his sister had kept her at court near his person, yet his marriageless state allowed men to attend the King without the attendance of their wives.

Had Father not died, had Mother remained at court, this never would have happened, she reasoned. However, when upon the Marshal's death Lady Marshal had returned to Chepstow, the seat of her power on the Welsh border, anxious to return to that which she loved most after her husband: the lands.

Margaret deBurgh, the justiciar's wife, could have, and most certainly should have, changed the complexion of the court, Isabella thought. Sister to the king of Scotland, she was a prize for the ambitious deBurgh, though it was said to be a love match. But Lady Margaret preferred to remain almost totally in seclusion in their residence in the keep known as William's Tower, after William the Conqueror, who had built it for the defense of London.

Disgraceful. These three totally unsuitable wretches as companions and maids for the princess—Will's betrothed—*her* sister? Isabella caught a glimpse of movement from the corner of her eye. "Seaton!" she snapped.

"Aye, milady," came the resigned voice as he appeared at her side.

"Now that Princess Eleanor's ladies have been . . . well fed, you must see that they are quartered," she said smoothly, though the steward's eyebrows rose perceptibly at the slight edge to his mistress's voice. "A chamber in the bailey, I reason—the outer ward. Poor dears, they must be weary from their efforts in their lady's behalf. See that they are comforted accordingly. We shall assign new attendants for our sister so that they might have some time to reflect."

The steward's gaze shifted to the objects of their discussion, and a small smile touched the corners of his mouth. His practiced and astute eye had already settled upon the women in question, and conclusions in perfect tune with his mistress had been drawn. "Aye, milady," he answered with what almost amounted to a smile. "I shall see to it. Also, you will want to be advised that a bath has been readied for Her Grace."

Light from the flickering wall torches cast uneven shadows about the hall, dancing across the massive tapestries on the walls to lend a feeling of movement to the characters etched in threads and shot of gold. The tall, two-story beamed ceiling lay in darkness, well out of the reach of the meager light afforded by the torches, the banners of those nobles in residence hidden by the shadows. The trestle tables had been cleared, linens removed from the dormant table on the dais. The soft sounds of the sleeping servants could be heard as they lay upon their straw-filled palliasses in the recessed alcoves of the walls. Beyond the dormant table, at the back of the dais before the massive hearth where a low warming fire could be heard to snap and hiss against the escaping gases from wood slightly green, occasional soft laughter and the hushed sounds of women's voices broke the silence. Accustomed to these nightly gatherings, not even the hounds chained for the night against the wall near the outer doors to the hall stirred in their sleep.

Knowing that no one would approach the area reserved for the family, the Marshal women sat at ease, sharing moments from the day as had been the custom of their family since before any of them could remember. There was something exceptionally peaceful and blessed about such moments, time taken when others were abed, when the world slept.

"I managed to speak with Alan Wadley before he left," Sybile said, pouring herself a goblet of watered wine from the table near her chair. Her sisters exchanged an amused smile at the comment. Was there any doubt that Sybile would manage to learn every detail of their husbands' activities before Will's knight departed Hertford? They had depended upon it. She explained the plan of siege to her attentive listeners and then fell silent as each considered the tactics from her own point of reasoning.

"Even now they should be within the inner bailey, to face the keep at dawn," Eve said, finally breaking the silence.

"Aye. The Duke of Cornwall's miners will be brought in tonight and the new tortoise set against the wall to cover them. With an intense attack against the keep throughout the day, the miners will have done their work before the sun begins to set again. With the wall undermined and timbered, the tunnel packed with wood, straw, and grease, the mass will have been fired, bringing that section of the wall down. Should those within the keep try to countermine to head off our forces, Will is certain that our miners, being the faster, will have the fires set before the tunnels can be met. In that event, smoke will ferret them out."

"We understand about mining, Sybile," Matilda said impatiently. "However, perhaps none of it will be necessary if the Archbishop successfully pleads with those within. I have to admit, I am stunned that the King thought to send for him."

"Aye, it is not the act of one seeking only glory," Isabella put in. " 'Twould seem that Henry is capable of demonstrating good sense. It is certainly encouraging."

"Well, we shall know the outcome readily," Sybile offered as she curled her legs up beneath her. "I sent a man with Wadley and he will bring us news, whatever happens."

"We can thank the Good Lord that the endeavor does not appear to be fraught with danger," Eve injected quietly. "With His blessing our men will soon be restored to us. In fact," she added with a twitch to her lips, "I surmise that they are having a perfectly grand time of it."

"Of course they are." Isabella smirked. "I was discussing the plans for the market with Gilbert when the missive came from Will. He tossed it off and pretended interest in what I was saying, but I vow I saw him tremble with excitement he was ill put to conceal. I won't say that he wasn't listening to me, but he suggested that I could do anything that I wished."

"Ha!" Sybile blurted. "You should have used the moment to suggest replacing the glazed windows you've been continually asking him for!" Her eyes turned to the cracked and drafty leaded windows.

"I did." Isabella smiled with satisfaction.

The quiet was broken by a burst of feminine laughter, causing the servants to mumble and stir in their sleep. "Tell me," Matilda asked, lowering her voice. "How was Eleanor when you saw her to her bed?"

Isabella sobered at the question. "Exhausted, of course. And slightly overwhelmed, I fear. And . . ." She paused, glancing at her sisters as she sighed heavily. "She has begun to bleed."

"Oh, sweet Mother of God," Matilda muttered. "Did you talk with her about it?"

"Nay. 'Twas only an observation as I helped her ready for bed."

"Do you think Will knows?" Sybile asked softly as she stared into the fire.

"More important, what will he do?" Eve interjected. "By custom and law he must now consummate the marriage. She is such a child."

"Do you not think he knows that?" Matilda snapped. "Damn!" she hissed furiously. "Damn Levene deFountaine!"

"Matilda!" Eve whispered, shocked. "How can you damn a dead woman? Moreover, what has she to do with this?"

"Everything! If she had not bewitched him so, he would have fallen in love with someone else long ago, and he would not be suffering this!"

"She did not bewitch him, Matilda. They loved each other," Eve said soothingly. "Whatever sins Levene may have committed, and we are not in a position to judge, were absolved when she died bearing the babe—"

"It was not his!" Matilda spat. "I will never understand Will's loyalty to that woman!"

"It is not for us to understand," Isabella pressed patiently. "He loved her. Love forgives everything. The question is no longer an issue—she is gone and so is the babe as she bore it."

"Nay, the question is real, for he loves her still!" Matilda protested. "It is that love which has caused such grief for him all of these years—and will continue to cause trouble, for him and that poor child who is sleeping abovestairs."

"You underestimate Will, Matilda," Isabella countered. "I accept that he lives with memories which haunt him, but I do not believe that he will allow them to destroy his future—or hers."

"What future?" Sybile snapped, then sighed sadly. "Lord, she is so terribly young. Some men would be panting at the thought of empowering such tender flesh. . . ."

"Sybile!" Eve snapped. "Are you suggesting that Will—"

"Of course not! But what choice does he have?"

"That is the issue," Isabella said thoughtfully. "Matilda, we know that Will loves Levene's memory still; he will always love her. Should we forget those we love because they die? But it is not our affair; Will's memories belong to him alone. What does concern us is that child abovestairs. Will has sent her to our keeping, and that alone is what concerns us. John Plantagenet was her father—what shadows has he left on her life? Her mother abandoned her. She has been raised in a male court without the influence or caring of a woman. At the age of nine she was betrothed to a man who loves her like a brother, but one who may never be able to care for her as a lover. Moreover, Sybile is right. The relationship, by necessity, must now change. Yet neither of them is ready for it. We can only imagine what it will do to them."

Matilda's gaze had turned to stare into the fire as she listened, and when she turned back to her sisters, her expression was set with resolve. "There may be precious little time before Henry takes her from us, and God knows he is pliable. Until the vows are reaffirmed and the marriage is consummated, the attempt to take her from Will, and the Marshal influence, will continue. Will has lived with this for five years; moreover, he must know that time is running out. Therefore, our position is clear and painfully simple. We must prepare her."

"I agree," Isabella enjoined. "Moreover, she is our sister. Before she leaves here, she must be strong enough to face whatever is to come."

A prolonged, silent moment followed as each of them thought about what had been said. "I cannot help but to wonder," Eve said quietly to the silence. "Would any of us have been strong enough to face this?"

7

"RODGER Bigod, you give that back this minute or I'll snatch you bald!"

Eleanor reached for the feeper, the green stalk of wheat the children had made into a crude whistle, as ten-year-old Rodger held it out of reach of the small towheaded girl who was alternately crying and screaming at her older cousin. Secretly Eleanor was disappointed when the boy shrugged and tossed it back to the sobbing child; she wanted to smack him. Instead, she could only glare at him as the other children crowded about, pulling at her skirts with entreaties to continue their game of blindman's buff. She gathered little Eve deClare up into her arms and wiped her eyes as she coaxed her to blow her nose on the kerchief she had drawn from the pocket of her bliaut. She would deal with Rodger later, she silently promised, eyeing the cocksure grin on the boy's face. Soothing the child, who began to hiccup between plaintive toots on the precious whistle, she bade the children follow her across the inner bailey to the base of a large elm, their favorite storytelling place. Or so it had become since Eleanor had discovered the joy of hours spent with them. As they settled beneath the shade of the tree, Eleanor stifled a smile at the predictable pairing that occurred as they sat about her. Six-year-old Richard deClare with his deFerrars cousin, John, of the same age. Isabella Bigod, six, who was angrily ignoring her older brother, sat arm in arm with Joan deFerrars, who was barely a year younger. Gilbert deClare wedged himself between Matilda Bigod and Eleanor, the three chestnut-haired five-year-olds appearing as if they were cast from the same mold, their rosy-cheeked faces flushed with anticipation, their large blue eyes eager for the story. Only Rodger, too impressed with his age to join the others, stood apart while acting nonchalant in his reluctance to miss the telling. Eve snuggled into Eleanor's lap as a thumb replaced the feeper, which was still clutched tightly in her small hand.

"Now, where did we leave the story? I simply cannot recall. Did we finish?" she teased.

"Nay!" Gilbert blurted anxiously. "The dragon had burned Beowulf's hall!"

"Ahh, now I recall." Eleanor sighed, her eyes dancing. "That nasty old lizard belched fire and flame and burned everything in sight. What," she whispered, her eyes widening as they rolled over the children, "do you think King Beowulf was doing all of this time?"

"He ran for his sword!"

"He got his army!"

"Nay, something far more important!" Eleanor answered in a hushed voice. "He had a special shield made. A great magical shield of iron."

"Pah!" Rodger snorted from where he leaned against the trunk of the tree. "My father's shield is made from pressed steel! Iron could never withstand the blows of a steel sword—much less the heat of a dragon's breath."

"This was a very, very long time ago," Eleanor explained to soothe the doubts which Rodger's contempt had brought to the children's faces. "A time when shields were made of wood. You can well imagine that a shield of iron would truly be a wondrous thing. And, of course, shields of iron worked against dragons—you don't see any of the loathsome creatures today, do you?"

The children brightened at the truth of Eleanor's words, and they dismissed Rodger's skepticism with relief, their attention again firmly caught. "Now," Eleanor continued, "as Beowulf prepared himself for battle, he thought back over those of his past, all those we have heard about thus far: when he cleared the evil hall of Hrothgar; when he destroyed Grendel's terrible kin; when he killed Hygelac, and even when he swam the great ocean weighted by thirty sets of armor. . . ."

The afternoon wore on gently, passing in a fixed moment. Eleanor recounted the end of the story, her lilting voice entrancing the children, who sat transfixed as she told of the magnificent funeral given by the people of Gent in homage of the years of their wise and mighty king. The walls of the bailey began to cast deepening shadows about the listeners as she finished: ". . . and so, the people of Gent, and the friends of his hearth, bemoaned the loss of their mighty lord."

Her final words fell on silence, and it was a moment before Eleanor realized the change in those gathered about her. She gasped softly as she realized the small audience of household knights stood nearby and she wondered with amazement how long they had been listening. They turned and drifted away, even as they gifted her with a smile before departing, but it was another listener that brought a deep flush to Eleanor's cheeks.

"Come, now, children, your nurses await with your suppers. Hurry now." Isabella gathered up the protesting children and firmly sent them scampering toward the keep. Even Rodger, who had resigned himself to settling at a spot behind Eleanor to hear the story, walked off, a bit behind the rest, at his aunt's firm bidding. "Well, now," Isabella said, turning back on Eleanor, who was self-consciously brushing the grass from her skirt. "You have a gift, Eleanor." Eleanor's eyes widened, and then she felt a tingle of delight as she saw the approval in Isabella's eyes. "If you were to work a little harder to develop your voice, I believe you could well rival any troubadour."

Eleanor flushed at the compliment from one whom she had grown to respect with a feeling akin to awe. Isabella was unsurpassed in voice and ability to entertain with song and story.

"You are too easily embarrassed by a compliment, my love." Isabella laughed kindly as she wrapped an arm about

Eleanor's shoulder. "You have many gifts and talents, Eleanor, many of which you have not yet begun to realize."

"I?" Eleanor blinked, glancing up at Isabella.

"Of course you!" Isabella laughed again as she gave Eleanor's shoulder a squeeze. "Eleanor, you truly don't realize what a breathtaking and disarming woman you are going to be, do you? Perhaps it is just as well, for I fear that you are destined to be the cause of many a broken heart!"

Eleanor regarded Isabella with a look of disbelief, then dismissed the statement as outrageous. "There is only one heart I wish to conquer, and not to break it, but to capture it," she stammered.

"You will, sweetling, give it time," Isabella said softly.

"Time?" she whispered. "It has been five years!"

"Five years for you to grow, to mature. Eleanor, what do you expect from him? Would you love him more if he had used your child's body?" She saw a flicker of surprise and doubt cross the girl's eyes at the question, and her own blue-green eyes narrowed as she determined that it was the moment for some plain speaking. "Eleanor, do you understand what happens between a man and a woman in the marriage bed?"

Eleanor flushed at the blunt question. "Aye," she stammered. "Well—more or less."

"More? Or less?" Isabella asked kindly. She gestured for the girl to sit with her on a bench along the wall beneath the spreading reach of the tree. "Eleanor, tell me exactly what it is that you need from Will that he does not give to you."

Eleanor frowned as she sought to answer the question. Her thoughts mingled, tossed confusingly with her emotions, as she sought for a way to express herself. "He treats me like a child!"

"And so you have been," Isabella said firmly. "And now you are becoming a young woman. In fact, I would venture a guess that this restlessness you feel, this dissatisfaction with Will's treatment of you, is a relatively new experience."

Eleanor stared at the Countess with amazement. "Aye! I did not used to feel this way! But then he changed. He—"

"Nay, Eleanor, he has not changed, love, you have. Where once you were well content if he would play draughts and merrypeg with you, your heart now reaches for something more. Give yourself time, love. Your body has begun to change and with it your emotions, and your needs are beginning to change as well. But just as the changes in your body cannot be hurried, all else must be given its proper place in time. Now come,'' she finished briskly, rising from the bench as she held out a hand. "Our supper is waiting. But tonight we shall talk more about this, and of all the wonderful things that are going to happen to you.''

Eleanor sat in the solar the following morning, her needle-work lying idle in her lap, and thought upon the astounding things Isabella had told her. In moments she thought she had almost caught the answer, the realization that would bring everything into focus, define her life in a way that would allow her to proceed unafraid, sure of herself at last. But answers remained elusive, just out of reach, leaving her with a continued jumble of confusion and fear—and doubt.

A heartbreaker? She? Perhaps it was something only others could see. It certainly could not be seen from inside, where she was. In a moment alone, before Isabella had joined her in their shared chamber and her new maids had gone to fetch fresh towels and water for her bath, she had ventured a glimpse of herself in the silvered mirror above her toilette table. She had looked haltingly at the image reflected, hoping beyond hope to see a different vision staring back at her. As she had stared into the mirror her optimism had plummeted. The same thin, too-long face peppered lightly with freckles stared back at her. The same straight black hair. The same narrow, shapeless body. All desperately the same. Totally untransformed.

Later that evening, when they were alone, Isabella had patiently explained the emotional and physical aspects of marriage. Surprisingly, Eleanor had found herself more fascinated than embarrassed. Perhaps it had been due to the easy manner of Isabella's recounting, or because it served merely to fit together pieces of the puzzle Eleanor had already speculated about.

She had lain awake for hours, armed with her new knowledge, speculating now on how it would apply to her and Will. She had blushed more than once in the dark chamber, but with it came an excitement, an anticipation of discovery. With Will it would be beautiful, she knew it. Only one thing plagued her, that which she could not rectify with what Isabella had told her—Father Latius's teachings. His words pressed and she squirmed against their memory. She was a spiritually weak creature prone to carnal sin. As the original temptress it was woman whose desire led man to sin, the essence of her own sinful nature as given by Eve. A good wife, he had said, was a Martha, allowing her husband his duty in order to beget children. A good wife understood her sinful nature, the wickedness of her soul. Only the grace of God and her husband could help her to redeem her soul.

Oh, she did not want to be responsible for leading Will to sin! Yet Isabella had said it was beautiful, not sinful. She said that the joy they would find together would enrich their marriage. And then, suddenly, not knowing why, she remembered the precious piece of tapestry safely tucked away in the bottom of her wardrobe chest. She had almost forgotten it—but not the image it carried.

Woman as the chaste and pure Virgin. But that could not be! A wife could not remain chaste. Nay, a wife could only be a Martha—or an Eve. Oh, it was all so confusing! And then she thought of Will. The mere thought of him made her body tingle, but more. A happiness settled over her, a feeling of peace and trust. He would know. He would never hurt her or let her fall into sin.

She sighed softly, picking up her idle needlework and she began to work it absently. In the time spent at Hertford she had begun to learn patience. She had been given a hint of what lay before her as reward for patience, and she clung to it, vowing to take each step as it came. She had been given so much here, in so short a time. She looked up and her gaze touched each of them: Matilda, Sybile, Eve, and Isabella. They had become a family in the weeks since her arrival at Hertford. Oh, not like Henry and Richard, but something different. They bossed her about, chastised her constantly, ever demanding this and that. Isabella made her spend hours with the lyre and psaltery, training her voice with John, Hertford's minstrel. Sybile drilled her in numbers and accounts until her fingers ached so that she could not bear to hold a quill and her

brain felt as though it would burst. Eve provided her with new
clothes and lectured endlessly on deportment, ever reminding
her of her carriage and manners. Matilda seemed to be always
there, watching, giving advice to the others when she was not
closeted with Eleanor on the duties of a chatelaine, listing the
endless matters involving a large manor and the proper attitude and supervision toward servants—including those of
her new maids. But all was done with kindness, an underlay of
love and attention that touched something deep and undefined
within her. It had been unspoken, but it was there like a
lifeline.

"Milady."

The women looked up as Seaton entered the solar and approached his mistress. Upon his next words the passing weeks
melted into new meaning and energy as if they had only been
the marking of time. "Milady," he repeated in his haughty
manner, "my lord deClare has returned in the company of my
lords Marshal, Bigod, Derby, and deBraose. They await you
in the Great Hall."

Eleanor stood back and nervously watched the boisterous
gaiety of the homecoming. The long hall was reduced to a
state of bedlam. The men's voices, women's laughter, and excited squeals of the children added to her own feeling of anticipation as her eyes fixed on Will. He was grinning at the
antics of his nieces and nephews as he held two-year-old
Joanna deClare in his arms amid the added hubbub of the servants setting up the trestle tables for midmeal.

It had taken all of her self-control not to follow the
children's example and throw herself into Will's arms. Instead, she had caught herself just in time and had held back,
garnering all of the hard-won restraint she had tried so
diligently to acquire under the firm tutelage of the Marshal
women. "Well-bred ladies do not scamper about," she mentally repeated Matilda's voice in her mind. Her fingers played
nervously with the folds of the rich burgundy velour of her
bliaut and she swallowed against the lump that was forcing
itself into her throat. She tried to picture how she looked, hoping for once that no stubborn strands of hair had escaped their
combs and that the short, sheer veil of sarcenet she wore made
her look older. Glancing down, she bit her lip in dismay to

note a smudge on the snowy-white sleeves of her chemise. She licked a finger and rubbed the spot, only to smudge it worse. Tucking her hand behind her back, she looked up and was appalled to find Will's eyes upon her. Oh, why at that particular moment had he chosen to notice her?

With a light kiss upon little Joanna's head Will passed the child to her mother, then crossed the span of the hall to Eleanor. Eleanor's eyes met Isabella's as Will turned, and the Countess deClare smiled supportively before her attention was taken by her squirming daughter.

"Eleanor, could this be you?" Will said solemnly as he came to a stop before her, but his eyes flickered with amusement. "Whatever happened to my page?"

" 'Tis not very gentlemanly to remind me of my follies, my lord," she sniffed.

His mouth worked at her retort, but he stifled his laughter as he gave her a gentle bow from his waist and took her hand to bend over it. "Forgive me, milady, for being so insufferable as to remind you. Little one, you look lovely."

She stiffened. The delight of having him kiss her hand mingled with the despair she felt at being reminded of her tender years. Her clothes, her new manners, yet nothing had changed one wit! Gratefully, she did not have to reply, for the children were being whisked away to their chambers by their nurses and the family had begun to take their places at the tables for midmeal. Swallowing back tears of bitter disappointment, she laid her hand on Will's arm and walked by his side the length of the hall to the dormant table. Keeping her eyes lowered as he handed her into her chair next to Gilbert deClare, she fixed her gaze steadily on the saltcellar directly in front of her. She closed her eyes as the chaplain intoned the blessing. But she heard nothing, aware only of numbing disappointment.

The ending of the blessing brought a scurry of activity as the servants entered the hall laden with their burdens. Eleanor's gaze shifted and fixed upon Will's hands as they trimmed a trencher of day-old bread for the plate they would share, and her brow furrowed pensively. Her attention was caught by the sight of his long fingers, the tanned muscles of his lower arms revealed by the rolled-back sleeves of his chanise, and she suddenly pictured those hands as they gripped a sword.

"Henry!" she blurted, and she turned to stare at Will.

He looked up from the frumenty he was dishing into her silver-lined bowl and a dark brow cocked with surprise. "What about him?"

"Bedford—what happened—is he well?" she gasped, horrified that she had not thought to ask before.

"He is well." Will chuckled. "Would I have not told you immediately if he were not?"

"But—Bedford—what happened?" she pressed. Suddenly she became aware of the conversation about her, and she flushed, realizing that the matter was being discussed by the others at the table.

Will smiled at her earnest expression as he offered her a slice of entrayle, sheep stomach stuffed with pullets, pork, cheese, spices, and boiled eggs. She squirmed impatiently. "Well?"

"The keep was taken, the leaders were hanged in the presence of the King's justice, who had been kept prisoner these many months. The castle was razed to the last stone, given to the Church for a new abbey."

"Then the mining worked," Eleanor observed with satisfaction.

"Faultlessly." Will grunted as he dove hungrily into a beef marrow fritter.

"Henry must be well pleased."

"Far more than William deBeauchamp," Hugh Bigod observed ruefully. "He requested to the Crown for the return of his keep and is given a bare plot of ground in answer."

"He will rebuild." Will shrugged. "It was important to make the point with deBreaute."

"And deBreaute is finished—once and for all," Gilbert deClare observed between mouthfuls as his gaze rose and his brows gathered. "Isabella . . . are those new windows?"

"The man is indeed finished," Isabella said quickly. "Mercenaries such as deBreaute are responsible for the cruelty brought down upon the people of England. They have no loyalties. Greed and avarice are their only motives."

"Do not overlook the fact that the barons opened the way for them, Isabella," Hugh said grimly as he motioned for his squire to refill his goblet. "England's peers grasped all too readily at the concept of knights' fees to be paid in coin in lieu of service to their king. My father decried the act, as did yours, Will, but few heeded their warning."

"Humph!" Sybile snorted. "It was not that simple. King John encouraged knights' fees to be paid in coin as he comforted himself by buying loyalty—the only kind he could expect."

Eleanor tensed at the mention of her father's name. She bit her lip against the contempt she heard in Sybile's voice, her own emotions ever in conflict between the truth and the loyalty she felt she should have for her father. But how could she defend him? She was only too aware of the errors her father had committed. His greed, his ambition, his lack of concern or feeling for others. And his use of mercenaries to subjugate the barons. All had eventually forced him to the table at Running-Mead and the signing of the Great Charter.

Eve saw the pain which crossed the young princess's face, and she glared at the thoughtlessness of her sister. "You are correct about my father's feelings regarding knights' fees, Hugh, but it never influenced the matter of his loyalties. He cared not for deBreaute, nor his kind, but he would never speak against a man who fought at his side in the service of England—and he was ever loyal to his king," she added, her voice giving heavy emphasis to her last words. Glancing in Eleanor's direction, she saw the approval in Will's smile.

"You have not told us why Richard, Gilbert, and Walter did not return with you," Isabella said to no one in particular as she sought to change the subject.

"They traveled to Oxford with Henry." Will grinned, leaning back in his chair. "Hugh and I managed to convince Henry that pressing matters required our attendance here, but that my brothers could act for us."

"With a set amount to spend toward the new chapel there," Hugh added glumly.

"Do not fear, Hugh." Will chuckled at his brother-in-law's discomfort. "They will hold to it."

Will sat before the hearth in the silent evening hours, his long legs stretched out before him and crossed at the ankles. His hands held a goblet on his chest which he turned idly in his fingers. He hadn't felt so relaxed in months, and his eyes turned lazily to the others, touching on each in easy affection. Only one was absent, her youth drawing her to an early bed. His wife—his mind twisted with the thought. Heaving a sigh, he shifted uncomfortably.

Matilda refilled her husband's goblet, returning Hugh's smile in a moment's exchange of love. Brief moments alone with Hugh in the afternoon hours past touched her memory, and she flushed in the remembrance. Their eyes locked in understanding, and with it Hugh sent her a promise and Matilda tingled with anticipation. The day's mundane matters receded as her body rushed with the realization that these were the best hours, the moments spent in quiet reflection and sharing before a time alone. A deep sigh from her brother brought her about and she fixed upon it, drawing from its reality to remember what had been planned. Exchanging a long look of understanding with Isabella, she crossed to the small table between Sybile and her husband. Setting the pitcher on the table, she nodded to her sister, then crossed to stand before the warmth of the fire.

Sybile yawned loudly, drawing a speculative look from her husband. DeFerrars rose and offered his hand to his wife as his eyes widened in a comic gleam. "We had best be to bed wife, posthaste judging from that yawn."

The comment was met with laughter from the others and a dimpling smile from Sybile as she rose to take her husband's hand. Eve left with William deBraose soon after, even as Hugh and Gilbert rose from their chairs to retire. Will, who was staring thoughtfully into the flames beyond his outstretched legs, missed the looks of understanding they exchanged with their wives before they quietly left. Long moments passed before Will looked up to find that Matilda and Isabella had remained. In the emptiness of the hall he looked from one to the other as a dark brow arched speculatively. "Well?" he asked quietly as his eyes glittered with fond amusement. "Out with it."

"You have a problem, Will," Matilda answered.

"Indeed, and I am certain that you are going to tell me what it is." He smiled.

"Eleanor," she said, ignoring his barb.

"What has she done?" His smile dissolved into a glower.

"Done?" Isabella shook her head. "Nothing, Will, except grow up."

He snorted. "She's a child."

Isabella rose from her chair to refill his goblet before taking the chair next to him. "You would like to believe that she is, still. But she is becoming a woman," she said with soft entreaty. Taking a deep breath, she plunged forward. "Will, she has begun her monthly cycle."

His goblet paused halfway to his mouth and he stared at Isabella. "Is this true?" he asked tightly. His eyes darted to Matilda, who confirmed it with a nod. "Jesu," he groaned, then threw down a large draught. He swore under his breath as he wiped his mouth slowly with the back of his hand. "It matters not—she is a child still."

"Surely you knew this day would come, Will," Matilda pressed. "Will you now insult Henry—and your vows—by rejecting her?"

"I do not seduce children!" he retorted, throwing himself from the chair. He turned before the fire and began to pace. Pausing, he ran his fingers through his hair before spinning back on them. "Sweet Mother, I never asked for this marriage."

"That, my dear brother, changes nothing," Matilda said firmly. "We cannot keep her here much longer, as dear as she has become to us. Henry will soon demand her return to court—and is certain to learn that she has passed from child to woman. The only reason no one knows of it now is because of the indifference of those wretches Henry gave her as tirewomen. He will face what you will not—if you do not reaffirm your vows and consummate the marriage, there are those who will take her from you."

"No one will dare." He laughed bitterly, drawing from the goblet still gripped in his hand.

"No one? Not even Peter desRoches?" she pressed.

"DesRoches can do nothing as long as he is kept from England!"

"Will, I have never known you to be so blind!" she persisted. "His son is still here and Peter desRevaux will press his suit with Henry. How long do you think Henry will hold out against the pressures that will be brought to bear?"

"Stop it!" Isabella blurted. "What is the matter with both of you? What is of the most importance here is Eleanor herself! You speak of her as if she were nothing more than a pawn!"

"She is a princess royal, Isabella," Matilda returned. "As such she is exactly that!"

"She is a frightened, confused young girl, Matilda. Moreover, she is our sister! I agree with Will. She is not ready for the responsibilities of marriage."

"Pah. She was ready the day she was born in a Plantagenet bed, and responsibility was thrust on her the moment she first drew breath. She is stronger than you give her credit for."

"And what of her life, and Will's?" Isabella looked up at her brother. "I could not bear to see you both unhappy, as you are certain to be if this matter is forced now."

"You are both right," Will said as he took the chair across from them. "I have no intention of turning my back on Eleanor, or this marriage. Nor will I take a child to my bed, for any reason. I care about her as well, Isabella," he added, his voice softening as he smiled at his sister. "You have grown to love her in just a few short weeks. She has been part of my life for nine years."

"What are you going to do?" Matilda asked with a catch in her voice. A feeling of dread washed over her as she studied the resolve in his expression.

"What I have planned to do all along when this moment came." His brow furrowed as he was distracted by another thought. "It is hard for me to understand why women are considered to be so when they are still children. Sweet Mother Mary, this should not happen to you until you are ready for it."

"For those of us who are blessed with loving parents—and are not mere pawns for men," Isabella added, throwing a glare at her sister, "it is not a problem."

Matilda ignored Isabella's chide and leaned forward in her chair, her eyes fixed on Will. "What *are* you going to do?"

"It was left in Father's will for Richard to see to the lands in Ireland; for Gilbert, our estates in Normandy; and Walter is for Wales. It is time they began. I shall take each of them to their lands and help them to settle their demesnes."

Isabella looked blank as she tried to make sense out of Will's words, but Matilda grasped his meaning instantly. She sat back heavily in her chair and stared at her brother.

"What is it?" Isabella asked as her eyes darted between them. "I do not understand; what has this to do with anything?"

"It is the solution, Isabella," Matilda said quietly. Her eyes had brightened suddenly as they filled with unshed tears, but she continued to stare. "Will is leaving us." She turned her head to regard Isabella sadly. "Can you not see? It is so simple. If he is not here, he cannot consummate the marriage. Yet he does not break his vows—and unless he were to do so, the marriage is valid."

"Oh," Isabella whispered. "Oh, Will—how long?"

"Two, three years, perhaps." He shrugged as he leaned forward to refill his goblet.

"But—what of matters here?"

"Your husbands will see to my estates. I have no fear that they will be well cared for."

Isabella swallowed heavily as tears began to fill her eyes as well. "You—you will be taking Richard, Gilbert, and Walter from us as well," she observed with a catch to her voice. She felt as if her heart were tearing in two. Until this moment she had not appreciated fully how close they were nor how unique among families of their time. She felt a door closing on something dear and precious that would never be found again, and it pulled at her like a small death.

"Will Henry allow you to go?" Matilda asked, her voice stronger than it had been moments before.

"He cannot deny me the right to fulfill the terms of our father's will. Now heed me well. It is vital that you say nothing to anyone about this. I will speak to your husbands and I know they will keep my confidence. In the morning I will leave for Chepstow, even as messages are sent to Richard, Gilbert, and Walter to join me there. It will give us the chance to say farewell to Mother and Joanne as well. From Chepstow I will send a missive to London informing Henry of my deci-

sion—the matter must seem to have been decided upon at
Chepstow. It will be said that our Lady Mother demanded that
the letter of the will be executed.''

"What of Eleanor?'' Isabella gasped. "Surely you are not
going to leave without bidding her farewell!''

"Isabella, I cannot,'' he snapped impatiently. "Can I tell
her of plans not yet made? It must never be learned that I
knew she had come to her time before I left—or be suspected
that it was the cause for my departure.''

"She—she will be so terribly hurt, Will.''

"Isabella, it is for her own good,'' Matilda snapped; then
her voice softened as she sighed heavily against her own grief.
"Can we fault Will for saving the child from the alternative?
Consider what he is giving up to allow her the time they both
need. Our grief is the least of it. Everything will be done as you
say, Will.''

"I had no doubt that it would be.'' Will smiled as he leaned
back in his chair and regarded his sisters affectionately. "Do
not be overly concerned by this; it was to come in any case.
Father's will might prove the excuse, but it certainly is a reality—one long overdue. I fear that in his attention to provide
for his many sons, he overlooked how reluctant we would be
to part. Amazing,'' he added as his eyes took on a distant
gaze. "There shall be Marshals from Normandy to Ireland. I
wonder if any family before has held such power?''

"Not in England,'' Matilda observed, her own eyes clearing
as she considered the question. "And to this you must add
the strengths of the Bigods, deClares, deFerrarses, and
deBraoses.''

" 'Tis clear that I must choose Joanne's husband with great
care.'' Will laughed and his brow rose speculatively at the
prospect.

"You have forgotten one most important,'' Isabella interjected, drawing the attention of the other two. She smiled at
the question in their expressions. "Young, tender, a mere slip
of a girl,'' she tossed with a smile that belied the seriousness of
her meaning. "One that should never be overlooked, for she is
a Plantagenet.''

PART TWO

Troubadours and Players

8

ELEANOR'S gaze lifted with the flight of the bird as it arched heavenward, only to lose it momentarily as it vanished against the blinding aura of the sun. Squinting, she turned her head away for an instant and blinked to regain her vision. Looking back, her entire body tensed in fear that she had lost it. "There you are!" she whispered, concentrating as if to aid the merlin in its quest. Unconsciously her gloved hands gripped the reins as she murmured encouragement, her eyes now darting between the circling falcon and its unsuspecting prey, which had lifted from the trees to her left.

"There! I told you!" she cried as the merlin seemed to pause and hang suspended from some invisible support in the sky. Instantly it plummeted earthward, its wings tucked back against its small body as it cannoned downward. Soundlessly the linnet was struck, feathers flying from the force of the impact, evidence left floating innocently behind as the merlin glided to the trees with its victim. "I told you she was ready!" Eleanor cried happily.

"You have not yet won your bet, milady." The young brown-haired nobleman at her side grinned at her. "Three to

105

your one that she does not allow the falconer to recapture her.''

"Done!" Eleanor laughed, spurring her mount as she called back over her shoulder. "You part with your money too easily, Rolph!"

The hunting party rode in the direction of the falconers through the trees, pulling in their mounts at a discreet distance so as not to frighten the young bird. Eleanor held her breath as her man moved toward the merlin, which was perched on a low-slung branch with the linnet in its talons. The falconer spoke in a slow, soothing voice as he approached, depending on the familiarity of his voice to gentle the bird. Clucking deep in his throat, he swung the lure in his hand and held out his other, heavily gloved, toward it. The bird hesitated over its victim and turned its head to stare at the man. Ruffling its feathers, it stepped a few inches down the branch and regarded the falconer with its intense yellow eye once again.

"There, I told you—"

"Shhhhh!" Eleanor hissed.

Fanning its wings for a moment, suddenly the bird lifted from the branch and came to rest on the extended glove of its trainer. With rapid skill the man wrapped a leg of the falcon with leather tresses and in a smooth movement had replaced the rufter, the soft hood used with new birds. Then he turned, grinning, to Eleanor, his weathered face fused with satisfaction and pride in his charge.

"You owe me three marks, Rolph!" Eleanor tossed, laughing at the disgruntled look on the face of the young knight.

His displeasure quickly disappeared in the face of her delight, and he grinned good-naturedly. "You shall have it, milady, before supper."

"Speaking of supper, we have not even yet had midmeal."

Eleanor turned and her smile dimpled. "Alan, Earl Newbury, do you think of nothing but your stomach?"

The young noble, who had brought his mount alongside Eleanor's, looked down at her from his greater height. His sandy hair fell carelessly over his forehead, tousled by the effort of the morning's ride. Warm hazel eyes looked deeply into hers, his mouth easing into an attractive grin. Eleanor felt her stomach flutter as the handsome knight smiled at her, and she struggled to suppress the unwanted reaction of her body.

"There are other things my mind dwells upon, milady," he said softly. "But such things must necessarily be left unspoken at this time."

Her mouth softened into a smile. "Indeed, Alan, as they properly must be. The only love of value is that which is pure. Only the heart that is given nobly has true worth."

"Aye, lady, and so you have mine."

Their eyes held for a long instant, until the moment was broken by the sound of a feminine voice. "This would be the perfect place for a picnic, Eleanor!"

"Oh—aye, it would, Katherine." Eleanor pulled her gaze away from the knight to glance about her. "But I fear that we must return to Windsor. The King has bidden me attend him for midmeal." She laughed lightly at her friend's disappointment. "I suspect he is planning a surprise, for he was most insistent."

The small party returned to Windsor, their mood lightened. Henry's surprises were well known to be memorable occasions, and the group speculated heavily on their ride back as to what it could be. Eleanor half listened to the light banter of her friends, but soon her thoughts drifted apart from the conversation. They were dear friends, she mused, and the time spent in their company had given her joy and companionship. Odd, in all the years of her life, with so many constantly about her, she had never really had friends of her own until the past few years. She owed it to the Marshal women, she thought begrudgingly. When she had returned to court after Will . . . She forced aside that thought as it pressed to enter. Nay, she would not think about him. When she returned to court, she thought with deliberation, Isabella and Matilda had accompanied her. They had closeted themselves with Henry for over two hours. When they left, Henry was solicitous, acting with a tender concern she had never seen in him before. Soon other young people were brought to court, and not just gentlemen for the King's chamber but young ladies for her own household.

Katherine of Kent, Constance Bramber, Margaret of Lincoln. Her dear, dear friends. While she had never spoken of it to Henry, she knew she owed their presence to Isabella and Matilda, and the pressure they had brought to bear on Henry. Not that she had seen the Marshal women again. Nay, like their brother, they had chosen to absent themselves from court.

Laughter drew her attention to the couple riding a few lengths ahead of her. Margaret has set her sights for Richard Chilham, she thought, suppressing her amusement as she saw the look that passed between them. And Katherine is smitten with Wayland Harvey, though I fear her suit shall go unrewarded. That one has no sense of nobility within him—he would use her and move on to another. She vowed to speak to her friend. Rolph cannot take his eyes from Constance— though she sets her sights for Alan. The realization brought a crease to her brow. Nay, Constance, she affirmed. Alan of Newbury is mine.

They rode into the courtyard of Windsor and went immediately to their chambers to prepare for the banquet planned for midmeal. By the time Eleanor had bathed, having dismissed her ladies to see to their own preparations, they had returned. Setting the servants to other tasks, the ladies-in-waiting to the princess began their usual happy chatter as they helped her to dress.

"Do you think Alan is the one?" Katherine of Kent whispered conspiratorially as she brushed Eleanor's hair, leaning to her ear so the others might not hear.

Eleanor stared in the glazed mirror at Katherine. "The one who what?" she asked, feigning ignorance.

The maid's green eyes sparkled. "If he was the author of the verse Darcy sang last eve, of course!"

"Oh." Eleanor shrugged. "Perhaps . . ."

"It must be," Katherine insisted. "Oh, Eleanor, you know that the verse was written for you!" Katherine's gaze floated dreamily as she whispered the words sung by the goliard:

> *My deepest sorrows abide with thee,*
> *A kiss to give me life.*
> *Beyond our time you shall be mine,*
> *In sorrow, my love,*
> *We cannot now but pine . . .*

"I vow that Darcy visibly winced as he sang the verse."
Eleanor laughed, remembering.

"Oh, Your Grace!" Katherine exclaimed. "How can you be
so cruel? The verse was given from the heart, the very soul—"

"Of course," Eleanor answered abruptly, seeing Katherine's dismay in her reflection in the mirror. Good Lord, she
could not have it said that she ridiculed the efforts of the
courtiers. Nevertheless, she had to drop her gaze so that
Katherine would not see the humor that persisted. When she
thought of Darcy having to sing those lines . . . laughter bub-
bled up in her and she coughed. Oh, Darcy, she thought, why
do you remain at court? Each night, to act as minstrel, to
spend your efforts carrying the lyrics of lovers.

Her toilette completed, she stood to allow the ladies to dress
her. Finished, she stepped to the full-length mirror and
critically appraised what she saw. Large eyes of vibrant blue
stared back at her. Plantagenet blue, she had heard them
called. Her hair, unlike those others of her illustrious
ancestors, was raven. The blue-black of her father. Hopefully,
to her way of thinking, the only thing she shared with him.
Many times she wished she had taken the blond glory of the
Plantagenets, as had her brothers, but, she reasoned, the effect was not displeasing.

As she studied the image, she ran her palms over the lush
sky-blue velvet of her gown. It clung to her body in soft folds,
girdled about the hips with links of gold, amethysts, and sapphires. The costly jewels were repeated at her shoulders where
they held the gown, the luxurious velvet falling to wide sleeves
short enough to show the tightly layered folds of the snowy-
white linen of her chemise. Her face was flattered by the gentle
folds of the white sheer wimple of sarcenet and the blue velvet
coif framing her face to fall beyond the shoulders, and topped
by a saucy pillbox cap, similarly encrusted in a delicate pattern
of the jewels.

Her eyes had particularly taken objective note of the form
of her body, the full breasts, the narrow waist, the swelling of
her hips, which were accentuated by the girdle that rested
lightly on their gentle fullness. Satisfied, she turned to the
others. "Well, ladies, we are ready. Shall we find out what the
King has planned for us?"

*   *   *

Darcy sat in the wide window embrasure, his long legs bent to hold the book on his lap as he enjoyed the unusual warmth of an early spring sun. His brown eyes moved over the words written, pausing occasionally as a dark brow arched in disbelief or blatant disapproval. Finally, he slammed the book shut and it fell idle on his lap. "Blathering idiot," he muttered. "Marcabru's mother should have drowned him at birth. At the very least she never should have allowed him to read or write."

Instantly bored, he glanced about even as his mind drifted to thoughts of Leona. Now, there's a woman, he thought. A real woman, not one caught up in this tripe. She was waiting for him in London, and he wondered why he hadn't departed Windsor before this. What was holding him? He could not have said why he had spent the past weeks at Court. Certainly not at the King's bidding—he could disappear and Henry would forget him soon enough. He turned his head and looked into the courtyard below, and his bored gaze fixed into a disbelieving stare. "By the blood of Saint Peter," he murmured. Watching the activity below, he fixed intently on the new arrivals. Feeling an infusion of excitement, something he had not felt for a long, long time, he suddenly realized what he had been waiting for—or for whom.

As the chamber door opened Darcy turned from where he was standing before the hearth with a tankard in his hand, and he grinned widely. "What in God's good name took you so long?"

The door closed with a sharp click. "Darcy! I don't believe it—is it really you?" Will Marshal stepped into the room, his tabard dust-ridden, weary lines of fatigue etched into his face.

"Who else would greet you?" Darcy grinned, leaning an elbow on the mantle. "Marshal, you look beaten."

"How kind." Will smirked. "We have not stopped since we left Normandy."

"I presume, since you have returned, that everything went well for you?"

"Aye. The lands left by William Marshal are in good hands. But no more of that now, I am much too weary to recount it.

By the blood, tell me how you came to be here?"

"You know me. . . ."

"I know—an ill wind." Will laughed. "Darcy, whatever fate brought you here at this moment, I am glad to see you."

The goliard merely mumbled assent as he shrugged his shoulders and stepped from the hearth. "Perhaps 'tis fate which has designed it after all," he offered as his eyes narrowed for a moment. Then his nose twitched. "God's breath, Marshal, your odor surpasses anything of my experience."

"Then call me a bath, you damn scoundrel. Landon and Meryle are seeing to the baggage, so you might as well make yourself useful."

"So I am finally reduced to a lord's servant," Darcy grumbled. "Would you also require some food?"

"I'm tempted—but I cannot; I must see to Henry."

Will sighed heavily with pleasure as he settled into the warmth of the bath. Leaning his head on the rim of the copper tub, he closed his eyes and mentally reaffirmed his pleasure at finding the goliard at Windsor. If anyone was aware of matters of importance, it would be Darcy. "Anything I should know about?"

"Would you like to know who is dallying with whom, or something more substantial?" Darcy responded, pressing a goblet of wine into Will's hand where it dangled over the side of the tub.

"Humph." Will grunted, relaxing in the soothing warmth. "Regrettably, the weightier matters. The rest I shall look forward to at a more leisurely moment."

"Well, then." Darcy paused, appearing to think on the matter. "There was that full-scale riot in London. Would it interest you?"

"What riot?" Will's eyes were now open and staring at the goliard.

"It involved deBurgh," Darcy answered, soberly watching Will's reaction. "A group of young apprentices had constructed a quintain beyond the walls of the city where they sought to practice their skills at tilting with homemade lances. Unfortunately, a group of nobly born sons happened by, and they took serious issue with the event. They took it upon themselves to teach the common-born a lesson, and the result of the confrontation found our young courtiers emerging the losers.''

"That caused a riot?'' Will said with disbelief. "A group of boys—''

"Nay, that came later,'' Darcy interrupted, leaning over to refill Will's goblet. "Henry—that is, the council decided that the apprentices should be punished. It might have ended there, with a mild rebuke, but a citizen by the name of Fitz-Arnulf used the situation to incite the people. At the scene of the whippings he called for the people of London to unite against Henry—reminding them that they had once pledged themselves to Louis of France, where, he cried, justice could better be served. The riot followed.''

"And deBurgh? What had he to do with it?''

"He was outraged against the offense to the Crown. He ordered that Fitz-Arnulf be hanged . . . without trial. Similarly, he punished many of the ringleaders of the riot.''

"Oh, God.''

"Feelings are strong against deBurgh in London, Will. They will not soon forget that he did not grant trial to one of theirs.''

"Dammit!'' Will swore, leaning his head back against the tub as he stared at the ceiling. "A plague on those accursed London guilds! They think themselves above the law, unless it serves them to use it! And deBurgh, he was in the right; why could he not act with aforethought! He has lost London.'' He sighed heavily. "Dear God, London's support of him was the only thing Henry feared.''

"Perceptibly accurate. Henry has accused him of treason —not formally as yet, but it is only a matter of time.''

Will groaned and sank deeper into the tub. "I wish I had not asked.'' After a long pause, with his eyes still closed, he asked the next question that came to mind. "Now to who is dallying with whom. How is Eleanor?''

Darcy choked, nearly strangling on a swallow of wine. "You jest, Marshal! If she were involved with anyone I would certainly be the last to tell you. I have too much regard for my own well-being.''

"Perhaps I should rephrase the question." Will grinned. "Is Eleanor well?"

"She is beautiful, Will—but you shall see that for yourself."

Will noticed that Darcy had taken a sudden intense interest in the depths of his goblet. "Of course she is beautiful!" Will frowned. "Do you not think I could reason that for myself? Stop mincing with me, you damn bard, tell me what you are thinking. I swear not to run you through regardless of what you tell me."

"Will, you have been gone a long time—almost four years." He sighed.

"I know how long it has been, Darcy. Tell me. All of it."

"Will, in truth, there are some things you must discover for yourself, they cannot be explained." How could he explain that Will was as a man who had slept, only to be awakened in another time. "Life at court is . . . changed. You must see for yourself if we are to speak of it."

Will's expression grew grim as he regarded Darcy's feeble explanation. "Is she chaste?" he asked bluntly.

"As far as I can know," Darcy countered, waving his hand to dismiss Will's suspicions. "I am certainly not privy—"

"Then, if that is not what you are attempting to prepare me for, what is it?"

"As I said, my friend, some things you will have to discover for yourself."

The sweet, mournful sound of the troubadour's lyre infused Eleanor's mind as her thoughts floated dreamily to the suggested imaginings of the lyric. The soft laughter heard about them, the colors of the bright gowns and tabards of the courtiers, fueled her emotions, which were further tantalized by the fact of Alan's presence. Raising her gaze to Alan's, she drank headily of what she read there.

"He sings of my love for you, Eleanor," Newbury murmured softly, bending toward her so that others who stood nearby might not overhear. "As Percival sought his Grail, so I do seek the joy of the sight of you, the privilege to stand in your company. To be near to serve you."

"Sir Alan," Eleanor protested lightly, the thrill of his words intensified by the danger that he would speak so in public. "Sir Percival's quest of the Grail was a holy one."

"As is mine," he countered with a smile of longing. "The search of my soul is completed, wisdom and all truth found in the shining light of your presence. To know that our love . . ."

It was a moment before Eleanor realized that he had stopped speaking. Her thoughts wafted on his words, and it was not until she looked up at him that she realized that his attention had been drawn to a point behind her. She felt a moment of alarm as his face turned pale with apparent shock. "Alan?" Puzzled, she turned, and her world began to spin. She felt the blood rush to her head and her knees threatened to buckle. She would have fallen but for Alan's hand which grabbed her arm, pulling her against him for support.

"Oh, God," she breathed. "Will."

Incredibly, he was standing with Henry deeply engaged in conversation. Lamely, she stared at him. Deeply tanned, his dark hair, still slightly damp from a recent bath, curled over his ears, his teeth flashing in a grin at some comment from the King. The rich black velvet of his tabard, cut well to his broad shoulders, lent startling contrast to the stark white linen of the collar and sleeves of his chanise and the deep burnished gold of his wide earl's belt. Her eyes involuntarily lowered to the deep slit of the tabard, the well-muscled legs beneath clad in chausses and the crossgarters that reached to his knees. "Will," she murmured, years melting, memories rushing, leaving her lightheaded.

Then a voice from behind her reached her ear as Richard Chilham nudged Alan. "I'll be damned, Will Marshal. So our illustrious Marshal of England has returned. I wonder what has brought him back?"

"I wonder," Alan responded quietly as his gaze turned speculatively to Eleanor.

Chilham's question registered in Eleanor's brain, numbing it with pain. Slowly, she became aware of those in the crowded hall, the dimmed conversation and the heads bent with hurried whispers. The covert glances thrown from Will to Eleanor where she stood with her companions. And other memories invaded, dulling her first response to Will's sudden, unexpected

presence. Hurt and pain welled up inside of her, the sharp
memory of betrayal, abandonment, a time when she thought
she would perish. Then the anger came, the hatred that had
sustained her, cleansed her, that which had allowed her to
function, to find a new life.

She turned back to Alan and her mouth lifted into a smile.
"What was it that you were saying to me, Alan?"

The knight's expression grew doubtful as he glanced in
Will's direction and back to Eleanor. "My lady, I . . ."

"I would hear what you would say to me, Alan," she said
evenly, fixing his eyes with her own.

Alan stared at her for a long moment, and then his hazel
eyes grew warm as a flickering of determination passed over
them. "I am ever here, milady, whenever you should need
me."

Eleanor's manner grew forcibly light as she engaged in conversation with her friends. She laughed easily and quipped
with her companions, pointedly ignoring the activity about
them in the hall. And then she heard Henry's voice even as her
companions deferred to the approach of the King, the men
bending at the waist as the ladies dipped into deep curtsies.

"Eleanor, sweetling, I have brought you a surprise!"

She turned slowly. Anger flared in her that Henry had
known—and had not warned her. Warned her? He had
planned it this way! Her eyes met Will's and for an instant her
anger wavered. The deep, warm blue of his eyes held hers, the
sparkling touch of amusement and humor she remembered so
well. But there was more. Surprise, appreciation for what he
beheld? And then his gaze dropped to where Alan's hand lay
on her waist and the eyes silvered to a dangerous glint. She saw
the suggestion of anger in his smile, as did Alan, who removed
his hand from her. "You were correct, sire, my wife has
grown into a most beautiful woman," he said quietly, his gaze
locked with hers.

And her anger returned, in a rage that made her tremble.
How dare he reenter her life like this and reclaim his rights!
Her mind was jumbled with the things she dearly wanted to
say to him, and it took all of her control not to scream. She
was vaguely aware of introductions being made, light comments tossed between Henry and Will, and some idiotic thing

Henry said to tease her as he bent to bestow a brotherly kiss on
her cheek. Turning away abruptly, Henry left their company
for others requiring his attention.

She, too, began to turn away and then stiffened as she felt
Will's hand on her waist. He drew her casually to his side as he
addressed those in her company. Gritting her teeth, she stood
there, knowing she could do nothing else that would not cause
a scene and be the source of court gossip for a fortnight.
Gradually, she managed to still her rage and began to breath
normally again, even with the burning sensation of his hand
where it touched her. At last she realized that Rolph was
speaking, his voice tense with frustration.

"The song the minstrel was singing was of the glory of
knighthood, milord."

"Is that what you perceive from the song I heard upon
entering, Sir Rolph? I think not. The story of Arthur's court is
the embodiment of chivalry. The flummery I heard reduces
knighthood to that of a fop pining at the hem of his lady's
skirt, begging for the bare promise of her smile. Is that how
you carry your vows, Rolph of Walpole?"

The young knights stiffened in unified outrage. "With
respect, sir, you are in error, Lord William," Sir Wayland
countered.

"Indeed?" Will's brow raised as he regarded the young
knight. "Is it your intent to instruct me on the details of the
Code?"

The knights had the sense to look momentarily chagrined as
they realized with whom they were speaking. As Marshal of
England, Will was the protector of the Chivalric Code by
which each had taken their vows, and upon which the tenants
of knighthood were based.

"Times change."

Will's gaze shifted to the speaker, the young man who had
momentarily had his hand where his own was now placed.

"If there is to be progress, times do change," Will
countered with a patient smile. "However, humanity must
always endeavor to change for the better if it is to survive. The
Code was written for a purpose, one that you cannot appreciate in the luxury of this court. The myth and the magic
that are given to us in the legends of Arthur, and have been

brought down in the Code, are there to assist a man in reaching beyond himself, to find the courage and strength that he otherwise would not be capable of attaining. Have you been in battle, Alan of Newbury?''

The anger in the young man's eyes dimmed with confusion. "Nay, milord." he answered. "There has been no chance to do so, to my regret.''

"Regret? Sir Alan, war is not the glorious quest you deem it. As you will know, should you ever have the . . . opportunity to find yourself in battle. The purpose of our Code is to give a man the strength to face what is demanded of him on the battlefield, in service of his country and king, not in the court for the servicing of his lady.''

"Ah, Lord Marshal, you are correct, yet you do not understand the meaning of the lyric.''

Heads turned as Darcy joined them, resplendent in his goliard's bardy coat of red. Will blinked at the man's audacity of wearing the coat at court, and then, realizing that the others were openly gaping, his eyes began to spark with humor. "Then I am gratified that you are here, goliard, so that you might explain it to me.''

"With pleasure.'' Darcy swept a bow to Will. "My esteemed predecessors, those nobly born troubadours who wrote with elegance and wit, did indeed endeavor to encourage man to draw on the myths and magic of which you spoke. And for the purpose of giving him the courage and strength he would need in time of war. But alas, they overlooked a most essential truth.''

"And that would be?''

"Our fair ladies, milord,'' he offered humbly, bowing his head to the ladies in their company. " 'Tis woman who ennobles a man, who allows him to gain access to his own soul. The quest of her can only make him wiser, a more sensitive, seeking member of humanity. Moreover, 'tis the unrequited love that brings him to his highest glory, for only by his descent through hell, the byways and defeats of life, can he truly find himself.''

Will's eyes narrowed as he regarded Darcy's calm declaration with amazement, and he wondered if he had misjudged the man all these years. And then, as he encountered a gleam of challenge in Darcy's even stare, he began to understand the goliard's message. "Then, by what you are saying, only lovers who are free from sin, who hold themselves chaste from the pleasures of the flesh, can truly find fulfillment."

Eleanor had used the moment to slip from Will's possessive arm, and she turned to stand at Alan's side. As much as she wanted to rail at him, for once she controlled her Plantagenet temper as her hatred focused on taking the moment. He was her husband and she faced the loveless years of duty ahead of her, the baser side of her life that she must now accept without question. But now, just this once, he would know how she felt. When she spoke, her voice surprised her. It betrayed none of her inner emotions but was smooth and controlled. "Darcy is only partly correct, milord. The bittersweet aspect of love does lie between desire and fulfillment. However, while tradition once bound a knight's fealty to God and his king, now the only true fealty is that which binds a knight to his lady. Moreover, the purest love declares that love be given freely, without earthly bounds and complaints, whereas marriage implies obligations and coercion, which is the death of love."

A heavy, nervous silence fell over the group at Eleanor's words. Eyes turned to Will to note his reaction, but he merely raised his brows slightly as he regarded Eleanor. "You place fealty to God and to your king in a place below that of your own pleasures?"

"Ah, but God is the patron of lovers."

Will stiffened at the silkiness of the voice, and he turned to find Peter desRevaux standing at his side. "Was it not your father who was the most vocal supporter of the evil nature of women?" Will asked coolly.

"As the young man said, times do change." DesRevaux shrugged as his dark eyes rested blatantly on Eleanor.

Will flashed a furious look at Eleanor as he realized that her words had been overheard by the Poitevin. Covering quickly, he took Eleanor's hand and brushed his lips against them possessively, ignoring the tremble he felt as he touched her. Straightening, he looked down into her eyes, holding them with a look of warning as he spoke easily. "Be as it may, my sweet wife, other matters require my attention. I must regrettably leave you to discuss this topic, as fruitless as it may be, among yourselves."

He turned and walked away toward the doors to the hall, his brain fuming with what had happened and not trusting himself to remain. As he approached the large double doors his gaze lifted to a large tapestry which dominated the end of the room and he stopped. Dumbfounded, he stared at it. It depicted a scene in a shadowed copse of trees. At the center a virgin sat in repose, clad in the purity of white, and in her lap, a unicorn rested its head. "Oh, my God," he whispered.

"I warned you that things had changed."

Will turned his head to find Darcy standing next to him, staring up at the tapestry.

"You had better come with me," Will gritted. "I think we have some things to discuss."

9

WILL stormed into the room. Tearing off his earl's belt, he dropped it on a nearby table before he spun back on the goliard, who had followed him into his chamber. "By the blood, what is going on!"

Startled from sleep, Landon and Meryle jumped from their pallets, rushing to Will to assist him, only to step back quickly at the glare he threw them. "Go back to sleep," he snapped, returning his glower to Darcy. The squires returned to their pallets, rolling their eyes at each other over the unlikely prospect of soon again finding sleep.

"Well? Who was that fop Newbury that Eleanor was clinging to? What madness has developed in my absence? And how did that tapestry come to hang in the place of honor in the Great Hall?"

"Which question would you like me to answer first?" Darcy asked quietly, crossing to a table near the fire to pour them each a goblet of wine.

"For starters, identify Eleanor's admirer." Will grunted, taking the goblet Darcy offered.

"Alan of Newbury. Knighted by Prince Richard and sent to court two years ago."

"Two years?" Will's eyes narrowed. "Then their . . . relationship is of long standing."

"He has been in her circle of closest friends." Darcy shrugged. "The, ah, relationship as you call it, appears only to have changed in the past months. But do not expect him to challenge you, Will. You are her husband; he would not deny your rights."

Will, who had stripped to his chanise and chausses as Darcy spoke, paused to stare at his friend with incredulity. "Not deny my—it would appear that my rights have been well denied, you idiot!"

"Insults will not stir me, my lord earl." Darcy smiled. "I fear that you are the stranger here, and more the fool. I told you that things have changed at court—now you will begin to understand. Actually, I have little doubt that your wife remains as chaste as when you left her."

Will dropped into a chair and glared at him. "From what I observed and heard tonight, now I know you're demented."

Darcy took the chair across from him and stretched his legs out toward the fire. "Will, answer a question for me. Which would you prefer: that people spoke ill of your lady and that you should find her good, or that she were well spoken of and you should find her bad?"

"The question is absurd. I would choose neither."

"Ahhh," Darcy sighed. "But therein lies the problem. In our father's day they would have answered to the former. Our sires' first concern would have been the faithfulness of his lady, even to the exclusion of her reputation."

"I cannot account for your sire, Darcy." Will smirked. "But I assure you that mine would have happily split the head of anyone unwise enough to besmirch the name of my lady mother."

"Will, that is not the point," Darcy countered with exasperation. "If they *had* to choose, they would have chosen to have her faithful."

Will's gaze lowered, hooding his eyes. "Are you suggesting that the coin has been turned? That as a husband I should now prefer that my wife be well spoken of, even should I find her faithless?"

"More than that, Will. The matter of her faithfulness is irrelevant; only the appearance of chastity is of value. All manner of effort is given to that end.''

Will's eyes darkened with anger, but then they turned to puzzlement. ''The tapestry. Its place of honor suggests that its tenets have been accepted by the court. It depicts the Virgin, the purity of the Holy Mother as the representation of women. If the priests have finally accepted it, then what you are saying cannot be.''

''Now we have reached the core of the madness. The Church *has* embraced the concept of the Virgin Mary and woman is no longer Eve. And thus have our knights of chivalry—nay, wait, let me finish. The courtier embraces chaste love, the epitome of purity, the idealism of women, each a part of the Holy Virgin. For the Church it is taken in its purest essence. But for man, the image is what sustains him.''

''Then they are living a farce—''

''Of course they are. Regardless of pretty words and avowed declarations of love, little has truly changed. Man could not exist in such a state.'' He paused for a moment, his smile fading. ''Except for a few. Those who have found fulfillment in the teachings, a need answered. Will, you doubted Eleanor's chastity and, after observing her with Newbury, called me mad for insisting it to be so. But I fear that you left a girl and thought to return to a woman, only to find an image. One you cannot touch.''

''You can't be serious!'' Will sputtered.

''Nay? Here.'' He picked up the book on the table next to him and tossed it to Will. ''Read this, my friend. I think you will find it enlightening.'' Rising from his chair, he regarded Will with sympathy. ''When you have finished, if you wish to talk about it, I believe that we will find many points of agreement. Sadly so, for I fear that we are men of another time. Sleep well, my friend. And—welcome home.''

Will entered the Great Hall as the court was gathering in the first measured steps of morning. He stifled a yawn as he glanced about the large room, regretting hours of sleep he had lost. He had retired with the book, intending only brief interest in an attempt to sleep, but the words had kept him caught in entranced horror well into the early hours before dawn. Feeling irritable from what he had read, as well as from his lack of sleep, he glanced about the hall defensively. Fops, jackanapes. It was not just the bright colors of their costumes —he could appreciate the rich, bright new dyes brought to England through its expanded trade with the Middle East. Nay, it was the cut of their clothes, the way they were worn. Attitudes blending with the astounding words he had read through the night.

Not quite four years, yet it seemed a lifetime. He had not intended to remain away for so long—but the demands, lands unattended by a master for too many years. Finally there were the letters from his sisters, which began to arrive with regularity. Anxious, chastising letters, suggestions that he was needed in England, that brought him home.

Sweet Lord, she was beautiful. How could he have known how much she would change? He had left a boyish slip of a girl, and in spite of logic he realized now that he had dwelled on the freckled face and childish voice he remembered. Never had he imagined the astounding beauty that had turned to face him the previous night. The grace, the large, resplendent eyes filled with . . . nay, that had changed too. He had expected the laughter he remembered in those eyes. The excited defiance, the challenge. The trust. Instead he had read only anger, bitterness—and hatred.

Glancing briefly up at the tapestry, he smirked, nodding imperceptibly to its presence and challenge, and he turned back to the hall, his eyes moving over those gathered. It was then that he spied Eleanor with her ever-present companions. And one in particular. Striding across the length of the hall, he grasped her firmly by the arm and, with a few muttered words of greetings to the others, led her away.

"Will Marshal, let go of me! What are you doing? How dare you," she hissed, attempting to pull her arm away from his grip.

"Smile, sweetheart," he whispered. "You would not want anyone to think that you were any but the serene, poised lady."

He led her into a darkened alcove and released her abruptly. She spun about, intending to flee, but found him blocking her way. "Let me pass!"

"Oh, I think not." He smiled, lifting a brow to her protest. "There are a few things that need to be said."

"Ohhh, why now?" Her eyes flashed with fury. She opened her mouth to say more but quickly closed it. Words flashed through her mind as Father Latius's voice rang in her ears. Shaken and confused, she had left the court the previous evening and had sought out the priest, desperately needing answers to the turmoil she was feeling. His words had been stern and she had clung to them, needing the comfort of his peremptory instructions. He reminded her of the words of Saint Paul, that man is the image of God, but that woman is the image of man.

"Your place is found in duty to your husband, child," Father Latius had said. "If you are to arise above that of the original temptress, to absolve the sins of Eve, to seek the higher glory of the Holy Mother, you must still the flames of passion, leading your husband from the temptations of sin."

"Passion?" She had not understood his meaning. "But Father," she had stammered, "I do not feel so for my husband."

"The passions of our darker side are many, my child. Anger and bitterness are each disguised parts of our carnal lust. All must be denied. If you are to be saved you must submit to your husband in all things. Bear it, my child, while striving to live as a shining example of chastity and purity. It is your duty to bring him from sin."

Standing now before Will, her face drained of color, Eleanor wavered. Alarmed, for a moment he thought she was going to faint, and he reached out to grab her, but she stepped back, flinching as her gaze fixed on his outstretched hand.

He watched with horrified fascination as her face passed through a gamut of emotions he could not read. She slowly straightened, her expression becoming placid as she opened her eyes to look at him. She merely stood and stared at him. After a long moment he realized that she was waiting for him to speak.

"Eleanor, are you all right?"

"I am fine, milord," she answered listlessly.

"There are many things we must settle between us," he began, irritated by the sudden, drastic change in her. "Now is not the time—except for one matter that cannot wait. Our conversation last evening was overheard by desRevaux. Nothing would suit that one more than for him to believe that we do not want this marriage. Nothing has changed since the day we were betrothed; the reasons for our marriage remain. I will not release you from your vows, and I will not allow you to jeopardize it. If you are displeased, if you would have words with me, you shall tell me of them in private. Never, never again in the presence of others. Do you understand?" He braced himself for the fury he saw was coming.

"Aye, milord. I ask your forgiveness for what can only be considered inexcusable behavior."

He frowned, staring at her with disbelief. He could sense the rage in her, but she stood before him, calmly accepting, acquiescing to his demand without the slightest complaint. Sweet Mother, he groaned inwardly, what *had* happened to her? "Eleanor, do you understand the importance of what I've said?"

"Of course, milord."

He felt totally at a loss for what to do or say next. Taking her arm, more gently this time, he led her back into the hall, wondering for a moment if this could possibly be the female he had left. The change in her body was nothing compared with the change in her manner, and he began to suspect that he had lost something dear in the bargain.

As they returned to the court he stopped suddenly, turning her to face him. He searched her face, trying to understand what had happened moments ago. Something was terribly wrong and he could not leave matters as they were. By God, he would take her somewhere where they could talk.

"By the blood of Saint George, Marshal!" he heard a voice bellowing from across the room. "It is good to have you home!" The King was striding across the hall toward him, and Will released Eleanor's arm with regret, noting that she used the opportunity to step away from him. He turned just as Henry reached his side. "Your Grace," he murmured.

"Come, come, Will. Walk with me! There is something I would show you."

They walked along the gardens of Windsor, among the winter-bare shrubbery and trees, which were just beginning to show the budding promise of spring. The morning was overcast and grey, a light misting fog hanging about them as they pulled their heavy, fur-lined cloaks about them, their breath clouding the air as they spoke, their voices low in shared privacy.

"I noted your scowl last evening when I was holding forth about deBurgh," Henry said quietly. "You think me to be unreasonable toward him, don't you, Will?"

"I believe that you feel justified in your reasons."

"But you think that I am wrong."

Will considered his answer for a moment. "No man is without faults Henry, and deBurgh is no exception. But he is honest and he is for England, as desRoches was not."

"He conspires against me," Henry mumbled, bending to pick up a smooth rock which lay in his path.

"How so?" Will's gaze dropped to the rock, which Henry was working with his hands. "I am aware that you have accused him of treason. Do you believe that he seeks the crown—for himself or for another?"

"Nay, not that—but Will, he stops me at every turn, criticizes my every decision! *I* am being blamed for mishandling the Welsh—how can I have foreseen that they would revolt? Besides," he added sulkily, "it was his fault. He built that new castle of his in Wales and the Welsh are furious about it. He shouldn't have done it; he should have known that it would inflame them."

Will shook his head at the whine in Henry's voice and his continual blindness. He sighed softly. Some things never change, he thought. Henry should have known that the Welsh would rise up against the Throne—they had done so against each English monarch since the time of the Conqueror— always testing for a weakness that might throw the English boot from their necks. As for deBurgh's castle in Wales, Will had thought it an unwise decision at the time, but Henry had given his consent—a matter which he had apparently chosen to forget. He opened his mouth to comment, but Henry's next words pushed other thoughts from his mind.

". . . Besides, he seeks to keep me unwed."

"What?" Will paused to gape at Henry.

" 'Tis true. You know that I had much admired the Scottish

princess when we were in Corse Castle as children. Yet, when I would have married Marian, deBurgh took Margaret to wife, knowing perfectly well that it would make my marriage to the younger sister unsuitable. Proposals were made to the daughter of the Count of Brittany, to the daughter of Leopold of Austria, and a Bohemian princess as well. All have refused me. Me! The King of England, and I'm not a bad-looking sort, after all. Why, Will? Rather than face the prospect of marriage to me, the Austrian wench ran off with the son of Henry of Germany!"

"Perhaps she was in love with him," Will countered. He tried not to smile as he kept his gaze on the path before them as they resumed walking.

"Ah! But you do not understand! It is deBurgh! He has been undermining every proposal!"

"How can you be certain of this?"

"I have it from a reliable source that the Count of Brittany was informed that I was squint-eyed, impotent, and incapable of enjoying the embraces of a woman."

"A reliable source?" Will countered, attempting to keep the obvious doubt of such an absurdity from his voice.

"Aye, the Earl of Newbury. He has close contacts on the Continent and informs me that rumors to the effect were carefully spread in Brittany upon the arrival of my envoy."

"Alan of Newbury?" Will stiffened. "He has not even tested his spurs—"

"It matters not as to the source, Will. It is deBurgh's duplicity which is at issue! He means to keep control of me—even as to whom I shall marry—and I will not have it!"

"Have you spoken to deBurgh about this?"

"Of course, but as I would expect, he denied it. Here, this is what I want to show you!"

Workmen were busily engaged in the construction of a series of low wooden buildings along the far side of the keep, connecting the additions to the larger structure by means of covered passages.

"This?" Will asked doubtfully, seeing no particular significance to the haphazard structures.

Henry laughed heartily as he realized what Will was staring at. "Nay, those are merely spare chambers I am throwing up for the Bishop of Carlisle and his retinue. They are arriving in a few days. Nay, Will, it is not what is, but what I want you to envision. Windsor, not as it is now, but what it will be. A residence worthy of a king, and of England." As Henry enthused, sharing his dreams, Will's gaze moved over what remained of the structure built by Henry I for his Saxon bride. Badly damaged as it was by centuries of sieges and little care, all that remained standing were the Hall and Saint Edward's Chapel. "Three baileys, there," Henry said excitedly, waving his hand in a sweeping gesture to the west of the old Norman keep. "In the lower, a magnificent residence worthy of my queen—whomever that might be," he added, rolling his eyes. "And there, a glorious new chapel in the name of Saint Edward the Confessor, an edifice worthy of his name. And there, a Great Hall, the likes of which has never been seen in England. A hall where foreign dignitaries will be received with pride—and honor."

Will listened to Henry's words, but his attention was distracted. "Henry, what substance are they using for that fireplace?"

The King frowned as he followed Will's gaze to the framed structure being prepared for the Bishop of Carlisle, and then he brightened. "Plaster, Will!" he said cheerfully. "I've discussed it in great detail with the architects and we saw no reason it could not be used. Much easier to use than stone, Will, and faster. Just think, it would take days to construct a hearth of stone, and this will be up before nightfall!"

Will's frown deepened as he watched the workmen, in spite of Henry's assurances, but he was soon distracted by Henry's next words.

"Well, what do you think of her?"

"Who?" Will asked perversely, knowing full well to whom Henry was referring.

"Eleanor, of course!"

As the two men stood watching the workmen, Henry's eyes shifted to his friend when he did not answer. "I warrant she has changed since you last saw her. She's become quite a beauty, has she not? Not quite the skinny little simp you left."

"Aye, she is beautiful," Will answered without looking at

Henry. "And—she has changed, Henry. In ways I could not have realized."

Satisfied, Henry grinned, locking his hands behind his broad back as he rocked back on his heels, his eyes again fixed on the industry going on before them. "She was quite upset with you when you left, Will," he said at last. "She was bitterly hurt that you never said goodbye."

"It was unavoidable. I wrote to her, explaining my reasons."

"Ah, aye, your reasons," Henry repeated, pursing his lips. "Let me attempt to recall your request. Your mother, the Countess Marshal, pressed you to fulfill your father's will. By the way, are your brothers well settled?"

"Aye, Your Grace. It is kind of you to ask."

"Aha!" Henry exclaimed. " 'Your Grace,' is it now? Will, the only time you call me 'Your Grace' when we are alone is when you are ill pleased about something! Have it your way then, my Earl of Pembroke. Your king is displeased with you. We are not fooled by that sorry excuse, nor were we when it was given. Indeed not. Although we took it into our gracious favor to grant you leave due to the fact that, in our wisdom, we understood the dilemma facing our loyal subject. In other words, you sorry ass, I understood what you were going through."

Will burst into laughter, drawing puzzled looks from the workmen, who paused in their tasks. Henry grinned, tossing the rock in the air to catch it. "I did understand, Will, even though you never spoke to me about it. Just as I was well aware that my little sister never made it any easier for you. She worshiped you, you know."

"Only when we were apart." Will smiled. "When she was with me, she fought like a cat."

"Well, she has mellowed considerably," Henry answered, missing the grim look that his words brought. "But you are here now, Will, and as your king—and brother—I would know what you plan to do about our little princess. I have kept Peter desRevaux and his kin at bay for as long as I can. Are you aware that they began to pressure me for an annulment even as your ship left port for Normandy? If the truth be

known—and it never will from these royal lips—no one was
fooled by your mission. Except, perhaps, Eleanor. But"—his
voice softened with emotion—"your reasons were deeply felt,
Will. Your tender concern for her was well noted. She was
young, so young. I admit that I could not withstand the
pressure from desRoches when he set sights on her for his son.
That is why I pressed her on you. I—I knew that you would
never—harm her. And, indeed, it was the right decision. I
married her to the right man," he ended with a warm, if
sheepish, grin.

"Please—do not thank me, Henry," Will responded. He
did not add that in spite of Henry's and the court's suspicions,
nothing could be proved. An annulment would have had to
come from Rome, and under the circumstances, without
Will's consent, it would not have been granted. "But for the
past four years I have been with you and Eleanor almost continually since you were but children. She—she is—"

"Like a sister?" Henry finished for him. "Do you think
that I do not know that? Will, there are far worse beginnings
for a marriage. My friend, since that day when the Good
Knight, your father and mine—for he was so to me, far more
than ever my own—placed me in your care, you have been
brother, confidant, family, and friend to me. Eleanor and
Richard are the dearest things in my life. Richard—well,
Richard can look out for himself." He paused with a chuckle.
"But Eleanor. I have never regretted my decision to give her to
you. Nor does it occur to me that you will ever cause me to do
so."

"Then you will not mind that I am going to take her to
Wales with me," Will said with a grin.

Henry looked stunned for a moment. "Wales?"

"I was wondering how to tell you. I must see to Striguil.
Norfolk has done well in my absence, but he has his own lands
to see to. You spoke of the trouble with the Welsh. It is my domain they most threaten, Henry. Prince Llewelyn has been
raiding Striguil's borders. I mean to send him back to
Snowdonia. A fact which, I might add, will benefit both you
and me."

"But you just returned!" Henry argued, a pout edging his
voice.

Will drew in his breath, intent upon making Henry see reason. "You asked me about my intent for Eleanor. There is no doubt that I can no longer avoid what must be. I feel that it can best be done if we have a time alone—away from the court and its influences."

Henry drew a deep breath. "I—do not like having to accept—what I do not want. And I do not want this. But I know that you are right." He took another breath. "Go then, with my blessing. *After* you have reaffirmed your vows," he added, glancing at Will with an amused flaring of his eyes.

"Of course, Your Grace," Will answered with mock solemnity. "I would never have considered anything else."

Leaning a shoulder against a wall deepened by shadows, Will watched the activity in the long hall of the Norman keep of Windsor. He had entered the hall quietly, seeking this private moment to sort out his thoughts. The past week had been a revelation, an uncomfortable one, and still he could not reconcile reason with discovery.

A mask of virtue. The thought turned in his brain yet again, the sum of what he had discovered. Stifling a sudden impulse to yawn, he shifted, reflecting on the hours he had spent the previous night with Darcy, talking into the early hours of the morning. On one matter they were in total agreement: the Gascon Marcabru, author of the book Darcy had lent him, was totally mad. His madness had caught part of a world, bringing it to the fire of his insanity. But Will was convinced that it had begun with Guilhem, the seventh Count of Poitiers, ninth Duke of Aquitaine. They had argued heatedly about the matter, trying to find a reason for what had happened to the social changes of the time. Will had never given much thought to such matters before; his only interest in history had been political. But with what he had found upon his return it seemed to be of vital importance, if for no other reason than what was happening, or was not happening, in the bedchambers about Windsor would eventually, he strongly suspected, affect what would happen in the King's Council.

The duke of Aquitaine, ironically a great-grandfather of Eleanor's, had led a life of free sensuality, only to find his activities condemned and thus curtailed by the clerics of the time, particularly one Robert d'Arbrissel. Finding that the ladies of his acquaintance had begun to believe that their activities would lead them to an eternity spent in the fires of hell, Guilhem devoted himself to writings developing a new thought. He wrote that love was divine, yet a mystery. That when a lady offered herself to her lover she was nothing short of a goddess in human form. Darcy should know, Will thought with amusement. He had made his wealth singing Guilhem's lyrics—tempered with his own. Innocent enough, however, Will reasoned, until the Gascon had taken the thought a step further with his own fiery words.

"I am certain that there is a reason that you are hiding here in the corner."

Will turned his head to find Darcy standing near. "I cannot yet face that mob. I see no reason why I should join them until the guest of honor has gifted us with his presence, and, as yet, there is no sign of the Bishop Carlisle. But I am glad that you are here. I have been giving a lot of thought to our discussion."

"And, of course, you know now that I am correct—in all things."

Will snorted at the comment but he fought a grin over the goliard's audacity. "I am willing to agree that Marcabru stole from Guilhem's ideas, but I still feel that it was the duke's words that began the problem."

"The duke's words were innocent, Will." Darcy scoffed. "Throughout time lyrics and words of worship have been given to a woman's beauty. It was Marcabru who made them into something dangerous. Guilhem declared that beauty and position set woman upon a pedestal, there to be admired and worshiped—and *loved*," he emphasized, "while our Gascon misogynist insisted that, in addition to those first two attributes, 'twas her chastity and virtue that set her apart."

"Marcabru would advocate the end of the human race." Will snorted, turning his head to the sound of laughter across the crowded room.

"My conclusion exactly. Unfortunately he is avidly read and listened to." Darcy saw the disgust on Will's face as his attention was drawn to the bard singing at the far side of the hall. "Minstrels are entertainers, Will. They sing what their audience wants to hear."

"I still cannot accept that men of good reason have taken such tripe to be truth. And in such a short time."

"It has been happening slowly. But you, like most of us, did not see it coming. We live life, viewing it from our own standards and morals, and are stunned, even to fear, when we discover that it has changed. Youth, of course, takes readily to new ideas and we blame them for those changes we cannot comprehend."

Following the goliard's pointed gaze, Will returned and his brows drew into a frown. Eleanor had entered on the arm of Alan of Newbury and in the company of her newfound friends. "If you are correct, Darcy, I need not hurry to her side. She is safe enough."

"Aye, milord, her virture is well kept," Darcy mumbled, watching the group with his own disapproval. "Unless, of course, I am wrong about Newbury."

Will glanced sharply at the goliard, and then his gaze returned speculatively to Eleanor, his interest shifting between admiration and anger. She was breathtaking, resplendent in a blaiunt of gold brocade which clung to her beautiful body, girdled about her narrow waist with rubies and amethysts. The wimple formed soft folds about her chin, flowering her face beneath a soft gold coif of sarcenet, crowned with a diadem of rubies, amethysts, and pearls. He shook his head slowly, watching her. Virtue, he mused, chastity. The European harem. Eleanor, he thought, what will you mean to me, to yourself? You look up at him, your face aglow with pleasure. He represents love to you, yet you do not have the slightest idea of what that means. If he were to touch you, and there is no doubt in my mind as to his intentions, what would you do? Perhaps it would have been best had I not returned quite yet, giving you time to face him as he really is.

His thoughts brought Darcy's poignant question to mind and he forced himself to consider it. Which *would* I prefer? he thought. A wife of ill virtue who is well thought about, or one chaste who is not? Yet the answer remained elusive, its consideration serving only to stir him to anger. God's breath! I will have her faithful *and* well thought about!

The horn sounded, announcing the arrival of the King, but Will barely noticed Henry's entrance as his eyes remained fixed on Eleanor. Before he realized what he was doing, he was crossing the room. Attention was focused on the group surrounding Henry as Will reached her side. Taking her arm, he ignored her startled gasp as he faced her companions. "You will forgive us," he offered smoothly, but the edge to his voice caused the others to stare with surprise, though none would have attempted to confront the powerful Earl of Pembroke.

"What are you doing—what have I done now?" Eleanor cried out as he led her from the group.

"Nothing whatsoever, my sweet. I am merely claiming my wife to join me for midmeal," he countered grimly. "I suggest that you keep your voice down if you do not wish to draw everyone's attention."

"Why would you want me to share your dinner?" she hissed. "You have barely gifted me with so much as a polite word since your return! Could it be that you have at last managed to forgive me after humiliating me beyond measure!"

"Enough, Eleanor. We will speak of this later, if you must; for now we must repair to the dais. The event requires that we sit with Henry, and everyone's eyes will be upon us. Now calm yourself." He heard her breath draw in sharply and he had to fight a smile. That's the Eleanor I know, he thought. Fight me, sweet, tell me to go to the devil.

As they followed the King's example and took their chairs, Will turned to Eleanor, expecting to fix on the bright blue of her Plantagenet rage, only to find her eyes downcast. With sinking dismay he noted tears had formed at the corners of her eyes. "Eleanor, stop it," he murmured. "Would you have everyone see you cry?"

"I have displeased you." She sniffed.

"Oh, Eleanor, not now. You—you have not displeased me. Sit up. Oh, good God, Henry's looking over here. . . . Your Grace"—his voice lightened—"'twould seem that our guest of honor has absented himself."

"Indeed, I have excused our esteemed bishop from our

company for the moment. Weary from his travels, he begged a time of rest, but he will be joining us before evening's end." Henry noted Eleanor at Will's side with a smile of approval, and he winked at Will before his attention was drawn to another point at the table.

Eleanor watched Will as he served their meal from the platters held by his squires, who had appeared behind their chairs to serve their lord and lady. What did he expect from her? She caught her breath raggedly, trying to control the anger she felt at being so rudely claimed from her friends. She could not look in their direction, inwardly cringing as she speculated upon what certainly must be their topic of conversation.

How could she never have seen it before? Will Marshal was a crude, insufferable bore. He was so—so—physical. A shudder took her and she bit the inside of her lower lip, recalling the moment before he had reappeared in her life. The sweet words Alan had spoken, the love he had pledged, and then . . . the fact of Will's sudden, unexpected presence, his anger. And now this. To pull her so ungraciously away from her friends. She had tried to forgive him before, attributing his insufferable behavior to his lack of understanding about her relationship with Alan. But this was too much! Not once had he sought to apologize for all the years past, the abandonment. In fact, he had ignored her. It wasn't fair! How had she ever caught herself in such a marriage?

"Eleanor?"

She looked up to find him watching her.

"Lampreys?"

"What about lampreys?"

"Do you wish to have some?" he asked.

"Oh. Nay, I hate lampreys!"

"So I remembered. But then I thought perhaps you had changed more than I realized," he countered, shaking his head at the manservant who moved down the long table.

She answered with forced sweetness. "It seems probable, milord, that due to the passing of these years, you would know little about me."

Will's brow arched as he regarded Eleanor's retort, and his eyes gleamed hopefully. "I remember everything, Eleanor. Including what a little snip you were."

Her breath drew in sharply, and she glared at him, bereft of speech. Her mouth opened and closed like a gasping fish as she struggled between what she wanted to say and her reason, which cautioned her to retain her poise. The latter won out, sorely. "You are most cruel, milord," she responded tightly. " 'Tis unkind to remind me of the past, a time when I was untutored. But I shall forgive you, for the sake of the moment."

He said nothing, but angered disappointment crossed his eyes as he accepted her answer. "Then let us speak of something else." He served her a portion of currant tart, which she accepted graciously, wondering if he remembered that it was her favorite dish. "I must leave soon for Wales, and upon reflection 'twould seem a good time for a bridal journey."

It took her a moment before his words registered fully. "Bridal?" The word struck her like a broadside.

"Aye. Are you not pleased, my sweet? How long we have both waited. It is time, Eleanor, for you and me." He smiled at her wickedly, only mildly regretting the horror that had entered her eyes.

At that moment, the hall reverberated with a rolling tremble and a deafening roar. The company fell to stunned silence, then the sound of women's cries rose, and the room was quickly reduced to the scraping of chairs and the confusion of voices.

"Silence!" Henry's voice bellowed above the bedlam. Those in the hall obeyed as the King's steward was seen rushing toward the dais in apparent agitation. "Well, Sir Tomas, what is it?" Henry boomed.

The man drew up before the King and attempted to respond with his customary unshakable demeanor. "There has been an unfortunate accident, Your Grace."

"We assume that! What is it?" Henry roared impatiently.

"The Bishop of Carlisle, Your Grace. That is, it seems that there was an explosion. The roof to his residence . . . it blew clean off."

"Good God! And the Bishop?"

"Shaken, sire."

"I should think so! See to him, Tomas—and inform him that he need not attend us. Tomas," Henry added, leaning forward to the steward, who had halted as he began to turn away, "do you know what caused it?"

"I believe that it was the fireplace, Your Grace. By all accounts it just seemed to . . . disappear."

Will rose quickly from his chair and went to Henry's side. "Your Grace, perhaps I should see to the bishop," he offered as he struggled painfully to retain a serious composure.

"What? Oh, aye, Will, perhaps you should," Henry answered absently, his brows furrowed, and he mumbled thoughtfully, "More lime, I should think; too much water, perhaps."

Will had to bite his lip furiously to keep from laughing, but as he turned to leave the hall he spied Darcy, their eyes catching at the inopportune moment. The goliard sat at the far end of a trestle table, his face was purple with repressed laughter and his dark eyes watering. Turning quickly, Will coughed as he forceably worked to control the shout of laughter which threatened to explode like the plaster of Henry's fireplace.

10

ELEANOR watched the activity in her chamber without really seeing. She felt detached, with only occasional stabbing pains of reality to remind her of what was happening. She watched the packing, listlessly answering questions from her ladies, unaware of the tension which had begun to build within her until suddenly she thought she would burst. Without a word she leapt up and rushed from the room. She ran down the long halls of Windsor, oblivious to the odd stares of those she passed until she had reached Saint Edward's Chapel. After pausing for a moment to catch her breath, she entered the cool, dark chamber and slowly approached the altar. She genuflected, then moved to the spot before the statue of the Virgin and bent her head in prayer. But prayers would not come. She moved her lips silently, but it was as if a wall had been set in her mind against her thoughts. She could not even cry.

Gradually she became aware of another's presence. She opened her eyes and gasped softly as she found the spare form of a cleric kneeling next to her, his withered hands grasping the prayer railing as his head bent to them, his lips moving in prayer. "Your Eminence," she breathed, not needing the crimson cloak or mitre to identify her silent companion.

Stephen Langton completed his prayer and looked up at her. His blue eyes defied his age, clear and penetrating, holding a kindness that brought a release of unshed tears from her throat to her eyes. "My child, I fear that these bony knees of mine can withstand only so much kneeling. My curse, I fear, as it forbids me the hours I would spend in supplication to Our Lord. Would you sit with me?"

She obeyed, sitting next to him in the shadows which fell across the rows of pews, her hands clasped tightly in her lap, worrying her fingers as she sought desperately for what she could say to him. "I am leaving today," she blurted.

"I know," he answered calmly, ignoring her discomfort. "It is that which has brought me from Winchester, as Will has asked me to reconfirm your vows. I am pleased that you seek this time with Our Lord before you are required to join your husband." His expression remained passive, but there was a softness in his eyes which played on the deep feeling of guilt she felt. Looking quickly away, she drew in her breath, willing herself not to cry. "Father . . . I cannot pray," she whispered miserably.

"The Lord knows of our needs before we ask," he reminded her gently. "Perhaps, in your inner self, you are unaware of those needs. You cannot ask for what is not right for you."

"Why does Will want to take me away?" she blurted, gulping back her tears. "I want to be a dutiful wife—I know that I must. But my life is here, my friends! There is no reason for him to do this!"

An uncomfortable thought tempted Langton for an instant. He was so very weary, suddenly overwhelmed by the confusion of humanity. The easy way was to tell her simply that indeed her place was with her husband, to remind her of her duty as so many in his place would have done. The temptation brought a momentary flaring of rage he had not felt in many years. Smiling to himself, he mused, you've lived too long, Langton, you've outlived all those mortals you ever felt really close to—except one: Will Marshal. Glancing at the girl, he smiled. "You came to pray to the Holy Mother," he said softly. "Look upon her now. What do you see?"

She followed his gaze, then looked back at him with confusion. "I—I see the Mother of Christ, the Virgin," she stammered, confused.

"What else?"

She frowned, trying to understand what he wanted from her. "The Blessed Virgin of virtue—innocence. All that I must strive to be."

"You pray to her to maintain the life you have set for yourself, what you feel to be your path, one of virtue, innocence, and purity of action and thought, yet you receive no comfort. Eleanor, when you realize why, you will have the answer to what you seek. And only when you realize it for yourself, will you be able to accept the truth and be granted the peace and comfort you wish for." He waited, but when she did not respond he patted her hand. "Come now, there is someone waiting for you without." He rose and crossed to the altar, genuflecting before he began to walk down the aisle, leaving her to follow behind.

As they stepped from the chapel, Langton nodded to someone beyond him then he turned to smile at Eleanor. When she looked over his shoulder as he turned away to leave, her eyes widened with surprise. "Isabella!"

Smiling, Langton turned and went back into the chapel. As he came into the shadows, he looked up at the candle-illuminated figure of the Virgin and his face softened. Slowly his smile began to fade. "The insanity of man," he mumbled, shaking his head. "Dear Lord, will we ever take the best that you offer and twist it to our own reasonings." Turning, he continued on his way to the small chamber where he sought the escape of his own prayers.

The two women walked along the path edging the Thames within the sight of Windsor. Their companionship was silent after the warmth of their greeting; the past years had filled them with questions, yet neither seemed anxious to press for answers. Finally, it was Isabella who spoke. "It has been a long time since we have seen one another, Eleanor. I have missed you."

"And I, you, Isabella," Eleanor answered. Until this moment she had not realized just how much.

"I have been at court for two days. Why have you chosen to remain in your chambers? Did you not know that I was here?"

"Aye—I knew," Eleanor said softly.

"Did you not want to see me?"

Eleanor shook her head, stumbling for an answer. "I—I did not want to see anyone."

There was a protracted silence, the only sound coming from a sassy mocker perched high in the trees above them as they walked beneath the spreading sycamores lining the graveled path. "Eleanor, do you remember the first time you came to me? You confided your fears to me then; you told me that you feared you would never become the woman you wished to be. Can you still doubt?"

"It does seem a long time ago," Eleanor mused softly as her mouth spread into a gentle smile, remembering. "How you put up with me, I'll never know. Sweet Mother, I was such a child. Such inane things I would fret about!"

"And now?" Isabella peered at her for a moment before she shifted her gaze back to the walk ahead of her. "What fears do you harbor now? Can you still share them with a friend?"

A friend? Eleanor glanced at Isabella and bit her lip. She loved Isabella, a part of her always would, but the question had stirred a feeling of anger. Everyone seemed to be challenging her to accept what she did not want. How could they claim to know what was best for her when it was against everything she wanted for herself? And there was another reason for her anger. "Why have you never come to court?" she asked.

The Countess answered without hesitation. "My husband's needs and those of my lands keep me quite occupied, Eleanor. There is little time for dalliance at court."

"But you should be here with your husband. A castellan could see to your lands."

"That is not our way, Eleanor. The lands are in our trust; many depend upon us. If a castellan were to fail, the fault would lie with Gilbert and me, not with those in our employ. The lives of our people lie at our door; no others can be held accountable."

"But I needed you too!" Eleanor argued.

"I was there, always, if you needed me."

"But I wanted you here!"

"Why, Eleanor?" Isabella stopped and turned to face the young princess. "Why did it have to be here?"

Eleanor's brow furrowed with her answer. "Because this is where I belong!"

"Do you?" Isabella asked softly.

"My brother—" Eleanor said lamely.

"Your brother is King," Isabella returned. "You cannot be part of that. Today you will reaffirm your vows to your husband. Once you dreamed of this moment. Have your dreams changed so much?"

"He is not the same man!"

"Oh? How is he not?"

"He—he does not want the same things; he does not see things as I do!"

"Do you know what you want?"

"Of course! I . . ."

Isabella laid a hand on Eleanor's arm and her eyes softened as she regarded the young woman's agitation. "Nay, do not tell me, Eleanor. Tell him. Find the courage, find the words, and tell him."

The chamber where Henry Plantagenet, King of England, performed his daily devotions was of soft green, a color favored by the youthful monarch. The tapestry hangings and rugs were of soft, muted colors, and precious items of antiquity were placed about with studied attention. The candles were lighted and braziers had been carried in and set about to warm the small room. There, before God and company, Eleanor Plantagenet knelt before Stephen Langton, Archbishop of Canterbury, and reaffirmed her marriage vows to William fitzWilliam Marshal, Earl of Pembroke, Marshal of England.

Eleanor repeated her vows absently, neither hearing the words of the Archbishop or those of her response. She was aware only of the man who knelt beside her, the way he looked in his deep blue velvet surcoat, his masculine presence as he had entered the room moments before. His manner had been firm but not without kindness as he had turned to her to take her hand in his to lead her before the waiting Archbishop. And then it had become a blur as her silent inner voice cried out against the finality of what was happening, the sealing of her life. Only weeks before her life had seemed to move along a path of her own making. And now it would never be hers again.

She felt a gentle but firm pressure at her arm, and she was lifted to her feet and turned to look at him. She forced her eyes up to his, dreading the encounter, fearing that he would read the anger, the frustration, the fear in her own. But her eyes widened in surprise. He drew her into them, deep blue depths of laughter, warmth. A memory, a moment forgotten, rushed back to her senses—laughing eyes challenging her—and for an instant, as memories floated, she was unable to catch herself from the hint of a smile.

As he turned her back to the gathered company she felt lightheaded, staring at a sea of faces. She felt Will's hand on her arm, and she was walking toward them as slowly they took form. Her friends, nobles of the court, and Henry. She was drawn up into his welcoming bear hug, and she clung to him, never wanting to let go. "I have a surprise for you, mouse." He smiled broadly, well pleased with himself as he turned her around. "Look who is here."

"Richard!" Eleanor cried, throwing herself into the arms of her brother. She could not believe it—Richard, with his blond Plantagenet handsomeness, tall, broad-shouldered, and tanned. "I thought you were in Germany!" she gasped between spurts of laughter.

"Ah, would I miss such an occasion, little sister?" He grinned. His warm blue eyes bore down into hers, holding all of the remembered mischief of their youth. She momentarily forgot her problems as treasured memories came rushing back. "You have forgiven Will for taking your miners for Bedford Castle?" She giggled as she whispered conspiratorially, in a voice that carried to all.

"I would have preferred to have been consulted beforehand." He grinned, glancing at Will, who feigned a look of innocence. "However, they were well used. A neat trick, Will. I doubt that others could have done the job; the battering of those walls would have withstood a normal sapper's talents, from what I am told. However, now that you have returned, you may expect a hearty fee for their services."

"Send it to your brother!" Will chuckled. " 'Twas for him the work was done!"

The company burst into laughter at Henry's sputtering. " 'Twas all in the family, Richard! Come, come now, enough! There is a fine banquet prepared in the solar. Let us be to it!"

The meal passed all too quickly for Eleanor. The laughter and gaiety of the company seemed in total contrast with what was tossing about inside of her. After her initial joy over Richard's presence, her happiness dissipated to a renewed depth of depression. Only Will seemed as quiet as she, but the knowledge merely served to make her more irritable. Attributing his quiet demeanor to his usual resoluteness, she tried to ignore him. Looking about for more interesting conversation, she fixed upon Richard, but he was staring oddly, with great cow eyes, at Isabella and was hanging on her every word. Eleanor's gaze strayed until it came to rest upon Alan, who sat at the lower trestle table. At that moment he looked up and their eyes caught. The look he sent her was filled with love and sorrow, so intense that she flushed and dropped her gaze, unable to look into such intent sadness. Drawing in her breath, she could not stop the sob that caught in her throat.

She tensed in horror, fearing that Will had noticed, but he merely reached across her and refilled her goblet. "Drink this," he said quietly. Numbly obeying, she took the goblet in both her hands and raised it to her lips as she willed her fingers not to tremble so. "In a few moments we will be leaving," he murmured. "I prefer to do so quietly. Henry knows of my wishes; you need not excuse yourself from the table. Wait for me in the hallway. I shall join you presently."

She wanted to argue, to delay their departure by any means, but she realized with a dreaded certainty that there was nothing she could do but bring more misery upon herself. She rose unsteadily, feeling Will's supporting hand at her arm, and she dipped a shallow curtsy in the direction of the king, who winked at her over his supper companion's shoulder. She turned away to leave the hall, willing herself all the while not to look again in Alan's direction, knowing that if she did so she would lose what little courage she had.

She found Landon waiting beyond the solar doors, her

cloak over his arm. She ignored the tentative smile from the squire, turning her back to stare sightlessly down the long hallway. It was only moments before Will joined her. He took her cloak from his waiting squire and laid it about her shoulders, then, with his hand at her arm, led her silently to the courtyard and their waiting horses and retainers. He lifted her into the saddle of her mare, and as he fixed her foot in the stirrup she stole a glance at him, but his expression was unreadable. As they rode from Windsor, taking the road northeast toward Wallingford, she fixed her eyes on the road ahead of her, knowing that if she were to look back she would be lost.

11

DREAMS were lost, replaced by reality born of disillusionment, acceptance of that which could not be changed. Eleanor thought of little else, even as a voice within her struggled against the feelings of self-pity and sorrow that threatened to overwhelm her. She hated such weakness in herself, yet she could not reconcile the loss of her dreams. She would not allow herself to think about Alan. He was gone, belonging to another time, she told herself. Yet she would never forget the joy, the promise of sweet, innocent love he had given her. And now . . .

She glanced at the man who rode beside her, silent but courteous as to her well-being, as he had been for the week they had been traveling. The vows had been reaffirmed, he was her husband, yet amazingly he had not pressed himself on her. The first night out she had expected him to come to her; the realization when they stopped for the night caused her to nervously pace the small chamber of the inn as she waited for him. But only a brief written missive had come from him, bidding her a good rest. She had lain sleeplessly in the large bed and for the first time allowed herself to think rationally. She had been so immersed in self-pity and grief that it was not until then that she faced the amazing fact that they had been allowed to leave Windsor without fanfare—and without the usual required bedding to consummate their vows.

Looking now about her, she fixed on the size of their company: fifty knights and over one hundred yeomen and men-at-arms who had joined up with them soon after they left Windsor. There was little doubt as to the display Will presented, his power as Marshal of England, or that he would brook no interference by anyone in his decision to bed his bride when and where he willed. His decision was obvious to her; what she could not begin to fathom was, why?

Will could not reconcile the young woman who rode at his side with the child he once knew. Had his visions, in the years of his absence, been so far afield of the reality? The change in her, beyond the physical, was so vast that he was left feeling that there was nothing familiar about her. Yet she was Eleanor. He was her husband. Moreover he knew that he must be husband to her. Time, he thought, glancing at the long column of men about them. For now I can give us a little more time.

She fancies herself in love with that twit Newbury, he mused. The imbecile actually seemed satisfied with staring at her with great cow eyes, or writing senseless love lyrics to her. All in the name of their distorted version of the Chivalric Code. Inane document. Henry had shown it to him—who else would allow such an interpretation of the code but Henry, the romantic fool. What was that one line? Something about defense of fair and chaste damsels. But with the impulse to laugh came a sobering thought, and Will remembered Darcy's warning. She believed in it. Moreover, she lived by it. The priests had fed her with it, and her own needs had deepened the distortion. Jesu, he had only been gone four years, yet it seemed a lifetime for the changes that had occurred in his absence.

Compelled by his thoughts, Will's gaze shifted to Eleanor as she rode by his side, and he was struck uncomfortably by her beauty. It fused with the dissociated feelings he had for her, tumbling his emotions into confusion. He had struggled to send the note to her, the first night of their journey, forcing himself to send it even as he chided himself for being a fool.

He recognized that the desire he had begun to feel for her was physical, only that, and in contest with feelings of protectiveness. A child-woman, she taunted his conscience. And it was his conscience that plagued him. The deep hurt, the hatred he read in her. The memory of Henry's words as they had walked together in the garden following his return. He knew now how much he had hurt her by leaving, and the realization cut him deeply. He also knew that, given another chance, he would have made the same decision. What other choice could he have made that would not have hurt her far more?

They passed through the western reaches of England, and to Wales, dropping into the richness of the Wye Valley and the lands of Striguil, the powerful seat of the Marshals. At last the massive round towers built by his father and the vast, elongated battlements of Chepstow came into view, stretching its unconquered parapets along the lazily reaching river Wye.

Will noted approvingly Eleanor's obvious appreciation of Chepstow as they approached the gate tower. Will's square banner, declaring the Marshal coat of arms, was noted as shouts from the tower guards reverberated along the walls. The groaning of heavy chains could be heard as the massive iron portcullis was drawn up, allowing the party entry as they clattered beneath the gate tower. They passed through the outer and inner baileys amid shouts and a scurry of activity as farriers, household knights, and menservants rushed from their duties to see to the arrival of their lord and his party.

Oblivious to the confusion about him, Will dismounted and lifted Eleanor from her saddle. With a supportive hand at her back, he ushered her up the wide steps to the main floor of the keep. The huge oak doors, banded with heavy iron, were swung open by the porters, and Eleanor found herself in a Great Hall of immense proportions with a high vaulted ceiling cross-beamed with rafters from which hung brightly colored banners of over seventy household knights. Large, rich tapestries covered the walls. Passage screens were covered with silk, embroidered in exotic colors and designs from the Middle East. The floorstones were scraped, void of rushes, and scattered about were sumptuous rugs of heavy damask in deep, flourishing colors. The high, arching windows were of leaded glass, opaque but unshuttered, allowing bright streams of light which crossed the hall, lending a glow of warmth, which was emphasized by the dancing movement of the dust motes that moved freely in their path.

At the far end of the hall a raised dais held a long, heavy table of dark wood and a row of massive, high-backed chairs before an enormous hearth. Breathlessly, Eleanor consumed it all in a sweeping glance. Then her eyes moved to the staircase on the wall to the far right of the dais. A beautiful woman of middle age, her waist slightly thickened, her eyes and the corners of her mouth touched with the lines of her maturity, was descending the stairs, her mouth drawn into a pleased smile as she noted the arrivals. Crossing the span between them, Eleanor saw that her eyes, a fascinating, changeable grey, were sparkling with pleasure.

"You sent no word of your arrival, Will!" The woman chided. She turned to Eleanor and her smile softened. "No one need tell me, least of all my thoughtless son: you are Eleanor. Good Lord, child, I have not seen you since you were but nine years! Welcome to Chepstow, daughter." Turning back to Will, she frowned, but the light in her eyes defied her irritation. "You should have warned me that you were bringing your bride to Striguil. I would have had time to prepare a proper welcome."

"The Lady of Striguil is always prepared, Mother." Will grinned, bending to kiss her cheek. "Had I sent word, you would have only fretted our arrival."

"Rude!" She snorted as she turned her attention again to Eleanor. "As you surmise, Eleanor, in the absence of my son's manners, I am Lady Isabel. But not Lady of Striguil. That honor is now due you, as wife to my son. Welcome, my Lady of Striguil and Pembroke."

Isabel's words struck Eleanor with a different note, and she wavered momentarily as she absorbed them. It had not occurred to her before that she was now Countess of Pembroke, Lady of Striguil. Isabel's graciousness in relinquishing the titles with such warmth was noted. Eleanor knew it was often not the case. But what struck her hard, for the first time, was that she was no longer first a princess of England. So much . . . gone, she thought.

"You shall have your grandparents' chambers," Isabel was saying as she flicked her fingers at the waiting steward.

"Nay, Mother," Will said quietly. "Eleanor shall have them. I shall repair to my chamber. She . . . will rest more gently there."

Isabel's eyes flashed knowingly as she glanced at her son, then his bride, but her expression did not change as she gave orders to the steward. "Your journey has been long," she said at last, turning again to Eleanor. "Perhaps you would wish to retire to your chambers before supper."

Eleanor was touched and gratified by Isabel's sensitivity. She wanted nothing more at this moment than to be alone. "Aye, lady, it would please me greatly. I am fatigued." Without looking again at Will, Eleanor followed the steward toward the stairs, grateful to be away from the strain of his company and the wise, knowing look in his mother's eyes.

But as Eleanor disappeared up the stairs, Isabel spun back on her son, and there was no dismissing the accusation in her expression. "Will—"

"Not now, Mother. Here, there is someone I would have you meet."

Darcy had entered the hall, and he knew instantly that something was amiss as the pair turned to him. He did not miss the divergent looks in their eyes, Isabel's anger, or Will's look of appeal as they settled on him. "My Lady Marshal . . . ," he offered, bending to her hand.

"Mother, this is Darcy. He is, I fear, a goliard."

"A goliard, is it?" Isabel scowled at the bard but her eyes had begun to dance. "Well, if we must put up with one of your measure, I imagine we must, seeing as my son apparently holds you in regard. I do recall that my husband favored those of your kind for some elusive reason. Something about honesty and cutting truth regarding matters of the realm, as I remember. Are you a true goliard, Darcy?"

"Aye, lady, I fear that it is so," Darcy responded, his eyes leaping with amusement as they met Isabel's.

"Good," she said. "Now, then, food. You must be hungry —all goliards arrive hungry." She snapped at the waiting servants, ordering a meal to be brought. "As for sleeping arrangements, you shall have the wall chamber, there." She gestured to the far wall to her left as she began to turn away.

"Ah, milady, I am touched by your kindness."

The hours since supper had passed quickly, spent in the welcome, treasured company of her son and of Darcy, who had proved as astute and amusing as the goliards she remembered from her past. Moments of tender yet painful nostalgia had touched her, memories recalled of similar hours spent when William's voice had carried the conversation, the arguments, the bantering. But as the windows of the Great Hall had darkened and the fire crackled and hissed behind her, Isabel's thoughts kept drifting between the words of the conversation and, with unease, in the direction of the stairs. She shook her head slightly as if to clear it of her disturbing suspicions, and her brow furrowed as she glanced at her son. She tried again to fix her attention on the conversation. I must be getting old, she mused; my mind seems intent to drift.

"But life is not like that!" Darcy was protesting. "You must accept what is; how else can you change it?"

Ah, she thought, I remember now. "What is, Darcy, is seen by each to his own accounting."

"You Marshals," he snorted. "You live in a world of your own making!"

"Perhaps." She smiled. "Indeed, perhaps we do. We have that power, to mold much of our world as we wish it. Power, Darcy. Look around you. What you see is only a smattering of what we hold. Lands in England, Normandy, Wales, and Ireland."

"Land and power," Will interjected. "And responsibility which increases with power and position. Responsibility and dedication to those who depend upon us, those who cannot speak for themselves."

"Aye." She sighed. "Your father taught you that. You did not learn it from me. The land is what has been important to me, its trust and care. Perhaps only my husband truly saw the world as it is, part and whole of his humble beginnings, I imagine. Perhaps it was that which led him to assist Langton in writing the Great Charter. And, when Pope Innocent abolished it, to invoke it once again when he became Regent."

"I wonder what Father would have thought of our new 'code,' " Will mused out loud.

Isabel frowned, then her expression lightened with understanding. "Ah, I have heard of it. Nonsense, total nonsense."

"Of course it is," Darcy offered. "But it is real, nevertheless, and part of our lives, for good or ill."

"For ill." Will grimaced.

Darcy interjected a comment about Marcabru, even as Will countered with his feelings of Guilhem's ill-given contribution, when suddenly Isabel began to laugh. Silenced, the men turned to stare at her with amazement. Seeing their puzzlement, she smiled. "Every generation believes their ideas to be new. Yet each idea is simply borrowed from one before and added upon. When my mother was a young woman, newly wed, she spent a time in Normandy, there as lady-in-waiting to Queen Eleanor of Aquitaine. Lud, it was her concept! Ideas born of a queen bored with life. The Courts of Love, she called them. Oh, Sweet Mother, how she would agrieve if she had known where it would lead! 'Twas an amusement! A study, considering the aspects of love. And now others have taken what was given lightly, adding to it, presenting it as truth, a way of life!"

"Milady, I think you are right!" Darcy enthused, his eyes agleam with speculation.

"Perhaps," Will mumbled, his own countenance set in a sullen glower. "But it changes nothing. Facts are facts, and the concept of the Virgin was not introduced in the Courts of Love."

"Ah, yes, the Virgin." Isabel shook her head. "We women have at last been released from the bondage of Eve's sin. No longer are we condemned souls to be saved and brought to the Kingdom of Heaven by the good grace of our husbands, sons, fathers, or brothers. Now it is the perfection of womanhood that man, most particularly the knight-errant, must protect." She smiled at the dumbfounded expressions on the men's faces. "Oh, I am aware of it. In fact, I have watched it beginning over many, many years. Will, your father and I discussed the matter upon occasion.

"Personally I believe that the concept was brought home

from the Crusades. Guilhem and Marcabru only embellished upon what had already begun. They have long believed in the perfection of womanhood in the East, and men came home from the Crusades dazzled by the idea. A much more tantalizing picture than Eve, after all, or even a Martha, the drudge of her husband's existence, wouldn't you say?" She paused, her eyes dancing as she smiled wickedly. "However, men, as usual, overlooked the reality of their women. In his absence she had learned new skills, authority she was not about to relinquish merely because he had a new role for her to play. How to resolve the dilemma? Create an image, a model of perfection to dream about. We now find ourselves living with that fantasy. We sing to her, write poetic verse, safely to fix upon the ideal, whereupon we can ignore the reality."

The men stared at her, their mouths agape. "Good God, Mother," Will drawled, his eyes rolling comically, "Darcy and I have been debating this for weeks. In a few words you have managed to sum it up, quite concisely, I might add."

She merely smiled in return, though her eyes danced mischievously. " 'Tis the nature of youth to debate. I do not have the luxury of that time."

"Milady, you have given me much to think about," Darcy said thoughtfully. Then his eyes seemed to focus, and he rose from his chair and bent over Isabel's hand. "As for that, I beg your leave lest I overstay the hour—and my welcome."

"Sleep well, my friend," Will called, then was caught by a sudden yawn as the goliard departed, and he also began to rise.

Isabel held up a hand to stop him. "I would speak with you, Will."

"Mother, I am most weary," Will protested, sensing that she had been waiting for the moment.

"It will not take long," she answered firmly. Ignoring his pained expression, she gestured toward his vacated chair.

Sinking back with a resigned sigh, Will met his mother's determined gaze. "You have it, then; say your mind."

"Aye, I shall come straight to the point. What trouble is there between you and your bride that you do not share a chamber? Surely in this brief time that you have been wed matters cannot have come to the point of such difficulties."

Will shifted uncomfortably in his chair, unwilling to discuss the matter. He could be firm in his authority, ordering his mother not to meddle, but he knew that Isabel would not be put off indefinitely. Sighing heavily, he faced it. "As you say, I have only been home a short time. We have been apart many years. I would give us time to know one another before I make her my wife. Is that what you would hear?"

Isabel stared at her son with horror as she absorbed his meaning. "What? Do you mean to tell me that you have not touched that girl yet? Will! What can you be thinking of? Surely you must know that if your enemies learn that you have not consummated the marriage, all that you have done these past years will be for naught! And what of her? What must she think—that you have not . . ."

"She can only be relieved." Will snorted. "She takes readily to the nonsense at court and is, without doubt, repelled by the thought of consummating the marriage."

"Will, I have heard what you and Darcy have had to say, but it will hardly change human nature. The rules may have changed, but the game is the same. This—this code will not be the end of the human race, I assure you."

"You do not understand. Most of what I observed at court was hypocrisy and much of it amusing to see. Men and women we know well, their former openly lusty habits now hidden behind the guise of innocence, though I have no doubt that their private lives are as before. But for one as Eleanor, growing up among the playacting, the result has been far different. She believes in it; she is totally beguiled by what she has learned."

"Will, you are still treating her as a child," Isabel answered bluntly. "Take her in hand."

"And do what?" Will's brows rose. "Force her? Tell her that all of what she knows is wrong and now she will submit and be a wife to me? I want more from my marriage than just my wife's submission. I have no hope for a great abiding love, but some measure of happiness for us would be preferred to what you are suggesting. As for treating her as a child, perhaps I am. It is hard for me not to think of her as I have always known her. This . . . beautiful young woman I have returned to is someone I do not know."

"What are you going to do?"

"I am going to see to the matter of the Welsh," Will answered with a slow grin. "Llewelyn is someone I know about. As for Eleanor, I was hoping that you might talk with her, now that you understand the situation. I had thought to wait to speak with you until you had seen for yourself. . . ."

"Me?" she gasped, finally understanding his meaning. "You want me to settle this for you?"

"Well . . ." Will shrugged as his smile turned sheepish. "You are a woman, and I trust your judgment. If you would speak with her, work with her."

"Oh, nay." Isabel shook her head. "Nay, Will, I do not need this in my life. In fact, now that I think upon it, it has been too long since I've seen Matilda, or Isabella. Joanne is with Sybile, and Eve is expecting again. A progress, I think, is what is called for."

"Mother!" Will pleaded. "If you could only—"

"Will, every marriage—and your father's and mine was no exception—has its difficulties. This problem must be worked out between the two of you."

"You insisted upon involving yourself," Will observed sulkily, frowning at the determination in his mother's manner. "Why did you insist upon interfering if you were not willing to help?"

"A mother's concern." Isabel shrugged. "You are dear to me, my love; I care about you. Advice I will give, to be used or discarded by you as you wish. But to lead your life—that I will not do. You must resolve this yourself if you are to make a life with that young woman. Will, I will give you this, the same advice that a wise old woman gave to my mother, and she to me: It is in the discovery of each other that you will find all that you seek. There is no easy way, Will, but I assure you, the outcome will be well worth the effort."

12

GLACIAL winds from the snowcapped peaks of Snowdonia swept across the reaches of Wales. The earth frosted, sheeting the land in boreal white, declaring unease for those who resisted its laws, promising victory of survival only to the strongest, the blessed, the brightest. Before its threat became reality, harvests were hurried in the lowlands, hedgerows were opened to allow cattle and flocks of sheep to forage on the remaining stubble in a final attempt of survival. Bloodmonth began, the weakest of the herd culled to allow the strong to continue, and those of the demesne of Striguil worked endlessly in the curing, salting, and smoking of meats, the preservation of vegetables and fruits, in preparation of winter.

The soul was protected. The feast of All Hallows was reverently prepared against the threat of those gone before, and chill fall evenings slipped into winter mornings swept with white, breaking slivers melting beneath the weakening sun's warmth.

Drawn against the lonely howl of the wind without the hall, Eleanor drew to a corner on a stool near the warmth and safety of the shadows of the hearth. She watched the proceedings in the Great Hall with disbelief. She could barely contain her frustration. The comments thrown carelessly about layered the weight of her own problems so totally ignored by the others. Three months she had spent in this godforsaken land, three long months with these barbarians, she thought miserably. She closed her eyes, visualizing what she had left behind, and she filled with longing for the graciousness, the ease of court. The laughter, the gaiety, entertainment of plays given by the ladies and the knights of the court, the riotous performances of traveling entertainers drawn to perform before the King with their monkeys and dogs . . . Lud, she thought, there had not been so much as a bear-baiting. . . . Gossip, the anticipation of dalliances upon discovering the unknown one whose sweet words were carried by minstrel and bard. Alan. She swallowed, willing herself not to think upon him, but he formed in her thoughts like an unwanted specter, dear and cherished, and she thought she would suffocate from the pain of remembering. Sweet remembrances. The broadness of his shoulders beneath the fine, rich cloth of his surcoat, his sandy, tousled hair that would break over his forehead, the loving brown depths of his hazel eyes. . . . Her eyes strayed to Will where he sat at the high table, and she drew them quickly away as a shudder took her body. Why, in the years he had been gone, had she not remembered that he was so . . . so big. Tall, muscular, without the long, slender refinement of Alan's body. Will's skin had tanned in the long hours he spent in the saddle, his dark hair and brows a sharp contrast to Alan's fair handsomeness. He was so *earthy*, she thought, unable to come up with a more apt description. He laughed too easily, too loudly—though his smile was pleasing, she conceded, his teeth white and strong without the signs of decay which had begun to show on Alan's, his breath sweeter. She flushed at the thought, remembering the moment the day before when that mouth had come so frighteningly close to hers.

It was that damnable goliard's fault, she reasoned, glancing at the bard with a furious look. Following supper he had begun to sing, not his accustomed barbs laden with political overtones but sweetly, his beautiful voice lulling her into a sense of lightness with words of love and dreams. She had found herself alone with Will, the others having gone to their

beds. They sat together before the fire in a quiet, intimate moment. He had seemed different, somehow. Companionable,
comfortable. They had discussed simple matters that had
taken their day, and soon it had slipped into reflections of the
past, moments Eleanor had thought forgotten. They laughed
together, recalling times with Henry, and sobered as they
touched upon shared moments of grief: the loss of the Marshal, Eleanor's loneliness when her mother had left for France
and her sisters for Scotland and Germany, the years she had
spent alone in Corse Castle. She had wept, and found herself
in Will's arms. For a moment she had felt the comfort she
had known with him as a child. She could not recall when it
changed, and she had begun to sense the difference in him.
Only the terror had been real, the sudden gripping fear that
caused her to fling herself from him, ignoring the pained, sor-
rowing look that came into his eyes as he regarded her with
silence. Even that only caused a feeling of revulsion to well up
in her as she staggered back from him and turned to flee to the
safety of the locked door of her chamber. Did he know that
she locked her door against him? Certainly, if he had ever
tried it, she did not know of it.

But she doubted it, much to her constant relief. Nay, the
only thing he seemed to expect from her was to be a Martha, a
chatelaine to see to his comfort. It had not been easy. Justin,
Chepstow's steward, had seen to her instruction. At first
fascinated, she had taken readily to the running of the manor,
wearing the bulk of keys at her girdle with a feeling of pride
and purpose as she learned to handle the household accounts
and the supervision of the chaplain, butler and brewers, the
porters who watched the doors, the cooks and food dispens-
ers, cupbearers, fruiterers, slaughterers, bakers, candlemakers, poulterers, launderesses, and the workers of the stables:
the farriers, grooms, smiths, carters, and clerks. She had
hardly been aware of such at court, though she knew they
existed, and for a time her lessons had served to occupy her
thoughts and energy.

Soon, however, it became little more than a pastime that
served to irritate her and add to her feelings of disquiet. Was
this to be the manner of her life? In the days before she had

left on her progress, Lady Isabel had seemed fulfilled by such, even enthused to greet each day with Chepstow's care. Though, in honesty, the lady's realm appeared to exceed Striguil. Many hours were taken with matters beyond its borders. Messengers came and went with their instructions and letters were written. Eleanor had drifted in a fog during those days, resentful and angry, hardly noticing what was happening about her. But she recalled the lady clearly and was glad that she had gone. An elusive element had drawn her to Isabel, yet she had felt fearful. Something in Isabel's eyes when they had come to rest upon her were speculative, as if waiting.

And she had been left alone with her husband. *Husband.* Eleanor shivered as she contemplated the word. Sitting near the fire but far enough apart to feel the chill at her back from the drafty hall, Eleanor pulled her cloak about her shoulders as she tried to dismiss the uneasiness that came over her. Once she had loved him, hadn't she? It was difficult to recapture those feelings. She remembered a different feeling, one of protection, of comfort. She recalled the child who chased after him, and she flushed with the memory of the childish protests, the demands. Oh, if she only had it all to relive! How her life had changed since that time! She was caught in a trap of her own making. Why are we allowed to make decisions when we are so young, she thought desperately, decisions we must live with for the rest of our lives?

Absorbed, she jumped when Will shouted, and she stared at him, wondering at his rage.

"The fool does not know he is beaten!" Will rose from his chair and began pacing before the flaming hearth, his hands clasped behind his back in an effort to contain them. "We have rousted him at every turn, yet he persists!" He turned back on his knights, who were gathered about Chepstow's dormant table, drawing of the warmth of the great hearth against the chill of the keep.

"They call him the Lord of Snowdonia," a knight ventured. "Llewelyn draws from it, resisting the fact that he is lost."

"Lost?" Will paused and turned to regard the knight with a wry smile. "A man has only failed when he is quit, Sir Rodger.

Ask Darcy." He nodded to the bard, who paused in the cleaning of his lyre where he sat on a stool near the fire to look up at the mention of his name. "I am certain that deeds of great glory could be given to Llewelyn's name by the right man, giving him further immortality."

"Do not look to me, milord." Darcy smirked. "I do not glorify lost causes."

"Humph." Will turned his back to the fire as he rubbed his haunches against its warmth. He turned his head and winked at the goliard. "You might do well to sing a verse to his praise. He may win yet."

"A successful bard, milord, knows well when to recognize the victor and remain in his camp," Darcy drawled with an easy grin. "And I, without doubt, am the most successful, as my full belly and warm backside will attest."

Will chuckled, but his demeanor again grew serious. "The King should have been forewarned when Llewelyn did not send his annual tribute of sparrow hawks and falcons. He took it as a personal jibe instead of recognizing it as an insult to the Crown. Instead, he wholly blames deBurgh for Llewelyn's actions. Damn fool, he can never see clearly ahead of him, and we now are paying the price for his short-sightedness."

"How dare you!" Eleanor's cry drew startled looks from the men. Vaguely, she was aware that she had cried out, but she was oblivious to their looks of horror, her troubled emotions focusing only on what seemed to be bursting from within her. She had leapt from her stool and was glaring at Will with hatred as the words tumbled from her unbidden. "You, his liegemen, yet you say such when you are safely from his hearing! Hubert deBurgh did indeed bring this upon the realm of our King, God save his soul. DeBurgh had been advised not to castellate in Wales, yet did he build at Arwystli, defying the Welsh lords with his power without leave of the King! Such is the loyalty of the King's men, and such with which he must abide!"

Unable to bear more, Eleanor fled to the stairs and up the torch-lit steps to the upper floor, seeking the safety and solitude of her chamber, away from the pain of the horrified

and accusing looks below. Suddenly strong hands took her,
spinning her about in the dimly lit hallway. She cried out and
tried to wrench away, but she was held fast as she looked up
into the fury in Will's eyes. "Never"—his voice broke in
barely controlled rage—"never will you speak thus in my hall,
before my men!"

"He is the King!" she cried, struggling to pull from the hard
grip of his fingers.

"And you are my wife!" he spat furiously. "I have asked
little of you, Eleanor, but I will have your loyalty!"

"Loyalty!" she cried. "He is my brother! And your King!
Yet you give him none of what you demand of me?"

She thought for a moment he would strike her, so great was
the anger raging in his expression, which he seemed to bring
under control with the greatest effort. "I will not justify
myself to you, Eleanor. But hear this, for you should know
the truth. DeBurgh *was* given license to build in Wales, by
Henry's own word. The King does not recall it, for he does
little of matters of state, his mind too often taken to matters of
personal concern. No one—no one, Eleanor—loves Henry
more than I, but I love him with his faults, not in blindness of
them as others do. Henry's hatred of the Welsh comes from
the moment when they insulted him by not attending his coronation, but he uses that hatred as food for bitterness, in lieu
of reason. He is the King and as such must compel them to
obey, as he should have years ago. I advised him of such
before I left for the Continent, but he chose to ignore it as he
does everything that would take him from his precious enter-
tainments. Now he has left us to face Llewelyn's strength,
which he has had years to build."

"Your words are traitorous!" she persisted, crying against
what he was saying.

"No one here is traitor!" he snapped. "Dammit, Eleanor,
we can love Henry yet disagree with him! But even if it were
not so, you are my wife! You will keep your council; your
loyalties are here!"

She began to struggle anew, fighting and squealing as she
kicked and wrenched her arms from his grip as she tried to pull
free. He swore under his breath, and suddenly she was in his

arms, wrapped tightly in his embrace as she struggled beneath the heat of his mouth as it closed on hers. Frightened, she whimpered against his lips, and just as suddenly she was free, stumbling back as she stared into the dismay and horror that was echoed in her own expression. Spinning about, he left her to stare at his departing back. She watched him go until he disappeared into the dark recesses of the hall, and a sob escaped, coming from the deepest recesses of her being and she cried out, damning him, even as she could not fully understand the depth and intensity of her hatred.

Will stared into the flames, seeking solace which would not come, even as he chided himself for his own foolishness in expecting it. Life does not offer up such simple solutions, he reasoned, a moment asked for and given. He knew that the answer would come only with time, the solution given quite possibly without conscious realization, pieces gathered and fitted, answers found without ever knowing whence they came. But he tried, as man will do, to draw from a moment of inspiration that would begin a day anew, leaving behind old griefs and doubts.

As always, he felt separated from life, a feeling of impermanence drawing him into another plane where he merely observed, preferring it to reality—particularly when it was pressing so hard. Damn reality, he gritted, reaching for the tankard near his chair in the silent hall. He wanted to shout, to cry out, to stir those who slept upon their pallets along the walls, for he resented the peace of their slumber.

Loneliness engulfed him. Memories passed over his mind of times shared before the hearth. Rich moments. Why had he been raised to value such times when they were no more, leaving him only to wonder if he would ever know them again? And if they never came? Would his life always seem so empty? Would he always have to pretend, to draw from memories, knowing that life would never again be so real?

How had he come to this? He had tried. He had thought to give her time, to live with him day by day, letting her come to trust him again. It seemed against his nature to force her; in that, perhaps he was odd. How much was because of Lavene?

He waited for the familiar catch to his heart, and he marveled that it had dulled with the passing years, though he accepted the fact gratefully. Lavene. He brought her image to his mind: her form, the beauty of her face, her large, dark, flashing eyes as they danced mischievously at him, and the pain returned. So short a time they had been given. So much pain. In his youth he had not understood, realization coming to give them only enough time to leave him with the regret, the anguish.

His mother's ward, she came into his unprepared heart, and remained. It had been a game at first; had she not loved others of his squire class? A soft groan escaped him as he drew from his goblet, a deep part of him not wanting to relive those years. Forgotten hatred welled in him, focused against her father, whom he had never met, by the grace of God, for he would have committed murder. Even now, no one but he knew her true reason for coming to be fostered at Chepstow. With her own demons driving her to do what she did, she had sought love, safety, security where she could find it. And she had done so, finding herself at last in Will's arms, the memory of her father's abuse finally receding in Will's comfort. But he had not realized his love for her then, or that it no longer mattered to him who was the father of the child she carried. Not until it was too late. Will groaned out loud, remembering, castigating himself as he had done so many countless times before, for not being with her at the end.

Unaware of his son's feelings for the young woman, his father had innocently brought him the news that Lavene had died in the convent where Isabel had sent her to bear the child in secrecy. And that the child had perished with her. And he had been left alone, without her.

A spark from the fire snapped, drawing him from his memories. He tried to return to her, but she remained elusive, her memory fading with his awareness of the hall, and a resentment grew in him with a sweep of self-disgust. He was doing it again, escaping reality. He thought of the young maid sleeping abovestairs. Eleanor was troubled, confused, and how could he blame her? Ever had he loved her as a child, and in his inability to accept what was expected of him she remained so. Oh, she had developed the body of an exquisitely beautiful young woman, but she seemed less capable of recognizing and accepting reality now than when she had been a freckled-faced, gangly hoyden. They both seemed to be guilty of that human error.

Things could not continue as they were. Time had run out. But what could he do differently? How could he make her see life as it truly was—and to want it? What spark had shone from her that was missing; what had stirred her child's passions . . . ? And then, as a hound whimpered from the deep shadows of the hall, an idea began to form in the back of his mind.

13

ELEANOR pulled her veil over her hair as she approached the chapel for mass. Her thoughts turned in anticipation of the peace she would find within the chapel's small sanctuary, when a tug was felt at her sleeve and she turned to find her tirewoman Dael at her side. "Milady, Lord William wishes you to ride with him this morning. He awaits you in the bailey."

Eleanor stared at the woman for a long moment, then turned without answering and entered the chapel. Nodding to Father Francis, she genuflected, crossing herself as she knelt at the kneeling rail. She bent her head to her folded hands even as her lips began to move in silent prayer to her Holy Lady. She was unaware of how much time passed as she concentrated on the monotone repetition of the cleric's voice, but she was aware of *his* presence even before the priest stopped speaking. A deep shadow cast from the tall, narrow windows of the sanctuary to fall across the pew. She refused to turn her head as she fixed her stare on the statue of the Virgin, newly brought to Chepstow at her request.

"Come with me, Eleanor." His voice was low and firm.

"When I have finished my prayers, milord," she responded with equal firmness.

"You will come with me now."

She turned her head to look up at him and saw the anger that sparked in his eyes. "This is a place of God, milord. Would you drag me from mass, from the very altar before the good father? And for what purpose?"

"My chaplain has been negligent," he answered, glancing up at the priest, whose eyes widened at the statement. "Father Francis, I wish you to instruct my lady in that which she is seriously lacking—obedience to her husband in all things. Does it not say in the scriptures that one can find God only when rebellion to his will is overcome?"

"Aye, milord, it does," the cleric answered, arching a surprised brow at the Earl Marshal.

"Then you will begin her instruction in all matters of a dutiful wife. However, I shall undertake the first lesson myself."

"You!" Eleanor leapt up, sputtering with fury. "You are no husband to me, Will Marshal! It takes more than mere vows to make a woman a wife!" she cried, oblivious to the shocked embarrassment that came upon the priest by her words. Eleanor gasped, horrified at her boldness, wondering what secret part of her had brought forth such words.

A dark brow arched and Will's mouth slipped into a smile as he looked down into her furious gaze. "Why, Eleanor," he said quietly, "I did not think you cared. But you are most correct and the matter will soon be rectified, be certain of it." He took her arm and led her from the chapel and by the passage screen to the bailey. Dael was waiting at the bottom of the steps with her cloak, and even in her rage Eleanor was aware of the stares of the knights who waited by their mounts. Fortunately, their attention was drawn by Alan Wadley, who barked orders for them to mount. She found her fur-lined cloak dropped about her shoulders and she was swung off the ground and plopped into her saddle. Her mouth worked with the words she ached to throw at Will. But she bit her lip, forcing herself to be still as she looked down at him, seeing the anger that, she suspected, would be loosed at the first utterance. He draped her skirt about her knee on the sidesaddle and tucked her foot into the stirrup before he turned away and swung atop Hamal.

They rode out through the bailey and onto the road leading to the northwest before Eleanor garnered the courage to speak to him. "Where are you taking me?" she asked churlishly.

"Where I bid," he answered offhandedly, ignoring her anger.

Eleanor turned her face to the cool morning air in a hope that the outraged tears that threatened would not spill, thus giving him the satisfaction of seeing her wipe them from her eyes. Again in control, she stole a glance at him, wondering if this man who rode by her side could possibly be the same man she had once loved. A child's love, the ignorance of innocence, but she had offered it to him, and he had rejected it.

She tore her eyes from his profile, unable to bear the pain of looking at him, and her gaze strayed to a large hamper fixed behind Hamal's saddle. Her eyes widened with surprise and she glanced quickly up at him, not daring to believe her suspicions, the thoughtful innocence it implied. "Will, what is that?" When he turned, she nodded at the basket. Following her gaze, he merely shrugged, muttering something incoherent. "Will Marshal! You brought me out for a picnic!" she cried, unable to keep sudden delight from her voice.

"A small thing," he answered casually. "Need you make so much of it? 'Tis an uncommonly warm day, most likely the last we shall see until spring. I felt it time that you came to know your lands, for they are yours now, Eleanor, as much as mine. Even if you have chosen to reject them—" "And me," he had almost said, catching himself in time.

Her delight died at his words as she realized the truth in them. How could she tell him, how could she explain to him that what was important to him never could be to her? Somewhere their paths had irreversibly turned and were now as diverse as summer's warmth and winter's chill. How she wished it were not so, that she could recapture something of what she once felt for him. She raised the corner of her sleeve to her eyes, wiping the tears that came, giving him that, a small offering for what could not be.

They crossed the rolling hills, deepening rich shades of green momentarily free from sheeting frost, kissed by mists

which edged the ragged mountains of Wales. The air smelled
heavily of winter while the sun warmed in a last, lost attempt
at fall, its warmth adding to the joy they stole from it in
desperately needed pleasure.

He showed her the lands. She spoke with the villeins, simple
people whom, but for a night at the edge of a meadow near
Wycombe, she had never really come to know. Isabella's
words returned to her, of the concerned regard for those in
their care, and she saw the same in Will. A spark began to kin-
dle in her, an unformed feeling that persisted throughout the
morning. Slowly, it began to flame a little more brightly, the
months of animosity between them fading as she turned to a
gentle reawakening of something of vital importance, once
known, then forgotten.

She found herself asking questions, listening to Will's
answers intently, wanting to know of things that had never
before existed for her. People, land, crops, the sounds of
children melded, the total forming within her. As they walked
through a field of harvested barley, the stubble catching at her
skirts, he filled her cupped hands with soil, and she felt its
coolness against her skin and it seemed to reach up her arms.
Was it his voice, low, touched with an emotion she had not
heard from him before, or something more elusive? Odd, but
there in the dirt, the hem of the rich, costly samite of her skirt
irrevocably ruined by the stain of soil, her hair disheveled by
the morning's ride, she had never felt so much that she was
a Plantagenet. A voice within her spoke softly, giving her an
awareness of her destiny. England. She had never had a sense
of it before, even as she suddenly felt filled with it.

They took of Will's picnic, though she hardly noticed the
food as she shot questions at him, unaware of his delighted approval as she sought eagerly for answers. She asked first of the
lands, then of other matters, not realizing she had asked many
of the same questions before in another time, in the more innocent way of a child. They talked of the Charter, politics, affairs that for so long had seemed remote.

As they rode back to Chepstow, she hardly noticed what
passed. Her mind was filled with what she had discovered even
as it tossed confusingly with what she had come to believe.
Lost as she was in her thoughts, it was moments before she

realized that Will had grabbed for the reins of her mount and
their knights had unsheathed their swords and had formed a
circle about her. Dazedly, she fixed on a party of men who had
seemed to form suddenly before them, and from their
garments she knew them to be Welsh. The danger of the situation gripped her with a stupefying rush of paralyzing fear. She
cried out as her breath caught, and her ears were filled with the
sound of war cries, the screams of horses, and the clashing of
steel against steel. Near her a man was struck, and Eleanor
was filled with terror that it had been Will. As he fell she tried
to look, but it was all that she could do to control her mare as
the crazed animal tossed wildly. Suddenly a destrier and its
rider crashed into the mare's haunches, swinging her about as
Eleanor fought to keep her seat.

Screaming, her mare reared, thrashing the air with flailing
hooves, and Eleanor felt herself falling. She twisted her body
and slid from the back of the frantic animal, miraculously
managing to land on her feet as she stumbled against the
tangle of her skirts. It took a moment to realize that she was
unhurt, and she stepped back from the fray as she heard the
retreating sound of her mare's pounding hooves. She heard
Will cry out her name and looked up to find him engaged in a
fierce battle with a Welsh knight as he tried to move Hamal
toward her. Amid the ringing sound of their striking swords,
from the corner of her eye she caught the movement of
another. Fear engulfed her as she realized that another Welsh
soldier was approaching Will on his left, his sword raised to
strike. A voice called from within her to move, and her gaze
dropped to a Welsh yeoman who had fallen near her feet.
Without thought she wrenched the bow from his lifeless hands
and notched an arrow. She could not have said how she
managed to draw the string, for its pull far outweighed her, its
tip towering over her head, but she drew the string back as far
as she could, every muscle in her arms and back straining, and
let fly. The bow recoiled, knocking her from her feet, and the
last thing she remembered was a thud and a sharp, blinding
light in her head.

Gentle hands took her shoulders as a soft voice spoke to
her. Crying out, she turned to the voice, drawing to its safety
and the warmth of the arms which held her. "Hush. You are

safe." It was Will's voice, his arms. "You saved my life,
mouse." She could hear the laughter in his voice, touched with
awe. He called her mouse. Distant memories touched, then
disappeared as reality entered and she drew back to assure
herself that he was safe. "They are gone," he said as he laid a
hand on her cheek, holding her gaze to his. "Nay, do not
look. They are felled, all but the few who escaped. The others
have gone after them. Come now, let us go home." He led her
to Hamal, who threw his head back, tossing it at the smell of
his master. She glimpsed the bloodied sight of the destrier's
hooves and looked quickly away, knowing the trained animal
had done his part in their defense. And she knew why Will
would not allow her to look upon the fallen.

In the saddle she slumped against him, drawing from his
comfort as the import of what had happened struck her fully.
She began to shiver uncontrollably and felt his arms tighten
about her. Resting her head against his chest as her arms went
about his waist, she clung to him, vaguely aware of the sound
of his voice as he murmured to her, soothing words of comfort. "Oh, Will." She drew in her breath shakily and it ended
in a sob. "Did I truly—kill a man?"

"You knocked him from his horse; Hamal did the rest. You
saved my life," he repeated, tightening his arms about her.
"God's breath, Eleanor, how did you manage to draw that
bow?"

"Did I?" She tried to remember.

"Aye, mouse, you did." He chuckled. "I will never understand how you did it, but I can thank God for giving you the
strength."

She opened her mouth to respond, but she felt his arms
stiffen about her and he hushed her in a drawing breath.
Suddenly he yanked Hamal's reins about, and dug in his
rowelspurs, and they plunged into the trees lining the road,
nearly upsetting Eleanor from her perch.

"What—?"

"Quiet!" he hissed as he drew them into a dark copse,
deeply hidden from the road. "Hang on to me," he
whispered. Pulling a kerchief from his surcoat, he leaned
across her and wrapped it about the destrier's eyes. Instantly
the animal quieted, becoming as stone, his only movement a

slight shifting beneath them. Her mouth opened with question but Will clamped a hand across it and shook his head. And then she heard it, the sound of riders moving along the road beyond them. Her eyes widened with recognition, and he relaxed slightly but as he lowered his hand he frowned at her with warning. She heard them stop and the sound of men's voices speaking Welsh, and her eyes widened with glassy terror as she stared up at Will. His head was turned to the voices —apparently he understood what was being said—and she bit her lip to keep from crying out.

Unable to stop the trembling of her body, she pulled at his surcoat, bringing his attention back to her. She tried to stop the wild panic that began to build, but she could only stare up at him, pleading for him to understand as the cry built up in her throat. Instantly he lowered his head and his mouth clamped over hers, making her cry a soft whimper.

She pressed against him, pulling his strength into her, her mind filled with pictures of rape, torture, death for her even as she saw him dismembered. Llewelyn's victory, the Marshal, and the sister of the King. She knew that should they be discovered, no quarter would be given. Just as she knew that Will knew as well.

His kiss of silence drew her fear and slowly she sensed the change as the fierce embrace became gentle and stirring. Sharpened by the prospect of death, her senses took over and her body responded as she felt a rush of something strong, pulling. An excitement, a rush of feeling hit her with a force of its own.

Her arms went about his neck, drawing him to her as her mouth opened under his. His tongue flicked over hers, touching the recesses of her mouth, and she struggled not to moan in her awareness of those nearby. As he drew his mouth from hers the shadows of the glade played across his face, but she could feel the burning question in his eyes. Fed by the rushing awareness of danger that coursed through her, she answered him, pulling his lips to hers once again. She pressed against him, needing to feel the comfort of his body against hers, the life-giving feel of his mouth, and she moaned softly against his lips as a shock of warmth washed over her, leaving her weak.

In the back of her mind she was aware of the retreating sound of horses' hooves, followed by silence. She knew as Will drew himself from her that they were again alone, and safe. He held her to him tightly for a long moment, and she began to feel the essence of reality return—and with it the shock of what had just happened.

Dazed, she felt Will shift behind her, and she was suddenly alone in the saddle. She watched numbly as he tied Hamal to a tree limb. She looked down at him, realizing that he was holding his arms out to her, and she shook her head, denying his meaning. "Nay," she whispered, her voice barely more than a breath.

"Come to me, Eleanor," he said softly.

"Nay," she repeated, her voice trembling.

He pulled her from the saddle and she tried to wrench away, but he held her against him and she could feel his breath against her cheek. "It is time, Eleanor," he murmured.

"Not here," she cried softly. "They will come back—"

"Nay, they will not. Would I take you here if it were so? The danger is passed, Eleanor; they ride into the arms of my men."

"I cannot," she pleaded, the sound coming as a soft cry.

"Aye, it will be now." He knew they were safe; he had known it as soon as the riders had spoken. They had happened upon the bodies of their fellows and paused only long enough to agree that the best decision would be to remove themselves from Striguil's borders as rapidly as possible. He had not planned to kiss her—it had only been meant to silence her—but then, to his amazement, she had responded to his kiss. He would not give her more time to think about it. All that had happened, the danger, the fear, had finally brought her into his arms. Were he to wait, to return her to the comfort of a bedchamber, the moment would be lost—and he had no intention of losing this moment. "Do not be afraid, sweetling," he said softly.

He removed Hamal's blindfold, knowing the animal would warn him should anyone approach. He drew her deeper into the shadows of the grove, drawing his heavy cloak to spread it on the dried leaves and needles of the forest floor. He pulled off his surcoat in a movement, and then his voice came to her softly. "Help me to disarm, Eleanor." She had stood watching him as she tried to breathe normally and to still the pounding of her heart. It was her duty, she mentally repeated, her duty. Disjointedly, her hands moved to his sides and she choked back a sob that lumped in her throat as she helped him with shaking fingers to lift his hauberk of jazerant-worked chain mail aside, then to the laces of the hardened leather hauberk beneath, then lastly, the gambeson padding above the linen of his chanise. Turning, he untied her cloak, letting it drop at their feet as he lifted her into his arms and lowered her onto the cloak.

His mouth took hers in a kiss, deep and stirring, as his hands went to the clasps at the shoulders of her blaiunt, releasing one, then the other, pulling the garment down to her waist. Slowly, as his kiss deepened and he felt the tension in her begin to ease, he undid the lacings of her chemise, and his hand slipped beneath to stroke the full, sweet softness of a breast.

As his fingers lingered, gently teasing the nipple, she drew in her breath sharply, alarmed by the hot spears that darted over her body. He drew her chemise from her shoulders, bearing her to him in the soft, dimming light of the glade. She moaned as his fingers were replaced by his lips, which circled the taut tip, then drew it into his mouth, pulling gently, drawing, and she cried out softly against the heat which seemed to fill her body at the touch of his lips. Her mind spun as a strange, driving tautness drew from her loins with each pull of his mouth and the teasing, burning sensation of his tongue. She closed her eyes tightly and fixed on the tingling rush of nerves which suddenly seemed to reach out to every part of her.

There had been a time when she had wanted this to happen, with this man. She had dreamed about it, speculating, wondering how it would be. And, ohhh, she wanted it now, even as she fought against it, knowing it to be base, apart from what was right, what was truly beautiful. The fact of where they were flashed across her mind, that he was taking her like an animal. But she did not care, for as he touched her she was lost to caring. She groaned, arching her back to his caresses, wanting him to touch her, wanting what he was giving her. Distantly, she heard the sound of her own voice, pleading.

He thrilled at her soft pleading. She was no more the child, but a woman, a beautiful, desirable woman. His wife. Forcefully, he brought himself under control in a determination to bring her pleasure. Aware of the conflict within her, he knew that if he failed she would use it against them. He would not let it happen; he would show her the joys of love, his own weapon for the future against what she had been led to believe, and his resolve firmed against the conflicts he felt in her.

He kissed her again deeply, then the corners of her mouth and eyes, light, tender kisses until he found the throbbing pulse at the base of her neck and teased it, lingering until he felt her shift against him with a soft moan. His lips trailed slowly across the tender parts of her shoulders to her breasts, teasing each again until she cried out softly in eagerness and her hands pulled at him for what he knew and she could only suspect. He took her mouth again with his as he lifted her skirts and his hand slipped beneath, touching her, gliding over her body lightly in sweet promise of discovery. Then his fingers slipped to the softness between her thighs, where they played and teased.

Her mind spun. It seemed as if she was on fire, each part of her aching in a bittersweet pain. She felt his fingers touch her intimately, but the shock she felt, along with lingering doubts, were thrust aside in her need and deep, aching curiosity.

His fingers played their game and he sought the sweet bud of his search, stroking it lightly, gently, as she gasped and moaned, her body moving with each touch. He claimed her breasts with his mouth, distracting her as his finger slipped gently within. He felt the resistance and smiled to himself. The pressure of the membrane was firm, and he wanted it so. He wanted her to feel the pain of his possession. He suspected the guilt she would feel later, and the pain was vital. But with it, pleasure—that he would give to her too.

Her fingers dug into his shoulders as she arched her back against the steady pursuit of his attentions, as she was driven by the burning tension, the contracting of her stomach muscles which seemed to overtake her, taking her unbidden as she felt her body tense in a surging thrust, a great trembling of unimagined sensation that carried her apart as she seemed to shatter.

He took her mouth in a tender kiss as she descended and she drew from it, needing him in an awareness that he knew what had happened. Her very soul had been drawn from her and he had taken it. She felt his body shift as he loosened his chausses and he moved over her, spreading her thighs to settle between. She welcomed the weight of his body, even as she tried to focus on what he was saying to her. "This first time there will be pain and I want you to feel it," he said softly. "Remember it. Surely, sweetheart, it is with the loss of your maidenhead that all sin is taken, as from this time you will know only pleasure."

Still seeped in sated peace, she vaguely wondered what he meant. As he thrust deeply into her she cried out in pain and surprise as he filled her, breaking her maidenhead. She began to sob, but he took her face in his hands and kissed her, lingering, touching the corners of her mouth, her cheeks, and the damp corners of her eyes until she quieted. She bit her lip and sniffed, feeling the aching between her legs and the awareness of him filling her. His eyes were warm and tender and she returned his look with a glare. Smiling, he lowered his head to kiss her but she clamped her lips and refused to return it. He nibbled at her lips, brushing light, fluttering kisses over her mouth as slowly he began to move with her. The strange, warm feeling began to return and she felt her body soften, her mouth opening against his pursuit as her mind began to swim against the renewed promise that began to spread over her, and her anger was suddenly forgotten. Gradually she started to move with him, following an instinct she could give no words to. She felt the tension build again, adding, filling her, taking her with him until she soared to that realm of indescribable sensation again, knowing that this time he had shared it with her. Gently they floated above the copse together, drifting, settling at last into the warm security of each other's arms. Languid, warm, sated, she snuggled her head into the crook of his arm as he pulled her fox-lined cloak over them against the chill of the deepening shadows.

14

ELEANOR opened her eyes dreamily and held to the deep, sated feeling of peace that clung to her body. For a moment she did not know why she felt so—a dream, perhaps—when memory flooded her consciousness and her eyes flew open to fix on the shadowing branches of the speading oaks overhead. The dreamlike quality of the grove vanished, leaving her chilled against the reality of her disheveled state and that of the man who lay reposed next to her, his arm lying heavily across her breasts, and she faced the enormity of what had happened. "Nay," she whispered, catching her lower lip between her teeth and bit as she could feel the rising hysteria.

Her subtle movement brought Will instantly awake. A swift glance about the thicket told him that everything was as before. Even Hamal, who would have been the first to warn him, was dozing peacefully in the failing light of late afternoon that stole between the natural canopy of the copse. "What is it, love?" he murmured, nuzzling her ear as he drew her close. "An ill dream, perhaps?"

"Let me go," she choked.

"Sweetheart, what is it?" He rose on an elbow to look down at her with concern.

"Do not call me that!" She squirmed away from him as she grasped her clothing about her as she leapt to her feet and backed away from him. "Do not come near me!" she hissed as he rose and took a step toward her.

"Eleanor, what in God's name—"

"Do not blaspheme more than we have, Lord Marshal!"

"Blaspheme? What are you talking about?" He stared at her, and his concern deepened at the wild look that had come into her eyes. "Eleanor, surely you cannot think that what we have done is against God's will!"

But she seemed not to be listening as she glanced about the glade, her eyes growing wider. "Have you no remorse for the bestiality of our behavior? I gave myself to you like . . . like an animal." Her voice broke as she turned back on him. "We —you tore at my clothes—"

"They're not torn. And it is too cold to disrobe, my sweet."

"We went at each other like animals!"

"Animals don't do what we did, not in the same way."

"Even in this place, a heathen temple of oak and spirits . . . Oh, Will!" she breathed, her eyes taking on a maddened look. "Surely I was possessed by an incubus, a demon spirit sent by the man I killed, sent to lead you to sin—"

"You did not kill him," he said wryly. "Hamal did—and he does not appear to be concerned about it." But the look she gave him dissolved any further attempt at humor. He straightened his chausses and went to her, grasping her shoulders in his hands, his long fingers biting into her flesh as his feelings tossed between abhorrence for what she was saying and concern for her sanity. "Eleanor, stop it! The only demons in this place are in your mind!"

"The Holy Writ says—"

"You are my wife! There is no sin in what we did!"

She opened her mouth to speak but suddenly, clearly, she knew the truth, and the words lumped in her throat. The wildness left her eyes, leaving them dull and resigned. "You are right, Will. There was no demon but that which harbors within me," she said, her voice now controlled. Relief flooded his expression and his grip relaxed. Using the moment, she stepped away and turned her back to him as she pulled on her garments.

"You are truly my wife now, Eleanor. It is not wrong. Can you find no joy in it?" he asked softly.

Still turned away from him, she answered in kind as she tried to keep the sorrow from her voice. "Aye, milord, that is as it should be. I am grateful to you for the time you have given me; I know it was for me that you have kept from my bed. It is written that a wife shall be dutiful and give all things unto her husband. I shall obey you in all things—but we have defied God's law by the base pleasure of our actions. I beg your forgiveness for how I have behaved to you; you were correct to remind me of my place before the good father this morn."

She turned and stepped toward Hamal as she heard Will swear under his breath, but she forgave him that, knowing that what had happened in the hour past was a sin which would remain heavily on her soul. As she approached the destrier she was suddenly spun about and yanked back, falling against Will. "Dammit, I told you to stop! What has happened to you, Eleanor? Can you remember nothing of common sense?"

"What are you raving about?" she shrieked, her emotions breaking in the face of his anger. "How dare you handle me thus! Let me go!" She clawed at his arm as she tried furiously to pull free, outraged that he would manhandle her like a baseborn, husband or no.

"Raving, is it?" he roared, shaking her. "Have the priests so addled your mind that you do not even remember not to approach a warhorse like that? Do you think it is a lamb you are seeking to mount?"

Her breath drew in sharply as she realized his meaning, and she glanced at Hamal, who was pawing the ground nervously as he pulled his massive head against his reins, which were tied to the heavy limb of a tree, his black eyes rolling wildly. "Oh," she breathed, "I did not think."

"You seldom do anymore," he snapped, flinging her from him and away from the frantic animal. Muttering to himself, he tied his armor into his cloak and approached the horse, his voice falling soothingly to allow the destrier to be calmed by his familiar sound and smell. Once mounted, he pulled Hamal's head tightly and held out a hand to her. "Can you remember how to come to me?" He frowned.

"Aye, milord, my addled brain can remember that much if I strain very hard," she snapped. Gathering her skirts about her so they would not rustle against the grasses of the forest bed, she circled downwind of the animal, beyond his vision, and held her hand out to Will. He pulled her up easily and settled her into his lap, holding Hamal's head tightly as the animal protested the shift in weight.

The ride back to Chepstow was silent, as they were both too angry to speak. It was dark when they rode into the inner bailey. Without a word, Will lowered her to the ground before Chepstow's keep, and he left her standing there in the dust as he turned the horse about and rode in the direction of the stables.

As Eleanor entered the Great Hall, William's knights, who were standing and pacing about the great length of the room, turned to a man and seemed to begin talking all at once. Alan Wadley silenced the bedlam with a roar, then turned to Eleanor, his own worry showing in his eyes and the deep furrow to his bushy brows. "My lady, are you all right? We knew not what had happened to you—there are still parties out searching. Earl William—is he with you—we feared that you had been taken—"

"He is seeing to his horse," she snapped, causing the grizzled knight's eyes to widen with surprise at her anger. "As you can see, no harm has come to us. Tell my lord that I am to bed—if he should care to inquire."

"Ah . . . milady." The knight hesitated. "There is a messenger who has come from the King."

"From the King?" She brightened and glanced about with interest. "Where is he, Sir Wadley? Bring him to me."

"I will see him." Will's deep voice caused the two to turn about, and Wadley's relief was obvious as he beheld his lord, who came to stand behind Eleanor. "I believe that you were to bed, milady," Will said, a dark brow arching as he smiled down at her. "I know that you are fatigued. I give you leave to go."

She had to clamp her mouth shut at the obvious amusement that flickered in his eyes. "Aye, milord," she answered lightly, recognizing the order that came with the calmly given statement. Damn him, she thought, he knew she could not protest after what she had said to him in the glade. Lud, did a woman have to be obedient to her husband in *all* things? Turning, she drew back her shoulders and left the hall with as much dignity as she could muster. All the while her thoughts turned to the messenger and what missive he carried from Henry. Dear Henry. Oh, how she longed to be back with him at court.

Once in her chambers, she allowed her women to draw her a bath. It was a matter she would have dismissed in her mood, but noticing the wrinkle of Dael's nose as she drew near, she allowed it. And with its need, the sharp memories of the past hours came rushing back, driving the awareness of Henry's missive from her mind. A feeling of loathing overwhelmed her, self-repugnance that she took into herself as a penance she knew she must face and accept. Fortunately, as her gown was drawn from her the other women turned away to other tasks, leaving only Dael to attend her. As the tirewoman drew her chemise away, Eleanor glanced down and she saw the traces of dried blood on the garment and her eyes darted to her thighs. Flushing, she grabbed at the chemise and tried to cover herself. Dael took the garment from her gently but firmly, her face impassive as she placed herself between Eleanor and the others and helped her into the bath. Handing her a cloth, Dael held her glance for a brief moment before she turned and set to lay out fresh garments.

Eleanor swallowed as she felt a rushing gratitude for the woman's sensitivity. Dael was lowborn, a mere servant, whereupon her other women were wives and daughters of William's knights, and Eleanor was amazed to receive such kindness from her. And then she remembered what had been pushed from her mind in the events of the past hours, the precious time before the appearance of the Welsh soldiers. Had she not been touched by those she had met, recognizing in them a simple, easy honesty? Thoughts played their normal game, tripping without form from one place to the next . . villeins . . . nobleborn . . . wives . . . marriage, and . . . She twisted her head about in time to see Dael lowering her chemise to a bowl of water.

"Nay! Dael, do not!" she cried, bringing surprised gasps from the other women. "Nay," she repeated more calmly to the woman's querulous look. "Joan"—she turned her head to Alan Wadley's wife—"as wife to Striguil's master-at-arms you are of the highest rank of my women. You will take my chemise to the men."

Joan Wadley took the garment Dael brought to her. As the woman's eyes fixed on the bloodstains, they shifted quickly to Eleanor, widening in surprise. Understanding, she nodded and left the room, leaving the others to wonder what had happened.

"Leave me," Eleanor ordered, unable to face the questions in their eyes. The sharpness of her voice broached no protest as the ladies fell silent and departed quickly to wonder at the foul mood of their lady. Only Dael remained, at Eleanor's bidding, to tend her mistress, ignoring, or pretending not to see, the sulking mood Eleanor had fallen into.

There, Will Marshal, it is done, she thought spitefully. The reason for the marriage—as he had so often reminded her—it was done. She could well imagine the tankards that would be lifted, the robust celebration and ribald jesting that would be given to Will for his accomplishment, and she was grateful to be spared it. No one could now deny that she was his wife. But why—why had it been this way, she wondered miserably.

I am lost, she thought. She had tried so to be good, to follow the Holy Mother's example of virtue. Yet she had felt the evil of Satan as he entered her soul when Will touched her. "I am no better than the Evil One," she whispered, unaware that she had spoken aloud or that Dael looked at her with curiosity before she again turned away and closed off her hearing. He is in me, driving me to turn from God, she reasoned silently. So shall the sins of the father be visited upon the sons—or daughters, for surely it is so. The greatest of lechers to sit upon a throne, of this land or any other, and he is in me. It is my penance for being born of his blood and I cannot escape it. Love is chaste, yet when my husband touched me I became forsaken. She closed her eyes in prayer. I saw none but him, wanted only what he could bring me, which shall surely bring me to damnation. Oh, sweet Lord, I promise I shall be good, I promise to try. To be a dutiful wife, in all things, to submit to my husband when he wills. But ever shall I resist the unholy lust that consumed me this day.

*   *   *

Eleanor sat before the fire in her chamber, working a length of samite with rich colors of silk for a tunic for Will. With each stitch she said a silent prayer for their marriage, and now that they were at last truly husband and wife in the sight of God, that a child might be brought forth to be raised in his name. Perhaps, she reasoned, if they were blessed with a child it would show that the Blessed Mother had forgiven her for the wanton passion of the union. Lost in her thoughts, she was unaware when the door opened.

He came to stand by her chair, and it was a moment before she looked up. Part of her was amazed that he was here in her chamber, even as she glanced about and realized that Dael had left quickly at the Earl's entrance. The thoughts vanished as she remembered Henry's missive. "What does he say?"

Will took the chair across from her, shaking his head as she thought to offer him wine or ale. "He is at Cardiff. We will leave in the morning to attend him there."

"We?" she asked hopefully, leaning forward.

"I will not leave you here." He shrugged, though he did not add that part of him thought it best. He had no desire to return her to court, but not knowing what Henry wanted of him, he did not know how long he would be gone. He would have her with him; to leave her alone at Chepstow for any length of time now would only give her the opportunity to draw further from him. If, indeed, she could be any further apart from him than she was at this moment.

"In the morning?" She smiled, her pleasure bubbling. "There is so much to do! I cannot possibly be ready!"

"I am certain that you will manage," he grumbled, shifting uncomfortably as he looked about the chamber. There was not one damn thing about the room that spoke of a man, he realized. Perhaps he would move his warchest in here—there, smack in the middle where she would trip over it. Or perhaps he should take her to his chamber. . . .

"May I take my ladies with me, milord?" she asked, even as her thoughts flew over all the things that must be done in the morning.

"Of course," he snapped, irritated by her rambling—and her obvious enthusiasm, so in contrast to the past hours—except for moments. . . . Damn, what had happened? He knew she had pleasured in him, as much as he had in her. And it had been good. More than he had dreamed, so much more. "Take whomever you want."

"Aye, milord." She blinked, wondering why he was so angry. "I only wished to know—"

"Stop calling me milord, Eleanor!" he barked, causing her to jump. Good, he thought, at least she is listening to me now. "You have ever called me by my given name and I shall have it so now."

"Aye, milor—Will," she amended with irritating contriteness.

They sat in a long, protracted silence, the only sound in the chamber the snap and crackling of the fire a few feet from them. Eleanor drew a long, nervous sigh, her mind tossing over all that she must do in a few hours, even as she wondered why he was sitting there, leaving them in this awkward silence, and when he would leave. Without realizing it, she sighed again and heard the deep sound of his soft laughter.

"I do believe that you are waiting for me to leave," he said bluntly. She stiffened at the accuracy of his thoughts. Seeing her redden, he laughed again, but the sound did not reach his eyes. "Oh, nay, my sweet wife. What is done is done and no more shall we sleep apart. Come here, sweetling."

She swallowed, realizing that she had known since she had looked up to find him standing near her chair. "Please, Will." Her voice trembled. "I shall be to bed—"

"Ahh, Eleanor, is that how you would have it?" He shook his head slowly. "Slip beneath the covers, draw them to your chin, and await the evil incubus?"

"Milord!" she gasped, crossing herself.

"I told you not to call me that—unless it is said with love, my sweet. But the truth, is that not how you see your marriage, Eleanor? With the demon in your bed?"

"Nay, 'tis not so! You are my husband! I shall give to you what you require; I will not withhold myself, I swear!"

"Be careful, love. For you shall be forsworn."

"Oh, how can you say such to me? I shall come to you, and I will not break that vow."

"As I will?"

"Aye!"

"Then come to me now," he said, holding out his hand.

She cringed at the way he was looking at her. Panicked, she glanced toward the large canopied bed and its heavy curtains. "But, I said—as a virtuous wife would have it, there—"

"With the curtains drawn, the darkness covering our love, as you withhold yourself?"

"I said I would not!" she cried, confused, fearing where he was leading her.

"There are many ways to withhold yourself. Come to me, Eleanor."

"Nay." Her voice was thready, pleading.

He reached over and took her hand as she gave a deep, anguished sob. He pulled her into his lap, holding her close as she trembled, and waited until her body had stopped shaking and she was still against him. Gently he placed his fingers beneath her chin and lifted her face. Tenderly he kissed her brow, the corners of her eyes, which were wet with tears, and the corners of her mouth, which trembled beneath his touch. "Eleanor," he whispered. "Once you trusted me. If you would let yourself but try, you could do so again." His mouth covered hers, gently, lingering, until her lips opened to accept him. He kissed her long, and yet again, until she moaned softly against his mouth. His hand slipped the ties of her bodice and lifted it apart to gently caress her, his fingers moving beneath to find and tease her nipples with a tenderness that spun her mind with wonder. She ran her tongue over her lips as her teeth ached at his gentle playing, and she swallowed, her mind filled with wonder as guilt receded and she focused on what he was doing. Surely this was not sinful, she reasoned as she arched her back to his steady attention. He was only touching her, and it was only a breast, and his fingers—oh, sweet Lord, it felt so good. Surely not a sin.

She thought she could not stand more. The growing, bittersweet aching from the deepest core of her had spread its drawstring tension over her body. He shifted in the chair, drawing her to him as he bent over her, and his lips touched her, replacing his fingers to draw light circles about the nipples, flicking the tender, sensitive tips, and she cried out softly. She tried to stay him, to push him away, but he drew a breast into his mouth and suckled, causing her to groan and press against him, and she knew that she was lost. She cared about nothing but him and what she now knew he would give her.

Dizzily, she felt herself lifted and carried as he placed her on the bed. He pulled her bedgown from her, and then he was there and she knew that he had withdrawn his garments as well. "Open your eyes, Eleanor," he said softly, and she obeyed, his voice drawing her against her will, and she looked into the darkness. "The curtains are drawn. But it is the same. Here, wherever we shall be together. Now close your eyes. Feel what I shall give to you, what we will share, what you will give to me. It is beautiful and it is right."

She tried to make her mind blank, to cling to the last vestiges of a virtuous wife, to remain chaste and placid while her husband did his will. But she was lost when he touched her as her body began to respond to his kisses. A warmth, a need she tried so hard to deny, flamed as he began to make love to her. His lips trailed down her body as she moved beneath his touch with pleasured groans. As he moved lower he anticipated her reaction, but he was determined to have none of it. He wanted her to know the full powers of love, its sweet promise.

His hand slipped between her thighs, separating them to his search. Gently he played, touching lightly in response to her body, which arched to his touch as she began to draw in quick, gasping breaths. He kissed the inner softness of her thighs as the pain in his groin increased, but he fought it back, determined in the importance of what he was about. He shifted, drawing her knees up, then placed his hand beneath her hips, drawing them up to him. The warmth of his mouth touched her, and she squirmed against him as she cried out.

She had been absorbed, her senses filled with total pleasure. Even the touch of his hands drew her deeper. But then, as she realized what he was about, she rebelled in horror. It had been so sweet—how could he . . . he was not actually going to . . . it was not natural! She cried out against him and pushed away as she struggled to free herself. "Nay, you must not! Oh, my God . . ." She tried to twist away but he held her firmly, his strength too much against her.

The steady touch of his tongue seared her with a fire that burst through her and began to drive all thought from her mind. As she felt the promise of intense, shattering pleasure begin to overtake her, she began to cry, wanting the pleasure he could give her, the tantalizing promise of what was building in her, the realization that what he was doing would surpass anything he had given her before. Cursing him, damning him, she clung to him, pulling him to her. Her body twisted beneath him and as feeling overtook reason, she cried out as she climaxed.

She felt alive, as if her body had returned to another time, before guilt ruled her emotions. She marveled at the sweeping tenderness she felt for him, now only wanting to give what she had found. She discovered him, touched him, relishing his soft sounds of pleasure, even while the recesses of her mind condemned and she knew she would feel the regrets later—much later. And she fought, and gave, taking until she was tossed again away from the world as they came together.

Awakening in the dim light of the chamber, Eleanor lay still for a moment and then flushed as she remembered the night past. Her body tingled with memory. She touched her lips, which were swollen from his kisses. Again and again they had . . . and once, awakening in the night, she had reached for him. . . . Oh, Lord, it had been so wonderful. How could it be wrong? And she knew what it was to be Eve. The Temptress. She stifled a groan and drew up her knees in a gesture of remorse. Oh, was she ever to awaken thus, the whole of her life from each slumber, filled with regret and guilt? She turned her head slowly and was surprised to find the bed empty. Had she imagined it? Pagan dreams sent to torment her very soul? But she could smell the spicy aroma of the scent he wore, and in the dim light from the openings in the curtains she saw the indent from where his head had lain. Nay, 'twas no dream. It was there to be borne, now and for all the days of her life, for she knew, in the deepest part of her, that it would ever be so. Her weakness, that given from her father and the mother who had fled to her lover barely upon the cold grave of her wedded lord and king, that she was wanton.

She pulled herself up, feeling almost physical pain, and

stared into the blackness of the shrouded bed. Unable to bear her own company, she flung herself from the bed, pushing back the curtain to stand in the light and the crisp morning air of the chamber. Drawing a deep breath, she steadied herself. Then, opening her eyes, she stared into Will's interested gaze as his blue eyes passed over her naked body.

"Good morning." He grinned broadly. He stood by the window, a robe laid about his shoulders.

"Ohhh!" she cried, flinging herself back between the bed-covers. The curtains were thrust apart and he stood with the morning light at his back, a shadow staring down at her, but she could feel him laughing, could hear it in his voice when he finally spoke. "Eleanor, would you hide from me? Could there be something I have not seen? I do not reason so, but your actions do give me pause."

"Oh! You are vile!"

He laughed at her protest as she sought to hide beneath the covers. He threw aside his robe and, lifting the covers, he slid beneath and pulled her to him. "Come here," he teased. "Let me see what you seek to hide from me. You have roused my curiosity."

"Let me go!" She struggled against him but he proved stronger as he pushed the covers aside and held her squirming body still. A hand moved gently over her and she twisted to look at him, cringing at the way he was looking at her as his eyes traveled boldly over her in the open light of morning.

"Oh, you are truly evil!" she choked.

"Oh, Eleanor, if this be evil, then truly I be damned." His easy laughter defied his words as she renewed her struggle. "Sweetheart, hold still." His hands held her and she closed her eyes against him. "Lord, Eleanor, do you not know how beautiful you are?" he said softly. " 'Tis God's gift to see you in the sunlight." His eyes traveled slowly over her, drinking of the rosy softness of her skin, the full breasts with sweet tips of a darker hue, the tapering waist, the slender hips, the long legs crowned by the soft curls that held the sweetness of her inner being that drew his touch, his fingers and lips. Oh, Lord, could she not know how her body affected him? "Eleanor, open your eyes."

He looked into the blue depths, wincing at the fear and condemnation he read there, but pushed it aside. His hand began to stroke her lightly as his gaze held hers. "My love, do you not know how beautiful you are to me?"

"It is wrong," she whispered.

"What is wrong, for us to love each other?"

"Nay, for us to enjoy . . . Will, the pleasures of the body must be denied. We must struggle against these forces. My body is given to you to bring forth children, but it is wrong for us to . . . to pleasure in . . . the act itself."

He pulled back from her and stared at her for a protracted moment. "You truly believe that, don't you?"

"Of course! We are taught—"

"I do not need further lectures, Eleanor," he snapped, now furious as he rolled away from her. He stared sightlessly above him as he digested her words, their meaning twisting painfully inside of him. Lord, what had happened to her? He had left a child in his unwillingness to use her body, yet one filled with enthusiasm and an eagerness for life and all of its discoveries. He returned to a woman, one of exquisite beauty of form and face, a woman beyond his expectations, yet filled with fear, denying the depth of her passion—and it was sweet—consumed by values which only could keep them from the discovery and fulfillment their marriage could offer. He drew a slow, deep breath as he thought of the emptiness that faced them. What could he have done differently? What could he do now? He would not accept it, for either of them! Yet what choice did he have?

15

FOG hung in a heavy grey blanket about the docks of Portsmouth, shrouding the movement of men among the endless rows of bundles to be loaded aboard the ships that stood silently moving on the gentle swells in the harbor. Will stood among the small group of knights who had accompanied him, half listening to the low murmur of their broken conversation as he awaited the arrival of the one he had come to meet. His eyes moved slowly over the activity on the docks when his attention was drawn to the sound of footsteps on the gangway leading from the ship nearest them. A man of medium height, heavily cloaked against the October morning, approached them, the hood of his mantle allowing Will only a slight glimpse of his face.

Will grasped the man's wrist in greeting. "My lord Peter, Count of Brittany," he said in greeting as he introduced himself. "The King is waiting. Nay, we can walk the distance," he added, noting that the man glanced about with question. "His Grace chose to be lodged nearby; 'tis his pleasure to personally supervise the loading of the ships." They turned down the wide street leading to the inn where the King was lodged, walking in silence but for the sound of their footsteps against the cobbled street. It was Will who broke the impasse, his voice firm with a determination to know the manner of the man who accompanied him. "Peter of Dreux, before you give your oath to Henry, I would know, can you truly deliver what you have promised?"

"This matter has been settled, Lord Marshal," the man answered firmly, though there was a tinge of irritation in his voice at being questioned on the subject. "It was assured past Christmastide, a delegation sent to assure His Majesty that all would meet him well upon his arrival on the Continent."

"I know that the delegation was led by the Archbishop of Bordeaux—a man for France—and would meet with Henry only in the privacy of his chamber to discuss these matters. I would be more comforted had English peers been present."

"His Grace has been assured of what we present," the Count of Brittany answered with an edge to his voice.

"As Marshal of England I warn you that I cannot advise my King as matters now stand," Will countered firmly. "I am convinced that to lead an English army into France at this time would be the worst sort of folly and would lead to certain disaster."

"The barons of Normandy and Poitevin await him as their liege lord, Earl Marshal, and I am here to give our oath of fealty in confirmation of that fact. Do you tell me now that my oath will not be received by His Majesty?"

They fell to silence, as Will could not give this man the answer he most desired to give him, that which would return him to the Continent without the aid and support of English armies. His mind turned thoughtfully, painfully, as it had countless times since, to those moments when he arrived, with those who had accompanied him from Striguil, at Cardiff where the King awaited.

In the early hours of evening, as the sun had turned to a red-gold blanket of dusk, Henry had come to the steps of the manor to greet him. After taking a moment to welcome his sister with brotherly affection, he dismissed her with her ladies in an eagerness to have news of Will and to give of his own. Will had assured him that the matter with Llewelyn was at hand, giving him a brief accounting of his recent encounter with the Welsh raiders, which Henry met with proper abhor-

rence, then enthusiasm. But he assured Henry, in truth, that
the remaining resistance consisted only of a ragtag lot, soon to
be set down before the power of England. Will did not add, as
had been the wise policy of his forebears in dealing with
England's monarchs, that Striguil would handle its own, dealing with the Welsh with diplomacy over the sword. It had
worked for over a hundred years, and he would not be the one
to defy such success. Indeed, he had learned the lesson well at
the knees of his father, and before him his grandfather,
Richard deClare.

While Henry had listened, it soon became apparent that the
young King's reason for calling Will to Cardiff was of another
matter. Will had never seen Henry so animated. And then he
had learned of the deputation's visit from France. They had
come first while Will was in Normandy, and it was only
recently that firm plans had been made. Will had listened in
silence, a feeling of dread creeping over him even as he
wondered how he could possibly make Henry see reason in the
face of his enthusiasm. It rankled him, yet stirred a feeling of
pity, that this should be the first time he could see a true sign
of kingship in the young Plantagenet. Over a lost cause.
Perhaps it would serve, Will had thought at the time, the
catalyst to form Henry into what he could become, to awaken
him from his apathy toward England and her needs. She
would benefit, in time, if the war were not too costly. Aye,
perhaps his dreams, to restore all that his father had lost,
would make him into the man, the King, he could become. But
even as he thought it, reason defied it. He would have heard
from his brother Richard if the provinces on the Continent
cried for Henry. To the contrary, Richard's missives did not
fix with what Henry was saying. But Henry was firm, moreover driven by a dream given form by those who had convinced him of the rightness of his purpose. Will could only
pray that those dreams would not be crushed, without re-
course for England and her people.

Those thoughts stayed with him as he watched Peter, the
Count of Brittany, kneel before Henry in the common room
of the inn in Portsmouth where they had taken quarters, and
offer his oath of fealty for himself and those of France who
awaited the might of England. The youthful King took the

shorter man's hands in his, offering the kiss of acceptance, and it was done.

"It is not well given this day," Hugh Bigod muttered for Will's hearing as they stood watching the ceremony.

"Would you step forward and so say?" Will asked quietly, watching.

"If you will not?" Hugh snorted. "I am not such the fool, my brother. If Henry will not listen to your advice, he will listen to no other. It appears that we go to Normandy. William deFerrars is here, as is deBraose," he added. "It would seem that your sisters' husbands would support you in this. All but deClare. He would be here but that he is not fit. Isabella sent a letter to Matilda, the day of my departure, that he has been taken by a pain in his chest that will not allow him from bed. He will join us when he is able and sends his prayers to the success to our mission."

"Would that there would be no need," Will muttered under his breath. "I had hoped that when Henry saw how few had come to sail with him, he would realize the folly of another war. The people lack heart for another campaign with the French."

"All have advised him that it is so; he will not listen. DeBurgh has pleaded with him to let be; I have been present when the justiciar has sought to make him see reason. He will have none of it."

"Particularly from that source," Will confirmed, glancing at the broad-shouldered man who stood near the King. DeBurgh looked weary, he thought, and older than he should, a far cry from the powerful and energetic man he once knew. Little wonder Henry ever used him as an excuse for his own restlessness and inadequacies, and more the pity. Henry could have no man at his side who cared more for England. "With Walter abed, it seems that the women will see to the demesnes," he said suddenly with a smile, needing to change the subject. "Think you they can manage in our absence?"

"You jest!" Hugh snorted. "I think they feel that they are well rid of our interference in what they hold dear. And since we are speaking of it, there is a matter I have meant to discuss with you. Will, there are scant women I respect more than your lady mother, but she does try a man! What she does not interject by her person she leaves to her daughters. She as much told me to see to my war and leave my lands to Matilda's care where they would be better seen to." Will's sudden laughter fed Hugh's purpose. "Your mother has seen to us all," he added sulkily. "I was the last to be honored by her visit."

He chuckled at Hugh's pained expression. "Be advised, Hugh, my lady mother's estates made her the wealthiest woman in England after the death of Eleanor of Aquitaine, our Queen. She ruled those lands, allowing my father to govern England, while providing him the funds to save England from bankruptcy. You might do well to take her counsel."

Hugh only grunted. "Speaking of Eleanors, I do not see yours," Hugh observed, scanning the gathering. "Is she with you?"

"Now you jest. She would not be left behind. She is with her ladies but will join us for midmeal."

"Would not be left behind?" Hugh grinned. "Can it be that England's Marshal cannot manage his fragile bride?"

"As well as you can handle your own," Will countered with a smirk. "She is not aware of it as yet, but there is a reason I brought her with me, beyond that of the pleasure of her company. I am going to ask Matilda to take her with her to Framlingham when we depart. I am not inclined for her to remain at court in my absence."

Hugh glanced at Will with surprise. "I assure you that Matilda will be pleased to have her company, but should not the lady remain at her own demesne in your absence?"

"Aye." Will sighed heavily. "But in honesty I do not think she would do so. I fear that the court would prove too great a pull."

"Could not your lady mother say nay to her? I do not notice that the Countess Isabel cringes from what she feels to be her duty."

"I would not do that to either of them," Will countered. "Nay, I feel it better that Eleanor be treated as an honored guest in your home than to find herself in a subordinate position to her husband's mother. By the blood, Hugh, 'tis a problem which plagues me. Can you see my mother quietly retiring to a convent, as others do in the face of their son's brides? And I would not have that for her if she would, yet the alternative is to become a buffer between two strong-willed women, each seeing life from her own, diverse beliefs. God help me, I think I am yearning for a war with France after all.''

They fell to silence, each thinking thoughts they would not voice. To Hugh it came that Isabel was garnering years and her death would eventually provide the answer, but he would not say so, out of kindness to his friend and brother. The conversation had brought Will's thoughts to Eleanor and that which he continually tried to keep from his mind.

Steadfastly she clung to her beliefs, her mind closed to reason and her emotions held from him. In the moments that they shared in companionship, at times they almost seemed close, at least normal, giving him hope—until he touched her. Even a look cast in her direction as his thoughts turned to moments of love with her, would bring over her eyes the walled gaze he was becoming so accustomed to seeing. She had made good her promise: she never refused him, and plying her patiently, gently, he could bring her to passion. But ever would she cry out, damning him, even in those moments he knew she found fulfillment. The more he tried to give her satisfaction, the more she withdrew from him. Damn, there were moments when he was tempted to take his pleasure and leave her to her pious emptiness. And then there was the quiet. The accusations and guilt he read in her expression, until he could bear no more of it and found himself keeping from her bed.

Perhaps if he could only come to truly love her. Not just the abiding affection he felt for her, the tender regard in which he held her. But he could not, those dreams had long ago been taken by another. . . .

''Ahh, now I see the reason you would not have her at court,'' Hugh murmured, drawing Will's attention from his thoughts.

His jaw tightened as he followed Hugh's gaze. Eleanor had entered a doorway across the room in the company of her friends, particularly with one on whose arm her own lay with a relaxed intimacy he had not enjoyed. Even across the span of the large common room of the inn he could see the raptured expression she wore and hear the easy lilting laughter of her voice as she pleasured in some comment made.

"Nay, Hugh, I do not worry about that source."

"Oh?" Hugh looked at him with puzzlement. "If she were my wife and were carrying on so with that poor excuse of—"

"She is not your wife, nor would you ever find Matilda behaving thus, and for *that* you may thank the Countess Isabel. Would that Eleanor had been so reared, with the pragmatism of a strong woman instead of the admonitions of the priests. As for my lack of concern, I know what you are thinking, but I assure you that I am not oblivious to Alan of Newbury's intent, though Eleanor is blind to it. Henry has taken up my suggestion that Newbury test his spurs on French soil."

"Ha!" Hugh laughed appreciatively as he glanced across the room. "Forgive me for ever doubting you, Will. Does she know yet?"

"Nay." Will smiled, watching the pair. "Nor does he." He watched Eleanor's hand pause before it was withdrawn from the young knight's arm as she turned to leave the room again in the company of her ladies. He drew in his breath slowly as he fought against a sigh. There would be no better time to tell her that she was for Framlingham with Matilda, he thought. He had already put it off too long. He started for the door when he heard Henry bellow in rage.

"Old traitor! By all that is holy, I shall have your blood!"

Will began to move even before he could reason what was happening. He reached Henry as the King lunged at deBurgh, and before his drawn sword could fall on the stunned justiciar Will had pinned Henry's arms. Hugh, who had moved as swiftly, wrenched the sword from the King's hand even as Ranulf deBlundeville, the Earl of Chester, threw himself between Henry and deBurgh.

"Let me be!" Henry roared. "By the Blood, Will, I will have him!"

"Your Grace, deBurgh cannot be to blame!" deBlundeville pleaded for reason. "Would not I, who have more to gain than any other should my lands in Normandy be regained, seek to know who has done this! But it is not Hubert, I would swear to it!''

Even in his fury, Henry's expression began to touch with doubt at the Earl of Chester's reasoning. Will felt him relax under his grip and he eased his hold, but warily. "God's breath, Henry, what has happened?" Henry pulled his arm free and continued to glower at the justiciar. "A portion of the coffers sent to finance the campaign are found to contain naught but sand and stone," he snapped. "Am I to believe that you had nothing to do with this, deBurgh? You have resisted this campaign from the start!"

"Sire, I do not deny that I feel this campaign to be ill-advised, but I swear to you that I had nothing to do with the theft," deBurgh said as color began to return to his face.

"Your Grace, there are many, I among them, who have advised you not to go to France," Will said quickly. "Hubert's voice has been no louder than mine."

DeBlundeville nodded in agreement. "Our justiciar is responsible for the coffers, milord. Would he be so foolish to tamper with that under his care?"

"We will find the one responsible," Hugh added. "Moreover, additional funds will be found. It will not delay us long."

Henry looked from one to the other, the deep blue of his eyes taking on a determined gleam as they turned on deBurgh. "Have I your pledge to now support this venture, with your whole heart? Say it, or I do swear that I will not let the matter rest!"

The nobles exchanged uncomfortable glances, knowing that the justiciar's support would be given to a cause they knew to be doomed from the start. In Chester's eyes Will saw the hope to regain what had been lost to him, in spite of the insurmountable odds which faced them. In deBurgh's eyes there was frustration and hopelessness as he faced, perhaps for the first time, the danger threatening him in opposing Henry's wishes.

"You have my pledge, milord," deBurgh said quietly.

The King seemed instantly mollified by the response, almost too easily, to Will's thinking. He sensed that Henry had won his objective. The atmosphere of the room eased as the nobles drew apart, the outburst quickly forgotten. Will exchanged a speculative glance with Hugh, wanting to know more about what had just happened, while knowing that nothing more could be done until Henry was calm. With nothing else for it, his thoughts turned to his earlier concern. But as he would have turned from the room to seek out Eleanor, the bell was sounded for midmeal. Softly, he swore to himself, even with a feeling of relief that the encounter would again be put off.

Taking his place near Henry, he glanced at the empty chair next to him and looked up at Hugh just beyond, noting his friend's quizzical glance. Where was Eleanor? He saw Matilda's puzzlement where she sat on her husband's right, and he looked away quickly, unable to bear the penetrating question from his sister. His gaze shifted, almost with reluctance, to scan those of the king's company until it came to rest upon Newbury. He almost sighed with relief to find the knight within their company. And then another realization struck him and he almost laughed out loud. The knight had not been placed beneath the saltcellars, but his position at a trestle table was dangerously close. Will glanced at Henry, who was busily engaged in conversation, and he grinned, noting the King's fine hand in Newbury's position at the table. Newbury came from an illustrious house, his position at court dictating his person to be placed much closer to the body of the King. Who else would have dared the insult? The disgruntled expression on the Earl of Newbury's face only served to add to Will's merriment, though he successfully struggled to conceal his feelings.

His humor rapidly vanished as he fixed, as did all in the room, on those who appeared in a far doorway. His thoughts passed through a gamut of emotions: puzzlement, shock, and horror. Eleanor had stepped from the shadows of the doorway, flanked by her ladies. She was draped in a soft gown of crimson silk, girdled about her breasts and waist with twisted cords of gold. Her long, hip-length hair was loose as a maiden's, intertwined with winter roses of brilliant red. Her attendants were similarly clothed in white, their eyes downcast, but the eyes of those in the room were firmly fixed on Eleanor and the burden she carried as surprised murmurs spread about the room. In her hands she bore a mazer bearing a peacock in full plumage.

"By the Blood," the Earl of Chester was heard to exclaim. " 'Tis the vow of the peacock! It has not been done for a hundred years—perhaps even to Arthur's time!"

Indeed, she stood as a priestess, bearing the noble peacock to claim the vow of the knights pledged to duty in service to their King. Will remained transfixed, oblivious to the conversation about the room as he wondered what Eleanor was about. She did nothing without a reason—and the obvious one seldom was where her mind was fixed. Slowly, with her maids following, she passed about the rows of tables, ignoring the knights who leaned forward expectantly when they thought she would stop before them. Each man's thought was the same, that the peacock would be placed before him as the bravest, the most noble knight. Thus honored, he would lay his hand upon the bird before the image of the priestess and give his vow, declaring his courage in the face of the battle to come, even unto death before dishonor. In fact, if memory served him, the dubious honor of the peacock had often led to the death of that particular knight. Fools, Will thought. Or bad luck. Will watched as she approached Newbury and he frowned with a moment's doubt when she paused, only to pass him by. She continued to move beyond, passing the tables in another round, tantalizing each, until she came to stop before him.

Will stared at the plumaged bird that was placed on the table in front of him; then his gaze rose to meet Eleanor's. Her expression was unreadable but for a hint of expectancy. His surprise dissolved in a surge of anger even as he heard the room erupt in boisterous excitement. Eleanor, he thought, attempting to control his rage even as it contested with a deep sorrow, do you truly hate me so much? Holding her gaze, he reached out and placed his hand on the full back of the brightly plumed bird. Evenly, with conviction, his voice reached to the corners of the room.

"I pledge, by this vow, to be first to the wall, to be first to vanquish the enemies of my liege lord, Henry, and that of England." He paused, his eyes holding Eleanor's. "Even unto my own death."

He ignored the flicker of her eyes as they widened upon his last words. He smiled, and his voice rose to the company. "I call upon all those here to attend me. Let no man's voice be stilled by cowardice in the face of England's enemies. Each in turn shall go forth, placing his hand upon the peacock in pledge—the first to be Alan, Earl of Newbury." He saw the glimmer of doubt, then the horror that passed over her eyes, and fixed upon it. Smiling, he sat back, his gaze locked with hers, daring her to complete the vow.

PART THREE

. . . And Wise Men Shall Come

16

1231
In the Fifteenth Year of Our Reign
Henry III, Plantagenet

ELEANOR stared at the high monastery walls. It was a moment before she realized that Father Latius was speaking to her, and she nodded with a sigh that brought a scowl from the priest. She followed him into the atrium of the chapel attached to the monastery's outer wall. They were met inside the dark chamber by a nun, who nodded to Eleanor, then led her to the loft where she would observe the mass behind the heavy latticework which separated the nuns who lived in an adjoining convent from the brothers of the order who lived in the monastery.

She took her place among the silent sisters, and her eyes fixed vacantly on the sanctuary below. She barely heard the words of the mass and twice struggled to stifle a yawn in the oppressive stuffiness of the crowded loft. What was the matter with her? she wondered. She should be feeling joy. Father Latius had assured her that her redemption would be found by such a selfless act. She was providing the funds to build a new wing on the ancient monastery, a new library with tall, glazed windows where the brothers would be better able to continue their work of transcribing the scriptures. But she found herself facing the coming day with the same lack of enthusiasm that she had been feeling lately for everything in her life.

She could not have attempted to explain her mood, or even when it had begun. She only knew that nothing seemed quite as important as it once had. She found herself moving through her days automatically. Her friends did not seem to be quite as interesting or amusing, though she could not have said that they had changed.

As she sat there her mind drifted and she gave in to it, accustomed of late to having it so. One moment seemed to press, her guilts driving her to remember it again and again, the peace she had been promised by Father Latius held from her as she relived the moment. Haunted, she could not forget the look in Will's eyes as she had set the peacock before him. Oh, Lord, what had possessed her to do such a thing? It had begun innocently enough, an amusement, nothing more. It was not until his gaze had locked with hers that she realized the enormity of what she had done, what the gesture had meant to him. Horrified, she could only stare at him, seeing the anger and hatred in his eyes as he repeated his vows. She had tried to find him later to explain, but he had left the tavern immediately after midmeal and she had not seen him again before he had sailed. Not a word had passed between them—he had simply left her.

Again and again she had tried to write to him, explaining. Then, remembering the hatred in his eyes, she had torn up the pages, knowing that he would never believe her—and why should he? She was not certain of her own intentions. Oh, Lord, had she truly wished, even for a moment, for his death?

Tearfully, she had confessed to Father Latius, eagerly grasping to the heavy penitences he gave her as well as the endless lectures that followed, instructing her in the manner of a dutiful, obedient wife. She clung to his words, struggling to feel them in her heart. But she felt nothing, only a hollow emptiness that would not allow forgiveness. No passion, no joy, no interest in anyone or anything about her, and most especially, in the future.

Vaguely she became aware that the sisters were standing, waiting silently, staring at her. Flushing, she realized that the mass had ended. Rising quickly, she crossed herself and turned to leave the loft. Father Latius was waiting for her at the bottom of the stairs, and he took her arm to lead her into the chapel as the brothers filed out.

"You must realize that this is a singular honor, milady," he said quietly, his usual firm tone implying disapproval. "A woman has never been within these walls before, even in the transcribing room. Of course the room will be reblessed following your visit."

"To rid it of contamination?" She responded quickly, immediately shocked that she had spoken so to the priest.

Latius apparently did not note the sarcasm in her voice. "It is so, milady. Frankly, I am amazed that your request to make your bequest personally was granted."

As they entered the large room, Eleanor's curiosity was pricked in spite of her mood. Robe-clad monks sat working on high stools at large tables, each covered with stacks of books, piles of prepared parchment, and tools of quills and various inks. But what caught her attention most was how gloomy the room was. Small, high windows afforded the only light, and the room was bitterly cold. Lud, Eleanor thought, how could they work in such conditions? Her bequest was certainly needed, she reasoned. A large, airy room was called for, plenty of light from tall glazed windows, a decent fireplace— one made of stone that would not explode. Suddenly, compulsively, she giggled, remembering Henry's plasterwork.

Latius' head jerked about at the sound, and he glared at Eleanor. Biting her lower lip, she attempted to look contrite as she lowered her gaze to stare at her slippers, which peeked beneath the rust velvet of her gown. As the folds of her coif fell to cover her face, she hoped that he would not see the smile that lingered.

The brother superior came forward to greet them, his face drawn into a pleasant smile as he greeted Eleanor with a pleasure he did not attempt to conceal. "My lady, Countess of Pembroke, greetings. We are most honored to have you visit us."

Well, apparently *he* was not going to treat this as a visit from the devil, she thought with amusement, glancing at Latius with a smile. Seeing the angry disapproval on the priest's face, she again dropped her gaze, confused by her mood. What had gotten into her? Of course the man would

not treat her with disdain. She was about to give him what
amounted to a small fortune.

As the brother superior drew the priest's attention away
from her, Eleanor almost sighed with relief and stepped away
from them. Momentarily forgotten, she began to walk around
the room, trying not to disturb the monks who sat bent over
their desks working. She came up behind one of them and
watched the round-shouldered figure as he worked, deeply absorbed in his task. He was different from the others, his robe a
soft muted grey instead of deep brown. She recognized by the
shaved top of the man's head that he was of the order of Saint
Francis, and she wondered why he was here in the monastery.
Even as he sat on the tall stool she could tell that he was short
of stature. He was heavier than most Franciscans she had
seen, their vows of poverty tending to reduce them to thinness.
The small, plump hands holding the quill defied their ability to
work with any sort of ease, and her interest was caught.
However, as she stepped nearer and looked over his bent
shoulders, she gasped softly. The chubby hands were deceiv-
ing. The work she saw as the quill moved over the margins of
the page was breathtaking. Colors exploded, forms took life
beneath his hands, seeming to breath.

Compelled, Eleanor stepped nearer. She picked up a book
from the edge of the table, hesitating only for a moment when
the Franciscan looked up. To her astonishment he smiled, a
warm smile that reached to the soft brown depths of his eyes.
He did not seem in the least surprised to find her there, and
with only a moment's hesitation he bent his round face to his
work and seemed to forget that he had been interrupted.

Shaken, she watched him for a moment, then remembered
the book in her hand. Opening it, she feasted her eyes on the
beauty of the margins, the scenes depicting the text within.
Her interest caught, her eyes shifted to the words written, and
without realizing it she began to read.

Lost in words that drew her into the pages, not understanding yet drawn to meanings that were strangely compelling, she
cried out as the book was suddenly wrenched from her hand.
Looking up, she stared into the controlled fury of Father
Latius' face. "You have overstepped yourself!"

"There is no harm done," the brother superior protested

lightly from where he stood beside the priest. "As our benefactress—"

"A woman cannot possibly understand the word of God without guidance," the priest reprimanded. "Moreover, in her uncleansed state her hands must not be allowed to touch holy work." He had raised the open book to emphasize his meaning and laid his hand on the pages with a reverence. "Herein lies the word . . ." He stopped speaking and stared at the book, his face draining to a deathly white as his eyes scanned the page. His body seemed to jerk with a spasm and his head twisted to the Franciscan and then to the brother superior with horrified disbelief. Suddenly his face rushed with blood and his voice raised to a roar of exploding rage. "In the name of God, what is this!"

Eleanor stumbled back in alarm. The priest raved, screaming something about blasphemy and perdition. Wildly he began to grab up the books off of the Franciscan's table, piling them in his arms. She cringed, even as she wanted to do something for the cowering friar as the priest continued to rail at him. Vaguely she recalled the priest demanding the Franciscan's name, and then she was aware of being propelled from the room and into the blinding sunlight.

As they rode back to Windsor, Eleanor's shock began to dull. Her mind repeated the astounding events and her gaze shifted to the saddlebags in which the confiscated books lay behind the priest, and she shook her head in wonder. Why had he been so angry? What was written there to cause such rage in the Poitevin? While it had stirred something elusive in her, she had not understood what she had read. The memory of the timid Franciscan brought her a deep pang of regret. What could the little friar have been transcribing that was so dangerous? Another memory entered, one of years before, and its similarity to the astounding day's events shook her reason. Always stern and opinionated, the priest had only once before shown such rage before her—when he had entered the morning chamber to discover the tapestry of the unicorn. He had decried, then destroyed the precious work and what it represented. Yet a few years later he embraced the concept with as much fervor as he had first condemned it. She stole a glance at the priest and her brow furrowed with doubt. Suddenly, for the first time, she saw him in a different light. Pompous, overbearing. A priest? Aye, but a totally insufferable man, one who used his powers to terrify and control.

Then an earlier outrage returned, one stifled in the moment of the priest's outburst, and she glanced at the priest with a look of contempt. Overstepped her bounds, had she? Uncleansed hands without the right to touch a holy work? What has happened to the purity of women, priest? she mused. Those teachings which you embraced with such fervor?

Eleanor's escort rode silently as their glances swayed between Eleanor and Father Latius. Their puzzled glances were not just for the priest's unexplained anger but more for the look that had come upon their lady. They quickly deferred to one among their company, an aging knight who had served under three kings of England. It was his look of warning that had caused his companions-in-arms to fix their eyes upon the road and withhold their comments. His eyes were watching his lady guardedly. He had seen that look before, and years of experience had taught him well not to confront a Plantagenet's rage.

The dim, flickering light of oil lamps played off the canvas of the tent, casting the spare furniture and those within into its deepening shadows. Will ignored the deep, throaty chuckles of the men and the lighter voices of the women of his company as he endeavored to listen to the stern admonitions of the priest who sat across from him at the camp table. Fr. Maslin had been with them throughout the campaign, his voice heard above the tumult of battle, in victory and defeat. The cleric seemed unaware of what was going on about him, his mind ever on his purpose. Even now he had sought him out, apparently oblivious of Will's company as he fired with his reasons for being there.

"Must I remind you that the treasury of England was depleted for this venture?" the cleric pressed, leaning across the table. "Can you so soon forget the sight of your king when he arrived at Saint Malo, bedecked in his armor and mantle of white silk—or the armada of over two hundred vessels that sailed in the name of this noble cause?''

"I remember that the French cooled at the sight of the hated foreigner upon her soil,'' Will drawled, his attention drawn to the burst of laughter nearby. "Those pledged to Henry ran back to Louis with their tails between their legs. We entered Bordeaux, with all of the glory of England, and they paid Henry the supreme insult of ignoring him. A rather anticlimactic entrance, I would say.''

"The King . . . was needed in England,'' the cleric offered uncomfortably, knowing that Henry's departure would be mentioned next.

"The King developed dysentery,'' Will scoffed, raising his brow as he regarded the priest. "He returned home because he had lost heart. And yet he bade me remain to hold what we could in the face of what the people of England have spent on this venture. The time is done.''

"If the venture is lost it is because there is no support for the cause!'' the priest insisted. "Those with you spend their time in drink and wenching instead of pressing their might against France!'' The man glanced about the tent as his expression filled with disapproval.

"My men are in desperate need of release, as each, to a man, has given all he can to aid Henry's cause,'' Will said with an impatient edge to his voice. As he struggled to keep his temper, his thoughts flashed to the doxy he had reluctantly sent away at the untimely appearance of the cleric. He glanced at his brothers-in-law, each heavily into drink and in pursuit of feminine attention, as were his squires, and he felt himself giving into anger. "Dammit, man, we have been here for most of a year, left with little but the order to take France! And with what? A half-hearted force who never believed in the cause, against a people who shift and disappear, ignoring our very existence! We have done well against those odds, gaining more than I would ever have expected to, but it is time to cease and let be! We are going home, have no doubt of it!''

Fr. Maslin opened his mouth to speak but clamped it shut as a yeoman entered the tent and sought out Will in the dim light. "Milord, a message from England.'' The youthful soldier handed Will the parchment, and Will could not help but to smile at his earnest and intent manner. "My thanks,'' he of-

fered to the young man. "There is food and beverage there."
He gestured to a table cornered in the tent. "See to your
needs."

Will opened the missive, his eyes moving to the signature,
and he smiled with pleasure to note Darcy's name. Unaware of
the deep sigh of the departing cleric, he bent the letter to the
flickering light of the candle on the war table and began to
devour each word, suddenly aware of his hunger of news from
home. It had been four months since Darcy had pleaded to
return home, and he dearly missed the bard's easy manner and
pragmatism.

Hugh Bigod opened his mouth to receive another sweetmeat
from the fingers of the doxy on his lap. His proximity to Will,
and the fact that he was for the moment less involved than the
others, allowed him to react first to the sound of anguish that
emitted from his friend. His head jerked about to Will's direction. Seeing Will's stricken expression, he pushed the woman
away, spilling the full-breasted wench from his lap as he
snapped orders to the others. In a protest of confusion the tent
was cleared in a rash of feminine oaths. "Will, what is it?"
Hugh asked anxiously as he noted that all of the blood seemed
to have drained out of Will's face as he stared at the parchment in his hand.

At the sound of Hugh's voice Will looked up and glanced
vacantly about the tent. He looked back to Hugh and swallowed, shaking his head as if he could not speak. Hugh turned
to the silent men and gestured for them to leave, then turned
back to Will, who was staring silently at the missive, which
had fallen to the table in front of him.

Now alone, Hugh took the vacant chair across from Will
and waited in the heavy silence. Finally, he reached across
slowly and slid the parchment to him, turning it to the
candlelight. As he read his eyes widened with surprise and then
his brows furrowed with doubt. When he finished, he pushed
the letter back and slumped in his chair. "My God, Will, I
can't believe it," he said softly. "It can't be true!"

"He knew all along," Will murmured thickly. "I thought it
was for Henry that he came, but it was for me."

"Will, what are you talking about?" Hugh pressed, leaning
across the table. "Dammit, tell me what is going on!"

"You remember how we came to meet Darcy." Will smiled vacantly, leaning back in his chair. "At the time I felt it to be more than mere coincidence, but I could not give reason to it. I even noted that his accent was of Northumbria." He laughed shortly. "Though, at the time, he would not confirm it. Now at last I understand."

"Will, this is insane!" Hugh pleaded. "All of these years —it is impossible!" He pulled the letter back across the table and stared at it angrily. "How can this child he speaks of possibly be Lavene's? We all know that the babe died with its mother in childbirth!"

"So I was told," Will said reflectively. "By those who knew I would claim the child for my own, had he lived."

"Will, be reasonable. How could Lavene's tirewoman secret a child out of the convent and across the length of England to Northumbria?" Hugh scoffed, tapping the parchment with his finger. "And why would his existence be kept from you all of these years? Will, it is a ruse, it must be! That damn goliard knows how you felt about Lavene and it is a trick to use you for some purpose of his own!"

"Perhaps." Will smiled grimly. "Or perhaps he speaks the truth."

"What are you going to do?"

"Do?" Will's brow arched with surprise at the question. "I am going to Northumbria, of course."

17

ELEANOR moved quickly along the dark, narrow path. She was heavily cloaked against the possibility of discovery as well as the drizzle that swirled about her, almost obscuring her escort, though he walked but a few paces away. Pausing at the wall, she gestured for him to remain with their mounts as she slipped through the narrow opening that would lead her to the small door set in the curtain wall of the castle. She made her way slowly up the dark staircase, knowing each step as she moved through the blackness, stopping as she reached the door at the top of the stairs. As she pushed against its weight, the door opened slowly and she stepped into the small room, feeling relief as she spied the candles that flickered in the dim light which they cast in uneven shadows about the chamber.

Her eyes fixed hungrily upon the books set on the table that centered the room. Throwing off her cloak, she pulled out a chair and drew a heavy book toward her. Opening the cover with reverence, she sighed, her eyes passing over the words, not wanting to waste a moment as she began to read.

The candles flickered, having lowered to stubs, when Eleanor looked up as the door leading to the hallway opened.

"I apologize for being late, milady." Eleanor smiled as the

plump little Franciscan entered. "A sick child . . ."

"Is he well?" Eleanor asked with concern.

"Aye, he will be fine. I suspect that the culprits were too many green apples behind cook's back."

She laughed softly as she regarded the little friar with affection. She had been right to bring him here to Odiham, the small castle southeast of Windsor that Henry had given to her for her own. And then she frowned as an unpleasant reality entered. "Brother Vincent . . ."

The friar paused as he lit new candles and looked up at the hesitation in Eleanor's voice. "Aye, milady, what is it?"

"I fear that this is the last time we shall meet for some time."

His bushy brows drew together with apprehension. "What has happened?"

"You know that Father Latius has never ceased looking for you—or for the books that so mysteriously disappeared from his room." Her eyes danced momentarily, meeting the twinkle in the Franciscan's eyes, and then they sobered. "I fear that he has begun to suspect me."

"You, milady?" The hazel eyes continued to dance. "The most chaste image of the suppliant, the supreme example of the good priest's teachings?"

"Well . . . for that—I fear that of late . . . that is, I find myself saying the most outrageous things. Thoughts just pop into my head and I find myself speaking without afore-thought."

"When first studying the great philosophers, one tends to do that." The monk chuckled.

"To the point of scandalizing the court," she added wryly. "Even Henry has begun to look at me strangely. But it is not him that I fear, but Latius. I think he knows. Therefore"—she sighed deeply, with a heavy regret—"you must leave here. It is no longer safe for you. I have arranged for you to become the household chaplain at Devizes. The castellan there despises Father Latius, a personal grievance of long standing that will serve us well. You will be safe there."

"I will miss the time that we have spent together," Brother Vincent said softly.

"As will I." She swallowed with a sudden rising anger. "If

only Henry was not so pliable to the pressures of others, to
Latius and . . ." She paused, blinking back her tears. "You
have given me . . . life, new purpose."

"Nay, Eleanor, not I." He smiled. "These." He tapped the
open book before her.

She looked down at the writings of Aristotle, and her mind
flashed with what she had just read, something about happiness being an activity of each human being. "Not without
you to explain them to me," she laughed. "Little did I know,
that day I brought you here and struck the bargain with
you—that you could stay at Odiham to transcribe your works
if you would teach me of what was written—that I would be
the one to benefit the most greatly."

"Well . . ." The little man coughed, embarrassed but
pleased by her compliment. "Well, then, if this is our last day
together for a time, we have much work to do. Shall we
begin?"

The next hour passed quickly, and all too soon the bell rang
for mass. Brother Vincent stopped speaking as the distant bell
was heard and he looked at Eleanor with hesitation. "You
must go," she urged, "but I shall stay a little longer this morning. Surely our last time together—there would be no harm."
The friar smiled and rose to leave, but Eleanor stopped him as
he opened the door. "My man . . . by the curtain-wall gate. He
will worry."

"I will tell him—we cannot have him storming the castle
looking for you, now, can we? If you are correct about our
friend the priest, he undoubtedly has someone within Odiham
watching for just such an occurrence. I shall return as quickly
as I can."

When he had left, Eleanor tried to resume her reading, but
her eyes would not settle on the page. She rose and began to
pace restlessly about the small chamber, pausing finally by the
tall window. Leaning against the casement, in the shadows
where she would not be seen from without, she stared beyond
to the horizon as the dawn began to turn the sky to a rosy pink
against a heavy bank of clouds that had begun to roll in. I
should leave, she thought. Soon there would be a storm. . . .

But she did not want to go. Everything that had begun to
give meaning to her life was in this room. It was here that she

had at last found peace—unqualified acceptance and companionship from the little Franciscan, who had opened her mind and challenged her. And then she recalled what the friar had told her one night in the first week she had begun to secrete herself at Odiham. They had been discussing Aristotle's concept of man and nature. She had been appalled by the implication that the soul was not merely trapped in the earthly body, which was an instrument of sin to be constantly rejected in the search for holiness, but rather that the soul was form and the body and all of nature were matter, two intrinsic parts; and that the body was beautiful, a work of God as part of the whole.

Suddenly, without knowing why, she had begun to cry, with deep, racking sobs that shook her entire body. She was helpless to stop them, feeling the weight of the world on her shoulders as memories flashed of a small child alone, touched with memories of Will. The friar's arms had gone about her, his gentle voice bringing her from her unexplained grief. "My child, what is troubling you so?"

"Oh, Brother Vincent, I am truly damned," she choked, pulling a kerchief frantically from her pocket to stop the flow of tears.

A lesser man would have been surprised by the statement, but the Franciscan had seen too much suffering to be surprised by anything. "You?" he said gently. "I think not. Surely there is nothing you have done that cannot be forgiven by the graciousness of Our Lord."

"Not . . . not even wanting my husband dead?" she whispered miserably, unable to look at the Franciscan's face and the horror that was certain to be there.

"Tell me about it."

Sniffing, she glanced up at the friar, surprised at the calm voice, with no hint of condemnation in it. Instead the soft hazel eyes invited her to share her grief. Biting her lip, she drew in her breath raggedly, and told him everything, beginning with the day that Will had returned to England, the words halting at first, then pouring out in a rush that she could not stop. "I have done everything Father Latius has told me to do. I have prayed and prayed, asking for forgiveness. . . ." Her voice trailed off, the confession leaving her drained.

"Yet, you feel alone, without comfort. Your teachings do not sustain you. You feel that even the Holy Mother has abandoned you."

She stared at him with amazement and felt a shudder pass over her. "Aye. How did you know?" she whispered.

"Child, when we doubt ourselves, we cannot put trust in another."

"But the saints, the Holy Mother . . ."

"Will they push truth into a mind that has blocked all reason?" he interrupted gently. "If you are fixed upon a purpose, you cease to listen. Only in listening will you find the answers to what you seek. Be easy, my lady, let be."

"But Father Latius said—"

"Listen to me." The Franciscan stopped, swallowing against the surge of anger that passed over him. Nay, he would not allow himself to lose control, not even over that one. She needed him; that was more important than what he felt for Latius and his kind. "All that you seek *is*, waiting." Oh, dear Lord, it was in such moments that he felt inadequate, and he pulled to the serenity of his books and quills. The wrong word spoken and he could lose this one. He prayed for guidance, knowing that her problems came from that accursed new code—and the teachings of the French priest coupled with her own feelings of loneliness and inadequacy. "The truth will be revealed to you, Eleanor. You must cease being afraid. Follow the inner voice that speaks to you, leading you to the truth."

"But does not Satan speak, demanding that his voice be heard?" she asked, pulling on her inner doubts.

"Can Satan's voice be louder than that of Our Lord's?" he asked. "Nay, it cannot be so. Listen and you will know the truth, I promise you. You will know. Follow it, even in doubt, for such is our plight. When our heart speaks, it is the Lord; Satan's work to be done through the doubt in our mind. Follow your heart, Eleanor."

"Even when my mind contests it?"

"Especially when your mind contests it."

Since that day she had found her mind opening, like a flower reaching to warmth, and she had been stunned by what she had found. Oh, her heart did lead her, allowing her to trust her reasoning, and she found herself listening to things she had never heard before, seeing where before she had been blind.

If only one did not awaken from the nightmare too late to recapture the dream. As she stared from the window her thoughts turned involuntarily to Will. What had she done to them? She had clung to the rigidity of her beliefs as the only constant in her life. The beliefs she had grasped had been the antithesis of the hopes and dreams of her childhood, those early dreams that had left her hurt and bitter and filled with hatred.

Oh, the mistakes. Had she also been wrong about Will? Could someone who cared for her leave her so cruelly without a good reason? And he did care, even if it had only been the deep abiding affection one has for a little sister.

Soon after he had left her that first time, already filled with the bitterness and hatred of abandonment, she had understood that he could never love her as she needed to be loved. She could not live at court without knowing of Lavene de-Fountaine. The gossip, the innuendos, the looks of pity. And she had further withdrawn, deeper behind the walls of piety and bitterness.

Now, her bitterness gone, she thought of the moments they had spent together. Her body stirred and she drew in her breath at the longing she felt, remembering. Each time he had taken her as she had once dreamed about, beautifully, with deep tenderness. That from a man who did not care about her? And she had twisted it, rejecting it, and him, damning him for offering it to her.

A sharp clap of thunder shook her from her reverie, and she looked out the window to find that the day had darkened ominously with the first drops of rain. The door opened as the room glowed suddenly from a flash of lightning, and she turned as another clap of thunder rolled across the hills.

"You must go now, milady, if you are to return to Windsor before the worst of this storm."

"Aye, I must not be found here," she agreed, crossing to where her cloak had been thrown on a chair by the table. As she pulled it about her shoulders, she realized that he was stacking the books. "Nay, Brother Vincent, those belong to you."

The Franciscan's face worked with emotion, and it was a few moments before he could speak. Then, taking up one small volume, he handed it to her, his hands closing over hers for a long moment. "This one you must take, Countess Marshal. Perhaps, if you approach it from your newfound confidence, it may hold a message for you."

Clutching the volume in her arms, she smiled at him and nodded, unable to speak. As she turned to go, the wind whipped violently through the door he had opened for her, catching the pages of the opened book on the table so that they began to flip wildly. Alarmed, she stepped quickly back to the table to close the precious manuscript and something caught her eye. The candles on the table had been snuffed out by the whirl of air from the door, and as he closed it against the gale he wondered why she hesitated. She crossed swiftly to the remaining taper on the far side of the room. Returning to the table, she set it near the opened book and she stared, not believing what she saw.

"Brother Vincent, what is this?" she asked with a tremor in her voice.

He stepped to her side, looking to where she was pointing. "A unicorn, of course." He glanced at her, wondering why she had grown pale.

"Why—why have you depicted a unicorn in a manuscript of the philosophers?"

"It is quite simple, Eleanor. For the great philosophers the unicorn represented the wisdom to see beyond the superficial, to what really exists. Moreover, to have the courage to accept it." He watched her as she stared transfixed at the beast and its proudly arched neck as it restlessly pawed the ground. His eyes narrowed for a moment as he studied her pensively. Then, silently, he took the small volume he had given her and sat down to the candlelight. Dipping his quill in the ink, he began to inscribe something inside the leather-covered wood of the book. Finishing, he handed it back to her. With a hand at her back he pushed her firmly toward the door. Pausing as he again opened the door, he watched her tuck the volume beneath her cloak. "You are ready now, Eleanor; no more hesitation, no more doubt. All that you are seeking is out there."

Her retainer was waiting at the gate, and he lifted her into the saddle quickly and took to his own mount. The anxiousness on his face was readily apparent, but she took another moment to look back one last time. She hesitated as she saw the Franciscan standing in the dimly lighted window of the tower room. A soft smile touched her lips and she turned, spurring her mount and they rode from Odiham. They did not stop until they rode into the vast courtyard of Windsor, just as the storm broke with its full fury. It was not until much later, finally released from the demands of Henry and the court, that she was able to extract the small volume from the cupboard where she had hidden it upon her return. Opening it, she found it to be a volume of *Tristan and Isolde*. Her brow creased with puzzlement, wondering why he would choose to give her an Arthurian legend. Then, looking inside the cover, she bit her lower lip as her eyes filled with tears. There he had sketched a unicorn and on its magnificent back sat a lady, held in the arms of her knight.

Will pulled sharply on Hamal's reins, causing the destrier to toss his head angrily. He looked over the gentle slope leading to the cluster of buildings which lay on the rise before him, to the manor spread along the rise to its crenellated parapets. His eyes paused as they passed over the gap-toothed tops of the towers, bringing a grim, satisfied smile. His sources had been correct. His eyes moved on to the circular keep and beyond to the outbuildings, which lay to form a lazy village of undefended structures. They have been isolated too long, he thought grimly. Undefendable, they would be easily taken—indeed, with a pitifully small force. These northern lords thought themselves beyond threat.

As he approached the keep, he was filled with disgust as no shout rang out from the gate tower to challenge his approach. Good Lord, he thought, what manner of man resided within? This was the place the woman had brought him to; Darcy's letter had been explicit. Saebroc, Lord Aldtern, was lord here, and what he had discovered had given Will an uneasy feeling.

Will's jaw tightened with anger as he rode beneath the raised portcullis and into the inner courtyard. Pulling Hamal to a halt in the empty courtyard, he frowned more deeply. No far-riers, indeed no one, appeared to assist him with his mount. The place seemed deserted, unkempt. Spying a standing post, he dismounted and tied the destrier's reins to the post. It would serve anyone right should they appear now, he mused. He would leave them to see to the animal and pleasure in it, though he did have a moment's concern for the horse. Then he laughed, realizing that Hamal would have the best of it.

Ascending the steps to the heavy doors of the keep, he balled a fist and pounded. No answer coming, he glanced frustrated about the courtyard and was just about to depart to search the grounds when he was brought back by the painful sound of the heavy door opening. A short, plump woman of middle age with greying hair stood in the doorway, frowning with displeasure. "Well? Wa' de ye be about? The master is gone away till the new week. There's na one here."

Will controlled his growing anger. "It is not your master I wish to see. I am looking for Giles, a boy of about ten years. Is he here?"

"Giles?" the woman repeated. Her wrinkled brow drew into a doubtful frown, and she peered at Will and the device on his surcoat from the shadows of the doorway. "Why ye be wantn' 'im?"

"That is my business, old woman," he answered, now feel-ing his irritation over being kept standing at the doorway by a servant. "Tell me where I can find him."

As he spoke, he threw back the hood of his cloak and the woman started. She drew back as he heard her breath suck in through her teeth. "Ye'll find 'im in the stables," she snapped just before Will found the door slammed in his face. Part of him pulled to beat down the door and confront the woman's rudeness, but reason prevailed and his thoughts turned to the realization that the child was actually here, somewhere.

He found the stables, a low, thatched structure built against a wall of the bailey behind the keep. The heavy odor of un-mucked stalls met his nostrils, and he covered his nose and mouth involuntarily as he coughed against the offense. A sud-den, raging surge of anger overtook him against his position and the overwhelming feeling of helplessness that consumed him. Did he actually expect to find the child here? "Giles of Fountaine!" he bellowed, oblivious to the horses who startled and pulled against their tethers.

A small form stepped from the shadows at the far end of the building. "Milord?" The young voice carried to Will, deeply touched by a heavy accent of Northumberland and the untutored, but strongly given and unwavering.

"By the Blood, child, come forth and let me see you," Will snapped impatiently.

"Has my master sent you, milord?" the childish voice came nearer in the shadows. "He said not; do you require a mount?"

"If you are the one I seek, you have no master but for God Almighty and the King of England," Will answered. "Come hence, child."

The slight form came into the light filtering from the open doorway, and Will's eyes narrowed speculatively as he repressed the impulse to wince in a moment's repulsion. The lad was utterly filthy. His clothes were rags; his face and even the color of his hair were indistinguishable for the soil and grime. The body was painfully thin beneath the scanty layerings that covered him, and Will had to clear his throat before he could speak. "Are you Giles of Fountaine?" he asked at last.

"I am Giles, milord. I know of no other name."

"Was your mother Lavene, daughter of the Count of Fountaine?"

"I know not of my mother," the small voice persisted.

Will frowned. Perhaps, after all, he had been misled. "No other name has been given you?" he demanded with frustration, irritated by the child's obtuseness.

"I have the only name I have been given." Dark eyes glared at him, touched with puzzlement as if doubting the sanity of the large knight. "I need no other."

Pausing, Will studied the child for a long moment. "Come with me," Will growled, turning to leave the offense of the ill-kept stable. Hearing no sound of movement, he paused at the doorway and turned back. Seeing that the child stood where he had left him, his manner softened for an instant, sensing the boy's resistance. "Come with me child," he said more gently. "I will not harm you."

With the child in tow Will entered the hall of the keep with a vengeance. Fed by the frustration he had felt since first laying his eyes upon the manor, he stood at the center of the hall, his rage bringing servants who seemed to appear miraculously from the shadows. Orders were dispatched and seen to with haste and confusion, and Will waited with a deep feeling of satisfaction, knowing it would only be moments before what he now dearly sought would be given to him.

It came in the form of a portly, well-dressed man of middle age who entered the hall in a huff of fury. Short of stature, wider at the waist than he was tall, his jowls shook as he sputtered, drawing up in rage to face Will, only to be countered by a grim, easy smile.

"You are Saebroc, Lord Aldtern?"

"I am! And who may you be to enter so and give orders to mine? God's blood, you have gall, man. I shall see you thrown from the tower if I do not see you to my dungeons first!"

"Dungeons? You have dungeons here?" Will countered with interest. He had heard that there were those who had converted the wide spaces beneath castles normally used for the fattening of livestock to other, more devious purposes. "I have heard of such, I should like to see them, but it is not to that I have come. Rather it is to the design of your walls that I am here. You have crenellated your walls, Saebroc of Aldtern, without license as given by your King. Can you give cause to this?"

"What?" The stocky man's face deepened with color as he regarded Will in a moment's hesitation. Will saw doubt and fear flicker across the man's expression before he drew up and answered the accusation with contempt. "Who are you to come here and accuse me of treason? I assure you that you are in great jeopardy! Give me a reason, if you can, why I do not have you drawn and quartered for pleasure."

"If you do, it will be the last pleasure you shall ever know," Will answered with a grim smile which he allowed to fade effectively. "I am here in the King's name. By his grace, I am William, Marshal of England. And you are Saebroc, for the moment Lord Aldtern, who has crenellated walls for defense without license from His Gracious Majesty."

"The Marshal—" The man seemed to shrink visibly. "The
. . . the parapets are not used for defense!" he choked, his eyes
frantically grasping for an answer. "They were set by design,
they are not used, not meant to—"

"Would you treat me as a fool? You know the law! Your
walls are topped with crenellations, yet no license was given by
your King to do so. Therefore they can only have been built to
be used against the will of His Majesty—"

"Nay!" the man squeaked, stepping back as he shook his
head against Will's reason. "Never against the realm! Nay!
Only design, I inherited from my brother and did not know,
truly, 'twas an error!" the man finished weakly, as if seeing
his doom.

Will was inclined to believe him; not that it mattered. It
could not but pass Will's mind that if he were in the simpering
fool's place he would note that, Marshal of England or not, he
was alone, quite alone, and would simply do away with the
menace, then deny that the incident had ever taken place.
Moreover, the jackass could claim that license had been given
by the crown under John Plantagenet. John was poor upon
keeping records. But those thoughts were Will's; he knew at
the first instant in meeting the wretch that such reasonings
would never occur to him. "I have a favor," he drawled,
pressing his position.

"Aye, milord, anything!" the man groveled as hope for his
salvation appeared.

Will gestured to the boy, who had stood to one side, watching the encounter with amazement and an intelligence that
Will did not miss, even in his baiting of the vainglorious
nobleman. "I want him cleaned up. A bath."

"Him?" Saebroc regarded the child with surprise and obvious distaste. "He is merely my stableboy, milord." Then a
new thought struck the Lord of Aldtern as he smiled slyly.
"Aye, milord. I shall have him bathed and readied for you."

Will stiffened as he realized what had passed through the
brain that resided behind those piglike eyes, which were
watching him with renewed interest. He forced down the impulse to bury his fist in that fleshy face. "See that he is
bathed," he ordered in a strangled voice. "And while he is

gone, you shall answer some questions for me. And I warn you, Saebroc, if your answers do not please me I shall take great pleasure in seeing that fat stomach of yours mix with the filthy rushes of this floor.'' Will's hand moved to the hilt of his sword, and it served to be all the emphasis that was needed, and his will was done with much haste.

The next hour proved a frustrating trial. The worthless Lord of Aldtern could give little clues to the identity of the child. The woman who had brought him to the manor had long since died and Saebroc had no knowledge of the boy beyond that of his duties in the stables. Even that was vague except the assurance that the child seemed to have learned his responsibilities well, only an occasional beating being required to enforce obedience. Will's thoughts while he listened to the fatlipped noble swam with the realization of what Giles had suffered, added to the doubt of the child's identity. As he listened he was filled with a pressing compulsion to leave before the child's return and accept the fact that he had been duped. But even as his thoughts damned Darcy for the wild goose chase, he stayed, determined to find the truth.

The sound of soft footsteps was heard behind him and Will rose from his chair, as much to dismiss the company of his slovenly host as to face his answer. Lud, he thought, why had he come? So far, and for what? Why could he not leave his memories in the past where they should lie? But as he turned, those memories came rushing, impaling him where he stood. He felt as if he had been struck. Heat rushed over him and he felt for an interminable moment that he could not breath. He stared. The child stood before him, watching with large blue eyes, questioning, observing the horrified look he wore. A mere child, yet in that small face Will saw the undeniable truth. Truth unexpected, undeniable, unquestionable, standing before him. In that face, his son.

18

LANDON glanced about the crowded taproom and his nose twitched involuntarily over the heavy smells of ale and unwashed bodies. His eyes watered against the smoke that hung in the room from the poorly constructed fireplace as a barmaid arrived with the stew he had ordered, dropping the heavy wooden mazers on the table in front of him before she turned and swished away to more promising prospects for her evening's entertainment and profit. Her interest in the handsome young squire had been overt when she had first spied Landon, a matter that he had firmly, if regrettably, settled, much to her displeasure. He watched her full hips sway as she moved away, and he sighed.

Meryle dropped onto the bench next to him and stared at the unpalatable mutton stew. "Lud, is this the best you could do?"

"It's that or goat."

Heaving a resigned sigh, Meryle dipped his spoon into the greasy stew and took a bite. Swallowing heavily, he cast barbed glances about the room in silent accusation for what he had just suffered.

"Easy, Meryle," Landon drawled, stifling a smile at his

friend's discomfort. "We are here to wait for Will, and to stay out of trouble while we're doing it."

"Then where is he?" the sandy-haired squire grumbled. "He's been gone three days. Dumping us here, without a word of where he was going . . ."

"He didn't 'dump' us."

"Didn't he? Are you going to tell me that you're not worried? Why here, for God's sake? There's nothing—just rocks and . . ." He paused, grimacing at the bowl in front of him. ". . . Sheep."

"He'll let us know when he's ready." Landon answered, grinning at his friend as he took a mouthful of the stew. "God." He shuddered.

Meryle laughed at Landon's pained expression. "Eat hearty! Or perhaps we should go out back and see if the innkeeper is holding out on us. At least the chicken we had last night was better fare than this."

"Now I am worried." Landon winced, pushing the bowl away. "Another night of this . . ." Motioning to the barmaid, he ordered tankards of ale.

"What?" Meryle's eyes rolled. "Is this the example of the squire under petition? Could this be Landon d'Leon, risking his spurs?"

"I'm not going to get drunk," Landon tossed irritably. "I only want to get that taste out of my mouth."

"Of course, of course." Meryle grinned broadly. "So do I."

As the barmaid brought their third round of tankards, she leaned over the table and Landon's gaze fixed on the low cut of her bodice, feasting on the bounty that fell open to his gaze. Grinning up at her, he slid his arm about her waist. "Good ale," he said, his eyes returning to the creamy tops of her breasts.

"Aye, milord." She laughed throatily, pressing against him. " 'Tis almost the best thing we offer here."

"Indeed," he countered with a lazy smile. "I would like to see what else you have."

"Landon."

Shrugging off Meryle's hand from his arm, he drew the girl more tightly against him.

"Landon!" Meryle hissed.

Puzzled, Landon turned to look at his friend, and Meryle nodded to a point beyond the barmaid. Turning, Landon realized the cause of Meryle's urgency. A large, extremely large, man stood watching, his burly shoulders topped by a head that seemed to have no neck. He appeared to roll rather than walk up to the table, his ham-hock arms sticking out of his shoulders, his clublike fists clenching and unclenching. The man fixed on the girl possessively, and his small eyes returned to Landon.

"Is there something I can do for you?" Landon tossed cheerily.

"Jesus," Meryle groaned.

The bench fell back as the squires stood up in unison, their hands on their sword hilts. Handing the girl away from him, Landon countered the villein's stare. "She can choose for herself," he said evenly.

The villein's gaze dropped to the swords and a flicker of doubt slowly crossed his brain. And then chairs and benches were heard to scrape across the worn boards of the tavern floor and the beady eyes began to glimmer with nasty pleasure.

"I'm ready when you are," Meryle murmured behind him.

"Sorry, Meryle."

"Think nothing of it."

The two squires slowly stepped back to the wall and their swords were out of their scabbards. The villeins moved toward them in unspoken agreement, their eyes grim with hatred of the young nobles. They moved closer, the menace of their intent evidence that no quarter would be given. The squires braced themselves for the attack, their swords raised, prepared to give as good as they got before they fell beneath the rage that approached them.

"Hold!"

Bodies froze and heads turned toward the voice. A sharp wind from the doorway whipped into the room, snow drifting about the cloaked figure that stood in the door frame. The newcomer's cloak was pushed back behind his shoulders and his hand rested on the hilt of his sword. As the speaker stepped into the taproom, the villeins paused, seeming to lose their desire to fight. Angry mumbles were passed, but the men reluctantly returned to their tables and the tankards that waited for them. Two young, raw squires were one thing, but a fully armored and armed knight was another—particularly, as evidenced from the well-kept but aged condition of his hauberk and helm, an experienced one. Not to mention the fact that the squires, who each had obviously shaved for some time, would be at his back.

Landon's and Meryle's thoughts were one. They focused on the effort to lock their knees that threatened to buckle as their gazes fixed sheepishly on the controlled fury that approached them.

Will came to stand before them, his gaze passing over them with annoyance. "Well?"

They both began to talk at once, and he waved off their protests with a wave of his hand. "Never mind. We will speak of this later." From the tone of his voice, they had no doubt of it. "Meryle, see to the innkeeper and request that a meal for two is brought to our room. Landon, see that the fire in the room is going well. God, it's freezing out there!"

They began to react immediately, and then they froze, jaws slackened, as they stared in dumbfounded unison at the small form at Will's side. "Well?" he snapped. "See to it!"

They moved, their brains spinning with what they had seen as they rushed to Will's bidding. Will followed Landon up the stairs and down the hall to the chamber, his hand on Giles's shoulder as he gently guided the silent child. He tossed his cloak on a chair as Landon fed the fire, bringing it to a warming blaze, and then he stood as the squire came to disarm him. Landon's fingers worked expertly, unbuckling the armor swiftly even as his mind tumbled with the realization about the child who stood nearby, watching. Meryle entered the room with a tray as Landon was finishing, and the two exchanged a puzzled glance as Meryle passed to set the meal on a table near the hearth.

Shrugging wearily, Will stepped to the table and stared down at the tray Meryle had brought. "What is this?" he asked churlishly, eyeing the tray with doubt.

"Mutton stew, milord," Meryle answered.

"Is it edible?"

"Nay, milord."

Dropping into a chair, Will sighed heavily. "Wonderful." Turning to Giles, who still stood at the center of the room, he spoke more softly. "You might as well try to eat something." When the boy did not move, he held out his hand. "Come here, Giles." The child came obediently and stood before him. "Eat." Will ordered firmly, nodding at the tray.

The child took the chair on the other side of the table, and to Will's amazement he began spooning the greasy mutton into his mouth with a fervor. Glancing at his squires, Will saw them wince as the child began to eat, but their expressions became frowns as they realized the child was half starved, and their gazes shifted to Will. Seeing that he was watching them, they flushed.

"Undoubtedly you realize that this is my son," Will said wryly, answering their unspoken questions, unaware that Giles paused and stared at him, his large blue eyes widening with surprise. Then the child's eyes went blank, hesitating only for a moment before he returned to the stew.

"That is most evident, Sir William," Landon answered stiffly, his eyes showing a disapproval that Will noticed to be matched in Meryle's. Will studied the two with narrowed eyes. "I will strike a bargain with you," he drawled. "You will not be quick to condemn me and I shall grant you the same consideration for what happened belowstairs before I arrived." Flushing, the two young men nodded sheepishly. "Well enough," he grunted.

When Giles had finished his supper, Will nodded toward the bed. "It is late, Giles. See you to bed." Giles glanced at the straw-filled mattress and looked back at Will with puzzlement.

"There, milord?" the child asked.

"Of course, there." Seeing the dilemma on the child's face, Will suddenly realized the problem. Good lord, he thought, the child had probably never slept in a bed. "Aye, Giles, you shall sleep there with me."

"But . . ." Giles looked to Landon and Meryle, who were listening to the exchange. "What of them?" he asked.

"They shall sleep on pallets—there," he answered, indicating the rolled pallets that lay near the hearth.

Seeing the child's dismay, the questions he seemed to be

struggling with, Landon stepped forward to take the child's hand. "Come with me, Giles." He led the boy to the bed and paused to help him to remove his tunic. "You shall sleep here, as befitting the son of the Earl of Pembroke. When you are a squire, as we are, you too shall sleep upon a pallet by the fire, there in readiness to serve your lord shall the need arise. For now, relish your bed, Giles, for you shall not again know its comfort until you are a knight in your own right."

Tucking the child into the bed, Landon turned to meet Will's gaze. He shrugged away the gratitude that he saw in Will's expression, answering it with a smile. "Will there be anything else that you need, milord?"

"Nay, Landon. See you to your pallets. And sleep well," he added. "We will depart this place at first light."

"Thank God for that," Meryle remarked.

Will sat staring into the fire long after the others had fallen asleep. Weary, he longed for the release that sleep would give him, but his thoughts would not allow it. His child lay sleeping nearby. His son. Faith had been a strength of Will's life, yet he felt that the pledge of protection and trust, long ago given to one dear to him, had been broken.

He was filled with horror as he considered the lost years, the life his son, her son, had lived. But for a meeting in a forest with a minstrel, he would never have known and Giles would have lived out his life in squalor, without any who truly cared for him. A tumult of questions raged in his mind: why? how? Yet he could not set reason to it.

Everything seemed to suddenly emerge to confront him. How would Eleanor view the child? Would she seek to cast Giles aside, even as she had sought to reject him? She had let him know, without qualification, how she felt about him. What could she possibly feel for his child by another woman?

Damn. Eleanor had tossed, nay, placed a vow before him with that blasted peacock. It was not for his honor that she had deemed him the bravest, the most noble knight. He laughed softly, a sound touched with sadness. She wanted him to make that pledge, knowing that he would do so by his own measure of pride, not hers. To be first to the wall—and first to die.

He had been first to the wall, not just the first time but in each battle. How disappointed she surely would be when he returned. But he had been careful, oh so careful, to see that Alan of Newbury had been kept safe. That one had pledged to fight bravely, for the honor of England, and Will had to begrudge him that. The man had fought well. But Will had been determined that Newbury would return safely; she would not have Newbury's death to throw up to him.

Eleanor, he sighed, what did happen to us? But why should I wonder, when it had begun so badly? Always was I expected to be father, brother, and then husband to you. Little wonder you would seek one to give you something new, exciting. . . . And then there is now. If I endeavored to place aside the past, it has found me. And I did try, I did try. Lavene had begun to meld into my deepest thoughts as I tried to turn to you. But now there is this child. Had he merely been hers, I would have loved him for that, but put him apart for you. But he is mine—and hers. How can I look at him, yet not remember?

His son. Giles was a bastard, and would ever be. By law, even if Lavene had lived and Will had taken her to wife, the child, having been born before the vows, would remain outside the protection of Will's name. Not that it made a great deal of difference; bastards were common enough. But he would never be able to inherit the lands or the name. But—and Will made the vow silently—Giles would never want for anything again. He would have that which was given to him by his father.

A persistent knocking brought Will awake and he sat up quickly. Glancing at the small sleeping form at his side, he nodded to Landon, who stood by his pallet, sword in hand, and to Meryle, who had already reached the door. Armed as well, Meryle opened the door, only to step back with a stricken look of surprise. He had no time to announce the visitor as the door was pushed open and Matilda swept into the room, her dark blue eyes flashing as they came to rest upon the bed. They softened for an instant as they fixed on Giles, who was sleepily rubbing his eyes as he tried to sit up. Then they shifted back to Will with a killing look.

"Good morning, Matilda," Will drawled, adjusting the pillows at his back.

"Do not 'good morning' me, Will Marshal!" she snapped. "Oh, Will, why did you not warn anyone? Can't you do anything right?"

"I believe that I did," he countered, smiling down at the child.

"Oh, really, Will," she deplored, but her eyes moved eagerly to Giles.

"Giles, you had better wake up and bid greeting to your Aunt Matilda." Will grinned, realizing that his son was about to be mothered.

"You do not seem to be surprised that I am here," she scoffed.

"Matilda, nothing you do surprises me. Obviously Hugh . . . by the way, where is he?"

At that moment Hugh came through the open doorway and stopped, his dark eyes taking in the scene before him, and he groaned. "Will, I apologize. Matilda, I told you to wait for me!" Glancing back at Will, he shrugged. "I was delayed in arranging another room for Isabella. . . ."

"Isabella is here as well?" Will blurted as a strangled sound drew his attention. "Stop that damned grinning!" he bellowed at Landon and Meryle. Looking back at Hugh, he saw that the Earl of Norfolk was staring at Giles. Hugh's gaze shifted to Will and he nodded slowly, his mouth drawn into a smile. Feeling the boy move closer to him in the bed, Will smiled gently down at his son. "Giles, this is your family, a very small part of it, I fear. It will take you time to come to know them all, but they shall love and comfort you as they do me—when they are not driving you mad."

"Will, how could you bring that child to a place like this?" Matilda said archly as her eyes flickered over the room with distaste.

"Where should I have taken him, dear sister?" Will countered with patience. "You may have noticed that it began to snow yesterday. Should we have slept in it?"

"Well, at least I thought to bring some things with me that he will need," she said as two of Hugh's squires struggled through the doorway with a large trunk.

"*Some* things?" Will gaped.

"Well, from what Hugh told me . . . ." She paused, glancing

at the boy, whose large blue eyes were fastened on her. "I suspected that he would need clothes, so I brought some things Rodger has outgrown. I believe they will be the correct size. Now, if you gentlemen will retire to the taproom, I will see to Giles's needs."

Giles's needs, indeed, Will thought wryly. His sister just wanted to get her hands on him so that she could smother him against her motherly breast. On the other hand, he thought soberly, if any child was in need of her pragmatism and warmth, it was Giles. "I would be happy to remove myself, Matilda," he drawled. "However, as things are, it would prove rather awkward." Seeing the doubtful look that crossed his sister's face, he grinned. "Since it was never the custom of the women in our family to attend to the baths and dressing of male visitors—or brothers—"

Matilda grasped his meaning as her eyes dropped to the sheet that covered his body. Flushing, she drew herself up with dignity and threw him a murderous look. "Oh, Will—really!" But she spun and left the room just as it filled with male laughter.

Settled in the taproom at a table near the fire with Hugh, Will felt himself relax for the first time since he had left Normandy, knowing that Giles was well cared for. He glanced in the direction of the stairs with a wry smile. He could well imagine his sisters fluttering about the boy, dissolving that wall the child had protectively fixed about himself. The smile faded as he recalled the moment when Isabella returned to the chamber with Matilda. It was, of course, the first time he had seen her since he left for Normandy, and the first since her husband, Gilbert deClare, had died.

He had pulled her into his arms and kissed her forehead with tenderness and held her to him for a moment. "I am sorry about Gilbert, Isabella," he had murmured.

"I know." She pulled back from him and smiled but her eyes were moist. "But it has been almost a year—and it is not quite so painful now. I think . . . what hurt him the most was that he was not able to go to Normandy with you. But he did what he could to see to everyone's affairs in your absence —until he became too ill, even for that."

Thinking on it now, Will tapped his fingers absently on the table. Indeed, it had been almost a year. In respect to Gilbert, as well as for Isabella's sake and that of their eldest son, Richard—Richard, he must find some time to spend with the boy—soon he must begin to look for another husband for Isabella. She was wealthy, beautiful, and in the prime of her years, a ripe apple, ready for picking. She was safe now, but if anything were to ever happen to him . . .

"So, then, Darcy was right."

Will's gaze shifted to Hugh. "Apparently."

"Good Lord, Will," Hugh muttered. "What you must have felt when you saw him."

"A bit more than I was prepared for."

"Do you want to tell me about it?"

Will sighed deeply, reaching for his tankard. Taking a long draught, he set it down again and fingered the pewter absently as he spoke. "You should have seen how he lived, Hugh. In the muck of a stable without any to care if he lived at all. He did not even know who his mother was."

"Have you told him?"

"Not yet. It's going to take time. He's not an easy child to talk to—he's awakened in another world and built a wall around himself to keep it out."

"Can you blame him?"

"Of course not. But he blames me. I see it in his eyes when he doesn't know I'm watching—the anger and distrust. How can I explain all of the years of neglect?"

"It would seem to me that you do not have to. You are not guilty of anything, Will. Someday he'll realize that."

"Perhaps. I hope so."

They fell to companionable silence as they sipped from their tankards and took a light breakfast of wheaten bread and cheese. Hugh had argued when Will had declined bowls of stew for them, protesting that he was hungry. "Go ahead," Will drawled, "but don't expect me to watch you eat it." Taking the hint, Hugh had ordered cheese.

As he ate, Will kept his eye on the tables where Hugh's knights and squires sat, and those occupied by the locals. His mouth twitched with humor as he spied Meryle and Landon.

The squires sat with Hugh's men, but their eyes shifted with regularity to the villeins, and one burly local in particular. Seeing Hugh's puzzlement at his sudden humor, Will recounted the previous night's encounter.

"You should have known better than to leave them here for three days with nothing to do." Hugh chuckled. Then as he finished his meal he leaned back in his chair and his manner became serious. "Will . . ." He paused. "There is another matter that brought me here. Matilda believes that Giles was the reason I came . . . but there is news I must give you before the women join us."

"What is it?" Will braced himself for bad news but was totally unprepared for what Hugh said next.

"Peter desRoches has returned."

"What!"

"That is only the beginning. Henry has made Peter des-Revaux the treasurer of the royal household for life. Our esteemed bishop has done well by his son. Moreover, Hubert deBurgh's own man, Stephen Seagrave, has been drawn into desRoches's web. The slime turned traitor to Hubert and has supposedly given evidence of the justiciar's poor administration, and even misuse of funds from the royal treasury."

"Damnation!" Will swore savagely.

"There is more. Do you recall, years ago, when we warned Henry of the problems that would come from allowing the Italians benefices in England? While we were gone a faction of nobles—it is not certain even now who they were—rode at night, in disguise, attacking the Italians with the intent of driving them from England. At first the people acclaimed their actions, their hatred cheering anything that would drive the foreigner out. Not to mention the fact that the 'Brotherhood,' as it was called, made the astute gesture of giving the wealth they confiscated to the needy. A rather popular cause."

"Get to the heart of it," Will said grimly.

"You mean the worst of it. Public opinion changed quickly when the Holy Father excommunicated the members of the raid and all who assisted them. It is said that the group carried letters sanctioning their actions, with approval of the Crown. The missives were said to have been signed by deBurgh."

"Impossible!" Will blurted. "Anyone who knows the man knows he does nothing in secret! Moreover, he would not be that inane!"

"That is what is so odd about it. Everyone knows the documents were forged, yet apparently they are accepted."

"Not odd, Hugh," Will ground out. "Well planned. We need look no further than the Bishop of Winchester."

"There is no doubt about it," a feminine voice came from behind Will. "Peter desRoches has had his fine hand in everything that has been laid at Hubert's feet. The Brotherhood was only the fly in the ointment."

The men stood up and turned in surprise. "Matilda . . ." Hugh frowned.

"Oh, we know all about it," Matilda scoffed as she ran her hand through Giles's hair. The boy flushed at the gesture, his eyes taking on a pained expression. "After all, William deFerrars is with the court, reporting everything to you."

"And Sybile is with him," the men said in unison.

"Reporting everything to us," Isabella said sweetly, slipping into a chair. She looked down at the remains of their breakfast and frowned. "Is that all you are going to eat?"

Matilda took the chair next to Will's, leaving the empty one between Isabella and her. Patting it, she gestured for Giles to sit. He threw a pained look at Will, fortunately unnoticed by the Countess Bigod, and Will pursed his lips in order not to smile. "Giles," he said sternly, his voice rising enough to carry across the room, "are you just going to stand there? The ladies have left a chair for you!"

"Really, Will, you needn't shout." Matilda frowned. "Giles, do what your father tells you."

Landon turned at the sound of Will's voice and caught his eye. With a glance he quickly assessed the problem. Rising from his bench he crossed the room, his amusement dissolving behind a facade of solemnness as he approached the boy, who remained standing by the vacant chair, his small face filled with misery.

"Milord," he addressed Will. "As Giles will soon be a page, perhaps, if you deem it proper, he might break his fast with the squires and knights. There we can begin to properly assist him in the duties he will soon face."

Will appeared to study the request for a moment and then shrugged. "Perhaps you are right. Take charge of him, Landon."

The squire winked at the boy, whose face beamed with excitement as his eyes fixed eagerly on the table of knights. Taking the boy's hand, he led him away as Matilda grunted with disapproval. Will caught Hugh's expression and he had to look away quickly, only to see Isabella struggling not to laugh, and he was suddenly taken by a strangled cough.

"Well, Will?" Matilda asked, settling to the cheese and bread the barmaid had brought. "What are you going to do about all of this?"

"About what—oh, deBurgh." Will's expression changed, becoming stormy. "You can be assured that I will not allow him to pay for desRoches's duplicity."

"Will, there is one thing," Hugh said, pausing. "It has occurred to me that you have been kept from England this past year for a purpose. Nay," he added quickly at sight of the disbelief in Will's face, "look beyond the obvious. None of us did question the order to remain in France. Yet it has served desRoches's purpose well. Far too much so, to my thinking. It was your power that saw him into exile, and upon your departure he returned. Before you return to that hornet's nest, think upon it."

"Not a hornet's nest," Matilda mumbled. "A lion's den, a Plantagenet lion."

"One that needs the arm of another lion—a red one, rampant," Isabella added, glancing at the device on Will's surcoat.

"Since we have mentioned the sharpness of Plantagenet claws," Will said irascibly, "how is Eleanor?"

Those at the table fell silent at the angry remark. "She was with us at Framlingham, just recently," Matilda answered finally.

"But she is not now," Will observed.

"Nay, she—"

"You need not tell me. She fled back to court, after a compulsory visit with my family. But then, there is a matter which would draw her there. Newbury has returned with the glory of his won spurs."

"Will Marshal!" Isabella snapped. "That is not fair!"

"Isn't it?"

"Nay, it is not. She left reluctantly, but there was a purpose. Will, Eleanor is not—"

"Spare me," he said gruffly, drawing from his tankard. "I am certain that she had a purpose. Eleanor always has a purpose for everything she does. And I know too well what that is."

Isabella began to protest, but Matilda laid a hand on her arm to stay her. Though her own eyes glittered with anger, her voice was smooth as she regarded her brother whose attention was fixed on his tankard. "You are correct, as always, Will. When Eleanor's mind is fixed upon something, nothing will stay her. Why, in the past months she has been known to utter the most outrageous things—even at court. But then, you will have to see for yourself. Aye, I think, Will Marshal, that it is time you took her in hand. Your wife should no longer be left alone."

Will stared into his tankard moodily, missing the looks exchanged by his family. "Indeed," he muttered. "And so shall I. I am to London then, with my son. . . ."

"And with me," Isabella said, countering Will's eyes as they lifted to her with surprise. "My children are well cared for and will survive without me for a time. Your son, however, is in need of a woman's guidance. You will be busy and will need someone to watch out for Giles."

He considered her statement, accepting the logic of her reasoning, but his brow furrowed with concern. "It may not be safe, Isabella. The problems in London may be far worse than we fear."

"Pah, she would storm a wall to reach Richard of Cornwall," Matilda tossed.

Will's eyes shot to his sister, who flushed deeply at Matilda's revelation. "Richard?" he asked with surprise.

"You could not know, Will." Hugh grinned, stifling his laughter as Isabella squirmed uncomfortably. "Your sister has set her sights for Richard of Cornwall. It is said that he is at Winchester."

"Richard?" Will repeated, his eyes widening. Yet it should not have surprised him. Reason declared that his beautiful sister would not remain unattached for long. And he did not need to ask if her feelings were returned. If memory served him, the King's younger brother had been severely smitten by the Countess deClare when they had gathered at Windsor for the occasion of his marriage to Eleanor. "I would guess that my lord Richard has been a guest at Hertford in my absence." He grinned.

"He has seen fit to visit upon occasion." Isabella shrugged as she pinked with embarrassment.

"Indeed!" Will laughed. "I imagine that he has! Well, then, it is settled. As soon as you can pack up that damnable trunk Matilda has brought for Giles, we leave for London!"

19

A HEAVY drizzle hung about the travelers, adding to their misery as they entered the darkened streets of London. Exhausted as they were with travel, their feelings turned toward the comfort of a fire, warm spiced ale, and the weight of a fur counterpane and drawn curtains of the beds that awaited them. Will drew the hood of his cloak more tightly about him as he drew Hamal back so that he might check on his family who rode at the center of the long column. Two of his knights flanked the small, huddled form of his son on the small palfrey he rode, as did two others about Isabella. They were safe enough, even in their discomfort from the chill winter London weather, he reasoned, and soon they would be warm and dry. But an unease prevailed nevertheless, and Will trusted his instincts, having obeyed them far too long to ignore or question them now. Thus, he pulled the destrier closer to his family and rested his hand beneath his cloak near the hilt of his sword, even as his eyes swept over the large party, noting the position and alertness of his men.

Their destination at the house he kept in London took them along the Thames. As they neared the tower the sky before them began to glow in an unearthly light through the curtain of heavy drizzle, the ghostly aura outlining the irregular roof-tops of houses and shops. As they came nearer they realized that the source of the strange light was large bonfires set ir-regularly about the streets. The scene suddenly became a nightmare. The streets were filled with the dark forms of peo-ple, their voices raised crazily as they rushed about. Torches were carried in wavering patterns against the grey of the fall-ing rain, streaks of light trailing the shouts and cries that pre-ceded their uneven path. A deep, chilling fear passed through Will as he instantly recognized what was happening. A riot.

As Will's spurs sank into his flanks, the destrier shot for-ward and rounded the head of the column. Will fought the destrier's furious movement, shouting orders for Alan Wadley to take ten of the knights and see his family by the back streets to their quarters. Knowing that the knight would obey in-stantly, he shouted for the rest of the men to accompany him, and he turned in the direction of the riot. Fear pulsated through him as they made their way through the grey, il-luminated darkness toward the structure once known as William's Tower. They pushed their way through the throng, the angry mob separating before the sharp hooves and bared teeth of the warhorses as they moved steadily toward the tower, now barely visible through the light rain. Will could hear painful cries as his men occasionally pressed their prog-ress with the flat edge of their swords, and curses were thrown at them by the outraged Londoners.

Arriving at the tower, they rode beneath the barbican of the Lion's Gate and along the wooden drawbridge leading to the Middle Tower. Hamal snorted nervously at the sounds from the menagerie, as Henry's "pet" leopards, buffaloes, and bears reacted unhappily to the sounds of the riot from with-out. Will frowned to find the portcullis of the Middle Tower was raised, and he rode beneath and across a second causeway over the inner moat of the Bell Tower. His alarm grew to find it also open with not a sign of a guard. He spurred Hamal for-ward, and as they rode along the high curtain wall of the outer ward the sound of the hooves of the destrier echoed the pounding in Will's chest. As they pulled up before the flat, vaulted roof of the Garden Tower, Will suddenly felt weak with relief. The massive iron portcullis was firmly in place, and they were challenged by a shout from the guard above.

Will identified himself and waited. Finally, a guard leaned over the crenellation and called down, "My Lord Marshal, it will be a moment before we can raise the portcullis; I've had to call for more men. All have fled but those of us who wear the badge of my Lord deBurgh."

Will swore fiercely under his breath. "How many are left?" The answer came back, "Enough to raise the gate, milord." Will drew in his breath sharply. That meant thirty. Just thirty.

Once the gate had been raised, Will fortified it with his own men, taking the remainder with him to man the doors of the tower. He slipped from Hamal and threw the reins to one of them with orders for them to block the entrance. He entered the tall, squarish keep, making his way through the dimly lit passages to the family quarters.

To his relief, his worst fears had not been realized. His hand grasped Hubert deBurgh's in a brief moment of understanding. He tried to keep the sympathy from his eyes, knowing the justiciar would not welcome it. "Is your family safe?" he asked quietly.

"Aye, my Lord Marshal, though I would wish that they were far from here."

"I vow to you, they shall be kept safe," Will said with compassion. "Hubert, tell me what has happened." Will could not but reflect on the greatness of this man, friend of his father, though many years younger. He was shocked at the change in him, how he had aged since he had last seen him. It was this man who, in defiance of King John, had refused to blind or execute the young prince Arthur, John's nephew and, in the despot's eyes, a threat to his throne. It was this man who, with a small garrison of 140 men had held out against the French army at Dover, allowing the forces of William Marshal time to effect Louis's final defeat. So much England owed to him.

"London will not forgive me my errors." DeBurgh shrugged with a fateful grin. "They hate me still for what I did to the traitor fitzArnulf."

"That is past," Will insisted, while knowing that the justiciar was right.

"Past?" Hubert smiled sadly. "Look you beyond these windows. They will never forget nor forgive me that moment.

All else that I have done is nothing to that. But it means much, Will, that you have come.''

"I will see the King," Will said sharply. "God's breath, Henry must realize—"

"The king is at Shrewsbury," deBurgh noted with a short laugh. "As ever he seeks to be from that which will cause him to face his responsibilities. Nay, 'tis to desRoches you must plead if there is anything for me."

"DesRoches shall not have you," Will gritted. "He sees himself as the power in England, but I do swear to you, Hubert, he shall know the might of the barons; that law in England is greater than the will of the Church—or of the Throne."

"You envision beyond you, my friend," deBurgh said softly, with infinite sadness.

"I was taught to dream beyond myself, Hubert." Will smiled. "There were two who showed me that nothing is beyond our dreams or reach. One is gone, though ever with me; the other resides at Canterbury. Would you deny either?"

"William Marshal, your father, and Stephen Langton?" Hugh shook his head. "Nay, I could not deny them their efforts, nor their dreams. But that mob without suggests that I am not to be part of it."

"And I tell you that you shall be," Will affirmed, turning to pull off his cloak. He tossed it to a chair as he pushed back the coif of his hauberk. "Hubert, if you are allowed to suffer at the hands of this lawlessness, then all that we worked for, dreamed of, is gone! I swear to you, it shall not be. Even now my brothers have been alerted. If we fall, they shall come, and the forces of those pledged to me with them."

DeBurgh stared at him for a long moment. "You would thrust England into war?" he asked quietly.

"Those damned Poitevins and their allies would see us reduced to nothing, the Great Charter and all that we have fought for, gone forever. Where Louis of France failed, they attempt to do now. I will do what I must to stop it."

A prolonged moment passed, then suddenly deBurgh laughed, a bitter, empty sound. "By the sweet mercy of God, I do believe that I shall be saved."

"Have I not told you?"

"Aye, you have. But now I believe it." They were staring at each other in silent understanding when a door was heard to open, and Will turned swiftly, his hand already fixed on the hilt of his sword. He froze, defying the shock of what met him.

"Eleanor!" he blurted. He could not reason the fact that she had stepped through the door and now stood there, watching him.

"I knew you would come," she said simply.

He was numbly aware that she crossed the span between them and felt the shock that ran up his arm as she laid her hand on it. "The children are sleeping," she said quietly to deBurgh.

He could not reason finding her here. "I was told that you returned to court," he said thickly.

"So I did."

"But . . . what are you doing here?" he asked tightly as a dark storm began to gather in his face.

"Oh, Will, the same thing that you are doing here." She smiled, ignoring his frown as she reached up on tiptoe and kissed his cheek lightly. "Welcome home, my love. Though how I wish it were of happier circumstance."

He watched her greet Isabella warmly like an old friend lost. Suspicions plucked at him, but he kept silent and bode his time, waiting. Each for its own moment, he thought as he held himself from the questions that pressed. She looked as he remembered her. Devastating beauty that tore at him . . . but not for an instant did he forget the anger, the hurt, the frustration. His stomach tightened, wondering what she was about. He had carried her away with him from the tower, to the house where Isabella waited, and now watched the touching scene before him, though his reason defied the sense of it. He had fully expected to find her with Henry. Or with Newbury.

Eleanor had felt the tension in him from the first moment she had entered the chamber in the tower to find him with deBurgh. She would not have expected less, nor was she surprised by the angry, doubtful glances he cast in her direction, but she was determined. There was no way for it but to see it through to its inevitable outcome. She had ignored his penetrating glances before deBurgh, and avoided his silent

questions upon their ride through the dark streets from the
tower. Even in her joy as she greeted Isabella, she knew that he
was watching, waiting. Not now, Will, she thought; words
cannot suffice. You must wait and see for yourself if you are
to believe, to accept what I have found.

She drew Isabella to a bench near the fire, and as she turned
back she smiled at one who had come into the room just
beyond Will's shoulder. Will turned and she puzzled at the
deep scowl that came over his face as it mixed with his surprise.

"Darcy!"

"Aye, milord," the goliard offered in unaccustomed hu-
mility. "I trust that you received my missive—and that your
quest was successful?"

"Indeed." Will's face flushed angrily. "We have much to
discuss, you and I."

"In its own time, milord. For now, it seems that there are
more pressing matters to concern you."

"Do not attempt to avoid the issue, bard," Will growled.

"I shall be here," the goliard replied. He glanced at the
women and offered a gracious greeting to Isabella, then exchanged a warm look with Eleanor, who gave him a soft smile.
The exchange was not lost on Will, who passed a speculative
frown to the pair.

"What of deBurgh?" Isabella interjected, feeling the tension in the room.

"Safe, for the moment," Will tossed irritably as he paused
to shout for Landon. The squire appeared instantly, then
disappeared again to fetch wine and food at Will's order. As
the door closed, Will turned back and slumped wearily into a
chair. "That rabble wants him. They have been incited to a
pitch. I have left men to guard him, but I cannot say what will
happen. Damn! How could Henry have allowed this!"

The answer came from an unexpected source. "He lives in a
world of his own making," Eleanor said quietly. "He wants to
rule in his own way, yet he expects the world to be beautiful
and pure; he cannot see the evil about him. Whenever he is
confronted with the ugliness of reality, he looks to a better
dream."

Will regarded Eleanor with surprise, but before he could

respond, Darcy intervened. " 'Tis too late an hour to find
easy solutions to such problems." He paused as Landon and
Meryle entered with food and wine, setting them on the tables
near the fire. Will dismissed them with a tired wave of his
hand, and as the door shut on them the goliard picked up his
lyre, which, Will realized, with a frown, had been propped
against the hearth. Sitting on a stool near the women, the
goliard began to tune the instrument.

"Not now, Darcy," Will snapped. "I am in no mood for
song and verse."

"I think, milord, this one you shall be. Bear with me, Will.
You must be weary. Give a moment to reflect upon all that is
happening, all that is needed."

Will rose, pouring goblets of wine, which he handed to
Eleanor and Isabella, taking one for himself, and returned to
his chair. Staring moodily into the cup, he ignored the goliard
as Darcy began to sing, but as his mellow voice filled the room
Will began to listen in spite of his growing irritation.

Darcy sang of a great king who had two sons, one who had
died, the other who lay near death. The king sent far and wide
for one to save his remaining heir. Counsel was given that only
the essence of a unicorn could save the boy. But how to capture the elusive, mystical creature seen only by a few?
Throughout the land they searched for the most beautiful
maiden, a virgin, who was taken into the deepest part of the
woods, where she was left in a secluded copse of trees. Four
swift dogs were taken out by the hunters and stayed hidden, in
view of the beautiful maid.

The unicorn came, drawn to the scent of the virgin. It drew
nearer. Overcome by the purity of the maiden, it lay down,
resting its head in the lady's lap. The dogs came forth, surrounding the mystical creature, capturing it for the hunters,
who drove their swords into the heart of the brave animal.

As the last refrain of Darcy's song ended, Will glared at him
over his goblet. "If you sought to soothe me by that song,
Darcy, you have erred. I find the verse depressing."

"I did not promise anything by it." Darcy shrugged. "As
ever, you must take what I have recited as you will."

Will glanced at Eleanor and Isabella. His sister looked sad,
touched by the verse as was he, while Eleanor had assumed a

glow as her eyes fixed brightly on the goliard. "You appear well pleased, Eleanor," he said irritably. "Does it not concern you that the animal should be so cruelly betrayed?"

"Nay, Will," she said softly, turning her eyes to him. "For truth can only give one joy."

"Truth?" He snorted with disgust. "Your 'truths' have always been a source of wonderment to me, Eleanor."

"As their discovery has always been to me," she countered. "Once the maiden would have represented the embodiment of the Holy Virgin, as we are taught. The blessed unicorn is the Christ, the huntsman the Holy Ghost, the dogs to be Mercy, Justice, Peace, and Truth."

"So I have heard," Isabella said, frowning. "Though I could never accept such. It seemed a terrible betrayal that the Holy Mother would draw her own son to be slaughtered."

" 'Twas his sacrifice that gave the world hope." Eleanor smiled. "And this is what the tale once meant to me."

"Yet we know that others who adhere to the tenets of the new chivalry find the unicorn to represent the courage and strength of the Order," Darcy offered. "To them the virgin represents the chastity of womanhood, her purest essence. Only that can lead him to his quest. In the slaying of the unicorn, he achieves it."

"That pitiful unicorn must be damnably tired by now as everyone seeks to make him his truth." Will snorted. "But tell me, Eleanor," he added quietly, his eyes fixed upon her. "You said it *once* meant that to you. And now?"

"I would answer you if I could." She sighed. "But truly, I cannot."

"Are you deliberately being evasive?" Will countered. "You said you knew the truth, therefore I can only assume that you are avoiding the question."

"I would not deliberately avoid anything you asked of me, Will." She returned his look unflinchingly. "I can only tell you that the song of the unicorn must be heard in each heart. If only truth would come unfailingly, in a brilliant revelation of clarity. Instead, it avoids me, taunting me in flashes of comfort, teasing me to seek, bit by bit."

His mouth drew up in a wry smile. "And what little bits of truth do you see now?"

"That if Peter desRoches's hand were on the sword, he would slaughter the unicorn and the strength, courage, and wisdom that reside within—while others would stand by and allow it, fearing to let the beast live."

Will's eyes narrowed to hide his surprise. "Then you are saying that the beast holds the secret of wisdom and truth, and in his ignorance man seeks to slaughter him rather than face what he cannot understand, thus fears."

"Has it not always been so?" Darcy asked quietly.

But Will did not answer as he continued to stare at Eleanor with a strange, penetrating look. She felt his eyes on her, and she would have spoken but for a sudden commotion at the door. Isabella's tirewoman stood in the doorway, her plump face flushed, her coif and wimple askew as she clenched her apron, her entire body trembling with agitation.

"Berta, what is it?" Isabella asked in alarm, rising from the bench.

" 'Tis the lad, milady. Won't have nothing done for 'im. Insists that 'ees leav'n this very night. Lyle caught him climb'n from the window and 'ee started throw'n things about. . . ."

"I'll see to him," Will said grimly, putting his goblet on the table as he started toward the door. He missed the puzzled look from Eleanor and the wide-eyed, silent question she turned to Isabella and Darcy. Her question turned to a frown as they avoided her eyes and seemed to fix suddenly upon distant points of the room.

As he approached the door to the chamber given to Giles, it opened suddenly and Meryle came backing out, followed by a candlestick, which flew by the squire's head and crashed into the wall behind him. A stream of profanities followed the missile, the depths of the words defying the young, high-pitched voice that issued them with vehemence. Increasing his pace, Will stepped into the doorway, just in time to duck another projectile.

The room was in shambles. Landon and Lyle, Will's manservant, stood on either side of the room, their legs apart as they braced for another round of attack. In the far corner, backed against the wall, was Giles, his face flushed as he held another candlestick above his head, ready to let it fly.

"Giles!" Will roared. "Put that down!"

"Bloody hell!" Giles cried, raising the candlestick higher.

Will ignored the appealing glances from the other two men as his eyes fixed on his son. "Now, Giles," he ordered quietly, with an iciness that caused the boy's darting gaze to shift to his father. Will saw a flicker of doubt cross the boy's expression.

"I ain't doin' it!" Giles said tightly. "They can't make me do it!"

"Do what?" Will asked firmly.

"Make me wear that thing!" the boy cried, jerking his head in the direction of the bed. "There's bloody lace on it! I ain't no fop!"

Will looked in the direction of the tousled bed. Among the disheveled covers lay a white linen bed gown, trimmed in the offending lace. Will's mouth twitched and it was a moment before he spoke. "Giles," he said sternly as his brows gathered in a frown. "We do not behave in such a manner; it will not be tolerated. Those here have sought to befriend you, and you have returned that friendship most despicably. Now, as for the bedgown. Apparently Berta did not realize that you are quite old enough to go without it."

"She said I had to—she called me 'poor lamb'! I ain't nobody's poor lamb!" Giles spat with disgust, although he lowered the candlestick.

Will had to clear his throat, but his voice remained stern. "That you are not. You are my son and shall henceforth behave as such. To begin with, you will apologize to those you have offended, and then you will put this room to rights—before you go to bed. As for your attempt to run away, if you should decide to do so, I must advise you that I am most weary. It would anger me greatly to give pursuit at this hour, in this weather."

"By the Blood, why should you care?" Giles sneered, turning his face from Will.

"We shall have to do something about that mouth of yours," Will observed grimly. "As to why I should care, you are my son. I have no intention of losing you again."

Giles turned his head and fixed doubtful eyes on Will. Puzzlement, then a glimmer of hope appeared, only to disappear quickly, the accustomed veil falling as he continued to stare.

"Now, do what you are told and get to bed. We will speak of this further in the morning." He turned to leave and stopped, freezing to the spot. Eleanor stood in the open doorway, her face paling as she fixed on the boy's face. Slowly, her eyes rose to Will's, and they were filled with tears. Before she could move Will was at her side, taking her arm as he turned her from the doorway and ushered her down the hallway. Throwing open the door to his chamber, he pushed her in ahead of him and shut it behind them. As he turned back to her he opened his mouth to speak, but no words came. Suddenly he was incapable of thought, of what to say to her. He watched as she crossed to the hearth and stared into the flickering flames that leapt and snapped, their sound the only break in the heavy silence. Watching the rigid set to her back, he drew a deep breath, letting it out slowly as he waited, bracing himself for the outburst that was certain to come. Oh, God, he thought, there was already so much between them.

"Why, Will?" she said softly. At first he was not certain that she had spoken.

"Why?" he repeated. He could not fathom what she meant. "There is no why of it—only the fact that he exists. I did not know, Eleanor, until Darcy wrote to me while I was in France. Even then I did not know that he was mine until I saw him."

"Darcy?" Her head came up at the name and she turned it slightly. "What has he to do with this?"

"I do not know," Will answered tightly. "But I intend to find out. All I know is that the boy was sent to Northumbria to be fostered when his mother died in childbirth. I had been told that he also had died. He was raised as a stableboy."

She turned on his words and a brow arched as her eyes flashed indignation. "A stableboy?"

"He lived in filth—half starved." He shrugged, not knowing what else to say.

"With whom was he living?"

"Saebroc of Aldtern, who is counting his last days as lord of Castle Fountaine." Will smiled mercilessly, his thoughts turning to the luckless lord. "The fool crenellated without license."

"Indeed?" Eleanor's brow rose speculatively. "Well, the lands should do nicely for the boy. Divine justice, as given from His Majesty, I should think. That should not be difficult to manage."

Astonished, Will could only stare at her as he watched the deliberation working in her face. "Eleanor." He smiled self-consciously. "I do not know what to say. Can you truly be so generous with—"

"Your son?" She finished, regarding him oddly. "Of course. Do you think that I would hold his birth against him? You are four and thirty years, Will. Can you think me so naive not to consider that you might have a bastard or two about? The child needs you, I would not deny him that."

Will stared at her as he tried to reason what was happening. "Then what was this about? The tears, the look I saw in your face when you came into the room . . . And . . . your question. What did you mean by saying 'Why?' "

She drew up and regarded him contemptuously. "Will, answer me truthfully. He—Giles—is *hers*, isn't he?" When he did not answer, she felt her anger rise, and she swallowed back the tears of rage that bit at the back of her throat. "Answer me, he is Lavene of Fountaine's son, is he not?"

"Aye." he answered quietly. "He is Lavene's. But how did you—"

"How did I know?" She laughed, but the sound drew into a ragged gasp. "Will Marshal, I have been wed to you since I was but of nine years. But never did you tell me about her! Never! I had to learn of her through the gossip of court, the whispers, the words said behind my back! Poor Eleanor! Does not everyone know that Will Marshal can never love the poor little princess as his heart has been ever given to another!"

"God's breath, Eleanor! It was in the past, it happened when you were a child! How should I have told you?" he answered, his own anger growing. "And when should I have told you—when you were nine, twelve, fourteen?"

"You could have saved me from the humiliation of finding out from self-serving, bitter ladies-in-waiting who reveled in the pleasure of watching my reaction as I tried to cover my true feelings!" she cried. "Damn you, Will, you could have told me why you could never love me!"

"Eleanor, I . . . ," he tried, words suddenly failing him.

"Do not say it!" she railed. "I will not listen to lame words, offered now to appease me! Oh, God, Will, leave me alone! There is nothing you could say now that I would want to hear!''

A moment passed as neither could bear to look at the other, and then Will finally spoke. His voice was quiet and filled with regret, even with the anger he could not conceal. ''God help us, Eleanor,'' he said quietly. When she did not answer he shrugged with defeat. ''You may use this chamber. I will find another until you are settled.''

''It is not necessary,'' she answered stiffly. ''I have my own chamber; I have been here for some time.'' Seeing his surprise, she added mawkishly, ''Do not look so surprised, Will. This is my home as well as yours.''

''So it is, my lady,'' he replied coldly. ''And I shall leave you to find your own chamber.''

She turned to the sound of the latch as the door closed behind him, and a tremor ran down the length of her body. Everything always began and ended so badly. At moments life seemed so well planned, but nothing came to be as she dreamed. She slumped in defeat and felt the chill of the room. Moving closer to the fire, she sat in a chair and curled her legs up beneath her as her eyes fixed comfortingly upon the flames, warm, bright, sure in their leaping movement. But she knew that their heat would burn out, extinguishing their warmth, just as her dreams seemed ever to do. Why? she had asked him. The question had been so encompassing that she had not expected an answer even as she had asked it. It had simply slipped out, unable to be retracted once spoken.

Lavene was not the issue, though it had been part of the question. For years she had known about her, and the pain had been there, lingering. Seeing the boy standing there, looking so undeniably like Will, a vividly real reminder of what he had known with another—all had rushed back to strike her to the spot with dizzying pain. Their son, defying her with his existence, challenging her to accept the reality that he would never, never love her.

But had she not accepted that fact years ago? He had wiped her nose when she was hurt, soothed a scuffed knee, scolded her for her childish antics. And, as a woman, what had she given to him when he came to her as a man? Anger and hatred for abandoning her.

She rose from the chair and crossed to the window, needing to see beyond the confinements of the room and the torments of her thoughts. She sat upon the cold stone casement of the window and her gaze traveled over the narrow streets trapped in the steady, light rain. London, she thought, and her senses thrilled at the realization. England. And it is mine. All of it. A line of kings passed through her mind: battles won, laws, great demesnes, people. A domain of people. Memories played, recalling a moment standing in a field of newly turned earth, the warm, rich smell reaching her senses as she had looked up at Will with amazement. Oh, she would have it! And she would have him who first gave it to her.

She had not planned on the boy's unexpected appearance, but then, to be fair, neither had Will. Her anger gone, her heart reached out to him, realizing the torment he must be going through to have found the boy after all of these years, in such a condition. Oh, why had she handled it so badly? A minor setback, she reasoned with renewed determination. Oh, Will, she thought, it was you I loved first, and it is you I love now. You will become mine, all mine, not by the lion—you would expect that. But by more the subtle courage of a mystical beast. Beware, Will Marshal, for I shall have you.

Will sat alone in the darkened main room of the manor. He stared into the fire, the only light the flames which flickered about his thoughts as they played against the walls of the room. He took a long pull on his goblet, the fiery liquid easing his thoughts as he sought reason for all that was happening. He had returned to that vortex from which he never had found release. Action suited him, gave him simple answers, a battle planned, and won. The manners of men and politics were comfortingly familiar, yet he had returned to his most private life where nothing seemed to remain but turmoil. Why not a simple life, a wife content to wait upon his return, greeting him with affection, raising his children. But somehow it did not fit, even as he thought upon it. Was it because he could barely remember a time without Eleanor? All of his adult life she had been there. He drew on his wine, thinking about the child. The woman. The surprising things she had said before Giles had thrown his tantrum, and she *had* surprised him. She was correct about desRoches, he did play upon the fears of others. He hadn't heard such sense from her since she was in britches, playing at being a boy.

He chuckled, sipping from his goblet as memories of Eleanor the Hoyden passed through his mind. Beautiful, willful, dogmatic Eleanor. And she was that; the hoyden was gone but the firebrand remained, if what he experienced a short time before was any indication. He laughed softly, raising his goblet to his mouth, then paused, stiffening as he stared into the fire. Good God. That is what was different about her! That is what had been taunting him since that moment when she had appeared in deBurgh's chamber! She was . . . Eleanor again. When had she come back? What had happened to her? He rubbed his lips thoughtfully with a finger as his brows gathered. Was he wrong? Perhaps it was merely wishful thinking. His mouth drew into a wry smile at the prospect of finding out. There was certainly nothing to be lost and the game could prove rather interesting, the prize beyond value if he was right. Actually, now that he thought upon it, when she had wished him dead it had almost been a hopeful sign. At least it had been better than that pious vacuousness she had willed herself into. And, he admitted with a deep chuckle, it had been cleverly done.

Aye, it was time to begin living again! By the blood of Saint George, he would give her a courtship, that which he had never given her before, the courtship of a man for a woman he desires. Alan of Newbury—he snorted at the thought of her thinking to be in love with that simp. Heavy doubts remained, but he was eased by his thoughts and he stretched his long legs out before him, crossing them at the ankles as he stared into the flames and began to lay out his plans. Beware, Eleanor, he thought with a smile, for I am in pursuit.

Will was unaware of when he fell asleep. Dozing lightly in the chair, he was rudely awakened by a commotion in the hall without. Struggling to pull himself up, he stumbled to the door and threw it wide, his expression blackened by the interruption.

"Milord!" Alan Wadley gaped at him, obviously surprised to find Will standing in the doorway, glowering at him. Will blinked at the sudden brightness of the lighted hallway, but he came fully awake at the alarm he read in Alan's face. "What is it?" he asked, pulling himself together to step into the hall.

"The justiciar, milord," Alan gasped. "He has taken sanctuary in Saint Merton's Priory. Do you not hear the bells of London, milord? Even now a mob moves to take him. The bells call for the people of London to take him from sanctuary, by order of the King!"

20

DREAMS tossed with the sound of running footsteps as Eleanor pulled herself awake and lay still, listening. The bells of London were ringing! She pulled herself from the covers and threw back the bedcurtains. Pulling a wrap about her shoulders, she ran to the door. Though it was not yet dawn, the hallway was mayhem. Servants rushed about and squires passed laden with armor of chain and mail on errand for their knights. She saw Landon rush into Will's chamber at the end of the hallway, and she covered the span quickly, stopping at the open doorway as her heart stilled with apprehension. Will stood at the center of the room in full armor. The jazerant work of his hauberk gleamed in the flickering of the candle-light, the bright red lion rampant of his coat of arms glaring at her from the chest of his green tunic.

"Will, what has happened?"

Meryle stood back from fastening Will's sword belt as Will looked up to find her standing in the doorway, clad only in her bedgown and robe. Her hair was tousled about her shoulders and her eyes, though wide with dread, were touched by recent dreams. He stared for a prolonged moment, until realizing that Landon and Meryle were doing the same. "See that

Hamal is readied," he ordered sharply, dismissing the squires, who left quickly as they recognized all too well that tone of voice. "DeBurgh has sought sanctuary in Merton Priory." He turned his head to listen to the bells, which were ringing all over the city. "Listen to them, Eleanor. The Lord Mayor has ordered them rung as a call to the people. Even now the mobs are marching on the priory."

"Oh, Will!" she gasped. "You must see to Henry! Only he can stop it!"

"Henry?" he snorted, shaking his head. "My love, 'twas by his order."

She gaped at him, taking a moment to digest what he was saying. Disbelief passed over her expression, which then hardened as anger began to glitter in her eyes. "You must hurry," she said levelly. "When DeBurgh is secure, come to Windsor."

"Windsor? Eleanor . . ."

"Milord, Sir Wadley bids you to come! He says the men are ready." Giles appeared from behind Eleanor, his eyes bright with excitement.

Will nodded, taking up his sword from where it lay on top of his warchest, and slid it into his scabbard. As he passed them, he paused and looked down at Eleanor. "I will return when I can. Pray I am not too late."

"I shall so pray, milord, with all of my heart. But do not look for me here. I have told you, I shall be at Windsor. I am certain that with all that has happened, the court has returned—and there are things I would say to Henry."

He studied her for a moment, then a hint of a smile touched his lips. "I think I pity Henry more than deBurgh," he murmured. Ruffling Giles's head, he laid his hand on the boy's shoulder. "I charge you to care for the women in my absence. I will return as soon as I can."

With that he was gone. As Giles tried to follow, Eleanor stopped him, pulling him gently back to her. "Nay, Giles. Your father has much to do, as do we, and quickly. I have a feeling that it will be a long day, and food must be prepared to send to them. Now come and help me."

The boy stepped back and stared at her doubtfully. "I—I do not know you, lady."

She realized then that indeed, he could not. "I am your
father's wife, Giles of Striguil. Eleanor Plantagenet, Lady
Marshal, Countess of Pembroke," she said formally, and then
smiled warmly. "And, I hope, your friend."

"Striguil?" The boy frowned. "Why do you call me that? I
don't know anyone there."

"While that is true, you are, in fact, Giles of Striguil. Your
father owns vast demesnes in England, Ireland, and Normandy, but the seat of his estates is Striguil. As his son, so
shall you be called. Until, of course, he gives you lands of your
own."

"Lands of me own?" he gasped, then snorted with incredulity. "Not bloody likely."

She blinked, and then remembered the scene in the boy's
chamber. "Giles." She smiled, recovering. "Do you know
how the King is called?"

"The King?"

"His name is Henry Plantagenet."

"Planta—. Bloody, 'tis the same as yours!"

"Aye, so it is. I am his sister, Giles. Firstly, a gentleman has
respect for a lady. Barring that, he holds respect for his bet-
ters. But last of all, if you can remember none of that,
remember this. If you ever say 'bloody' in my presence again,
I shall have the King throw you into his tallest tower and give
me the key. Can you remember that, Giles?"

His mouth dropped open, then he smiled tentatively. "Pah,
ye don't mean that, do ye?"

"Try me." She passed by him and paused in the hallway,
turning back to him. "Well, are you coming? We have much
to do."

Will watched the scene before him from beneath the
shadows of his helm. Shifting in his saddle, he tried to make
himself more comfortable. He felt chilled to the bone from the
soaked gambeson beneath his hauberk as the steady rain,
which had continued falling throughout the day, ran in
rivulets beneath the mail. His cloak gave him little protection;
it had been soaked through within the first hour. A brief
glance about him confirmed that he was not alone in his discomfort. Rain, as well as intense heat, was the most bitter

enemy of the knight—that and waiting. Although he should be glad of the last. The confrontation before the Priory of Merton had become a standoff. The arrival of Will and his knights, seventy hardened, mailed warriors, and two hundred men-at-arms and yeomen, added to the forces of the Earl of Chester, had taken considerable energy from the rabble, who stood about, waiting to rush the sanctuary.

Pulling Hamal's head about, he rode into the courtyard of the priory and dismounted. Throwing Hamal's reins to a knight who stepped forward from the doorway, he entered the cool darkness of the priory. "How is he?" he asked an approaching monk who came from the sanctuary upon his entrance.

"I have encouraged him to eat something, but he takes only a little water."

Will passed by the monk and entered the sanctuary, his eyes drawn to the form supplicated before the altar. "The good brother tells me that you are being difficult, Hubert. You must eat something."

DeBurgh looked up and smiled at Will as he shrugged in answer. "I confess that my stomach has troubled me of late, Will. I prefer the pain of hunger to that which comes when I eat."

Will stared at him for a moment, then turned to the monk. "Bring some warmed milk," he said quietly, turning back to the justiciar as the cleric departed.

"Milk?" DeBurgh grimaced. "Will, have I been reduced to a babe? Perhaps it is so; I feel as helpless."

"The milk is an old remedy of my mother's." Will grinned. "My father had problems with his stomach in his late years, and milk seemed to help."

DeBurgh laughed softly. "Put that way, how can I refuse? I will take the comfort of his memory with the milk. I—I am glad that he is not here to see my shame, Will. I respected him above all others."

"There is no shame upon you, Hubert," Will responded gruffly. "The shame is Henry's, though it grieves me deeply to say it. Or, perhaps, after all, the shame is mine. I have been Henry's companion since he was nine. What did I leave undone?"

"Now I must protest. Henry, though he is young, is his own man. He does not allow himself to be well advised, as the truth takes too much effort. He vacillates between being a king and a builder, a man of the arts, where his true interests lie. He should have been born for study in a great university, not for the Throne of England."

"Alas, we do not choose our kings, they are given to us from the marriage bed. Perhaps it would be better for all if we were to choose them from those fitted to the position."

"You have at last lost your senses, Marshal." DeBurgh smiled, shaking his head. "To elect a ruler? Impossible! We would be reduced to anarchy!"

"Perhaps." Will shrugged. "But somehow . . ."

"Will!"

The pair turned to find Hugh Bigod striding toward them from the east end of the sanctuary, his face elated.

"Sweet Mother, Hugh, where did you come from?" Will asked with surprise.

"From the Countess Pembroke, Lady Marshal." He grinned broadly.

"My mother?" Will blinked.

"Nay, you fool, your wife!" Hugh grinned. "Moments following your departure from that accursed inn in Northumbria, I left with deBraose to join deFerrars at Windsor. Wipe that foolish look from your face, Marshal. Do you think we would remain behind? Beyond that, as to why I am here—she's done it, Will! I would not have believed it had I not seen it with these two eyes! Damn, I remember her when she was a scrawny, freckle-faced child, following you about like a puppy."

"Would you get to the point?"

"What? Oh, aye. Hubert, even as we speak, the mob is dispersing." He laughed at deBurgh's dumbfounded expression. "They have been charged that no harm will come to you, upon their own safety. Will, you should have seen her. She swept into the King's presence without being announced and began to lay into him. But desRoches—that you should have seen. When she was through chastising Henry, she turned on him and her voice would have melted butter. Bloody damned if she didn't top him at his own game!"

"Hugh." Will cleared his throat as he noted the blanched expression of the monk who stood nearby. "Would you remember where you are?"

"Oh, of course." The Earl flushed, then quickly enjoined his story. "DesRoches was calling for your hide, Hubert—sorry, but I'm not saying what you do not already know. He accused you of seducing Margaret to claim the throne of Scotland, compared you to the despot Longchamp, accused you of being responsible for the war with Wales, and of defiling the treasury as well as the trust of London. And then she took it. She pointed out that if the citizens of London were allowed to achieve their purpose, might not their strength then be used against their grievances toward the Crown? You should have seen Henry's face on that one! She reminded the Lord Mayor of London, who was present, that the motto of the drapers, the most powerful of guilds, was 'Unto God only be honor and glory,' and that glory was not found in the actions of a mob. And then she reminded Henry of Thomas à Beckett and what Henry II had suffered by allowing the defilement of sanctuary. Will, she shamed them! All but desRoches, of course. He turned blood-red, but at that point it mattered not. Henry gave the order, and it is done!"

"Praise God," DeBurgh uttered in a choked voice.

"Praise Eleanor Marshal!" Hugh chortled.

"Hugh!" Will admonished, though he was filled with pride and wonder at what she had done.

"I must see to Margaret and the children," DeBurgh said as if to himself.

The words brought Will from his musings, and he turned to the justiciar with alarm. "Do not even think upon it! Hubert, I have sent men to add to your own and they have taken your family to Bury Saint Edmunds. So near to Framlingham and Hugh's forces, no one will dare harm them. You must not leave sanctuary until we can find a solution to this! Swear to me! God's breath, man, if you leave this place you are placing yourself in desRoches's hands! Swear!"

"Will is right, Hubert," Hugh agreed. "Your family is safe—on my word."

"I will not swear, Will. Such has been forbidden to us by God. But as I can give it, you have my promise."

"So be it." Will sighed wearily. "Give us time, Hubert, be patient. This will be resolved, on that you have my word."

Will rode to Windsor only to learn that the court was at William's Tower, to observe some "stupendous occasion." Baffled, he rode with a small party of his men to join the court—to the White Tower, they now seemed to call it since Henry had had the entire keep whitewashed. We move in circles, he mused, riding along the Thames toward his destination. All is the same as life appears to change, yet remains.

My God, he thought, a "stupendous occasion." Hubert deBurgh, the justiciar of England, a man who had given the whole of his life for what he believed, was being held in sanctuary, clinging to an altar of a minor priory and what remained of his life. Meanwhile, Will had spent the night and most of the day in the pouring rain, soaked to the bone, his soul chilled with the prospect of the death of a great man taken by an unruly mob, on order of the King of England, urged by a bishop of the Church. Now, changed into dry clothes he had found at Windsor—how had Eleanor thought of that among all of this—he rode toward a stupendous occasion. It had better be good.

The rain had stopped and the sun emerged between high, breaking clouds to warm the drenched streets as Will rode toward the tower. He left Hamal in the care of a farrier and moved through the throng that had gathered in the inner ward. The atmosphere was charged with gaiety as tradesmen, hawking their wares, moved among the brightly costumed members of court and many of London's wealthier merchants who had come for the occasion. This was Henry's work, he reasoned, there was no doubt of it. Only Henry could cause this in the midst of all that had happened. The contrast of activity on the green, before the imposing keep, to the moments only a night past when he had walked these same steps, struck Will uncomfortably and he felt a surge of anger. Gravitating to the center of the crowd, he found Eleanor flanked by ladies of the court and knights who stood about to hold the crowd from them. Coming up behind her, he bent to her ear.

"What is he up to now?" he murmured.

"Will!" She turned with delight and gave him a warm

smile. "Wait and see." She laughed happily as she slid her arm in his and leaned against him.

He looked down at her with a glimmer of surprise, which he covered quickly. Putting his hand over hers where it rested on his arm he bent his head. "Hubert sends you his gratitude," he said in a low voice as he glanced about at the gathering. "You amaze me, Eleanor. When you said that you had words for Henry—I could not realize. I am very proud of you."

"Indeed?" she said, turning to regard him with amusement, but a glow shined from her eyes which he missed as his eyes swept over the crowd. Looking beyond his shoulder, she squeezed his arm. "Oh, look!" she exclaimed. "There is what we have come for!"

He turned, and gaped. "Jesu!" he gasped. "What is it?"

"An elephant." She laughed. "Henry's newest pet."

An elephant. Aye, he reasoned, it was indeed an elephant. And Henry was there, as the animal's keeper led the enormous beast, scampering by its side like an idiot. The animal was truly awesome, there was no denying its grandeur. He watched, absolutely fascinated, but then it struck him. This was the stupendous occasion. At that moment he spied Giles, romping behind Henry, and something snapped. "Why did you bring him here?" he gritted.

"Bring whom?" She followed his gaze and glanced back at him. "He is a child, Will. This is the fantasy of a child."

He turned to Landon, who stood nearby, and curtly ordered him to fetch Giles. "I am leaving, as will you if you honor my wishes." He glared blackly, his gaze returning to the animal, which, to his mind, seemed as out of place and disquieted as he.

She opened her mouth to speak but shut it again as she noted the deep glower in his expression. Giles was brought, against his protest, and she gathered him to her, silencing him with a look of warning as he began to argue against the realization that they were leaving.

They returned to the London house, and over supper Giles enthusiastically recounted the happenings of the day to Isabella. She greeted his stories with the proper interest, punctuating his words with an occasional exclamation while her eyes surreptitiously noted the tension between Will and

Eleanor. Soon after Giles had finished his supper, she ushered him off to bed, closing the door to the hallway as they left. Brooding, Will leaned back in his chair and stared moodily into his goblet as he turned it in his fingers.

"Richard was there," Eleanor said lightly, seeking to break the tension. "I should not have allowed Isabella to remain behind; they would have had some time together."

"Perhaps she had better things to do with her time—not to mention the good sense not to participate in such triviality," he answered churlishly.

Her mouth worked with anger, but she repressed it with effort. "Will Marshal, life does go on. No one feels more for deBurgh than I, but there are others who have needs and are feeling pain in their lives. Your sister, for one. And your son."

His head jerked up at her criticism, but as his eyes met hers he softened, regretting the foolishness of his words. "How can I say such to you? You did it all, you saved him. I did not mean to criticize."

She answered softly. "Will, I—I do know how you feel. It was you kept him safe until something could be done. I know that you are worried for him, Will, but it will not help him to fret about it tonight. In the morning, perhaps answers will be found. There is always the morning."

He looked up and their gazes locked for a prolonged moment. Flushing, she rose and began to turn away but he stood up and reached out, taking her hand to draw her back to him. When their hands touched, both felt the shock of the encounter. "Will," she said nervously, "Darcy has been waiting to speak with you."

He reached up and touched her face lightly, trailing a finger over her cheek to her lips. His eyes followed his finger, lingering on the trembling of her lips, then his eyes raised to hers. "Sleep well, my love," he murmured softly.

Shaken, she stepped back and turned, practically fleeing from the room. He laughed softly, knowing how much he had unsettled her. Beware, Eleanor, he thought. It has only begun.

His thoughts were still fixed on pleasant fantasies when Darcy joined him. He looked up at the goliard and sighed, releasing his thoughts regretfully. "I am chilled," he growled. "There is a fire in the other room; let us see to it."

As they settled in the warmth of the small hall chamber, Will surprised Darcy by pouring them each a goblet of wine. As he handed one to the goliard, Will noted Darcy's amused expression. "I have told Landon and Meryle to retire. I think we need some privacy for this talk. Now, Darcy," he added grimly as he took a chair across from the bard, "no lyrics, no rhymes, no parables. The straight, unvarnished truth. How did you know about Giles?"

"Ah, well, it is not an easy story to tell. I might say that Eleanor's song came to me as well." Will glowered at him and he held up an appeasing hand and smiled. "No parables, Will, I promise. You shall have the truth, but I can only recount it in my way. I would ask a little patience—it may take a moment if you are to understand." He paused to take a long draught from his goblet as he stretched out his legs and stared into the fire. "You once asked me who I was. I was born in Northumbria, to the amusement of the gods, a bastard. Oh, I shall tell you no tales of a pitiful childhood. My father was titled, and while we did not particularly care for each other, he treated me well enough. My mother, a tirewoman to my father's wife, lived until I was fourteen. When she died, my father was generous enough to give me the choice of my life's work—to be fostered by another to learn the arts of warfare, or to enter the Church.

"There was really never any choice for me. When I was ten I had traveled to Rome with my father. There I had heard Francis of Assisi speak. It was on that day that I became his. In short, I entered the order of Franciscans, dedicating myself to a life of poverty and service. I saw it as the life most closely emulating that of Our Lord's, and of those in the order from which I learned, I believed to be saints. However, by the time I was twenty the ugliness of humanity had been revealed to me. Self-sacrifice is heresy, Will; it causes guilt in those who cannot understand it and they fear those who choose it. The order began to split into factions, Zealots on the one hand who demanded the extreme of poverty, and Moderates on the other who conceded to a measure of property and wealth. And a war began, as it always has, in the name of the Peaceful Christ. Oh, there was more, of course, that led to my decision to leave the order. In my position as one assigned to the Holy Office—

a lowly position, I assure you"—he grinned—"I became involved with many of the new translations of the Greeks. It was then that I began to hear the song. Not the song our unicorn sings to the Church, wherein the truth of nature is only that which gives spiritual and moral understanding; nor the one that warriors of your order have heard, whereby they gain the mystical purity of their soul. But the one of Aristotle, the truth of man's relationship with nature and the spirit of the soul. The true wisdom of the unicorn. It was soon after that I left the order."

"Now I understand why you agreed so readily when I asked you to take a position at the university in Paris as a translator," Will observed, raising a brow. "No wonder it was so easy for you to affect the guise of a monk!" Darcy shrugged as he drew from his wine, and Will sobered and his voice softened evenly. "Your work for us there was vital, Darcy. The knowledge you brought us saved many lives. But I can now understand why you wanted to leave so suddenly, and I can sympathize with your decision to return to England. It must have been very painful for you to work with Roger Bacon and Thomas Aquinas and then betray those you met there."

"You overestimate me, Marshal." Darcy smiled, shaking his head. "It caused me no discomfort to spy for you. My work with Aquinas and Bacon placed me in contact with those having the knowledge you needed, but there was never a time when I betrayed the trust of those great men. Nay, my reason for returning was not because of what I did—but because of what I could not do." Finishing his wine, he rose and refilled their goblets, then leaned against the mantle of the hearth, looking back to the flames in his inability to meet Will's gaze. "It was too late. The mystical beast no longer sings for me. Too much has happened, I have seen too much, committed far too many crimes against what I believe in, to have continued to work with them. And here the story becomes simpler. I returned to Northumbria, whereupon I saw Giles and wrote to you. And then I returned here to London to wait for you."

Darcy moved to his chair, slumping into it as he drew from his goblet with a moody expression. For a long moment the only sounds were the crackling of the fire and distant sounds from the street without. At last, Will broke the silence. "Now tell me all of it," he said quietly. "Nay, save that innocent look for someone who believes it. Let us retrace a little—to the years you are not telling me about. When you first left the order of the Franciscans—where did you go?"

"I returned home for a time, only to find less than what I had left." He shrugged. "My father had long since died and a distant cousin had inherited the estates. It really did not matter, however, I had not intended to stay. My anger with the Church, with the injustices I had seen by those in power over men's lives, the deep philosophical teachings of Aristotle, which had become forever ingrained in my soul, left me no choice but to become a goliard." He laughed at Will's shocked expression. "You believe all goliards to be outcasts, miscreants. And I imagine that we are. Miscreants, at least. But outcast? I had never been that. The choices in my life were fully mine. I chose the life with much deliberation as the only one which would give me the freedom to express my beliefs. That which would give me the occasional though intense pleasure of seeing a man's eyes widen with new thought, a new idea. Oh, eventually I will probably hang for it, but never again will I know the regret of stifling knowledge and whatever wisdom God may see fit to reveal to me."

Will listened, but as Darcy finished he pinned a steady gaze on him. "Why did you return to Northumbria, Darcy? Surely you knew that your father had died, and you say that you never intended to stay." When Darcy did not answer, he pressed. "For whom did you return, Darcy?"

Darcy sighed heavily but he did not avoid the question. "My sister—my half sister, that is. We had been very close as children. I think that she was the only human being I had ever truly loved. But she died a short time before my return. After that, there was no reason to stay."

"Darcy. Who are you?" Will watched the goliard's reaction to his question, and he felt the tension building in him as he waited for the answer.

The bard stared into his goblet for a long moment, then looked up at Will unflinchingly. "Even as Giles, I have no surname, Will. But I was once known as Darcy of Fountaine."

Will felt himself go numb, as if all the blood had left his

body. When he could finally speak, his voice sounded distant. "You are Lavene's half brother."

"I am. Or, rather, I was," he added sadly. "When I learned that she had died, far from Northumbria, I had to find out what had happened to her."

"Then it was as I suspected," Will murmured. "It was not a chance meeting between us."

"Nay, it was not. I had made it a rather studied hobby to learn of the Marshals. At first, the object was revenge. Later, when I came to know your family—and you in particular—it changed. There was little that I did not know about you by then, but most important was that you loved her—that you would never have done anything to harm her. Indeed, that your grief was as great as mine."

Will rose from the confinements of the chair and, for something to do, he topped off his goblet. Drawing a deep breath against the anger he felt pushing at him, he glanced about the shadows of the room before turning to face the waiting bard. "What of Giles?" he said derisively. "You returned to Northumbria; how could you turn your back on her child?"

Darcy rose from his chair to confront Will's accusation, his eyes flaring blackly. "Damn you, Marshal, for accusing me of that! You accepted her death and that of the child! You had the advantage of me; I did not even know how she died, or where, or that she had had a child, until long after the fact! When I finally found out, I wanted to murder you, Marshal! To let her die like that—alone! You condemn me easily, yet how easily you accepted what you were told! A little effort, a little time, perhaps you would have learned that the child had not died!"

"When did you discover that he had lived?" Will asked tightly, fighting the truth of Darcy's words and the echoes of his own guilts that had plagued him since he had first laid eyes on Giles.

"Rumors, suspicions." The goliard shrugged, turning away. His mouth drew into a wry, almost angry smile. "There are advantages to having a background as a cleric. A humble monk arrives at a convent. Solicitous attention is given to a nun ill-suited to the order, the type who is all too ready to confide in someone who will grant a little attention to her. You would be amazed at what secrets are revealed. I returned to Northumbria, and he was there. It took little prodding to gain the truth from Lavene's tirewoman.'' Seeing the deep look of pain, the questions in Will's eyes, he softened. "Lavene had bidden her to take the child to you if anything happened to her. But it seemed that my father had somehow learned of it. When Lavene died, he had sent someone for the woman and the babe—and had bestowed a rather large gift to the convent to keep the matter quiet. 'Tis a puzzle, Will, one I have never been able to reason. My father was . . . ah, shall we say, not the fatherly type. Why he wished to be saddled with another bastard I cannot fathom. I suspect that the answer resides with him in hell.''

Will turned away, unable to face Darcy as the painful truth tore through him. Oh, God. He could answer that question; perhaps he was the only one who could. Bile rose at the back of his throat as he acknowledged that the truth did indeed lie in hell. It was a confidence he would keep. He would not share his agony, causing Darcy the pain of knowledge he had carried with him all of these years. Should he tell Darcy of the licentious nature of his father? That he had ravished his own daughter, causing her a living hell until she escaped to be fostered by Isabel? Will could well imagine the Count of Fountaine's reasons for wanting the child, the child of the mother who had escaped him. He could only thank God that the despot had died while Giles was still a babe. Finally, he said only, "You are correct, Darcy, the answer must reside with your father. But I must know, why did you not tell me of the boy's existence when you first learned of it?"

"Why should I have?" Darcy responded, surprised by the question. "I had no reason to suspect that he was yours." His face softened as he recalled his memories. "As a babe his hair was fair. He was an imp, so like I remembered his mother. I swear to you, Marshal, his early years were tender, I saw to that. I visited him as much as possible and made sure of his welfare." Then his expression turned as if a storm had raised. "And then my cousin died without issue, and the estates were granted to the cousin of Saebroc of Aldtern. I was no longer given license to visit Giles. I sent what coin I could, wrote to him, though there is little doubt now that neither coin nor letter reached him."

"But when you discovered how I felt about her—why did you not tell me then? Knowing that I loved her, how could you keep it from me?"

"How can you ask that, Will Marshal?" a feminine voice came from behind them. Both men spun about to find Eleanor standing in the opened door to a side room. "Would you pour me some wine, Will?" she asked, coming into the room, the skirts of her russet silk gown sweeping over the floor as she moved. "I recall the day when Darcy entered our lives," she mused. "What was he to say? 'I am Darcy of Fountaine, my Earl Marshal, half brother to your cherished Lavene. There is a child, now residing in Northumberland. . . .' Really, Will! Would you have believed it? Besides, as he has told you, he had no reason to suspect that you would accept a child not yours—no matter how much you had loved the mother."

"That is true, Will, I swear. It was only when I returned from France and determined to see him, in spite of Aldtern, that I knew, seeing him grown. Having known you these past years, I could not but recognize the resemblance—it was quite a shock. 'Twas then that I wrote to you."

Will looked from one to the other as words and the confusion of Eleanor's sudden appearance tussled. The fact of Eleanor's presence won out. "Dammit, Eleanor, what are you doing in here?" he shouted.

"You need not raise your voice, Will," she said calmly, pouring a goblet for herself. "I have been listening to every word for some time."

"You've been eavesdropping?" Will gasped, his face flushing with rage.

"Now, I wonder who made that a crime?" she mused, sipping from the goblet. "If one is not prepared to accept the discomfort of hearing words spoken against one, then one should never listen. If, on the other hand, one had been raised as I have been, never trusting words spoken directly, the insincerity of flattery ever masking truth, one learns to trust only what is read between the lines—and I have become rather adept at that fine art—or when those who are speaking are not aware that one is listening. So much for your fine sensibilities,

Will. I assure you that I did not come with the purpose of
eavesdropping, but I will not apologize for doing so. As for
your other question, Will, the answer is painfully simple. Until
Darcy knew the child was yours, there was no reason to tell
you of his existence. Moreover, the question is now moot. The
only consideration now is Giles's welfare. Looking at his
prospects, they appear quite good. He has the love of his
father and a stepmother who accepts him completely. In
Darcy he has the tender regard of a doting uncle, and for the
rest—I should think that our only concern need be that your
family does not smother him with their attentions.''

The two men gaped at her, and it was Darcy who first broke
the tension with the sound of his deep laughter. Shaking, he
set his goblet on a nearby table. "In the love of God, Will,
there is nothing more to be said, as your lady has summed it
up quite nicely. With that I shall seek my bed. The hour past
has left me feeling slightly drained but, I will admit, with more
enthusiasm and hope than I have felt in a long, long time.''
With that he left them.

Will stared for a moment at the empty doorway left by
Darcy, his feelings muddled, feeling incomplete, and he spun
on Eleanor in his frustration. "Sweet Mother Mary and
Joseph!''

"Now, Will," she said sweetly, deliberately refilling his
goblet. "There is nothing more you can do tonight. You need
time to think on all that has been said.''

His brain worked furiously as he sought to respond, but it
melted into a frustrating blank. The past hours had left him
exhausted; it was too much to think upon. There was so much
more he wanted to say to Darcy, yet there was nothing; it had
been said. And then there was the unreal fact of Eleanor's sudden presence. This new Eleanor. The thought struck him that
even in the midst of heated battle, when hundreds of men
depended on the clarity of his thinking, he had not been so
struck. And now, in the presence of one frustrating woman,
he could not think clearly. One frustrating, breathtaking,
beautiful, woman. He glared at her as his gaze fixed upon the
dark curls of her tousled hair that hung over her slender
shoulders. He tried not to notice the graceful form beneath
the clinging silk of her robe, the fullness of her breasts, the

narrow waist, the full hips . . . and the fact that she was his wife. And they were alone. Suddenly, he wanted to grab her, pull her into his arms, kiss that neck just above the point where her robe fell apart. Swallowing heavily, he braced himself as a stronger determination took reason. He reached out and gently pushed back a wayward curl that hung over her shoulder. He felt her body tremble beneath his touch, and he fought the temptation to smile at the small victory.

"I thought you were in bed," he said softly. "Why did you come?"

For a moment she could not think except to focus on the heat in her body that his touch had caused. It consumed her, focusing on an aching need that spread from her middle and pushed everything else from her mind. Oh, sweet Lord, she thought, how could he merely touch me and cause this? She recognized desire, her memory sharpened to remembrances of what he had once given her. But she had not planned it like this! Oh, she had learned so much, and she knew it would not be as before. This time, when he took her, she would not hold herself back from him. She wanted him, and needed him, but as she would give, she had to have more from him. Not just the desire of a man who needed to expend himself on the body of his wife. She needed all of him, his body, his desire, and his love. She pulled away, stepping from him, and turned aside so that he would not see the torment in her eyes, the need. "You asked me why I came. A messenger came for you, Will, soon after you retired here with Darcy. Before I tell you of the missive, will you promise me not to rush from this chamber?"

He frowned, tensing at what she was not saying. "What was it, Eleanor?"

"Promise me!" she insisted. "If you do not, I shall not tell you!"

"Dammit, Eleanor, I promise. Now tell me!"

She turned back to him, regarding him steadily. "Will, Hubert has left sanctuary. He has been taken to the tower."

He stared at her for a moment, then his face flushed and he began to turn away toward the door. "Will, you promised!" she cried, grabbing for his arm. "Listen to me!" He pulled his arm from hers, but he turned back though his face had gathered into a dangerous storm. "Will, you cannot do anything for him now. Believe me, there is nothing for it!''

"You allowed me to sit by, dwelling in my own interests, even as he was being taken! By the Blood, Eleanor, how could you!''

"How could I? Because I know Henry! I tell you that nothing can be done now! DeBurgh spelled his own fate when he left sanctuary! You warned him, Will, pleaded with him to see reason, you told me so yourself! If you go there now, it will be worse than if you did nothing! Give it time, let Henry wallow in his moment of victory. Tomorrow, as always, Henry will see his decisions from a different light. Do not demand of him now! Tomorrow, Will.''

Will drew a deep breath, letting it out slowly. He knew she was right. Smiling sadly, he reached up and touched her cheek. "Eleanor, I have known him well, even longer than you. How is it you can read him so well while I seem to know him less and less as each year passes?''

"Because, my love, you can see beyond to that which is greater,'' she answered softly. "While I—I remain in that reality, the damnation that is my family. He is my brother and I understand him, I feel what he is feeling, I think what he thinks.''

"Nay, I do not reason that you think the same,'' he countered with a smile. "Perhaps that of Henry, your grandfather, but your reasoning is far beyond that of your brother, and most certainly that of your father.''

"You forget my namesake. Can you so easily dismiss my grandmother, Eleanor of Aquitaine?'' she smiled mischievously, her eyes now dancing. "There were women who gave to what I now feel. With each great Plantagenet, nay even back to the Conqueror, there was a woman of strength and wisdom. Think upon it, Will Marshal, Earl of Pembroke.''

"Oh, nay!'' He laughed, drawing away from her. "I shall not think upon that! Would you drive me to insanity?'' But his look was warm. He knew then, with startling clarity, why Eleanor was so important in his life—what he had seen in her, even as a child. Lavene would have depended upon him beyond what he could give, drained him, even as he needed the strength, the support he had so dearly known from the women in his life: those beautiful, gentle, loving, and damnably im-

possible Marshal women. How he pitied those who thought of
a woman merely as a supplicating object, never understanding. And Eleanor. Oh, she infuriated him, confounded him,
but was that not part of the whole? Would he not readily accept the same in a man whom he considered the dearest friend?
Ah, but the difference, the difference.

He reached out, laying a hand at her waist, and drew her to
him. "Eleanor," he murmured softly, his eyes filled with
questions that were answered in her own. He bent his mouth
to her waiting lips, the shock of their eager softness filling his
senses. They drank of each other, drawing dizzily to the reality
of the promise of that kiss. Well-laid plans escaped both of
them, dissolving in the warmth that washed in a rushing sensation. Thoughts tried to enter, but were gently and firmly
pushed aside. Now, only now, the past gone, a new beginning.
And they heard the soft, gentle song of the unicorn.

21

WILL was dizzy with pursuit; his mind swam with the realization that her desire matched his own. As his hand worked down the fastenings of her gown, she was pulling at his clothes. "Eleanor, I will take you to your chamber," he murmured huskily.

"Nay—I cannot wait," she breathed. She tried to work the lacings at the side of his tunic and swore as the knots would not give into her fingers.

"Patience, love." He chuckled softly with delight. "Someone might come in. There is no latch on this door."

"Then their embarrassment shall be greater than mine," she countered, breaking a knot. "Oh, Will, I do not care."

"Eleanor!" He burst into laughter, covering her hands with his own to stay them. "What has come over you?"

"You, if you hurry—please!"

"Please?" A dark brow arched. "Can this be the same maid who fought me, fought her own feelings?"

"Will Marshal, do you want to talk or make love to me?" she rejoined, stepping back to look at him. "There was a time when you did not give me a choice. You plied me, until I accepted you. Now I want you as much as you once wanted me,

275

and you stand there talking reason!''

"Do you want me, Eleanor, truly?" he asked softly, his eyes boring into hers. As her mouth drew into a gentle smile he stepped toward her.

She put a hand up to his chest to stop him and stepped toward the hearth. In answer, she began to undo her gown. She unclasped the shoulders, drawing each slowly from her arms as she fixed her eyes with a seductive message. He stood watching, his arms folded across his chest as he watched with interest, and an amused glint that made her blink with a moment's doubt. He wasn't suppose to be amused! She had planned this for so long—those eyes were supposed to be filled with . . . with passion! For a moment she panicked but as her hands went to the ties of her chemise, pulling one ribbon slowly, ever so slowly, his expression changed. She saw his body tense, and the blue of his eyes darkened with an interest that now held no humor. Thrilled, her eyes held his, brightened with desire and purpose, and she knew that their blatant meaning was burning into his brain. Encouraged, she continued to unlace the chemise, drawing the ribbons apart with slow deliberation. Then she reached back with one hand to release the final fastenings of the gown. Suddenly, the soft, purposeful gleam in her eyes faded, turning to dismay. Unconsciously her tongue caught between her teeth as she tugged and pulled at the fastening at the middle of her back that would not give. "Damn!" she swore softly, yanking at the fabric.

Firm hands took her shoulders and he turned her around, and she flushed at the soft sound of his deep chuckle. The gown slipped over her hips, drifting to her feet, and he turned her back to face him. She fixed on the buckle of his belt, not wanting to see the laughter in his eyes. Damn, she had wanted this to be so perfect, and she had botched it completely! What a twit he must think her to be. He lifted her face with a finger under her chin, but she would not look at him. "Eleanor." The tenderness of his voice brought her gaze up to his. She thrilled at the heated look in his eyes as they moved with blatant hunger over her body, now thinly clad in the linen of her chemise. "Want you?" he asked thickly. "I never wanted anything more."

He stepped back from her and withdrew his garments. Fascinated, she watched as another part of him was revealed, that which she had not brought herself to look upon before. Lud, Eleanor, she thought, what a fool you were. She feasted on the hardened muscles of his chest and arms, the flat, round muscles of his stomach, and, shyly, her eyes drew lower in curiosity. The full, erect strength of his member drew her eyes, which widened as she stared. Memory of the intimacy he had given to her, driven her to accept, now compelled her. She wanted to touch him as intimately, to become as familiar with his body as he had once been with hers. Her eyes rose to his and she smiled seductively, pleasuring in the slight flaring of his eyes as he recognized her purpose. Slowly, she slipped the straps of her chemise from each shoulder, allowing the garment to slip to her feet. A rush of warmth filled her at what she read in his eyes as they moved boldly, eagerly over her body. Now, Will, she thought, at last you will truly become mine. She stepped toward him, unaware that her feet had become entangled in the pile of clothing. As her mouth softened into a promise, the world suddenly disappeared.

"Eleanor!" he stared down at her as she lay spread-eagled at his feet.

"Damn!" she cried, the sound muffled in the garments. He knelt and tried to draw her up but she pulled away as a small fist pounded the floor.

"Eleanor, it is all right," he pleaded, trying furiously not not laugh.

She garbled a shriek into the clothing. "Ohhh, I can't handle this! Go away!"

"Not likely," he strangled. "Eleanor, are you hurt?"

"I—I think I bruised my leg," she said in a muffled voice. Sitting up, she rubbed the spot on her thigh, sniffing back her tears. "Oh, damn," she said miserably. "I have ruined everything."

"You fell," he said with a voice of reason. "It could have happened to anyone." But the strange sound that came from his throat made her jerk away. "Eleanor!" he protested, but he erupted into laughter. She squealed, twisting away, but he grabbed her and managed to pin her down under him. "Oh, God, Eleanor," he gasped, "My sweet, beautiful, fascinating

Eleanor. Life with you will never be dull." He started laughing again, and, suddenly seeing the humor, she started to giggle and then burst into laughter that joined his as she wrapped her arms about him. Her warm, soft body brought him back to his senses, and, holding her still, he bent and kissed the spot she had hurt. "If you think that I will let you go now, then indeed you have truly lost your senses," he said, his humor spent as his voice grew husky.

He lowered her to the rug as his lips covered hers, stifling the last gurgles of her humor. Years began to slip away. Memories danced, passing through them; understanding and trust long forgotten teased, then touched their emotions like a pervading spirit. Intoxicated, Eleanor reached up to slip her arms about his neck, this man who had been everything to her for more years than she could remember. So much time had been lost.

He pleasured in the sound of her soft sighs as his hands spoke for him. His lips trailed over her shoulder, lingering at the tender spot at the base of her neck and traveled unhurried to a breast. His fingers teased the full nipple, preparing it for the assault of his mouth and tongue. As his mouth took her breast she gasped, then moaned as she arched her back to him, and he felt a deep thrill rush through him. Even as she began to move beneath him and cried out softly, pleading, he would not surrender her breasts, knowing with dizzy anticipation that this time her pleading was for fulfillment. His hand slipped lower, stroking the silkiness of her body until it found the tender object of his search, and she thrust her hips up as a soft sob tore from her. He opened his eyes in surprise and raised his head to look down at her, amazed by her passion. Her head was turned, her face filled with ecstasy, and he marveled, watching her as his fingers expertly stroked and played with the core of her desire. She called out his name and he persisted, measuring the moment, feeling the muscles of her stomach begin to tense, then tremble beneath his arm. He slipped gently over her, replacing his fingers with his phallus, stroking gently, then he thrust into her. Her legs came up about his waist as she sought to feel him deeper within her, and she began to move with him, matching each thrust, until she gasped softly, tensing for a moment, then cried out with fulfillment. He groaned as he found his own release, all thought driven from him as his climax broke furiously over him.

She lay wrapped in his arms before the warmth of the fire. He had pulled the skirts of her gown half over them, as much for protection against an intruder as for warmth. Neither was willing to disturb the moment, even to retire to a bedchamber. Will's arm covered one breast as Eleanor lay with her back against him, facing the fire, and his fingers gently stroked the other. His thoughts had drifted. Relaxed and sated, he had not sought for reason but it had unmercifully invaded, and his brow was creased in a slight frown. She was an enigma. She had become the woman he had always hoped she would be—but what had happened? What had caused this change in her?

"Oh, Will." She sighed, an edge to her voice that echoed his own thoughts.

"What is it, love?" He bent and kissed an ear, seeing the disturbed frown she wore. "Are you . . . dissatisfied?" The thought struck that now the recriminations were coming, the guilt, the hatred, because she had found fulfillment. He wondered how they could go on, living as they had before.

Absorbed, she was unaware of the tenseness of his body against her back, but his words had gained her attention. "Hardly that, milord," she said softly. "I have never known such pleasure." She bent her head and kissed his arm. "It is me. I know it is unsuitably unromantic to say, but . . . this floor is hard. And I'm cold."

Relaxing, he chuckled, pulling the skirt up about her as he bent to kiss the spot beneath her ear. "Soft beds are always preferable to a hard floor—or practically anywhere else that I can think of for matters of love. Although, variety does add spice. It leads my mind to great speculation."

"Variety?" she mused, dreamily. "Oh, aye Will. Let us never become like—like—oh, those dried-up marriages where they have no interest in each other anymore—if they ever did. We won't be like that, will we?" She turned her head to look at him, and he kissed the end of her nose.

"I will do my best to prevent it, sweetling," he murmured.

She had already turned to look back at the leaping flames on the hearth, and her eyes had turned to speculation. "Do you think that it is possible for people—lovers—to really be like those told about by the troubadours? Oh, Will, could we be like, say, Tristan and Isolde?"

"I hope not!" he exclaimed with mock horror. "Tristan died, or had you forgotten?"

"That is not what I meant," she scoffed, miffed that he refused to take the matter seriously. "There was more to it than that, much more." She paused, thinking about what she had discovered in Brother Vincent's book. But this wasn't the time to tell him about that—not now. " 'Twas their eternal love to which I was referring. When she died, their love was so great that vines grew from their graves, to intertwine about the oak tree above where they lay, to last for all time."

"I cannot answer for eternity, Eleanor, but I can account for this life of mine, and it is pledged to you, now as it has always been."

"As it always has been?"

"Always."

"Then why did you leave me?" she blurted, the words coming unexpectedly.

"Eleanor, I had no choice, you know that. The war with France made it imperative—"

"Nay, I mean before!" she cried softly, turning in his arms to look at him. "Why did you leave me, Will? Without even so much as a goodbye. When I came to find you—I wanted to—oh, I do not even remember now, some childish concern that meant so much to me then—and you were gone! You did not come back Will, for four years!"

He sat up, wrapping an arm about a bent knee. What could he say to her? "Did I hurt you so very much?" he asked softly.

She sat up but did not look at him, turning her back to him as she stared into the flames, the hurt and sorrow of those years rushing back. Aye, she would have it from him, the explanations, answers to the questions she had tortured herself over. She had to know. "I hated you," she said quietly.

"When you returned, I hated you still. Nay, more. It had a long time to grow."

"Is that why you wished me dead?" he asked gently, without accusation.

"You knew."

"I knew."

She did not answer for a long moment. "It was quite a spectacle. They still talk about it at court." She laughed sadly. "The Vow of the Peacock. No one knew my true motive, not even I." She hesitated. "Except you. Will, please believe me, I did not realize what it meant until it was too late. I tried to find you, to explain, but you were gone."

He turned her about to look at him. "Eleanor, listen to me. I do believe you, and I am glad that you've told me. And as for leaving you, even now, knowing how I hurt you, I cannot think of a way to have changed what happened." Seeing the hurt in her eyes, he pressed. "Listen to me carefully. Think upon what we found together tonight, the fulfillment, that is the love between a man and woman. Even when you fought and struggled against your own feelings, the emotions you were capable of finding within yourself were those of a woman, giving herself to a man." He drew his breath, releasing it in a sigh. "When I returned from Bedford Castle I was told that you had begun your monthly cycle. It was then that I knew that I had to leave you."

"I had wanted to tell you!" she blurted, then flushed. "I had no one else to tell. You were my friend, you were everything," she added quietly, lowering her eyes.

He placed a finger under her chin and raised her gaze to his. "And had I been truly your brother, or merely your best friend, you could have told me. But I was more than that, Eleanor, I was your husband."

He paused, knowing the truth was more surely accepted when it came to oneself. "Oh," she breathed, staring at him as reason dawned at long, long last. Why had she not understood before? "You would have had to consummate the marriage then. You would not have had a choice!"

"Had I not, you would have been taken from me. Peter desRevaux was pressing Henry for you."

Staring at him, her eyes sifted to a distant spot and her expression worked with the possibility. "Bloody likely," she murmured.

"Eleanor!" he admonished, even as his mouth worked with laughter.

"Will Marshal." She looked up at him, her eyes bright with understanding and a good measure of accusation. "Oh, I understand now. You, the defender of your own strict moral code, would not take a child of fourteen to your bed. So, to save me a fate worse than death, you abandoned me."

"Abandoned you? Eleanor—"

"Nay, now I shall have my say! Abandoned me! For that is what you did. Men!" she spat, her face scrunching with disgust. "I understand your reasoning and I love you for it. But I was young, not stupid! If only you had been honest with me! I could have discussed anything with you! I would have understood. A ruse, a declaration by Henry that the matter had been resolved. Who would have dared to deny it? Even if you had left then, I would have understood!"

He listened, giving her the respect of hearing her out. His voice was quiet, tender. "I did what I thought was best, and I would do it again. Nay, listen to me! You ask me to have trusted the emotions and wisdom of a child of fourteen, and to have trusted Henry? As much as we both love him, Eleanor, you know that he cannot withstand pressure. If he—or you— had slipped once, just once, the results would have been disastrous—and I would not even have been here to stop it! And consider, truthfully, a child who would not allow me to go on a hunting trip without her—would that child allow me to leave England? I fully expect that I would have found you stowed away on the ship for Normandy. Can you deny it?" When she did not answer, he smiled at her affectionately. "Sweetheart, I have listened and I feel deeply for the hurt I caused you. We can only try to place these regrets in the past where they belong. As for now, we are a man and a woman who have, blessedly, come to trust and care for each other. And," he added with a wicked grin, "we are sitting here talking of these matters bare-ass naked. To be honest, I can no longer look at you, knowing what it is to touch you, to make love to you, and remain placid. In short, Eleanor, I'm going to take you to bed—or take you again, here and now."

"Purple braid, I should think, intertwined with threads of gold. Nay, like this, along the sleeves and neck." Henry III, king of England, tried to hold his temper as he patiently explained his wishes to the tailor, who seemed infuriatingly not to understand his meaning.

"Your Grace—" Will pleaded.

"A moment." Henry gestured with a wave of his hand. "Nay, like this, along the seam."

Will sighed, controlling his own temper as he sought another way to approach Henry on the matter for which he had come. Henry had kept him cooling his heels for the past two hours, first in consultations with his architects for the new Lady's Chapel at Windsor, and now with matters with his tailor. In a moment he would risk his head for the hangman, he reasoned, even that to end this ceaseless prattling! Sighing, he turned his head as the door to the King's privy chambers opened. A soft smile touched Will's mouth as Eleanor entered with ladies of the court and a group of courtiers. She paused only briefly to say something to her companions before joining him.

He leaned down to brush her cheek with a kiss. "Where is Newbury?" he asked solemnly as the corners of his mouth twitched. "He is not among your admirers this morning."

"I sent him on an errand." She shrugged, then her eyes began to dance. "To Wales."

"You didn't."

"Didn't I?" Her eyes grew innocent.

He stared at her for a moment, wondering if she was joking. Then his thoughts shifted to more vital matters. "What have you discovered?" he murmured.

Eleanor drew him aside and pretended to adjust the collars of his tabard and chanise. "My sources tell me that 'friends' helped him to escape the tower within hours after being taken there. He fled to Brentwood, to the manor of his nephew, the Bishop of Norwich," she whispered. "Geoffrey of Crowcomb led the party in pursuit and found him there. He dragged him from the altar, where he was bent, clutching a cross. They roused the blacksmith from his bed to bind deBurgh in chains, but that brave man would have none of it. He declared that the hero of Dover and Sandwich would not wear chains made by him. Thereupon they threw Hubert upon a horse, binding his feet beneath the animal's belly, and returned him to London."

"I would know the blacksmith's name," Will murmured furiously. "He will have reward for his courage. Where is Hubert now?"

She hesitated, not wanting to answer. Glancing at her brother, she shook her head. "It is said that he was thrown into a cell in the White Tower—and has been chained to the walls."

That did it. Will's patience snapped and he crossed the room in a few strides. He tore the garment from the tailor's hands and ordered the startled man to leave. Then he turned on the King. "Henry, I *will* have word with you."

Henry stared, his mouth agape at Will's audacity. Confusion took him, and he was unable to react for an interminable moment, even as his eyes shifted in the direction of the disappearing tailor. Thoughts tumbled: outrage, the necessity of bringing Will under his displeasure in the face of those in the room. No one could speak to him in this manner! But he realized then that the room was empty, but for Will—and Eleanor, who was shutting the door and had turned against it to fix her gaze on him. She looked angry. Why was she angry with him, what had he done? His gaze shifted back to Will. Will seemed angry too. "What is it?" he asked, baffled by their odd behavior.

"Hubert deBurgh, Henry," Will gritted. "The justiciar of England."

"Oh, him." Henry snorted, turning his attention back to the garment he picked off the table where Will had tossed it. "That one will no longer defy me. No one shall rule England before me. With deBurgh removed it is now assured."

"Henry, he has had no trial!" Will pressed. "You cannot—"

"I cannot?" Henry roared, his head jerking up. "You dare to tell me what I cannot do? Be cautious, my Earl of Pembroke, you overstep! The prisoner refused to be tried by a court of his peers and has thrown himself on the King's justice! He has had his trial!''

Will took the news badly, his stomach churning at the information, but he struggled not to let it show. He glanced briefly at Eleanor, who had paled. "Your Grace," he asked tightly, "what is your decision for him?"

"I have much to consider." Henry answered with a shrug. "The man has been accused of murder and the practice of black magic.''

"Black magic?" Will choked, staring at Henry with disbelief.

"Henry, you cannot believe such dribble!" Eleanor protested, drawing near.

"I must consider all of the charges," Henry answered, miffed by their questions. "Soon deBurgh will be taken to the Templars. There I shall—"

"The Templars?" Will interrupted, as his eyes narrowed. "You are taking him to the Knights Templars? I see. Now, at least, I know your meaning, Henry." The powerful Order of the Templars, with their unequaled military might, thus subject to no laws but their own, had become the protectors of wealth and possession. In their deep vaults, beneath their quarters along the Thames called the New Temple, the wealthy deposited their coin and jewels for safekeeping. Will smiled softly at Henry, the unamused grin that had ever made Henry squirm with discomfort, as it did now. "You did try, didn't you, Henry? You went to the New Temple, to claim deBurgh's wealth, but the Templars would not admit you, even you, as they pledge that no man but he who places it in their care shall claim it. What have you done to Hubert for him to agree to give all that he owns to you, Henry? His life?"

"You overstep!" Henry cried. Damnation, he was King! Will had no right. . . . But another part of him, a soft voice, knew that Will could bring him from his throne, even against the power of desRoches. But Will would never do that—he was his best friend! Oh, if only he could speak with desRoches now, for a moment. "DeBurgh has forfeited his rights to the Crown," he answered sulkily. "Two days hence we shall take him to the Templars. You may attend if you wish. All will be dealt with fairly—you shall see for yourself! It will be proved beyond a doubt that deBurgh has stolen from the Crown, from England! The proof will be there!''

"So be it," Will said evenly. "And you may comfort yourself, Henry, I shall be there." He turned away, taking Eleanor's arm, and they began toward the door. Pausing at the doorway, Will turned back. "At the New Temple there is the Round Church, Henry. As we pass on our way to the vaults you should, perhaps, pause for a moment to reflect."

As the door closed, Henry stared at it. The look Will had given him remained, causing him to tremble with feelings he could not, would not face. He turned away and fingered the velvet garment he had been holding. Silver braid, not purple, he thought. Aye, that would be better. But Will's meaning invaded, pressing, and he cried out in anguish, throwing the garment across the room. Next to the Temple, in the Round Church, there to rest for all time under the protection of the noble Templars, lay the remains of William Marshal, the one who had placed Henry, son of John, upon the throne of England.

Frowning, Henry crossed the room to pick up the garment he had thrown aside. Fingering the luxurious velvet, he sniffed. It was not fair, he thought, Will did not understand. And then he looked up and frowned, his attention caught. And he sniffed again, raising his head to the air. His eyes widened in outrage. Spinning about, he rushed from the room and began to bellow for his chamberlain. "By the Blood," he cried, bringing wide-eyed servants scurrying as the King bellowed in rage. "The stench of dirty water carries through these halls! I will not have the privies offending me!" And Henry tore down the hallway to see that the matter was rectified.

22

ELEANOR sighed heavily against the oppressive silence in the room. She rose from her chair, leaving the fire to pace, not wanting to disturb Will but knowing that she could not remain silent for much longer. She paused, glancing at him where he sat bent over his writing desk, the only sound in the room the scratching of the quill pen as it moved over the parchment. She felt the sound in her spine, and she fought not to scream in frustration.

"Damn!" Will broke the tension with the profanity as he leaned back and stared at his work with frustration.

Eleanor crossed to the desk and stared down at the vellum and quickly assessed the problem. "It was not prepared properly. Here, let me help you." To Will's amazement she took up another piece of parchment that had been scraped and worked a piece of chalk across it until it was properly softened. Blowing the excess away, she handed it to her husband. "There, your ink will not blot now."

"Where did you learn to do that?" A brow arched as he regarded her with amazement.

"I studied for a time with a Franciscan monk." She

shrugged. "I used to prepare his parchments for him while we talked."

"You?" He gaped, and then chuckled. "Eleanor, you never cease to amaze me."

She smiled at him, warming at the gentle praise. But the smile disappeared as he returned to his work. Pouting, she returned to her pacing, throwing occasional piercing glances in his direction.

"Sweet Mother Mary!" she cried at last, spinning on him. "I would strip naked if I thought you would pay attention to me!"

He leaned back in his chair and studied her, his mouth pursed as his eyes moved slowly over her, even as his eyes became intense with amusement. "That might do it," he said with feigned seriousness. "Try it. Although I cannot promise anything."

"Will Marshal! I have sat here silently for over an hour, yet you seem to have forgotten my very presence. What are you doing? To whom are you writing?"

"I will be finished soon, Eleanor," he answered, returning to his missive. "Why don't you visit with Isabella until I'm done?"

"Isabella took Giles with her to Saint Edward's for mass."

"Hummm."

Her eyes narrowed speculatively as she watched him seal the letter and add it to the small pile that had collected. Her frown deepened as he took another page of parchment and began writing again. So many, she wondered; whom could he be writing to? He had passed off her earlier questions, suggesting that he was merely dealing with personal affairs, but her senses told her otherwise. She moved closer to the table, hoping to see to whom they were addressed, but the bundles were turned down. It involved deBurgh, she knew it. What was he up to?

Casually, she moved around the table behind his chair. Leaning over, she wrapped her arms about him and began to nuzzle his neck. Her brows furrowed into a frown as she realized he was still ignoring her, and for an instant she had an impulse to bite his ear. Controlling herself, she flicked it with her tongue instead and pressed her breasts against his back.

He folded the vellum slowly, sealing it with wax and his seal, and dropped it with the others at the edge of the table. And then he moved. She squeaked as strong arms went about her waist, lifting her from the floor, and she found herself half spread across the desk with him on top of her. "Will!" she shrieked, flailing her legs as she squirmed under him in an attempt to stand up. "What are you doing!"

"Giving you what you want," he answered lightly. "This is what you want, isn't it?" She drew in her breath sharply as she realized that he was pulling up her skirt.

"Will Marshal, let me up! Someone might come in!"

"You didn't seem to mind the other night." She gasped as his hand went between her thighs, and he kissed the sensitive spot at the base of her neck. "Would you prefer the floor again?" he murmured. "For myself, I think the table adds a bit of variety."

"Will!" She struggled frantically, pushing against his chest with her hands. He raised his head to look down at her, and seeing the grin and the wicked gleam in his eyes, she blinked. And then laughter gurgled up in her and her own eyes began to dance. "Was I so obvious?"

"Glaringly. But I'm not complaining."

"Are you going to tell me what you're planning?"

"No."

"Are you going to let me up?"

"No."

"Then what are you going to do?" she said, exasperated.

When he didn't answer, she twisted her head to look at him. "Oh, Will." She swallowed. "Not here. Someone will surely come in. Oh!" Her heart began to pound as her breath caught in her throat. "However," she gasped, "Giles *is* gone . . . so is Isabella." She moaned. "No one else would . . . dare—without . . . knocking. . . . oh, sweet Mother Mary and Joseph . . ."

As their breathing became more normal, Will raised up and planted gentle kisses on her nose and down to an ear, nipping it lightly. "It occurs to me," he murmured, still breathing heavily. "There is a table in the kitchen that is higher than this one. It suggests some interesting possibilities."

"Will Marshal, you are impossible." She laughed breathlessly. "Now let me up, you brute, there's a quill sticking me in the shoulder."

"Brute?" He frowned, pulling himself away from her to stand up. Readjusting his chausses, he arched a brow at her. "I didn't hear you complaining a moment ago." And then he winked at her. "Besides, as I recall, you asked for it."

Sitting up on the table, she brushed down her skirts and smiled up at him sweetly, "Nay, milord, not exactly. What I wanted were these." She grabbed up the bundle of letters and slipped by him before he knew what she was about.

"Eleanor, dammit, put those down!"

"Oh, nay, Will." She backed away from him as he rounded the table toward her. Before he could reach her she had glanced at each of the names on the letters. She had only a moment but enough time to see the names of Will's vassals who were spread about England and Wales, knights not normally seen at court. Then, instantly, her mind sorted the information. Nay, they were not merely random, but held lands situated in a straight line, from London to Chepstow. As he took them from her she stared up at him, her eyes wide with speculation. "Oh, Will, what are you doing?"

"Eleanor, I do not want you involved in this," he said gruffly, tossing the bundle back on the table.

"I am involved, Will. As much as you are. Will, do not shut me out of your life! Not again!"

He stared at her for a long moment. Then, reaching out, he touched her face gently. "Never again, love, I promise you. But this is different, and you must not be involved with it." Seeing the hurt in her eyes, he sighed with indecision. Stepping away from her, he took a few steps, then stopped, turning back. "Eleanor, Henry does not understand what he is doing. He is not his father's son; there is no malice in him, only poor judgment. But he is being led by desRoches and his Poitevins, and the outcome will surely lead Hubert to the block. I cannot stand by and watch that happen. I will not allow an innocent man, one who deserves all that England can give to honor him, be reduced to that of a criminal. Moreover, the result will eventually lead England to civil war."

"War?" She shook her head with disbelief. "Surely not."

"Eleanor, Hubert is only the beginning. DesRoches will not

stop with him. He will continue until he has Henry totally under his control, as he tried to do before. He has nothing but contempt for England's peers, and he will persist until he has eliminated anyone who could threaten his power. War must inevitably be the result."

"Oh, Will." She listened, her heart twisting at the truth of his words. "What are you going to do?"

"What I must, to stop it."

She felt a rush of fear tearing at her. She fought it back, willing it not to show in her eyes. "Then do what you must," she answered softly, controlling the tremor in her voice, refusing to acknowledge the pain that filled her. "As shall I."

Aware of each minute in the hours that passed, she waited for Will to return. Moving through the morning, her thoughts slipped to him, to what must be happening, but she faced the reality that she would not know until Will returned to tell her of the visit to the Templars. Of Henry's decision. Of Hubert's condition.

The missives had been sent at dawn with Alan Wadley. She knew they would reach their destinations—and the die was cast. She had broken fast with Isabella, but reality proved to be too much for light conversation and she needed time alone to face it. She walked in the narrow garden behind the manor, the winter-bare shrubbery reaching down a gentle slope to the Thames. She stood on the gravel path running along the river as her mind fixed upon the current, allowing it to block her thoughts, its movement easing the torment. A memory pressed, an aroma of rich, newly turned earth, bringing with it a resolution. What must be done would be done. Duty, obligation, regardless of personal pain. It had to be done.

A sound from somewhere to her left brought her from her reverie and she turned. Giles sat with his back to a set of evergreen bushes at the river's edge, his knees raised to support his arm as his chin rested on the heel of a hand while he threw stones into the passing current. As she watched, unwanted memories of loneliness played, and she wanted to reach out to touch him.

"May I join you?"

He looked up and shrugged, turning his attention back to
the river as he tossed another stone. She sat down beside him
on the bank and watched for a moment, then she searched
among the pebbles about her skirt. "Here. This will do nicely.
Watch." She took the stone and threw it with a snap of her
wrist. The stone hit the surface of the water and skipped,
once, twice, three times before it sunk beneath the surface.

"Ga!" he breathed, watching, his attention caught. "How
did ye do that?"

Lud, she thought, the child does not even know the
rudiments of what every child would know, how to skip a
rock. She felt rage well up and struggled not to let it show on
her face as he watched her expectantly. " 'Tis simple, Giles,"
she offered lightly, choosing another stone. "See this, you
must select one that is flat and smooth. Then it is all in the
wrist, sending it along the surface to skip. Try it."

They spent the better part of half an hour searching on
hands and knees for the proper stones and tossing them.
Slowly Giles's reserve began to melt as he threw himself into
the challenge, and finally she determined to attempt another
tack into that wall of reserve he had built about himself, one
she could all too easily recognize. "I found a marvelous book
for you, Giles, one that I am certain you will enjoy very
much."

"I can't read," he said, pitching another rock.

"I know, and I shall read it to you until that matter is
remedied," she answered without sympathy. "Your father has
instructed that your studies shall begin tomorrow." She saw
the coldness that fell over his gaze at the mention of his father.
"I know that he has had little time to spend with you, Giles,
but he truly has no choice. There are matters he must see to,
though he would choose to be with you if he could."

"Not bloo—" He caught himself, hesitating for a moment.
"Not likely," he muttered at last.

She picked up another stone and tossed it. The stone
skipped four times before it disappeared from view. "See, it is
in the wrist. A snap, keeping the stone along the surface.
When I was a child, much younger than you are now, there
was a pond where I lived. I used to do this by the hour."

"What was it like?" he asked, sitting back as he eyed her with curiosity.

"The pond?"

"Nay, your home. Was it like this?" he asked, nodding toward the manor.

"Oh, nay." She laughed softly. "Nothing like this. It was a large castle, remote. 'Twas by the sea, I remember most how lonely it was. And the wind. It blew all the time, cold, howling though the high rafters. At night I would listen to it—wishing that someone would make it stop."

His small face screwed up in puzzlement. "But yer father was the king. Doesn't sound so fine and grand to me."

"Oh, I did not live with my father," she said casually. "Nor with my mother. My brothers were there at times, on and off, but mainly I lived with two Scottish princesses who had been sent as hostage to my father. And another, a sister to Arthur, a cousin of mine. We were sent there, it was said, to keep us safe. But it was very lonely."

"Did you see your father and mother often?"

"Hardly ever." She shrugged. " 'Twas when your grandfather became Regent of England that I was brought from the castle to London. 'Twas then that I first saw your father."

"What was he like?" Giles asked, caught with curiosity.

"Oh, he was magnificent! I was so frightened, everything seemed so strange. After all, I had lived alone, or practically alone, without real family. It seemed that everyone who should love me did not care about me. Suddenly I found myself at court, a new, strange life with people who seemed to expect something from me, yet I could not understand what. But your father was there, kind, concerned, tender. He seemed to understand. He did not ask anything of me, he gave me only love." She added, remembering, "And he made me laugh."

Giles's mouth tightened and he turned away from her. "I think you have to like someone to laugh with them."

Her breath caught and she swallowed, knowing that he did not want her pity. "Your father is a burdened man, Giles. I do not expect you to understand, but there are things that are happening that take all of his attention, very important things.

If he could choose, he would be here, with you. He loves you very much, Giles, though he has not had a chance to show you yet.''

She saw the rigid set to his shoulders and she sighed softly, knowing she had not reached him. She knew, even as she had tried, that there was only one who could.

She accompanied Giles back to the manor and took mid-meal with him while trying to amuse him with stories—with little success. Landon, who had joined them, listened for a moment, then took up with the conversation. With a little prodding Giles soon had him recounting tales of great knights and their deeds.

"Will I truly be a knight someday?" Giles asked hopefully as Landon finished a tale of Sir Gawain.

"Of course you shall, but first you must be a page and then a squire.''

Giles thought about it for a moment. "When can I begin?"

Affecting a serious demeanor, Landon tapped his mouth with a finger as he considered the question. "When your father feels that you are ready, he will pledge you to a knight's service. But I see no reason why we cannot begin your training now.''

"Now?" Giles's eyes widened then he squirmed with excitement.

With a wink at Eleanor, Landon's brows furrowed solemnly. "Come here, Giles, and stand by my chair. We shall begin with what every good page must know: his duties at the table. When needed by your lord, you will stand behind his chair, ready to serve his meat and pour his beverage, or to see to whatever errand he may request of you. Stay attentive, for it will anger him to ask you twice.''

He showed Giles the proper way to cut and serve and how to pour wine properly without spilling or dripping onto the goblet, thus causing his lord to have sticky fingers. Eleanor watched the lesson with delight, noting the determination in Giles's expression, which did not conceal his pride and pleasure. As her eyes caught Landon's, she silently sent him her gratitude.

"Now, then," Landon continued, "when you are not required to serve your lord, you may partake of your own meal.

At the end of the trestle tables, of course, with those of your own rank. However, there are strict rules of behavior to govern your actions there as well. Now listen to me carefully, Giles. When you approach your lord, you say, 'God speed.' Say greeting to all nearby. Do not sit in your place until you are bidden. Do not wiggle—it is important to sit as a gentleman. And *never* scratch yourself." He paused, ignoring Giles's giggle. "Do not put your elbows on the table. Do not spill, nor drink with a full mouth. Never pick your nose or your teeth. And never have your mouth so full that you cannot respond when someone speaks to you. Do you have all of that?"

"Oh, aye, Landon."

"Good." The squire grunted as he affected a very serious demeanor. "Now, Giles, and this is *very* important, we must speak of what is known as 'ill wind behind.' "

"The what?"

"Put it this way. While on occasion a polite belch is permitted, always with the hand covering your mouth, an audible release from the nether regions is not. Now, the rules are far-reaching. . . ." He paused, trying to maintain his serious mien, ignoring the strangled sounds coming from Eleanor. "The Roman emperor, Claudius—you remember, we talked about Rome in your lessons yesterday—saw fit to pass a law allowing for silent wind-breaking after learning that one of his more polite guests endangered his health by resisting his needs of release. Although, I cannot say who first passed a law making the practice illegal . . ." He had to roll his eyes heavenward as Eleanor burst into laughter, bringing a puzzled look from Giles. "However"—he coughed—"such is not considered proper in polite society, and you shall do your best to refrain. But I think that is enough for today's lesson." He paused rising from his chair. "How would you like to spend the remainder of the afternoon learning to ride?" He glanced at Eleanor. "Lord William will not require my attention today as Meryle has gone with him to Windsor."

"It is quite all right, Landon," she gasped as she wiped the tears from her eyes. "Take him—quickly. And Landon—my thanks."

"My pleasure, milady." The squire grinned, taking Giles's

hand to lead the beaming child from the hall.

She watched Giles depart the room with the squire, his youthful face filled with excited anticipation, and she sat back in her chair. Laughing again, she felt more relaxed than she had felt all morning. Refreshed, she suddenly needed activity, and she sought out the steward and checked the household accounts, then set to a detailed inventory of the pantry, finally returning to the hall in late afternoon. As she wondered how she would fill the remaining time until Will returned, he burst into the hall, crossing to the table by the hearth, which held an ewer of wine. Pouring himself a goblet, he took a long draught before he turned to acknowledge her presence. "It is gone, all gone, his wealth, his offices, his honors, all save his earldom. Henry took it all. They have taken him to Devizes Castle, there to remain until he takes the vows of the Templars. He is to leave England for the next Crusade."

"Oh, Will," she gasped.

Ignoring her exclamation, Will laughed bitterly. "Henry insisted on being taken to the vaults by a back passage. He would not pass by my father's tomb. He seemed disquieted, would not even look at me until the Templars opened Hubert's vault. Oh, deBurgh had amassed great wealth, Henry broke out in a sweat when he saw it. It's gone, all gone."

"And Hubert?"

Will glanced at her and his smile twisted. "He is in the round tower at Devizes, shackled to the wall."

Eleanor turned at a sound at the other end of the hall. Meryle had entered to attend to his lord's needs, and she shook her head. The squire read her meaning and left, closing the door behind him, and she knew that they would not be disturbed. Turning back to Will, she stiffened her spine and became determined. "Firstly, he must reach sanctuary if we are to help him. There is a chapel in Devizes Castle—and one there who will help him to reach it—"

Will turned to stare, and his look silenced her. "What are you talking about? You are to have nothing to do with this."

She returned his stare evenly. "Why not?"

"You are Henry's sister. I will not ask you to be part of what must be done."

She took a deep breath. "Will, you once told me that I

was no longer a princess of England, but your wife. You demanded that my loyalty be given to you. In that you were both right—and wrong. I am your wife, and as such you deserve and have my loyalty. But you are wrong that I am no longer a Plantagenet. Such is mine by right of birth, and nothing will change that. It was you who first placed England's soil in my hands, awakening me to what position and responsibility meant. Aye, Henry is my brother, and I love him. You have said it yourself, there is no malice in him. What will happen to him when he realizes what he has done? Moreover, I cannot stand by and watch him destroy England, to give her to the likes of Peter desRoches, not for her sake or for the sake of Henry's soul." Seeing the softening that came into his expression as he listened, she pressed. "Of course, desRoches has demanded custody of Hubert and Henry is considering it."

He regarded her with surprise. "How could you know?"

"I understand the workings of the minds of the Poitevin priests," she scoffed. "I was taught by them well. I am certain that Henry fears for his immortal soul if he does not give in to their will. Hubert's life is forfeit if desRoches gets his hands on him."

"You could not be more perceptive." Will smirked, drawing on his wine, and then stretched, rolling his shoulders against the torment of his thoughts. He peered at Eleanor keenly. "Could your man see him to sanctuary?"

"Without question." A flicker of amusement deepened her eyes to a twinkle. "Surely 'twas by the hand of God that deBurgh was placed in Devizes and the care of one in particular. Trust me, Will, it can be done. But then what? How will you effect his escape from sanctuary?"

"A ruse," Will answered quietly, his mind working with the plan that had begun to formulate since the moment deBurgh had first been taken. "The escape itself I have arranged, but a ruse must be effected which will draw both Henry and desRoches while the deed is done. I have not yet determined how to be in two places at once."

Eleanor took his goblet and refilled it as she thought about what he had said. She would not allow herself to think of the risks, the danger to Will, not now, instead focusing only on the plan. Then, as she handed him the refilled goblet, she smiled suddenly. "Send for Darcy," she said softly. "He is with Leona. I think that we are of need of him."

Eleanor slipped through the door as the storm from without lashed at her back, whipping the rain in behind her. "Shut it quickly!" she snapped at the lagging porter as she stepped into the hallway and pulled at the soggy ties holding her drenched cloak. Pulling off the soaked garment, she handed it to the man. "See that it is hung out and . . . Landon?"

The squire was crossing the hall, his face flushed with an unaccustomed rage. Hearing his name, he stopped short and turned to her, though it appeared to take a moment before he realized who it was. "Milady?"

"Landon, what is wrong?"

"Nothing, milady," he answered tightly, glancing at the porter, who stood nearby, a small puddle forming beneath the cloak as he watched with interest.

"That will be all," Eleanor said curtly. As the porter left, she turned back to the squire, who had also turned to leave. "Landon, come back here." The squire turned back reluctantly. "What has happened? And do not tell me nothing."

"It's—it is Giles, milady," Landon answered reluctantly.

"What about him?"

"Sir William is sending him to Framlingham, to be fostered."

"What? He cannot!"

"That's what I told him. Or tried to. He told me to mind my own business, that his son was his affair."

"Oh," she said quietly. "I see. Never mind, Landon, I will speak with him. And Landon . . ."

"Aye, milady?"

"Giles has a good friend in you."

"Aye, milady." The squire smiled.

"Where is he?"

"In the study." He nodded toward the door. "And he's not in the best of moods."

She opened the door and stepped inside, closing it quietly behind her. She stood there for a moment, watching him, and then braced herself. "Will, you cannot do it."

"Do what?" He looked up from the accounts he was reviewing with a frown.

"Send Giles away," she said softly.

"It is the best thing for him." He returned to the ledger.

She swallowed as her mind worked. How could she make him understand? "Best for him? I do not understand. Would you explain that to me?"

"What is there to explain? He is of an age for fostering. Custom dictates—"

"Custom? Oh, Will, you need not tell *me* of custom! Custom that dictates that children shall be raised by others. Left in remote manors with no one who truly cares about them! Custom that allows a child to be used as a hostage against the possible actions of his father! How did you fare in my father's court, Will, all of those years? Did custom sustain you?"

"Eleanor, that has nothing to do with this!" he answered, now growing angry. "I am not sending him to a despotic court or anywhere as a hostage! I am sending him to be fostered with Hugh. Anselem did well there. If you do not believe that, write to my brother and ask him."

"It is not the same thing. Anselem's early years were with a mother and father who loved and cared for him. He was strong, sure of himself, when he went to Matilda and Hugh."

"What would you suggest I do?"

"Keep him with you. He needs you, Will."

"The boy needs discipline. That which I cannot give him with all that is happening."

"Giles needs love, comfort—"

"And exile, along with his father? Are you forgetting what we are doing?"

"Exile?" she swallowed. "We do not know that—"

"It is a possibility, we do know that."

She could only shrug, letting the matter drop as he bent again to his work. She knew of the pressures he was living under, the agony of the decisions he was making. She did not want to add this to everything else—nor could she ignore it, knowing what it would do to Giles—to both of them. The

loneliness she had suffered was nothing compared to the in-
dignities, the horror Will had suffered as a young boy in
John's court. A hostage for his father? That was only the
name that had been given to it. It was for punishment, retribu-
tion by John Plantagenet toward William Marshal for defying
him. And the child had been made to suffer. Nay, Will had
not forgotten, and his memories could only be adding to his
burdens. Sweet Mother, she realized, he really believes that
what he is doing will lead to his exile . . . or . . . She drew in a
steadying breath, willing herself to be calm. That explained so
much. She knew that he still had not faced how much Lavene
haunted his memories. The guilts that were causing him to
hold himself from Giles. But now there was also this. The pain
of coming to love someone soon to be lost to him. Or was he
afraid that Giles would come to love him too much? Nay, she
could not add this to his other burdens. She would simply have
to handle the matter herself.

"Will?"

He looked up, his eyes touched with impatience and
wariness. "What?"

"Would you promise me something?"

"Not without knowing what it is." The beginnings of a
smile touched his mouth.

"Would you allow Giles to remain, just for now, a little
longer?"

He hesitated, then his face softened and he sighed. "If it
is so important to you, aye. For now." When she remained
standing there, he frowned. "Is there anything else?"

"Not much." She shrugged. "Unless you want to know
what happened this morning with Henry."

His eyes widened and he sat back abruptly. "You saw
him?"

"I saw him." She smiled, taking the chair across from him.
"Oh, you were right, desRoches did his best to interfere.
When I arrived at Windsor I was told that Henry was at Win-
chester."

"But you didn't believe it."

"It was Father Latius who told me."

"Really." He grinned.

"I thought he would have a stroke when I minced past him and went into Henry's bedchamber unannounced."

"That could have been, ah, rather compromising, Eleanor." He laughed.

"It was. But she was dressing."

"And Henry?"

"Surprised to see me." She dimpled as he laughed. "He soon forgot about my sudden appearance, however. He is absolutely ecstatic about our suggestion—he even had a few to offer of his own."

"I imagine." Will smirked, though he was pleased that she had gained Henry's unknowing support with such ease.

"Indeed, he has ordered that the entire court shall attend. A masque has not been held for some time, and he deems it as just what is needed to lift the gloom that has descended on the court of late—what with the distasteful matters that have occurred," she added with a smirk.

"And desRoches?" Will asked, his expression guarded.

A small smile broke at his question. "I suggested that the bishop of Winchester should be there as the guest of honor. In gratitude for all that he has done to aid Henry of late."

Will grunted with grim pleasure. He rose from his chair and went to the window, staring down into the street as he was momentarily lost to his thoughts. Eleanor came to his side, placing her hand on his shoulder as her own gaze turned to the view, sensing what he was feeling.

Darcy had come, grasping immediately what was needed. Days had been spent in painstaking preparation of the play until the goliard had set the final script before Will and then stood back, glancing hopefully at Eleanor while it was read. Will's reaction had been explosive.

"By the blood of Saint Peter!" Will rose from his chair, holding the final pages of the masque prepared by the goliard. "By the breath, Darcy, you must covet death! We cannot do this!"

"Will, it must be." Darcy's voice was calm as he countered Will's protest. "You need a masque which will draw their attention—and desRoches is no fool. No simple play will absorb him. Besides, my life has been directed toward this, the chance to write what I feel, what I believe. Would you take this opportunity from me? Give this to me, Will. It gives to both of us what we need.''

"You will not leave Windsor alive,'' Will countered angrily.

"Perhaps not,'' Darcy countered lightly. "But if that be the case, I will leave this world happily. Believe that, Will. Give me the satisfaction to know that I was able to say something of what I believed in this sordid world, and helped my friends as I did so. What more could a man ask of life?''

With steady pressure from both Darcy and Eleanor, Will had gradually relented, and the plans had been made. But watching him now, she knew that worry for Darcy only added to his other concerns. That, and the fact that he was defying Henry. The years, the close, easy affection they had once shared, the pain of its loss showed in the new lines about his eyes.

"It will not be long,'' she said softly. "Henry loves you; he will forgive this.''

He turned his head to look at her, his expression one of infinite sadness. "Not this. Eleanor, you must face what will happen.'' He turned and took her face between his hands as he gazed down at her. "You are so very dear to me,'' he said softly. "You shall ever be a part of me. But you must promise me that once this is done, you will do nothing to defy him.'' Seeing the look in her eyes, he tapped her nose lightly with his finger. "Must I remind you of a Plantagenet's temper, sweetling? His anger with me will be enough—but if he should learn that you have been part of this . . . The hurt of that betrayal, and he is certain to see it as that, will cause him to follow us to the ends of the earth to get at you. I will not do that to you, Eleanor, I will not give you that kind of life. You must promise me that you will stay here and do nothing to call attention to yourself until it is safe for me to send for you. Promise me.''

She thought she would perish with what he was asking of her. A life without him? Nay, she would not, could not accept it. Somehow, even with all that was about to happen, she could not face the possibility that they would never be together again. But she would not tell him that. He believed it to be inevitable, and her hope would only cause him more pain.

"Aye, I will do whatever you ask of me," she said softly. It passed her that he had not said he loved her, even now. Her voice broke. "I will love you always. Until the last breath I take you shall be part of me. But I will not defy him."

His mouth dropped to cover hers, drawing deeply of their sweetness as his arms folded about her. They clung to each other, the tenderness changing to resolve to remember this moment, not knowing if it would ever come again in this life.

23

THE Great Hall at Windsor swelled with the sound of
voices. The immense room smelled heavily of new mortar, but
the unpleasant odor was forgotten in the stunning magnificence of the room. Murmurs raised to exclamations, passing
over the gathering in appreciative awe. "Henry the Builder,"
Darcy muttered, his eyes lifting to the high arched beams, the
heavy lead glass of the breathtaking windows that lined the
walls. Finely set stone, rich woods, and the brilliance of rich
tapestries were evident everywhere.

"Is everything ready?" Will asked impatiently, drawing the
goliard's attention.

"Of course," Darcy answered, though his eyes automatically passed to his efforts, so painstakingly prepared. A false
wall of light timber covered with fabric, painted with bright
scenes, reached along the narrow end of the room where they
stood. Before the wall were placed large potted trees and
bushes set to resemble a thicket in a deep forest. Behind the
wall stood another set painted with the interior of a castle,
ready to be moved for the appropriate moment in the masque.
Satisfied, Darcy grunted and turned to Will with a grim smile.
"It will work, Will. You must not doubt it now."

"It better, my friend," Will murmured tightly. "If it does not, Eleanor's life may be forfeit as well as our own."

"Henry would not harm her."

"At the moment it is not Henry I am concerned about." Will's glance passed to the man sitting next to the King across the large room. His eyes fixed on Peter desRoches as the Bishop leaned his dark head toward the King to catch what Henry was saying to him above the din of the crowded hall. The cleric was lean and fit, attesting to his earlier years as a soldier, unlike most of his order, who leaned toward softness from years void of physical activity. His vestments were of the finest linen, yet displayed none of the ostentatiousness common to his order. Will begrudgingly admired the cleric's perception and intelligence in the picture he displayed. Feelings ran high against the extravagance of the Italian priests, but no one would lay such accusations against the Bishop of Winchester.

"Are you certain that he will not suspect?" Will pressed.

"God's breath, will you stop it!" Darcy snapped, his own nervousness showing in his irritation. "It will work, all of it! Have I not said so? May I remind you that you will be long departed; it is my life that hangs in the balance if we are discovered. I assure you that I have done everything possible to see that it does not happen!"

Will grunted and began to step away, then paused to turn back to the goliard. He smiled and reached out a hand to clasp the other man's shoulder. "I just realized that this may be the last chance I will have to thank you, Darcy," he said quietly. "You have been a good friend. I shall not forget."

The two men exchanged a moment's understanding, feeling the deep bond that had grown between them over the years. "Nor shall I, my Earl of Pembroke." Darcy gave him a small smile, then shrugged. "No matter what happens, Will, I only ask that you take good care of Giles. See that he grows to the man that I would have him be." Puzzled, Will regarded the statement oddly, as he had sent Giles to Framlingham just that morning. But before he could respond, Darcy shifted his gaze to the King. "By the blood of Saint Edward," he growled, his voice thick. "Let us be about it."

The two men slipped through the narrow door in the wall

behind the sets. Will's eyes swept over those gathered in the
small, dimly lighted room, and he marveled at the intricacies
of their costumes. Henry should be pleased by their efforts,
he thought grimly. The animation felt in the room supported
the pleasure the participants were feeling to be part of such
an elaborate masque, though none but a select few knew the
true purpose for the play. As he moved among the players,
stopping to speak to those who stayed him as he passed, admiring their costumes and brightly painted masks, he finally
found Eleanor. She stood near a far wall engaged in last-
minute preparations with a player. He paused for an instant,
allowing his eyes to feast upon her, memorizing each part of
her. She was draped in a soft crimson silk gown of Grecian
cut, not unlike the costume she had worn for the Vow of the
Peacock, he realized with amusement. Her hair was loose and
intertwined with garlands of flowers, the costume of the virgin
she would play in the first act of the masque.

Coming up behind her, he reached out and drew her into the
shadows of the wall, beyond the reach of the low, flickering
rushlights. Coming into his arms, she smiled up at him, her
eyes filled with love and pleasure. "You must change into
your costume, milord," she said huskily, pressing herself
against him.

"Is there another room where I might change?" he
answered, bending to nibble her ear. "I will need your help.
Surely there are fastenings that will require nimble fingers."

"As I recall, there are none more nimble than your own."
She laughed softly. Then, remembering the moment, she
sobered and leaned back to see his face in the dim light. "It is
time," she observed, realizing why he had come.

"Aye." He sighed, releasing her slightly while unwilling to
allow her to step away from him. "Where is Landon?"

She nodded to a door just beyond. "No one has been allowed in there, nor shall they be. Oh, Will, we shall not
fail."

He responded to the sudden desperation in her voice and
bent to kiss her, whispering to her as his lips met hers. "Nay,
we shall not."

Torches had been extinguished in the Great Hall, darkening

the room. Tall iron stands of candles had been set flanking the forest scene, drawing the eyes of the assembled nobility to the players who began the first act of the masque. Murmurs about the room had softened to silence as the players began, all eyes fixed upon Eleanor as she was led into the glade by her maidens, her face covered, not by a mask but by a soft veil of white.

The court settled back with murmurs of pleasure as they realized the play was that of Tristan and Isolde, a favorite Arthurian legend of the time. But none was prepared for the version that began. Subtly, the masque unfolded. Darcy's words came easily to Eleanor as the words of another Franciscan filled her emotions and her voice lifted. She could feel the attention of the court as the players spoke their lines.

The glorious world of King Arthur flowered, Darcy's carefully constructed lines gradually insinuating the courtly world of lies and deception, the delusion of the new concept of chivalry. King Mark, the epitome of all that was good and holy, the true, valiant, courtly king, began to unfold, portraying the inner weakness of man, the greed, avarice, the failure of his vows as he determined to win Isolde's love from Tristan.

As the players prepared for the next act in the masque, Will found Eleanor as she stepped from a side room where she had changed from her costume. As his eyes came to rest upon her, he drew in his breath sharply. He had not seen her costume for this act, for she had refused to show it to him, and now he understood the reason. Her hair was loose, tumbling down her back, covered by a light white gauze held by a garland of leaves and flowers. Her gown was of the same translucent gauze, artfully layered so as barely to cover her breasts and hips, clinging to the long lines of her body, leaving little to the imagination.

She looked up as he approached, and her expression broke into a warm smile. "God's breath, what are you doing?" he hissed, freezing the smile on her face as he drew her into the shadows. "You cannot wear that before the court!"

She opened her mouth to protest but shut it, realizing the shock he must have felt when he saw her. It was the very reason she and Darcy had not allowed him to see the costume before now. "Will," she said softly, reaching up a hand to touch his cheek, "Darcy will see that the lighting in the hall is muted, shadows will conceal me from full view, but everyone's eyes must be on me if this is to work, you know that! Do not be foolish; Landon is waiting, you must change." She saw the hesitation in his eyes and pressed the moment. "Now, Will, there is no time to argue."

As the soft strains of the lute, harp, flute, and psaltery began to play from the gallery above, Will moved to his place in the soft glow of the candles near the vine-enshrouded stone of his tomb. "My lady, Isolde, Queen of Cornwall, my heart . . . ," he began, his voice rising to his final plea as Tristan before his death. As his final words were given, he lay in the shadows of his tomb, concealed by the candles, which were gradually extinguished about him. Begrudgingly, he realized the wisdom of Darcy's decision as Eleanor appeared among the candlelight across the set from him. Soft gasps were heard in the darkness about the hall as she appeared, even as her voice was raised in anguish as Isolde, grieving for the loss of her heart's love. He knew that all eyes were fixed upon her, drawing attention from him where he lay in the shadows. He hesitated for a moment, in spite of the painstaking preparations, not wanting to leave her. Not like this.

"Milord!" An urgent whisper from Landon came from behind him where the squire stood in the shadows. Will slid from the slab of his tomb as the squire, dressed alike and in identical mask, took his place and Will stepped into the shadows where Landon had stood moments before. He felt Darcy pull at his arms, to draw him away from the edge of the scene.

Eleanor closed her eyes, drawing on the pain she felt, crushing her, allowing it to come as she raised her voice to say the lines which were certain to draw all eyes upon her. "Oh, false word, that which would deny the true beauty and courage the world would know. The unicorn did come to me, to lay its head upon my breast in trust, to offer its strength that I might go on. Oh, how cruelly betrayed! There is no longer truth. The age of wisdom is crushed beneath the dark hand of man's false faith!" She raised her gaze, feeling desRoches's eyes riveted upon her, but her next words were for Will, even knowing that he had gone.

"My heart, the deepest part of my soul without which I do not exist, you are lost to me, leaving nothing to give me ease," she cried, turning her head toward the crypt, to Tristan's body where it lay in repose. And then, in the shadows, she saw Will, watching her. She felt a shudder of terror pass over her—why had he not left? For a moment she could not speak as she felt her heart pound. "My life . . . though there are those who would keep us apart . . . my heart, ever shall reside with you. . . ." As she spoke, her gaze locked with Will's and tears began to trip over her cheeks as she saw him hesitate, then disappear into the darkened shadows. "My life is drained, it perishes with your loss. You have taken all love with you. Only courage is left to me now." Her voice softened to a whisper, tears streaming. "But I shall go on . . . until I am with you again." For a long moment she could not move. Then, slowly, she approached the bier and lay next to Landon's form in the shadows beneath the intertwined vine. At that moment, Darcy stepped into the light in the form of Percival, King Arthur's man, and the play continued.

Shadows flickered about the small green chamber, touching lightly on the richness of the antiquities that dotted the room. A room of perfection, she mused distractedly, Henry's room, the room where she had taken her final vows with Will. Will was right, Henry should be of the arts, not the ruler of kingdoms. The gods surely had a sense of humor, for how else could they play such cruel amusements upon man? The gods, not God, for only the lesser deities could so amuse themselves. Henry was King, while Richard, who was far more suited to such power and responsibility, had been second born. She—she had been born a mere woman, yet given the wisdom to see the mistakes, and was compelled to fight to undo the wrongs while only wanting to be with Will. And all had now been left in the hands of the one who could do the most harm. Her eyes met desRoches's and she struggled not to allow her contempt and hatred to show.

"You *will* tell me. Did you have a hand in that work of blasphemy you spoke tonight?" The Bishop asked quietly, his dark eyes boring into hers.

"Surely you do not expect me to answer that," she said,

regarding him without the flinch he expected, was used to encountering, in those he confronted.

"If you fear for your immortal soul, you will answer me truthfully," desRoches countered.

"Are *you* threatening me with excommunication?" she bantered. "The truths I have found leave me little fear of that dire prospect, so let us leave my immortal soul out of this."

"If you are responsible for the words I heard tonight, I believe that you are truly lost," desRoches said blackly, his eyes burning.

"If you mean that I am lost to the influence of those of your ilk, you are correct." She laughed. "But enough, desRoches, there is no one here but us, so let us speak the truth. My soul is not what is in question here but the loss of your power over Henry. You fear that Henry may have heard the truth tonight. I watched his face as he listened. He is thinking, and you cannot allow that."

Before he could respond, the door opened and her eyes widened slightly as Alan of Newbury entered. As his eyes met the Bishop's, she turned her head in disgust, recognizing where the young earl's loyalty lay.

"Your Excellency, the King is—" he began, only to be cut off by a stern look from the Bishop. He looked to where Eleanor sat, his eyes widening as they passed over her body, for she was still clad in the revealing costume of the masque. Without hesitation, he removed his mantle from his shoulders and crossed to lay it about Eleanor's shoulders.

"Nay!" desRoches said with venom. "Let the whore remain as she is."

She saw the look of horror, then doubt that crossed Alan's face, and she responded with contempt. "Do what your master bids, Alan. After all, one must choose between vows given when they are in contest with each other. What is your vow to the Code of Chivalry, that which you have so dearly embraced, when it lies in conflict with that of the Bishop of Winchester? What has he offered you, Alan? Wealth? Position?"

Alan stiffened at her rebuke and regarded her with disapproval, but she could read the doubt in him. "My lady, the code pledges us first to the word of God even before our vow to protect the perfection of womanhood."

"The word of God, according to Peter desRoches," she snorted with soft laughter. "Of course, Alan, do what you must. But, for heaven's sake, do not just stand there leering at me; you will lose your soul for your thoughts." As Alan began to bluster at her comment, she turned back to desRoches, dismissing the knight with all of the contempt she felt for him. "So, then, what will you do now? Attempt to condemn me to Henry? I would think twice about that, desRoches." She heard the intake of Alan's breath behind her and she had to fight a smile. "Trust me, desRoches, for all that I have said, and more. On your *mortal* body, it will not bring you what you expect."

The Bishop smiled. His lips turned up with pleasure as he regarded her coldly. "Would I harm you, my lady? Nay, never. But there is another, one who seems to be of importance to you, although I cannot imagine why it should be so. He is one sought after by the Church, a soul lost, one who can only find redemption through the heat of the flame. And it shall be so, I promise you. A cruel death, it is so said, to be bound at the stake and cleansed by fire. But so it shall be for Darcy of Fountaine. Even now he is being held in preparation for his sentencing."

As he spoke, Eleanor felt a cold settling over her, a frigid sweep that touched her, drawing from a deep inner core. She recognized it, welcomed it familiarly, drawing from the heat that stirred her anger, allowing it to push aside every feeling but her outrage. Oh, so welcome, the strength of that rage. She rose from her chair and drew herself up, confronting him, unaware that Alan had taken a step back involuntarily, his eyes fixed with fascinated horror.

Her voice was deceptively soft. "Peter desRoches, this I do swear to you. If Darcy of Fountaine is harmed, you will cry against the hand you had in it."

"Do you presume to threaten me?" desRoches countered, ignoring her as he tossed a hand at her words.

"Nay," she answered, her voice lowered, drawing his attention. "Not you, I would not give you that release. But your son, desRoches, you would do well to watch your son."

She had the satisfaction of seeing desRoches pale, though he attempted to cover it. "You would not dare—"

"Not dare? I am Eleanor Plantagenet." She smiled. "You would do well to remember it."

The Bishop's face reddened, his eyes fixing upon her with building fury. Though he opened his mouth to protest her threat, he was forced to bring himself under control with immense effort as the door swung open and the King entered, followed closely by Richard, the Duke of Cornwall. Henry's eyes took in the scene before him, and he hesitated at the door when he saw Eleanor, and his face flushed with rage. "By the Blood, cover her!" he roared, stepping into the room. "By all that is holy, would you leave my sister so clad?"

Eleanor fought a smile as Alan's mantle dropped over her shoulders, and she turned a sweet smile to her brother. "My thanks, Henry," she said softly, dropping her eyes demurely. "I was rather . . . chilled."

"I should think so." Henry snorted. "Light the brazier, Newbury, it is damp in here." He swung to desRoches, not noticing the glare the Bishop threw toward Eleanor before his eyes glazed impassively. "Will has secreted deBurgh out of Devizes. They are heading toward Wales," Henry said sulkily.

Eleanor felt her heart lift, joy rushing through her at Henry's words, but she fought to keep her face placid as she stared at the floor. Will had done it! They were safe. Soon they could cross the Wye. They were beyond the King's writ! She raised her eyes and bit her lip as she saw the rage in desRoches's face. Then she realized that Henry was speaking to her.

"Eleanor, did you know of this?" Henry peered at her seeking the truth.

She could feel desRoches watching her, waiting for her answer, his dark eyes beginning to gleam with speculation. She did not want to break the promise she had made to Will. But he did not understand. No one did, not even Will. But it was imperative that the Poitevin have an inkling, it was vital, more than ever, for Darcy's sake. Oh, Will, forgive me for breaking a promise, she thought. Then she raised her eyes to Henry and smiled softly, the curve of her lips touching her eyes. "Henry, he is my husband," she answered softly. "I know him to be

the most loyal man in England, even as was his father, the
Good Knight." Her eyes shifted to Richard, who stood by
Henry, and she was encouraged by the glint in his deep blue
eyes, knowing that she had an ally. "Aye, I knew. It was well
planned, and I was part of it. Henry, no man could be
everything England would have him be. Hubert deBurgh is a
man of faults, but he does not deserve to die. Will is your
friend, beyond all else; he could not allow you to regret a decision, forced by others"—she glanced briefly at desRoches
—"one that you would certainly come to deeply regret. Will
has taken the decision from you, at great cost to himself, for
he so loves you."

"He has defied me!" Henry roared, his face flushing with
anger. She noted desRoches's look of satisfied expectation as
Henry turned blood-red. A moment, Poitevin, she thought.
You do not understand, not yet.

"As I have said," she countered calmly. "And to what
gain? He could have chosen to bring the power of the Marshals upon you, challenging you, but he did not. Instead he
chose this way, involving only himself."

"Your Grace, he has defied the authority of the Throne!"
desRoches interjected. "By taking deBurgh from the reaches
of your royal writ, he has betrayed you! It is no less than
treason!"

"She is right, Henry," Richard interrupted, waving off the
Poitevin. "If his attack had been upon you, he would have
brought the forces of his power against you and taken your
Throne. Instead, he has chosen exile. Such a sacrifice must be
considered, Henry. Think on it!"

Henry glanced from one to the other, his face mixed with
the confusion he felt. Oh, why was nothing ever simple!
DesRoches was waiting with anticipation. Newbury, that fool,
was watching with an irritating awe. He was the King and his
word would be law, condemning a dear friend to death or
granting clemency to a traitor. And then his eyes fixed on
Richard, whose eyes gave warmth, confidence. And Eleanor,
whose heart shone in her eyes. Slowly, memories flashed, of
an isolated, windswept castle, two small, frightened boys and
a little girl, bound together in their loneliness, having only

each other to trust—until another came, bringing them into light. "We shall wait. I wish to think upon what has happened."

"Your Grace!" desRoches blurted. "Even now they—"

"Enough! I have said that I shall think upon it! Nothing, desRoches, nothing shall be done until *I* decide! Do you understand?"

The Bishop nodded tightly, his face flushed with frustration. "Aye, sire. Perhaps tomorrow—"

"Aye, tomorrow. We shall see." Henry dismissed him with a curt wave of his hand, wanting the matter done with.

"Tomorrow," Eleanor said softly as the Bishop retired, passing by her. He turned and glared at her, his eyes burning into hers. "Do nothing, desRoches, remember. . . ."

24

THE man stood before the dormant table in the Great
Hall of Chepstow, clutching his cap in his hands with nervous
fingers. The high-raftered hall was silent, but he could feel the
tenseness from the knights who stood about waiting, and a
trickle of sweat began to course down his back beneath the
rough wool of his tunic. Why had he allowed his shrew of a
wife to convince him to come? Surely his life was forfeit while
she remained safely at home in their cottage. He raised his
gaze gingerly until it met with the Earl Marshal's and he
flinched involuntarily at the stony blue of the other man's
eyes.

"Are you certain that it was my son who did this?" Will
asked steadily, his gaze holding the villein's.

" 'Twas 'e who was described, milord," the man answered,
shifting his weight.

" 'Twas described?" Will repeated, arching a brow. "Then
you did not see him. You come to me, asking for justice,
accusing my son of stealing what is yours, yet another has accused him. Who is this one?"

"M-me wife, milord," the man stammered, wishing he
could suddenly vanish before those penetrating eyes.

"Then why is your wife not here? You know the law, man; the accusing one must do so in person."

"I speak for 'er, milord, as 'er husband."

"And you may do so in matters of contract or issues of morality. But not in matters of crime." Will sighed, suddenly weary of the morning spent listening to requests and complaints from his vassals and villeins, culminating in this charge against his own son. His son. He still had not adjusted to the fact that Giles was here and not at Framlingham. Arriving at Chepstow in the dead of night, weary and travel-sore, he had settled deBurgh in, then entered his bedchamber, his only thoughts toward the comfort of his bed. Divesting himself rapidly of his clothes, he had thrown back the bedcurtains, only to find Giles sleeping soundly beneath the covers. Eleanor! She had done it again! Countermanding his orders —and for what? So that Giles now shared his life of exile. And now this . . .

"Enough, Ramsey, I pledge to investigate the matter. If Giles is responsible, he will be dealt with. In the meantime, regardless of the outcome, you will need stock. See you to the herdsman and he will give you four hens and two piglets to begin again. I will not see you and your woman starve, regardless of the identity of your thief. But I warn you, Ramsey," he added, leaning forward to rest his arms on the dormant table, "if I learn that your story is not as you have presented it to me, that also shall be dealt with."

Clearing the hall, Will rose and stretched against the deep, aching fatigue in his back. Stepping from the dais, he glanced at Landon, who was busily rolling up the vellums on the table. He fought a smirk as he realized the squire was avoiding looking at him. "Where is he?" he asked quietly.

The squire exchanged an uncomfortable glance with Meryle, who shrugged, and he finally met Will's gaze. "Milord, I cannot believe that Giles would do such. He is, ah, energetic, I admit, but he has lived as a villein, he feels deeply for their situation, he would not—"

"Dammit, Landon, you do not need to plead my son's case to me! Answer my question!"

"He is in his chamber, milord," the squire answered stiffly. "He has been there of a morning, studying his lessons."

Will merely grunted as he turned toward the stairs. He would not admit it, but Landon's furious defense stood well for Giles, even as it struck a sadness in him. He was well aware of his squire's closeness to the boy, the deep affection that had grown between them. While he was grateful for it, it made him more acutely aware of the lack of closeness between Giles and himself. Ascending the stairs, he tried to slough off the feeling. What could he have done for it, after all? With all that had happened—deBurgh's escape, the needs of Striguil taking every waking hour since his return . . .

He paused in the doorway to Giles's bedchamber, finding it open. He began to knock, then froze in disbelief. Giles was stretched out on a rug before the hearth, a small casket open on the floor before him, and the boy was dangling an object before him, swinging it gently as his large blue eyes followed it with fascination. Will swallowed, forcing himself to be calm as his rage threatened to erupt violently. The object the boy held was a slender gold chain supporting a priceless stone, a large emerald which had been in Will's family for many, many years.

"Where did you get that?"

Giles jumped with surprise, dropping the stone on the rug, and he looked up. He blinked at the fury on his father's face but recovered quickly as he sat up and glared back defiantly. "I did not steal it," he challenged.

"Indeed?" Will's eyes glittered angrily. "Then perhaps you will answer my question—as well as where you were on Sunday last, after mass."

"Why should I?" Giles glared, his blue eyes meeting the same angry blue glare of his father's. "You would not believe me anyway."

"Answer my question," Will stormed.

"Why do you want to know where I was on Sunday?"

"Just answer the question."

The boy shrugged. "I rode to Tintern Abbey."

"Why?" Will asked, surprised by the answer.

"Do you mean, 'Can you prove it?' " Giles said sarcastically.

"I want to know why," Will repeated stonily. "But since you mention it, can you prove it?"

"Ask Grandmere," Giles tossed, turning his head toward the hearth so that Will would not see the hurt in his eyes.

"What has your grandmother to do with this?"

"Ask her."

"I am asking you. Giles, look at me!" he growled, trying to control his anger. He felt himself wince inwardly at the look of accusation the boy turned to him and was shocked at the trace of tears he saw in the face so much like his own. Taking a calming breath, he sat on the rug next to the boy. "Giles, a man came to me this morning—he said that a boy of your description stole two of his pigs and scattered his chickens. Do you know what that can mean to a villein, to lose all that he has? The matter is quite serious."

Giles's face filled briefly with horror, but the mask rose quickly and became blank once again. "Then it must have been me." He shrugged.

But Will had seen the shock in the boy's eyes, and he sensed the truth even as Landon's words returned to him. He was filled with a sweep of regret, to know that his squire knew his son so much better than he. "You said that you were at Tintern Abbey," he said quietly. "Why were you there?"

"I could not have been," Giles countered spitefully. "Apparently I was stealing pigs."

"Giles, the only thing that a man has truly of his own is his word. It cannot be given to him, nor can it be taken from him; only he can destroy it. Therefore it is his honor, the true measure of him. Never treat it lightly; guard it as you would your life. If you give me your word, I will accept it as truth. I will do so, Giles, always—unless the day comes that you betray it, thus give it away. And what you give away, you cannot take back."

Giles's face worked with Will's words for a long moment, the conflict settling slowly as a glimmer of determination began to show. "I—I went to Tintern to pray for Darcy," he said in a small voice. "Grandmere said that I could go there when I wished—that we—you owned the abbey."

"I do not 'own' the abbey, Giles." Will smiled. "Though your grandmother would think so. Tintern was built by your great-great-great uncle and the family has supported it for two hundred years. It is the way of your grandmother to feel that anything she supports belongs to her." Seeing the flare of indignation that crossed the boy's expression, he laughed. "Giles, we can criticize those we love; it does not mean that we love them less. The true measure of love is to accept the faults in those we care about and not to love them the less for it. Can you understand that?"

Giles thought about that. He nodded, understanding the meaning, even as he wondered if his father could ever love him, even without his faults.

"Do not worry about Darcy, though he would be deeply touched to know that you prayed for him. I promise you, Giles, Darcy will return to us. There are many in your family, including Eleanor, who are protecting him. Darcy is your uncle—but do not forget that the King also is your uncle. Darcy will not be harmed, even though there are others, bad men, who would wish it so."

"Like the Bishop of Winchester?"

Will blinked with surprise. "How did you know that?"

"Grandmere told me."

"Your grandmother talks a lot," Will muttered.

"Aye, she does," Giles smiled. "But I love her. She tells me things. Even more than Landon or Eleanor. Why is Eleanor not here, milord? Why does she stay in London?"

"She must stay there for now, Giles." Will hesitated. He explained briefly about deBurgh. "The King is angry about what I have done, and if she had come with us, she too would now be exiled. DeBurgh must stay here with his family; if he left, his life would be in danger. However, as long as he remains, the King will remain angry with us. Do you understand?"

Giles listened to Will's explanation thoughtfully and nodded, then looked up at his father with determination. "When I lived with Lord Saebroc, I saw many who worked hard. They tried to do their best and to do their jobs well, yet Saebroc beat them, or took what they had, no matter what they did. That was not right. Sometimes I wished I were a knight, so that I could fight him. That is what you did for deBurgh."

"Aye." Will smiled. "That is what I did for deBurgh."

"Then, if what you do is right, why is the King mad at us?"

"Oh, Giles." Will laughed. "Why do you not ask me something simple, like why the sky is blue! Besides, we have been skirting the issue at hand, my lad. You have a question to answer first. Like where you came by this emerald." He picked up the stone and dangled it between them.

"Oh, that." Giles shrugged. "Grandmere gave it to me."

Will blinked, glancing dumbly at the stone and back to Giles. "She gave it to you? God's breath, Giles, do you have any idea what this is?"

"She said it belonged to my great-grandmother. That it was my inheritance. But"—he smiled sheepishly—"I do not know what that means. But I promised her that I would never lose it."

Will said something under his breath as he stared at the stone, fingering it tenderly while he shook his head with wonder. "Aye. You must never lose it, Giles. I will never pretend to understand your grandmother's mind—I gave that up in my own youth. But you must understand that this stone is very, very valuable. It alone will make you a wealthy man. But more than its cost, it is the first thing your great-grandfather gave to your great-grandmother. It was on the day of his knighting that he gave it to her, a pledge of their love, a new beginning." Suddenly he stared at his son and began to have a glimmer of Isabel's meaning, the thought filling him with an amazing depth of understanding. He almost laughed out loud—for once in his life an answer came sweeping, as a gift. He continued to stare at Giles for a long moment until the boy began to shift uncomfortably at the intensity of his father's gaze. "Aye, my son," he said softly. "This truly belongs to you."

"What do you mean, Father?"

The boy's first, easy endearment caused Will to smile, even as he knew that Giles had not realized that he had used it. "Giles, someone very dear to me once said that the song of the unicorn can be heard only by those who listen with the heart." Seeing the confusion on the boy's face, he reached out and laid his hand on Giles's shoulder. "My son, you have been born into a new age. My father, your grandfather, was the most renowned knight of his time. His nobility came of loyalty, his strengths used to protect England and to mold her into greatness. But a greater time is coming. A time of wisdom, of discovery. Oh, there are so many things I have to tell you about. The Magna Carta; a rediscovery of the ancients and their gifts of thought; science, literature . . . Do not attempt to understand this now; only forgive my rambling. Suffice it to say that the emerald is truly your legacy. That which was first, the beginning of it all . . . the pledge. It is yours, Giles—my son, it is yours, with all that is to come."

Will walked along the parapets of Chepstow's south tower. He paused to lean against the battlement and stared down into the river below, his eyes transfixed vacantly on the Wye's steady current as his thoughts fixed. How had Eleanor known —that in his son's eyes he would find such truths.

Ever had he been on the outside of his life, viewing it apart, looking upon the play acted within. Those early years, spent in John Plantagenet's court, he had withdrawn out of necessity. Loneliness, separation from his family, he had withdrawn for self-preservation. Hostage for his father, he had blocked the King's debauched activities from his mind, even as he now faced them. If a man could be a whore, John Plantagenet had been so. As a young boy, he had been forced to watch the King's activities with his paramours—those willing, and those not—as attendant to the royal bedchamber. John Plantagenet's punishment upon William Marshal, the son had watched.

Once he was returned to his parents' household, they had tried to undo the hurt, the horror. Will knew that they had tried. But even in the shelter of their love he had remained apart. And he now knew, at long, long last, what Lavene had truly meant to him. The abused woman. And in his need, in his pomposity, he had been her savior. His hands clenched the rough edge of the merlon, the stone cutting into his fingers as he shut his eyes against the realization. He had been incapable of love; it had been her suffering that had drawn him to her. Oh, God, had she known?

Eleanor, oh, Eleanor. He had allowed himself to marry her. Allowed himself—how many years spent as the martyr? He withheld himself, the big brother, suffering under the fate dealt him. Taking her finally in duty, leaving her for the same. Excuses were sweet, found, turned, used to a purpose. Yet she filled his thoughts, every hour since he had left her, her words spoken in the masque repeating over and over in his mind. He smiled, knowing that she was an indelible part of him, and he sighed. How like love it would seem . . .

He raised his head, looking out over the valley as if seeing it clearly for the first time. The smooth, rich valley of hamlets and farms, the craggy mountains with their splotchy green surface and sawtoothed ridges, and among the view of his beloved Striguil he saw the truth. He had told Giles that one heard the song of the unicorn with his heart; sage advice for one who had never listened. But he could learn. And there was only one, just one, who could teach him the song.

"Will, in the name of the blessed Saint George, you cannot! It would be suicide to return now!" Hugh deBurgh stood helplessly in the center of Will's chamber, his expression showing the frustration he felt.

Will smiled at deBurgh briefly as he paused in the orders he was giving to the hubbub of activity in the room. Servants scurried about, sorting garments and packing trunks as Will's squires, led by Landon and Meryle, set his armor and weapons to order, determining those in need of repair as the suspect items were rushed to the armorer.

"Will, listen to me, all that you have done has been for me and mine; is there nothing I can say to stay you from this folly?"

Before Will could answer, another voice was heard. "Nay, my lord deBurgh, you must not count this decision upon your conscience."

The two men turned at the sound of a woman's voice to find Isabel in the doorway. She stepped into the room, her eyes noting the confusion in the room, and a frown passed over her brow for an instant. A few curtly snapped orders and the room was suddenly changed to one of organization. Isabel's eyes softened as they came to rest on her son. "Alan Wadley tells me that you leave for London in the morning."

"Milady, you must say something to this fool to make him see reason!" deBurgh protested.

"My son makes his own decisions," she said quietly, stepping forward to lay a hand on Will's arm. "What of Giles? Will you leave him with me?"

"Nay, he goes to London with me."

"I relent! You are both insane!" DeBurgh threw up his hands and spun about, storming from the room.

Isabel smiled at deBurgh's departing back and turned again to Will. "He will feel better once he understands."

"And you will explain it to him?" Will looked down at her with amusement.

"You are your father's son," she said softly, reaching up a hand to touch his cheek. "Women of this family must be strong if we are to bear the decisions made by our men. Of course you must return; I've been waiting for you to realize how much you love Eleanor—and the fact that you cannot leave England in the grip of Peter desRoches and his kind."

Will's large hand covered his mother's where it lay on his arm as he looked down at her tenderly. "You realize that things may not go as you would have it. There is the possibility that I may not return."

"Pah!" She stepped away, snapping at a lagging servant before she turned back to Will with a determined glint in her eye. "All that you were born to is with you, Will Marshal. All that which you learned at your father's knee—a love for England, a loyalty to her . . ."—her eyes danced with mischief—"and an ability to handle Plantagenets."

"Are you forgetting that when Father brought King John to the table on the Thames, to sign the Magna Carta, I was on the other side with the barons?" Will grinned. " 'Twould seem that our loyalties were divided."

"Not so," Isabel countered. "You brought the Great Charter to the table; your father brought John. Could one have been effected without the other?"

Will's eyes crinkled and he laughed. "I had never considered it in that way."

"Well, you should." Isabel's smile became serious as she regarded Will, and she sought the right words for what she would say next. "Your challenge now is as great, Will. The fact that Peter desRoches returned without council from the barons proves him to be more powerful than ever before. Your defiance of his will, in bringing deBurgh here, weakened his power, but if it is to last you must restore yourself to Henry's favor. Will, I know that it is for Eleanor that you are going, but the issue is greater than either of you.''

"Mother, while it was the realization of how I feel about Eleanor that formed my decision, it is for Henry and England that I go. If it were not, the matter would be simple. One frail woman is secreted out of a city with little effort; it would not require my presence at court.''

"One frail woman? Are we speaking of the same damsel?''

"Give me my delusions, Mother.'' Will laughed. "At the moment she is all that the troubadours credit to womanhood, as such is my longing for her.''

"And Giles?'' Isabel asked, shifting the subject. "You were firm that the boy was of an age of fostering—''

"And I am still firm on the matter. He shall be fostered, yet I shall not part from him.''

Isabel regarded her son with bemusement, but as she opened her mouth with questions they were interrupted by another. Father Francis, Chepstow's chaplain, entered with a vellum in his hand.

"Milord, the missives have been sent. I would have you recheck this list you gave me to assure that none has been missed.''

Will took the list, his eyes running over it before he grunted assent and dropped it on a nearby table. "There is one other, I think. Send a like message to Richard of Cornwall.'' He turned back to find Isabel reading the list, her eyes widening with each name. She looked up at him with surprise. "You have sent for them? Why did you allow me to go on like that when all the while your plans were made?''

"Because you confirmed my own thoughts.'' Will grinned. "Besides, Mother, I would never rob you of your moment.''

He turned to leave the room, pausing to grab up his sword and scabbard from where it lay on his warchest, and she rushed to keep up with him, two-stepping to maintain his long strides as he strode down the hallway to the stairs. "What of Giles, Will? What do you mean for the boy?''

He answered with a smile. "Patience, Mother.''

When he entered the Great Hall, his eyes swept over the confusion, lighting with satisfaction as they came to rest upon one. "Landon!'' he bellowed over the mayhem, bringing the wide-eyed squire to his side.

"Kneel."

The young man did not comprehend the order at first, then began to sink to his knee even as his mouth opened to question what was happening. Before he could respond, Will spoke. "Before the grace of God and Henry of England, I bid you go forth as a knight of this realm. Ever be faithful to the vows of the order that God may ever look with favor upon you."

Landon stared vacantly up at Will; then his expression filled with amazement as his voice became choked with emotion, his words barely lifted to the silenced hall. "Aye, lord, so I do swear."

Then Will administered the *colee,* smiting the other a blow to seal the vow. Reaching down, he assisted Landon to rise and handed him the sword. "This, Landon, with the vestments of knighthood, shall be given you. I bid you hold this sword, in my name, until the day when my son comes to his knighthood, when I ask that it be given to him by your hand."

"It shall be so, milord, I do swear," the newly vested knight said with emotion.

"And will you so accept my son into your service?"

Landon blinked and slowly his mouth drew into a smile. "As page—and squire. Milord, I do accept."

"In whose service do you pledge yourself, Sir Landon d'Leon?"

"I would seek to pledge my service to you, milord, if you will have me."

"Most gladly, Sir Landon." Will smiled, resting a hand on the other man's shoulder. He turned to the expectant faces in the hall. "A banquet, such as can be prepared, I believe to be in order!"

"This is highly unusual, Will," Isabel mumbled at Will's side as Sir Landon turned to the rush of congratulations from his peers. "To keep Giles near you in such a manner? 'Tis not done."

Will grinned, wrapping an arm about her shoulders as he looked down at her and winked. "I suppose not. On the other hand, who is going to tell me that I cannot?"

25

ELEANOR moved among the rubble, lifting the hem of
her skirt as she stepped over a dusty pile of scattered lumber.
The heavy morning fog had burned off, leaving the August
day warm and muggy. She felt an uncomfortable trickle of
moisture trail down her back under the linen of her gown, and
she regretted the decision to wear the heavy linen wimple
and coif. Resisting the impulse to remove the headpiece, she
drew a kerchief from the pocket of her skirt and dabbed her
forehead as she looked up into the scaffold impatiently. Damn
Henry, would he never finish with this endless questioning of
the workmen? She had accompanied him this morning to
avoid the endless hours in the ladies' chamber, the endless
two-sided comments from those too wary of her position to
speak openly, yet too steeped in jealousy and resentment to
avoid comment altogether. Petty, insipid creatures, she
thought, she could not abide another hour in their company.

She looked up again to the framed structure that would
become the magnificent edifice built to the memory of Edward
the Confessor, Henry's obsession. But then, he had come by it
honestly, she admitted to herself. Queen Mold, their great-
great-great-grandmother, the Saxon queen of Henry I, had

made it a custom to pray at Saint Edward's altar in sackcloth. She had placed hair of Mary Magdalen in the Confessor's vault and had perpetrated many of the reverences and traditions given to the pious king's memory. Henry II had obtained canonization for Edward. When the tomb was opened, the body had been found miraculously to be greatly preserved— pale and fragile but with the features and magnificence known in the king's life. Respect for the Confessor's memory had been part of Henry's childhood, and his life. Often, with his nobles, he dressed in white robes to attend a night-long vigil before the tomb to pray for the saint. Now he was about to realize his dream, to build an edifice he felt worthy of his hero. And, as always with Henry, no timber, no stone, no window, nor tie bar would be raised without his approval and advice.

She raised her gaze to the high scaffolding, shielding her eyes with her hand against the early-afternoon sun as she tried to make out Henry's form on the rafters. She was so engrossed that she did not hear the sound of approaching horses or the footsteps that approached across the gravel path behind her.

"Eleanor."

She felt the timbre of his voice, even before the sound formed in her mind. She spun about, her heart thumping heavily in her chest as her mind flashed with thoughts she knew she dared not think. "Will!" she gasped. He was there, truly there, if this was not a dream. "Oh, my God, Will!" She was barely aware of the grin on his tanned face, the glint of his blue eyes she remembered so well, so lovingly. She did not know whether to laugh or cry as she beheld his dear face. And then panic rushed through her as she grasped the sleeve of his surcoat and pulled him with her into the shadows of the abbey. He went willingly, allowing her to draw him after her, as he chuckled deeply.

"Will Marshal! What are you doing here! You cannot be here! Henry is still furious with you!"

"Wife, we have been parted these long months. Is that the only greeting you have for your husband?" He grinned, pulling her into his arms and smothering her protests with a kiss, deep and longing.

Her mind spun, her nerve endings tingling with danger as her mouth and body responded to the feel of him. Long

months of dreaming of this moment overrode the immediate
danger, and she gave herself to the kiss, pushing aside the fact
of where they were, and Henry's presence, so dangerously
near. "Will, Will," she murmured against his lips as he kissed
the corners of her mouth. "Why have you come? Did you not
receive my last letter? Do you know something that I do not?"

He raised his head, planting a light kiss on the end of her
nose, then smiled down at her. "Aye, my love, I have learned
many things in these past months, things I shall pleasure in
telling you." He kissed her again, then pulled away, turning to
the waiting horses and riders. "There is someone else I have
brought to see you."

Giles had dismounted and stood next to Landon. The newly
vested knight stood with his hand on the boy's shoulder, the
device of his coat of arms, a hart lodged, or lying down, a
molet, or star, quartered to indicate his position as a third son.
Her mouth drew into a happy grin for the new knight, and
then her eyes widened to note that Giles bore a badge of Landon's white and blue colors. "You have pledged him to Landon?" she asked with surprise. He merely answered with a
smile. "Then . . . you are not angry that I sent him to
Chepstow?"

"I was furious," he murmured, giving her a gentle squeeze.
"But I came to know that your decision was the right one—for
both Giles and myself. I have much to be grateful to you for,
Eleanor."

She held her arms out to Giles, grabbing him to her as he
came into her embrace. She hugged him fiercely, then held
him at arm's length, reaching up to brush his tousled hair
from his face. "Are you well, Giles of Striguil?"

"Aye, milady, I am so." The boy grinned happily. "I am
Landon—ah, Sir Landon's page!"

"So I see." She smiled affectionately. Then she noticed that
Giles's gaze had shifted past her shoulder to something behind
them, and his grin faded as his expression turned to a puzzled
frown.

Eleanor and Will turned, following Giles's gaze, and they
froze. Henry Plantagenet stood a few feet away, his face pale
as his eyes stared stonily at Will. Slowly, a reddened flush
crept up his cheeks. "My Lord of Pembroke," he choked, his

face now filled with fury. "You do dare to come into my presence?"

Will stepped forward and bent a knee before the King. "I do so dare to throw myself on the mercy of my King and liege lord," Will answered evenly, rising.

"Henry . . . ," Eleanor pleaded.

"Silence!" Henry glared at her, then looked back to Will. "You have erred, Will Marshal. When you came once again under the power of my writ, you forfeited your life. Where is Hubert deBurgh?"

"At Chepstow, sire."

Henry's face flushed deeper as he regarded Will with amazement. When he could finally speak, his voice was strained. "I will say this, Will, you have more audacity than anyone I know."

"And you should know, sire."

Henry's mouth quivered at the statement, but he stifled the reaction quickly and set his brows in a deep frown. A heavy, long silence followed, the mood deepening by the silent group of nobles that had gathered and were waiting breathlessly for the outcome of the dramatic confrontation between the King and his former favorite. Finally, Henry turned his back and began to stride away. "Walk with me," he grumbled.

Eleanor thought for a moment her legs would give way beneath her, and she grasped to Giles for support as the boy looked up at her with alarm. "My lady," he whispered anxiously, "what has happened?"

"I do not know, Giles," she said weakly. "We can only wait and see."

They walked in silence as Will waited for Henry to speak, finally reaching the south end of the structure, where Henry came to a sudden halt, almost causing Will to plow into him. "Come, come, Master Henry!" the King roared at the chief builder. "You must do better for me than that!" Disregarding the fine green velvet of his tabard, he leapt across the lower scaffolding and proceeded to leave Will standing there while he engaged in a lengthy discourse over the size of the buttresses. Will leaned his shoulder against a timber and waited. Finally Henry returned, mumbling to himself unhappily as he brushed off his tabard.

"Some things never change." Will grinned.

Henry laughed in spite of himself, his strained expression easing with his humor. He reached up and rubbed the back of his neck. Then his eyes darkened as they met Will's. "Dammit, Will, why did you do it? I loved you as no other man, not even Richard. How could you betray me?"

"Who has convinced you that I betrayed you, Henry?"

"No one had to convince me!" Henry snapped. "Your actions condemned you!"

"Your Grace, I have returned because I can no longer remain apart from my wife, nor from you. I have never lied to you and I will not do so now. I believe in what I did. I believe it to be best for England, and for you, and I would do it again. DesRoches would not have rested until Hubert's neck was in a noose. If you had allowed deBurgh to die, the results would have been dire. Can you not realize that every peer of this realm would have come to view the offense as one against their own power?

"Many years ago I warned you against the growing threat of the Italian priests and the resentment against them. The results ended in bloody riots. But that was nothing, Henry, nothing to what will happen against the Poitevins and Gascons who seek to gain control. No Englishman will for long tolerate influence of the French—by lay or clergy."

"We Normans were French," Henry parried with a smirk.

"Are you condoning another Conquest?" Will countered.

The smile died on Henry's face. "Enough, Marshal, enough! I will consider what you have said, but you would do well not to rest with ease upon it. I have not forgotten what you have done. Do not attempt to leave the city, I warn you—it would not go well for others. That damn goliard is still within my reach—and your sister, Isabella, is at Winchester."

"Isabella?" Will felt his heart quicken.

"Aye." Henry smiled slyly. " 'Twould seem that Richard is taken with her. They would marry—but I have not yet decided. And then, of course, there is Eleanor. . . ." His gaze shifted in the direction they had come. "And your son."

"I did not return only to leave again before this matter is settled," Will answered, keeping his voice even. "I will remain, at your disposal, Your Grace."

"Good, see that you do," Henry grunted. "You will present yourself at court, one week hence. I will decide the manner of your . . . future at that time."

Seeing that he was dismissed, as Henry had turned to study the workmen, he added one more comment. "I know that I have no right to do so, sire, but may I beg upon your generosity to make a request?"

Henry looked back, his eyes widening that Will would be so bold, but his interest was struck. "And what is that?"

"A slight one, sire. Only that the Bishop of Winchester might be present."

Henry's eyes narrowed as he considered the request for a moment; then he shrugged. "He shall be there."

"My thanks, sire."

Will returned to Giles and Eleanor, who paled with relief when she saw him. He saw them wordlessly to their mounts, ignoring Eleanor's questioning glances as they rode to the London house. It proved agony to Eleanor as she forced herself to move through the normal activity of settling them in. Finally, as the door closed behind her in the chamber she would share with Will, the tension released.

"Sweet Mother, tell me what happened! What did he say?" she cried, spinning on him. Before she realized what he was doing, he reached out and removed her coif, then her wimple, dropping them to the floor. "Will?"

"Only what I expected, love," he murmured, pulling her to him. He silenced her with a kiss, immediately pushing all thoughts of Henry completely from her mind. It was gentle and stirring with a tenderness that spoke more than words. She opened her eyes and looked up at him with wonder. "Will . . . ," she whispered as her eyes searched his, fearing to believe what she read there.

He kissed her again as his hands slipped to her hips and held her tightly against him. He released her mouth to kiss the corners, her cheeks, and the point below her ear that made her body rush with tingling sensations down to her toes. "I love you, Eleanor," he whispered. "I love you as I have never loved anyone. I did not understand what the word truly meant until I came to understand what you mean to me."

"Oh, Will," she breathed. Oh, sweet Lord, she thought as

her mind raced wildly. He had said he loved her! She swallowed heavily as he began to unfasten the shoulders of her gown. "What has happened?"

"Happened?" He tossed the large garnet fastenings onto the table next to them. "Nothing. Everything."

"Will, those are worth a small fortune!" she gasped, watching the jewels roll across the table to the floor.

He grinned, drawing her back into his arms. "Materialistic little wench, aren't you? Your husband is trying to make love to you, to declare his undying devotion, and your only concern is a set of garnet clusters."

"Is that what you are trying to do?" Her eyes began to twinkle happily.

"Trying?" He snorted. "I thought I was fairly good at this. Apparently I'm not."

"Nay"—she laughed—"not that. The part about your undying devotion."

"Oh—that. One comes with the other, my love." His gaze fixed on her breasts beneath the sheer white fitted chemise. Sighing, he turned her to undo the laces at her back.

She swallowed heavily, reading the warm intent in his eyes. "Not always, milord. Devotion is not necessary for . . . for the other."

His hand paused on her back as he seemed to consider her statement. "Nay, you are correct. Love—even affection—is not necessary for a vigorous coupling."

"Nay, it is not—so I've heard," she amended quickly.

"So you've heard?" She could hear the amusement in his voice as his fingers lingered, caressing her back. "It seems to me that I recall your being quite swept away in the thralls of passion—even when you did not particularly care for me."

She stiffened and tried to turn, but he held her shoulders then continued to unlace her chemise. "I—I did not really hate you, Will," she stammered. "I just thought I did."

He bent and kissed her shoulder, and her skin trembled beneath his lips. "Nay, Eleanor, the hate was real. That born of what you thought to be a betrayal of your love," he said softly. She turned in his arms and searched his face, but his gaze was tender. "Never deny your feelings, Eleanor. When you are hurt you cannot heal unless you face those feelings. As

to your passion—you were a warm, passionate young woman,
awakened to your own sensuality. Even when you hated me,
when you knew I was going to make love to you, I saw the expectancy in your eyes, even as you fought it. It was only after
that the guilt and recriminations came.''

"That isn't true.''

"Ah, but it is.'' He laughed, linking his hands behind her
back. "Tell me the truth, did you tingle down to those tiny
toes?''

"Certainly not!'' she huffed, turning her face as he brushed
her cheek with a light kiss.

"Nay? No thoughts came into that pretty head? No tantalizing visions—not even for a moment?''

"None,'' she said stiffly as her toes began to tingle.

"Eleanor.'' He laughed softly. "Do not lie to me. And
when the hatred had passed and affection was reborn between
us—when you were able to accept your own sensuality without
guilt, how much sweeter it was. And now with love? How
much infinitely better it will be.''

"Infinitely,'' she agreed, leaning against him as her eyes
grew dreamy.

He grinned down at her, reaching up to brush a lock of hair
from her temple. "Now, then, sweetling, would you like me to
tell you what we are going to do?'' He lowered his mouth to
her ear and whispered.

Her eyes grew wide and she gasped. "Will,'' she protested
weakly, "how can you say such things?'' She realized then
that nothing between them, mutually given, could be wrong.

He kissed her ear, his lips moving in light, fluttering kisses
to her mouth, claiming it, at first gently, then with an in-
sistence that left no further doubt in her mind. She slumped
back against the support of his arms and looked up at the love
echoed in his eyes.

"Eleanor,'' he murmured huskily. "Everything that has
gone before us is part of us, not to be forgotten, nor even
regretted. Everything that has happened to us has made us
what we are and has brought us to this point. One moment
changed and we may have passed it by. I love you, Eleanor,
and nothing can change what I feel for you at this moment:
not the past''—he smiled—"not words, not what others

would do to our lives." Gently he pulled her chemise from her
shoulders and his hands touched her breasts, hearing the intake of her breath as his thumbs softly rubbed the peaks,
which were tightening under his touch. "Let me love you,
Eleanor. Love me, unreservedly, the past placed where it
should be, the future put aside in this moment. If this is all
that we have, no one can ever take it from us."

Joy and sorrow intermingled until she thought her heart
would break. Slipping her arms about his neck, she lifted her
lips to his. They clung to each other as tears slipped from her
eyes, trailing over her cheeks, where they mingled with their
lips, giving to the sensation of their love and grief. After all
the years, so much found. And to know that they had only this
brief moment. So late, and so little time.

Eleanor awoke slowly, still taken with her dreams and the
exquisite memories of the night passed in Will's arms. She
turned in the bed and reached out to touch his pillow, stroking
it lovingly in the absence of the one who had occupied it a
short time past. He had awakened her before dawn and made
love to her again, and she sighed, recalling his touch, the
tender way he had loved her before their passions had swept
them away. Later, too sated and peaceful to rise, she had
growled at him when he tried to get her up, and he had teased
her for being a slugabed. Then, tucking the covers about her
he had kissed her lightly before he had slipped from the bed
leaving her to another hour's precious dreams.

Oh, he had been so right, it was so much better when there
was love. Mutually shared souls, minds, hearts in the giving
and taking of their bodies. Her mouth deepened into a smile.
could have told you that, Will Marshal, she thought, laughing
lightly. But you had to discover it for yourself. Lightened by
her thoughts, she slipped from the bed, eager to find him, just
to be near him. She washed and dressed quickly, dispensing
with the wimple and coif as she ran a comb through her hair
and pinned it back with combs. As she turned to leave the
chamber she paused, spying the book Brother Vincent had
given her where it lay on a table near the hearth. Her brow
wrinkled as she crossed to it. She was certain that she had not
left it there. She picked it up and opened it, her eyes misting as

she looked at the inside of the front cover. Beneath Brother Vincent's sketch of the magnificent unicorn, its proud neck arched as it pawed the ground, bearing the lady and her knight, was an inscription in Will's broad hand: "From your heart, my love, I have seen truth."

Eagerly Eleanor threw open the door to Will's study, only to stop short as her brows lifted in surprise. He was sitting before the hearth with Hugh Bigod. "Hugh!" she exclaimed with pleasure as she swiftly crossed the room. He rose from his chair as she approached, his own expression lightening as he gathered her into his arms for a warm hug.

"It is good to see you, Eleanor. It has been a long time, too long."

"I agree, Hugh. Sit, sit!" She took a chair next to Will as the Earl again settled and she leaned forward eagerly. "How are Matilda and the children?"

"They are well, as are the deFerrarses and deBraoses." He grinned. "Although we are all anxious about the King's decision." His expression suggested what the conversation had been before she had joined them as his expression slipped easily into concern. "It does not bode well for you, Will. Foreign soldiers keep watch along the battlements of the ports. Mercenaries are everywhere, roaming freely about, swaggering as if they were indeed already in rule. I have not seen so many of their ilk since King John's time."

"I know," Will murmured grimly. "I observed many of their kind on my way here. It was for that I did strike my colors soon after leaving Chepstow and found it necessary to travel by little-used routes."

"Nepotism reigns in London," Hugh said angrily. "Daily the King makes appointments to the Poitevins and the Gascons that arrive from Angoumois and Provence. His mother appears to have an endless supply of favorites, and they are all seeking their fortunes on English soil. Moreover, since he cannot now count upon the barons' support, he hires foreign mercenaries to surround him. We have returned to his father's time."

"Ah, if it were so." Will sighed. "Unfortunately des-Roches's cunning supersedes John's. It would be deadly to underestimate him, Hugh. He will effect by flattery what John could not do by his sheer will. He will cajole the barons to support him. The fact that they did not rise up to confront the Poitevins when they first threatened deBurgh, moreover supported his downfall, gives proof that they do not realize the consequences of what is happening. In Hubert deBurgh they cast out an able administrator, one who was English and understood the people. In his place they accept foreign rule."

"Aye," Hugh agreed thoughtfully. "I fear that you may be right." Suddenly his temper exploded and he pounded the chair arm with his fist and leapt up. Striding before the hearth, he spun back on Will. "Why can they not recognize the contempt desRoches has for England! Arrogant, pompous, he has nothing but disdain and scorn for England, yet the barons will not see it! By the Blood, the cleric is now making open decisions for Henry in council! Only a fortnight past an emissary was sent from the Saracens to plead for our help and—"

"A Saracen? In England?" Will blinked.

"Aye. It seems that some Mongol—ah, Genghis Khan, I think—is threatening the Holy Land from the East. The Saracen came to us to plead for help to repel him. Many in the council, including Henry, saw the opportunity as a new crusade. But desRoches stopped it handily. His comment was 'Let the dogs devour one another and perish.' And his decision stood!"

"DesRoches does have a weakness, beyond that of his insufferable pride," Eleanor interjected, smiling at the questioning looks they turned to her. "His fear of the power held by the strongest family in England, not to mention their kin. Believe what I say, he fears you as no other, Will, and will do everything to garner his forces against you. Already I have watched him plying his wiles upon the earls Lincoln and Chester in an attempt to turn them from you."

"I am counting on it," Will agreed, smiling grimly. "It is that hatred which must expose him to the barons. They must see him at his worst. Until they see him for what he is, and the grave and present danger that exists to themselves and to England, they will not act. And they must—before it is too late."

Eleanor's eyes met with Hugh's and they exchanged a look

of worry and anguish. Drawing in her breath slowly, Eleanor smiled as her husband looked up at her, and she picked up the ewer to refill his goblet. She thought her heart would break, but she would not let him see it. "Might we persuade you to stay for supper, Hugh? Darcy will be joining us. I sent him a message when we arrived home yesterday," she added, noting her husband's puzzled but pleased look. "I thought you might want to see him. He has written a new song he planned to send to Giles, something the scoundrel wrote while he was in the tower—the lyrics of which, fortunately, have not reached the court. Have you ever pictured a certain bishop as a hedge-hog?"

Heavy, blanketing fog hung about London, casting smoky shadows about the Great Hall in the White Tower. Seeping softly, the grey light muted the vibrant colors of scenes depicting the history of Antiochus which covered the walls and the banners filling the high arching rafters. Sound seemed softened, even as colors, an oppressiveness drawn from the fog-shrouded morning to lay across the emotions of those gathered. A tension was felt among those of the court, affecting conversation, stilling the scattered, tinkling sound of laughter normally heard. Eyes shifted occasionally toward the large, iron-bound doors at the end of the immense hall normally used for state banquets, and then to the dais where sat Henry, King of England, and near his right hand a step lower, Peter desRoches, Bishop of Winchester, his dark head bent to the words of the King.

The silence crackled as the King's porter made his announcement, bringing conversation to an abrupt halt, even to those on the dais. The doors swung heavily open and the Marshal of England entered, his lady by his side. If the Marshal and his lady felt the impending doom which lay in their fate, they gave no evidence of it. Heads bent together as eyes fixed expectantly on the ill-fated pair. Then, as reality struck, gasps rose from the company over the bold audacity of the Earl of Pembroke.

Will was fully armed, the jazerant-work of his hauberk glistening as it caught the soft light from the windows. His gold surcoat of battle was emblazoned with the red lion of the

Marshals, its jaws ferociously agape. He wore his helm with its
gold and green plumed crest, the face piece set back to reveal
the stony blue of his eyes as they fixed on the dais before him.
His hand rested lightly on the hilt of his sword in its scabbard,
as Landon walked behind, holding his shield on his arms bearing the Marshal coat of arms. Next to Landon walked Alan
Wadley, his master of arms, representing Will's knight-fees, a
sum unequaled among English peers.

Eleanor, Countess of Pembroke, approached on her husband's arm, her eyes fixed on her brother as a confident smile
touched her lovely mouth. Her bliaut was of fiery red velvet,
matching the lion of her husband's device, rubies and pearls
embroidered about the hem and sleeves, a girdle of brilliant
sapphires encircling her hips. A mantle of red baudekin, shot
with gold and lined in precious ermine, hung about her
shoulders and was held there by enormous ruby clasps. Her
raven hair was loose, tumbling to her hips, covered by a sheer,
translucent veil of sarcenet. The veil was banded about her
forehead by a wide circlet of gold set with precious gems,
boldly declaring her lineage as a princess of England.

Ignoring the murmurs which began to rise from those
gathered, Will kept his eyes on Henry. He saw Henry pull at
his ear and recognized the nervous reaction. Peter desRoches,
whose face had flushed dangerously at the bold entrance,
leaned toward the King and whispered. Henry's expression
tightened at whatever hurried comment had been made, and
his face turned stony as he looked up at the pair, who had just
reached the foot of the dais.

Will removed his helm, handing it to Landon, and turned
back to the dais. "Sire, I am here, as you commanded, at your
will and disposal," Will offered in a voice that did not suggest
the seriousness of the crime of which he was accused. He bent
in a slight bow to Eleanor's curtsy.

"William Marshal, Earl of Pembroke, you do dare come
before this court armed?" Henry roared, flushing with rage.
"Is it your intent to declare war upon this Throne?"

Will fought an impulse to glance at desRoches, knowing the
satisfaction he would read on the face of the other. Instead, he
fixed his gaze upon the King and responded evenly. "My intent
is to declare war, sire, but not upon the Throne of England.

The war I seek is upon your enemies, those who seek to be close to your hand, those advising you to turn from our laws and our justice. Many here fought in a bitter war to cast foreign influence from our shores, yet they have returned. Not boldly, with arms to declare their intentions, but with guile. They seek to turn your ear from that of the barons, the peers of England, her natural advisers—"

"Marshal, you overstep—" desRoches protested, his voice rising.

Will ignored him, continuing to regard Henry as he spoke. "The peers of England, rights granted to them—"

"There are no peers in England!"

The stillness that followed could be tangibly felt. Then came outrage as a single, indrawn breath from the barons. Eyes shifted to the source. Peter desRoches was leaning forward, his hands whitened as they gripped the heavily carved arms of his chair. Feeling the eyes of the company upon him, he drew up and regarded the man before him with contempt. "You stand here as the accused, Earl William of Pembroke; do not attempt to draw aside the issue before this court. You are a traitor and so stand condemned!"

But Will's eyes were fastened on Henry, who was regarding the Bishop with horror, as did all in the hall. Puzzlement crossed Henry's face, and dismay. Satisfied, Will avoided referring to the Bishop's damning comment, allowing it to register fully with the court before he shifted attention slightly. "My lord, near here is being constructed, by your hand, a magnificent edifice to Saint Edward the Confessor, a godly king, who sought only to do God's will for England. She is again in need of one who will see her to greatness. Those who would bleed her, those who would turn from her needs, seeking only the fulfillment of their own greed and power, must be identified and exorcised. I do pledge myself, and all at my resource, to that purpose. To you, my King and liege lord, and to England, upon my life."

The movement was subtle, the sound a bare whisper among the rustles of the skirts of the ladies of the court, but heads turned involuntarily to the quiet change in the hall. The new arrivals had gone unnoted, a point having been silently but firmly pressed upon the porter, and now stood along points in the hall before the gathered company. Clad like Will, in armor bearing their devices, stood the Marshal brothers. Richard, from Normandy; Gilbert, from Ireland; Walter, from the depths of Wales; and Anselem, representing England's knight-fees under the power of the Marshals. With them stood Hugh Bigod, Earl of Norfolk, Framlingham, and Bungay, representing his control of over one hundred estates; young Richard deClare, now Earl of Gloucester and Hertford; William deFerrars, Earl of Derby; and William deBraose, representing the power of his family.

"My lord king," Eleanor said softly, though her voice carried through the silence of the hall. "Our sire was forced to the table at Running-Mead because he ignored the will of the barons. You, in your wisdom, have embraced the Great Charter, signed by our father that day in July. My husband has spoken as a peer of this realm." She glanced at desRoches as her voice rose meaningfully. "Indeed, England has its peers, those of wisdom and power. It is of their advice that a great king will seek, taking the best for England."

"We are here to consider the disposition of the former justiciar of England, Hubert deBurgh," Will continued smoothly. "And those of us who aided him to sanctuary across the river Wye, to Wales. I will not now dispute the fact that England has lost its most capable administrator; the point is sadly no longer an issue. What must be considered now is who shall rule England. Sire, if you believe that England truly has no peers, none of blood bred upon this soil who can nurture and lead her, then you must indeed find me guilty of treason. And in kind, all who stand with us in support of England and of Henry Plantagenet."

Henry raised his eyes to the armed barons declaring for the Marshals and to the barons who had stepped forward subtly to stand by them. So many, he thought, so many. He rapidly calculated the knight-fees represented, the power of those who stood beside Will. Settling back in the tall-backed chair, he rubbed his lips with his fingers as he thought desperately of what he should do. God, how he hated deBurgh! The man was a plague, set upon this earth to cause him torment! Even now, beyond his writ in Wales, he caused discomfort. His eye shifted, half hooded, to Will. Will had always been his best friend. His memory flashed on the years, the pleasures spent together, the laughter. The advice, the support, when there had been no one else. And then his gaze shifted to Eleanor. How he longed for the warmth, the love of their early years. Damn, she had hardly spoken to him in the past months. His eyes again lifted to the hall, to the armed barons who stood silently waiting. By the Blood, their wealth surpassed his own, by goodly measure. The Marshals alone . . .

"Sire, you cannot allow this," a voice whispered in his ear. "They seek to control you! You cannot allow—"

Henry turned his head and his eyes fixed on desRoches. "Enough," Henry grumbled. "I will hear no more. You settled the matter by your own words. They will have carried over England before a fortnight, you fool! You have well sealed my decision." Henry turned to the court, his gaze passing over the expectant company before it came to rest upon Will and Eleanor. Oddly, as he prepared to speak, a strange comfort settled over him. Somehow he sensed that it would be the last time he would feel satisfaction, even a moment of joy in giving a decision. "Will Marshal, I have listened to your plea and that of your lady. You have caused serious grievance to me in defying my will, but I have listened. While your actions cannot be condoned, I believe your motives to be pure, your intentions to be for the good of the realm. Therefore, I grant clemency in your past actions, and give you freedom. As to the matter of Hubert deBurgh, he shall remain in exile for a period of four years. At that time, the disposition of his lands and titles will again come under our consideration."

They walked along the Thames, their footsteps crunching along the gravel path beneath the spreading willows that lined the path. A sound from above drew their attention, and they laughed as a monkey jumped to a nearby branch, chattering at them as if scolding for the interruption.

"We should advise a keeper of the menagerie that he has escaped," Eleanor observed, watching the antics of the monkey as it settled upon a branch above her.

"Eventually," Will agreed, reaching out to draw her to his side. "Allow him a moment's freedom, love. I think I know how he feels. One comes to treasure freedom, when one has known its loss."

"But he might escape!" she pressed, her brow furrowing with concern as she watched the animal.

"Escape?" Will smiled, following her gaze. "Where would he go? It is part of nature to remain where it is familiar, even when the prospect of something greater pulls. Comfort is taken from what one knows." He pulled her into his arms.

"Comfort?" she sniffed, stiffening as she turned her face aside from his kiss. "Is that what I am to you, Will Marshal? Familiar, like an old shoe?"

"Nay, love," he mused thoughtfully. "You are certainly softer than old leather, though less pliable." He laughed as she began to struggle against his grip and tried to pull away. "Eleanor!" he chortled. "What I meant to say is that I need you. I can depend upon you, and your love, and it is my strength." As she relaxed, he pulled her tighter. "There is much to be said of comfort in a relationship, Eleanor. Good Lord, you must admit that it did not come easily to us."

"It certainly did not," she mused thoughtfully, leaning her body against his, a fact he acknowledged with a raise of a brow and a gleam in his eyes. "Lud, Will, it seems a lifetime. Could it be that I was once so young, following after you like a puppy, doing all of those . . . terrible things?" She buried her head in his tunic as she flushed, remembering.

"Aye, you did that." He chuckled, holding her firmly so she would not escape. "I recall a time when you desired nothing more than to be my best friend, to ride harder than I could, to shoot an arrow straighter."

She swore at him, her voice muffled in his tunic. But as she raised her head she was smiling warmly, her eyes glowing. "I did want to be your best friend, and I still do. You have no better friend, Will Marshal."

"Oh, I do know that, Eleanor Marshal," he answered, his voice becoming husky as he stared down at her. "My best friend, my lover, my wife." Bending, he kissed her, deeply, responding to the answer of her own willing response.

Remembering where they were, they pulled apart reluctantly and, after a moment, continued down the path as Eleanor locked her arm tightly in Will's. After a prolonged shared silence her brows gathered into a frown. "What happens now, Will?"

He laid his hand over hers where it rested on his arm and paused, looking out to the small boats and barges drifting down the Thames, his eyes fixing upon a distant spot. "If I could give you what I wished, it would be that we would return to Chepstow. To spend our years there, peacefully, raising our children." He paused as a deep sigh escaped. "But you know that it cannot be. We must remain here, taking what brief moments to return to Chepstow that we dare. Any time away from court will allow desRoches's kind what they require. Henry is pliable to whoever whispers in his ear, and it must be me, Eleanor, you know that, until another comes to take my place."

"I know." Eleanor reached up to lay her hand gently on Will's cheek, compelling him to look at her. "Will Marshal, there is none to me who shall be as you are. I ask only to share your life. Whatever time we are given, our purpose shall be the same, as it always has been, even when we reasoned it to be at odds. Life is so strange," she reflected, her eyes becoming distant. "We struggle to make it as we would will it. We see only desperation beyond our reason as we move through it, continually pleading to God to bring it to our dreams, while thinking He does not listen. Yet, in hindsight, we see evidence of the pattern we prayed for. No longer will I miss today while seeking tomorrow. I am content. Each moment, each part of a day with you, will be enough."

He drew her into his arms and raised her chin with his finger, his eyes holding hers as he smiled tenderly. "Eleanor, you make me hear the song. You have given that to me. No matter what else may happen in our lives, I have heard it."